Dante's Ballad

Eduardo González Viaña

English Translation by
Susan Giersbach Rascón

Arte Público Press
Houston, Texas

This volume is funded in part by grants from the City of Houston through the Houston Arts Alliance and the Exemplar Program, a program of Americans for the Arts in collaboration with the LarsonAllen Public Services Group, funded by the Ford Foundation.

Recovering the past, creating the future

Arte Público Press
University of Houston
452 Cullen Performance Hall
Houston, Texas 77204-2004

Cover art by Alejandro Romero
Cover design by Giovanni Mora

González Viaña, Eduardo, 1941-
  [*Corrido* de Dante. English]
  Dante's Ballad / Eduardo González Viaña
     p. cm.
   ISBN: 978-1-55885-487-1 (alk. paper)
   I. Title
  PQ8498.17.O55C6713 2007
  863′.64—dc22

                        2007060688
                        CIP

7 8 9 0 1 2 3 4 5 6   10 9 8 7 6 5 4 3 2 1

To the Peregrinos de La Santa Muerte
I sang with them in a bar in El Paso
I sang off-key and I'm paying for my mistake

We didn't cross the line.
The line crossed us.

—Sung by the Peregrinos de La Santa Muerte

1
The First to Arrive at the Party Was a Donkey

Dante Celestino was waiting for the guests at the door when he saw two long ears appear, outlined in profile against the southern sky. The silhouette gradually appeared more clearly. It was a donkey, coming from afar and limping on one of its hind legs, but advancing toward him as if it were an old friend, as if it had been invited to the party, or as if someone had told it that Dante was an animal doctor.

By its slightly sorrowful, intellectual manner, when it was still a distance away, a black silhouette inside a yellow sun, Dante took it for an angel. But angels fly and don't trot, nor do they limp or raise their ears like someone bearing an unbearable pain without complaining. Nor do they look at us with enormous, red, nostalgia-filled eyes. Nor do they flick away bees with their tails. Nor do they approach us and move their ears in greeting. And since the donkey did all of that, the man did not hesitate to welcome him, gesturing to him to sit down next to the front door, to see if he could diagnose the cause of his lameness and help him.

Although he was all dressed up, Dante took up the task he had been doing for most of his life in the United States. He took off his necktie and bright blue velvet suitcoat, rolled up his sleeves, knelt down next to the injured animal, and began to evaluate the extent of the break. It was not too large, but it was deep and needed treatment. In the forty minutes that still remained before the first guests would arrive, Dante managed to find a piece of wood and a long scrap of denim with which he wrapped the hoofed animal's injured leg. Finally, he placed the lame stranger next to the door of the hall. The

1

donkey, despite what was presumably great pain, had not complained during the splinting process, had not moved its ears or tail, but had been unable to prevent two heavy tears from spilling from its enormous eyes.

An hour later, Dante Celestino began to welcome his friends, inviting them into the community hall after an exchange of slaps on the back. Standing there all decked out in new clothes he had just purchased in Portland, smiling and accepting everyone's congratulations, the host of the party began to feel like the administrator of a circus as he greeted the ladies and gentlemen in attendance at the grand event. That thought soon passed and he remembered that the most important moment of his twenty-five years in the country had arrived and that he was keeping the promise he had made to his wife on her deathbed.

After straightening his shirt collar, Dante went to look with some astonishment at the expanse of the community hall. It was vast and elegant. The more than ninety families who lived in the complex had the right to use it, although at times they might consider it overly ostentatious when compared to their simple apartments. The apartments had only two bedrooms, but what had excited Mrs. Celestino when they moved into one of them was the size and elegance of the social center.

"We'll have Emmita's *quinceañera* here," she had proclaimed then, looking at her daughter who was just learning to walk.

But Mrs. Celestino had died a year earlier, without being able to participate in the solemn occasion that awaited Emmita, and in the hospital, near death, she had barely a moment to talk to her husband. She whispered in his ear the great commitment she was leaving him.

"You won't forget about the *quinceañera*," she said.

"I won't forget what?"

"Don't forget. You have to have her *quinceañera* next year, but a real *quinceañera*."

For the rest of his life, he would recall those words pronounced in an already distant, halting voice, the way the dying communicate their last wishes. Whether working with machinery or healing animals, when the moon grew large and yellow, or when the wind blew from the west, those words always came back to him. All the time, and now, moon after moon, Dante felt happy to be keeping his word. And in what a place!

"No . . . , *caramba*, these gringos are so practical," Dante said to himself whenever he thought about all the different uses one could make of the community hall. In all his years there, he would see it used as a basketball court, stage for the Christmas pageant, dance hall, and town meeting hall. Now, with the help of some generous friends and relatives and with several years of his savings, he was keeping his promise and turning the hall into a lavish party stage like those on which the lives and loves of soap-opera characters unfold.

Suddenly, on the same side of the horizon from which the lame donkey had emerged, an irresistible resplendence blazed, which turned out to be the front of a silver vehicle; the guests spilled out the door at the news that the queen of the birthday party was about to arrive. As it approached and while it progressed along the curves in the road, the silver shape came into view and finally revealed itself to be an extremely long limousine with fourteen doors and a blinding brilliance that forced observers to squint while looking at it. When it stopped, a chauffeur dressed in black leaped out to open the door that displayed a royal crown, and from there Emmita descended.

Her fingernails, red. Her lips, intense. One blue line below and another above her eyes. The mascara lengthened her eyelashes, turning them into floating wires. For the first time, the little girl was dressed as a woman or a queen. She was trying to step out of the vehicle, but she was wearing high heels and that made her descent difficult. Finally, she pushed against the seat of the car with her hands, managed to perform a graceful leap, and then walked down the red carpet that awaited her.

From that moment on, everything was shrillness. First, the applause was endless, and after the sharp, metallic blare of a trumpet that split the Mount Angel sky in two in order to proclaim to the winds and to everyone in the world that *"Éstas son las mañanitas que cantaba el rey David hoy por ser día de tu santo, te las canta-*

mos a ti." After half an hour, everything returned to its place or found the place where it belonged. King David went to Heaven, Emma was led to her throne, and the limousine parked proudly next to the doorway to the party, while, right in front of it under the red awning, sitting on his four feet, the lame donkey completed the scene.

Dressed in an electric-blue dress with blinding silver and glass sequins, the mistress of ceremonies' syrupy voice was announcing the endless parade of sponsors. The first to be introduced was Mr. Egberto Longaray from Guanajuato, about seventy years old, his cowboy hat tilted down to his nose. He was introduced as the sponsor of the limousine, because he was the one who had rented it.

Then came Don Manuel Montoya and his wife Socorro de Montoya, and when it was announced that they were the sponsors of the fireworks, an endless applause began, because Don Manuel had been able to achieve something that was nearly impossible in the United States. Throughout the country, the shining castles of fire were seen only on July 4th, but the irresistible congeniality of that Peruvian living in Oregon had won out, and he had managed to get the city of Mount Angel to allow him to bring them from who knows where and set them off on the day of the *quinceañera*. A palace of fireworks had been constructed next to the social center, and at midnight it would turn into sparks and stars, flowers of fire and firework doves, torches, radiancy, and thousands of lights capable of illuminating the entire density of the sky and of life.

The proprietress of the microphone then introduced the sponsors of the preparation of the hall: Mrs. Lulu, her husband Gabriel Escobar, and their daughters Lulu the second and Lulu the third. The four of them walked along looking worriedly at the floor, as though fearing they might have missed something and were ready to correct it immediately.

Next slid the alligator-skin boots of Carlos Montealegre, the sponsor of the music, accompanied by "his honorable wife Doña Guadalupe Alegre de Montealegre and their children Rubén, Martín,

Martina, Cleofe, Carlota, Carmencita, and Guadalupita, who add majesty to the party," as the hostess explained.

Each of those mentioned was greeted with a round of applause that became shouts of approval with the introduction of Doña Marisol Rodríguez, the wavy-haired sponsor of the *ballet folklórico*, who was dressed as a country girl and was followed by close to twenty young men wearing red pants and white shirts and as many girls wearing bright blouses and very long skirts. Their eyes revealed ostensibly that they had been dancing constantly for weeks preparing for the grand occasion.

Then came the sponsors of the cards, photos, veils, cakes, drinks, hairdos, prayers, video, makeup, phone calls, personal invitations, and many other things whose sponsorship showed the many ways in which they had collaborated in the event. Everything had been rehearsed for several weekends, but from time to time a nervous *madrina* or rushed *padrino* violated the protocol.

The mistress of ceremonies then said that the orchestra was going to begin the party with the Sponsors' Waltz, and the strains of the "Blue Danube" were heard, but there were so many *padrinos* and *madrinas*, and they represented such different generations, that a single musical selection was not sufficient for all tastes, so the Danube soon yielded to "La niña fresa," so the youngest could dance to it, and a *ranchera* for the enjoyment of the most elderly. When the time came that the music was only for the older people, all the men danced like Mr. Longaray from Guanajuato did, eyes and hats tilted downward toward the floor.

Seated in the center of the hall, the guest of honor smiled nervously. It was no secret that the town hairdresser had provided the throne in appreciation for all the hairstyling he had had to do for the Hispanic girls in Mount Angel. Bouquets of flowers and glittery trim gave that chair regal remembrances. A very dark woman with a hairdo that made her look like a fairy swore that Emma's dress, white with gold trim, had been ordered from Heaven by her mother, who likely remembered having seen that dress in the closet of one of her TV heroines.

Fourteen young ladies dressed in blue smiled nervously along-side the guest of honor while, facing them, fourteen young gentle-men wearing black tuxedos cast nervous glances at them, but none of them moved. Their suits looked too big in some cases, too small in others, but none of them looked uncomfortable but instead impatient to once and for all step toward their partners, as they had been rehearsing for several weeks. In the center of the hall, the *chambelán* was posing for a photograph. He was a young man holding a golden cane in his right hand, with which he was to give the order to dance as soon as the airs of the "Blue Danube" were heard.

All was silence and stillness. It was one of those moments when time stands still, when the world seems to pause and pose.

Never during his past life in Michoacán had Dante dreamed that he would ever throw a party like this one. Everything that he had spent, despite his friends' support, was the product of many years at minimum wage, the most anyone would pay a man without a green card. Twenty-five years earlier, he had crossed the line; ten years later the one who would be his life companion arrived, and Emma had been born to them here in the United States. They had planned to have more children, but after the delivery, Mrs. Celestino's doctor had said that she should not risk another pregnancy.

"Get all the *padrinos* and *madrinas* together for a picture," someone whispered to him, and Dante wondered if he could do that while holding the accordion. It was his inseparable companion and many were hoping he would play.

Meanwhile, two short, twin priests from Michoacán, the Fathers Pichón, were walking back and forth from one end of the hall to the other, blessing everything they came across: the throne and pots of food, chairs and trumpets, ladies' lilac silk-covered shoes and cham-pagne bottles, tables and goblets, steel-toed boots and the *madrinas*' makeup, purses embroidered with pearls and the *padrinos*' slicked-back hair, guitars, memories of the distant homeland, speakers, and the almost heavenly clothing of the guest of honor.

Then, they decided that it was time to bless the ring that would be given to the queen of the party, and they approached the young man who was the *chambelán*. He had spent the entire first hour of the party on his knees on a prie-dieu, his gaze fixed on Emmita, whom he was attempting to woo, apparently with little success.

"Do you have her gift here?"

The young man took a small package out of one of his pockets and unwrapped it slowly before the sponsors' expectant gaze.

"Oh, how lovely! Oh, how lovely!" a big-bosomed woman, apparently the most important sponsor, kept saying, sighing happily. "Isn't it beautiful, Dante? Oh, Dante . . ."

"Yes, of course, of course it is . . ."

Then the priests asked the young man to submerge the ring in a basin filled with holy water, prior to giving it to Emma. Very carefully, the *chambelán* did as he was told, and when the object entered the water, it made a rounded, effervescent sound, like *chorrrrr* . . . and caused steam and bubbles to rise to the surface . . . *chorr* . . . *chorrrr*, as if the young man's sins caused boiling upon its entry into the blessed liquid. Dante observed the young man with a worried expression, but calmed down when one of the Fathers Pichón assured him that it was natural and happened at all *quinceañeras*.

Suddenly, everything shook, and the band Los Vengadores del Norte, armed with very powerful speakers, again burst forth with the strains of the "Blue Danube." It was as if the light of the Holy Spirit suddenly descended upon the social center; the *chambelán* went into action, he raised and lowered the cane several times and, in English, repeated "one, two, three . . . one, two, three."

Something that bothered Dante was that the young people spoke among themselves in English and used Spanish only to communicate with their parents. Of all her group of friends, Emmita used the family language the least and did not seem to pay much heed to her father's advice about the kind of boys she could go out with.

"Hispanics, like us, that's fine," Dante would say, "but not those other *Hispanic* guys that don't speak Spanish and join gangs and make drug deals."

"One, two, three . . . One, two, three . . ." the *chambelán* repeated as he raised and lowered the golden cane. Then he went over to the girl turning fifteen and, taking her arm, led the group of fourteen couples who nonetheless were not yet dancing. Instead, they went first toward one wall of the hall where there was a statue of the Virgin of Guadalupe, and they bowed before it. Then they continued around the room, bowing and kneeling before Emmita's godparents, her father, the priests, the neighbors, and a group of gringos who were taking flash pictures nonstop.

But Emmita did not look very happy. During several of the obligatory bows, she was unable to hide an unpleasant expression of contempt or boredom. Finally, when the couples began to dance, their feet traveling with the triumphal strains of the waltz, she seemed neither to be in this world nor in the other one, and when it was time for her to dance with her father, she kept looking toward the door.

Dante realized that his daughter was no longer the same person. It was as if she had been replaced. No longer was she the little girl whose headache or stomach cramps he could cure by simply repeating to her *"Sana, sana, colita de rana."* Those spells no longer had any effect on her. He recalled a neighbor who had warned him to keep an eye on his daughter.

"I don't want to meddle, but I think I saw her with a boy that's not from here. He wasn't one of our boys."

Then she had described the interloper: he looked Mexican, but barely spoke Spanish; he came to town in a lowrider or a huge truck, the kind that gang members drive, and dressed completely in black. They had explained to Dante that the guy came around when he was working. Dante couldn't believe it. He imagined that—in order to not be seen or heard—his daughter's friend hung from the roofs at night like a sinister pouch and that his wings covered him completely, nocturnal, fateful, ominous, evil, hanging, flying, silent, deadly.

The day he talked to the neighbor, he got up the courage to tell Emmita that maybe it was time to talk very seriously about some matters.

"First of all, I believe that you're getting all grown up . . ."

"Please, Dad, don't interrupt. I'm watching TV."

Weeks after that failed attempt, Dante decided to try again because when he came home late, it seemed to him that a small shadow detached from the neighbors' roof and flew off screeching toward the blackest part of the sky; when he closed his eyes, he saw two small, piercing eyes that kept watching him; on other occasions the small beast's silence transformed into a screech, and it seemed that it was announcing the end of the world, or the end of *his* world.

"I've always told you that Mexican boys your age are very proper, and that if you're going to have a suitor, it would seem normal to see you with one of them."

Emma stared at him and turned up the volume on the TV and then, only then, did it occur to him that maybe, and maybe for the worse, the neighbors were telling the truth, and when he thought about the bat again, he looked not young, but old, dry, and perverse, like one of those faces that is always watching you from an accursed tomb.

❀ ❀ ❀

Y tú, quién sabe por dónde andarás, quién sabe qué aventuras tendrás, qué lejos estás de mí. The band Los Vengadores del Norte didn't know the words to this *bolero*, but Don Manuel Montoya had come prepared with recordings for those fond of old songs, and the leader of the orchestra was obliged to play it, and his musicians to accompany him. *Like a little moonbeam, asleep in the midst of the jungle, you gave light to my life, like a bright little moonbeam.* The adults began to dance. Like the sponsor of the fireworks, a dozen other men were singing into their partner's ear. Some of the women were sighing. And then, *Although the virgin may be white, paint little black angels for her, for all the good little black ones to Heaven too . . .* Mr. Longaray closed his eyes like one of the good little *negritos* in the song.

But the band was prepared to please everyone and continued with "El *corrido* de Johnny el Pachuco" by Steve Jordan, followed by "Ay te dejo en San Antonio" by Flaco Jiménez and then Joe

López's latest hits, causing the young people to go wild. They also played Pedro Ayala's "El monarca del acordeón."

Maruja Tafur took over the microphone. She was a large, South American woman, perhaps Argentine, perhaps Peruvian, who always sang at every celebration. She raised her face toward the sky as she closed her green eyes and warbled in an irrepressible voice. She had come to Mount Angel long before most of the Mexicans who lived there and had worked at the local school until she retired. Everyone respected her, and no one would have dared oppose her desire to sing, even though they would have preferred to go on dancing. Her strong suit was not *rancheras*, but rather some lyrical songs in which she revealed a voice that could shatter glass and turn the universe upside down. Once she took over the microphone, she took her time praising the age of fifteen as the best time of one's life and saying that she was going to announce the surprise of the evening.

"I've composed a song for Emmita, and I'm going to ask Dante to accompany me on the accordion," said Maruja, but no one heard her because, as she was speaking, the sound system had malfunctioned. Then came a silence and a raucous sound filled the hall. A whistling sound split the air.

Maruja took Dante Celestino by the arm and led him to the podium, where she helped him with the accordion. While the father of the guest of honor squeezed the instrument and pressed its keys, the singer began to warble in a strident voice, and her trilling flooded life on the planet with nostalgia.

A strange sound filled the hall, but no one noticed it because they were overcome with melancholy. It is impossible to say how long Maruja Tafur sang or whether it is true that some birds flew down from the four corners of the sky and entered the social center to accompany her. This will never be known because the only thing that is known is that, on the way to the sky, the warbling of the woman and the birds was interrupted by a ram, raaaammmm, ram-ramram. Rammmmmmmmmmmmmmmmmmmmmmmmmmm.

Don Egberto Longaray, from Guanajuato, states that from one minute to the next, it was as if everything were turned upside-down, the orchestra, the music, the sponsors, the guests, the sequined dress of the large mistress of ceremonies, and perhaps also life itself, because the heavenly warbling of Doña Maruja Tafur was abruptly overwhelmed by a brutal drumbeat and beams from headlights that invaded the social center.

"What we had thought was an explosion of snare drums became a thousand and one blasts of a motorcycle engine, or of many motor-cycle engines. I looked at the faces of the other people, and they were all confused. But they weren't regular motorcycles, they were lowrid-ers with their mufflers removed. From them emerged a group of young men who looked like gang members, and they entered the party uninvited."

According to him, when the gang arrived, many guests returned to their tables or slipped toward the exit without saying a word, but Emmita's face shone with a ferociously beautiful light.

"I tried to look toward the main door because it seemed odd to me that the gang members were trying to come in uninvited, but there was no one there anymore because the strangers were already inside and surrounding us without our realizing or wanting to realize it. The only thing I remember is having seen a young man dressed all in black enter the hall. Behind him, his companions had their hair slicked back, gleaming as if they had put Vaseline on it."

Dante will remember it for the rest of his life. He'll remember all of it, the stranger dressed in black, hair slicked, moving toward Emma . . . and reaching her although Dante tried vainly to step between them. In her syrupy, frightened voice, the mistress of cere-monies was screaming, "No, please! No, please! Leave us alone! Don't do this to us!"

They didn't do much. All they did was remove the orchestra and turn the sound system up to full volume with buzzes, roars, explo-sions and from time to time a raucous voice sang or shouted some-thing in English.

Some of the guests managed to say their good-byes, but others did not. Dante, standing next to the door, tried to stop them and explain that it was all a mistake, but they left him practically alone.

He collapsed into a chair, put his elbows on a table, and the planet ceased to exist for him.

Some say the gang members made Dante drink a strange substance. Others say he was knocked out by being hit on the head with the butt of a pistol and the gang took over the party. They became the masters of the *quinceañera* and, in the end, gave Emmita time to pack her bag and get into the back seat of one of the lowriders.

But Dante does not remember it like that:

"Nothing happened. What newspaper did you say you work for? No, sir, nothing happened that night."

"I'm taking notes to write a story. Perhaps that detail will not be included."

"Nothing happened."

"How many of them were there?"

Dante looks at the sky.

"The gang members. How many?"

"I repeat: nothing happened."

In any case, he awoke the next morning. Maybe regaining consciousness at the hall or in his bed if it's true that nothing happened. Maybe he decided to believe that he had dreamed it all.

According to what he says he remembers, it was late the next morning when he went by his daughter's bedroom door and wanted to invite her to go out for a walk to talk about life. He knocked three times on the door, and no one answered. He waited another hour and knocked again, but the door did not open. Then he pushed the door open and found his daughter's bed made, as if she had not slept there.

Never again, no matter how many times the world turns, would Dante ever be so alone. It was obvious that his daughter had left him and that the party planned during most of her life had been a failure.

He found nothing but his daughter's letter waiting for him. It was on her desk. He says that he saw the letter and that he could no longer see anything else. Since it would take him a long time to read it and he wouldn't understand it completely, he decided to go find a trusted friend.

But when he walked out of the house he met the huge eyes of the donkey to whom he had given shelter the day before. He thought that he would go find its owner later.

"I'm leaving, Dad, I don't feel right in this environment that you have for me. Remember, Dad, you aren't in Mexico anymore and I'm not a little girl. You and Mom always took me to the Hispanic parties, to church, to Spanish classes, and now you organized this ridiculous party for me. Dad, I'm an American girl. Johnny and I have been going out for a long time, like more than six months. Now I'm going to go live with him . . . How do you think I could have told you that, Dad, since you don't like boys who speak English, you can't stand guys that wear earrings or have tattoos . . . Dad, these aren't your times and you aren't in your country anymore. Dad, I'm fifteen years old now, and you don't even let me go out at night.

"Remember the party at the end of the school year? At ten o'clock you were already there to pick me up, I looked like an idiot in front of everyone. Nobody has to do that. You know that my grades are better than those of my friends, but their parents reward them even for getting a C+ and let them do whatever they want during vacations, even stay at their boyfriends' apartments. But you and Mom always insisted on treating me like a little girl. Wake up, Dad, I'm an American girl. I wasn't born in Michoacán.

"Papá, don't come looking for me. You have no right to. If you do find me, the police will ask me if I want to live with you or not, and I will say I don't because this is a free country. And if you fight it because I'm not eighteen yet, they'll send me to a home for adolescents, but they won't make me stay with you because, Dad, you're practically illiterate, and you can't offer me the future that you yourself don't have. Don't you realize that you can't even read this whole letter and that you'll have to ask someone else to read it to you?

"Don't try to stop me, Dad, because Johnny can pay good lawyers and, if you fight it, you could end up in jail. And don't worry too much, maybe someday I'll be back, but that will be after I've achieved my dream of being a great singer, like Selena. Johnny knows businessmen and has a lot of influential friends, and he'll get me an audition. I'm gonna be famous, Dad."

Like Selena. Como una flor. Like a flower.

And bidi bidi bom bom. And bidi bidi bom bom.

"I'm telling you, Dad, for your own good, don't try to stop me. For your own good."

A few days after the party Dante set off into the world in search of his daughter with no friend other than a lame donkey.

Como una flor. Like a flower.

And bidi bidi bom bom. And bidi bidi bom bom.

2
Those Who Think They Know Only Know Half the Story

The people from the *El Latino de Hoy*, the most widely read Spanish-language newspaper, had heard the story, but the editor did not know how much truth there was in it. The English-language papers in San Francisco and Portland had given a lot of coverage to the story of the Mexican who got lost on U.S. roads and highways searching for his daughter, and it was not right for *El Latino de Hoy* to be unaware of that information. Therefore, they asked me to write what journalists call a "human interest story" about Dante Celestino. When I asked how much space they would give me, they offered me as much as I wanted and suggested that they might even publish a special section devoted entirely to the case.

I arrived in Mount Angel, the town where Dante lived, in the afternoon and immediately headed for the Buenos Amigos restaurant-lounge-bar, where I had been told I could get information on the matter.

"What'll it be?"

"Nothing. I was in the neighborhood and I'm looking for . . ."

"What'll it be?!" repeated the authoritarian voice of the owner who, clearly, did not care for me. My camera equipment was too obvious.

"You know you can't take pictures here."

"I'm not here to take pictures."

"Then?"

I did not know how to respond, because he was not giving me a chance to explain.

"Then?"

I looked all around to try to locate the exit door, but the bar was very dark.

"Then?" repeated the authoritarian voice. I saw the exit sign and began to walk toward it, but a friendly voice spoke up behind me.

"Mescal?"

"Mescal?"

"Yes, mescal for both of us. You're going to pay, aren't you?"

These words came from a man who seemed to have been sitting in the darkest corner of Buenos Amigos his whole life. I accepted, although I had never drunk mescal. The bartender returned with two glasses full to the brim with the beverage, and then he disappeared.

"Are you going to talk to me about Dante?"

"No, about Virgilio."

I had learned earlier that the donkey's name was Virgilio and, honestly, that seemed irrelevant to me. I told him so.

"I said I'll talk to you about Virgilio," he insisted, and I was about to walk away, leaving him there with the two glasses, when I heard the rain and thunder outside. I could not see his face; all I could make out was a poncho that he wore like a shawl across his mouth. For that reason I do not remember his words well, although I am attempting to reproduce them here.

"Some say he entered the United States by sea, others swear that he came through the mountains like most of us, and still others want to see him flying. They see him floating over the rolling hills of Tijuana. They see him skirt the radar traps and evade the infrared lights. They see him rise up, weightless, above the gringos' helicopters. And finally they feel him land at the entrance to San Diego as angels alight, because Virgilio is small, furry, soft, a donkey through and through, and no matter how much of a donkey he may be, he is still light and airy, so light and airy that when he trots, he does so as if steadying himself on the ground, as if tying himself to the earth, fearing that the wind would carry him off.

"Someone says that the Espinos brought Virgilio across the border. It was during a sandstorm one day when the wind blew so hard that several Mexican mountains crossed the border without showing their papers and an eloping couple became hopelessly lost in the vast California skies. But that cannot be true, because not even God can hide Virgilio's ears when Virgilio gets nervous, or stubborn like a mule, or acts like an ass, and moves on through a storm to the United States, invisible, transparent, incorporeal, silent, philosophical, but still a donkey, and before him go the soft, furry, enormous ears of a donkey on the run.

"Or maybe they crossed during a night when there was an eclipse. The moon must have been bouncing from one side of the sky to the other until it finally disappeared into a reddish hole, and they took advantage of that moment to cross. The moustaches of the gringos at Customs shone golden beneath the eclipse, as did their hair, eyebrows, and eyelashes, and because of all that, if they did see Virgilio's ears go by, they looked reddish-gold to them, and they must have taken them for butterflies.

"Anyway, none of this is important. The important thing is to find out how the Espinos got the idea of entering this country with a donkey, when we all have felt the weight of the fear and poverty we bring from the other side. The truth is that we all would have wanted to bring our donkey, our house, the town clock, the bar, and our friends, but coming to this country is like dying; besides our hopes and sorrows, all we can bring with us are the clothes on our backs."

"Yes. That," I interrupt him abruptly, interested in the donkey. "Why did they bring him?"

"Maybe he was all the Espinos had, other than their son Manuel, who must have been about five years old and probably did not want to give up the donkey. Maybe they felt that without an animal, a human family is neither good nor complete, as God says in the Bible when he speaks of Noah who weathered the storm, taking with him, in addition to his wife and daughter, turkeys, ducks, pigs, sheep, dreams, a tiger, a lion, a butterfly, and an elephant that was in town. Whatever the case, in this memory there is always a glowing, yellow afternoon, and walking ahead of that color the silhouettes of a man, a woman, a child, and Virgilio, about to enter the United States.

"God gave the Espinos the largest house in the area. They came upon it there, on the banks of the Willamette River, on the side where the wild geese stop to rest every year, and it was such an old, empty house that it looked like it had been abandoned since the time of the Great Flood, and they took it because an Oregon attorney who defended immigrants told them that it was legal to take possession of abandoned houses. In it, Mario José and María del Pilar took the room with the west window and gave the child the east room. Virgilio spent the daylight hours grazing, sleeping, philosophizing and playing with Manuelito in a room adjoining the house, which was full of calendars and books about raising chickens. Neither the immigration authorities nor the local police would go look for him there because never, even in the land of gringos, has anyone heard of librarian donkeys.

"Their good luck arrived right when their son Manuel was getting past the age of learning the alphabet, that is, he was saved from illiteracy as has been occurring with children born in California who, unluckily for them, are children of undocumented immigrants.

"Manuelito liked school so much that, from the first day, he came home ready to teach Virgilio to read. This is not strange because little girls feed their dolls, although it indeed is dangerous if animals learn. Nor is the case strange if we keep in mind that donkeys cannot write because they do not have hands, nor can they talk because they bray, although there is no law preventing them from reading."

"Are you telling me the donkey knows how to read?"

"No one here is saying anything," the man replied, ordering two more mescals from the bartender.

"Just one. I don't think I can drink . . . ," I corrected him, but it was as if my voice were not there because the bartender showed up with the mescals and an order of tortillas.

"Besides, no one here is saying that the donkey really learned, but that is what Manuelito said, and his parents pretended to believe it. That's why every day when he got home, the little boy went into Virgilio's room, opened his book to the lesson the teacher had taught him that day, began composing words, phrases, and obsessions, and repeated that this word means 'elephant' and you won't forget it because the 'h' is a tall letter with its trunk in the air, just like the elephants in the jungle and in the afternoon, and that next one is 'world,' because the letter 'o' is deep and joyful, and this word is 'clouds' because it is dark and because it looks like it is always moving away, and you won't forget the word 'waves,' because the 'w' looks like the waves that come and go.

"Virgilio would look at the book that the boy had left next to his feed and could not believe that the words spoke and wanted to speak to him to tell him that the ships came down by the north and the south and went up through the west and the east. He could not believe it until he found the word 'house' and, without his teacher being there, identified it with the Espinos' house, made so neat and tidy by Mrs. Espino. Then the word 'child' seemed identical to Manuelito, and finally he sniffed the words 'farewell,' 'mountains,' and 'borders,' and it occurred to him that they should be with others like 'origin,' 'homeland,' 'grief,' 'nostalgia,' and 'love.'

"An illustration showed him the green delicacy he received every morning and tasted again in the meadow after playing with Manuelito. 'Feed,' 'pasture,' 'grass,' and 'hay' were words that varied from green to yellow, but which were without exception delicious and fundamental. 'Grass' is the most pleasant word in the language, Virgilio may have said to himself, and his eyes grew large, his enormous ears stood straight up, and he formulated his first complete sentence: 'I think . . . I think . . . therefore I am.'"

As the man spoke he drank his glass of mescal, and mine too, for which I silently thanked him. Then he stopped talking right when the rain stopped. I got up, paid the bill, and headed toward the door. Suddenly, I realized that I had not said good-bye and I turned back, but the man was no longer at the table.

"I'd like to know the name of the man who was giving me information for something I'm writing."

"Are you sure you were talking to someone?"

And when I insisted, his authoritarian voice returned, ordering me to drink or leave.

"What'll it be? . . ."

◈ ◈ ◈

That man in the bar was the first person Dante Celestino saw when he set off to find his daughter. He asked him if he knew the guy who had taken her away, but all he got were stories about donkeys.

Of course, the first thing he would do when he went to the police station would be to turn Virgilio in and report Emmita's disappearance. But first he had to find out some things.

Saturday and Sunday were not enough time to make inquiries about his daughter nor to be urged to give up and wait. Some neighbors avoided talking to him, not wanting to get involved. The worst was what happened at the home of Marisol Rodríguez, the sponsor of the ballet, who was having a meeting with several other women at the community hall. Seeing her, he could not contain himself, and he declared that he would go to the ends of the earth to find his daughter.

"I understand you, Dante, but remember that we're in the United States . . . Here you have to communicate with the authorities, and the truth is that here it's not considered so awful for a girl to run off with her boyfriend."

"I'll search for her until I find her," the man replied, and he said it vehemently. None of the women recognized in him the timid neighbor who never lost his patience.

When he repeated that he would continue searching for his daughter, the women stared at him as shocked as if he had suddenly sprouted wings and long blue feathers.

"Understand, Dante," said Aguirre, his next-door neighbor. "You're as illegal as I am. What do we stand to gain by making a scandal over something that in this country is perfectly natural?! What good would it do for me to go with you to the police station?! And what if they ask for our documents?"

He tried to call Doña Rosina Rivero Ayllón, Emmita's godmother, but she had moved to California a month earlier. The Fathers
Pichón had already left for the town where their parish was located.
The Mexican priest was not in Mount Angel. He went to see Juan
Pablo Medina, the pastor of an evangelical church, and the gentleman asked him to take a seat while he looked for the appropriate
quote in the Bible. Dante was thinking that he was wasting time and
that his daughter might already be crossing the state line, but being
the timid, courteous man that he was, he had to wait for the pastor to
finish reading him a long quotation from the Book of Job.

"Really, I wanted to ask you to check with your parishioners.
Maybe someone knows something."

But the pastor, not listening to him, began to look for another
verse, and Dante had to sit in the armchair, timidly tapping his foot
on the floor, not realizing that the pastor was also prescribing pru-
dence and acceptance of his fate.

To report the case to the police, he had to wait until Monday to
go to the state capital. He had thought that maybe the highway patrol
would set up roadblocks and ask all truck, car, and motorcycle drivers the whereabouts of a young Mexican girl named Emmita. What
still had not come to him was what to say if they asked him for the
name of her abductor.

"Are you listening to me, Dante? Dante?" repeated Pastor Medina, seated with his back to the window, but Saturday had come to an
end and instead of looking at him, Dante was looking behind him at
the endless night.

Very early Sunday morning, Dante traveled eight miles to the
neighboring town of Woodburn to the office of Josefino and Mariana, astrologists who for a few dollars told fortunes and provided
spiritual advice for Hispanics throughout the valley. He had known
them for a long time and had visited them often during the time
when Beatriz was sick.

"Here again, Dante, our friend. What brings you here this time?"
asked Josefino, and it seemed to Dante illogical that a fortune-teller

would ask him that, even out of courtesy. He showed him a picture of Emma.

"Your little girl, of course. You're looking for her, and you want us to help you. How old did you say she is? Ah. Fifteen. Then, she has run away from home. Don't worry; we're going to help you . . . Of course, you must carry with you the magical Cloth of the Three Wishes that we are now going to charge with power so that it will be a shield for you against the enemies you will encounter along the way. The magical cloth will allow you and your vehicle to become invisible when scoundrels are looking for you."

Meanwhile, Josefino continued talking and attempted to disguise the questions that stimulated his fortune-telling ability and caused ever-greater astonishment in the client. But when the time came to set the price to sell him the lucky charm, the fortune-teller looked into Dante's eyes and hesitated. Behind his eyes appeared an innocent man whom he saw traveling and becoming lost all the time, swallowed up by the distance and an evil fate. It was easy to see that within that man there was no longer anything, not even a soul, only stubborn hope.

"No, Dante, my friend. I cannot deceive you. I do not believe you are able to search for your daughter. I do not believe there is any charm in the world that can help you. Go back home and stay there; do not take any more risks. You've already lost everything."

Morning, noon, and night he asked, getting nothing in return but pats on the back and vague advice to accept life as it was. On Tuesday, he parked his vehicle at the Tapatío, the store that sold Mexican products and phone cards, and he went inside. Mrs. Quintana's youngest daughter was the only one there. She looked at him and then turned her eyes back toward the television where a soap opera was on. Dante took off his hat as a greeting, but that was an unnecessary gesture because the soap opera had the girl's complete attention.

Therefore, Celestino decided to wait for her mother to get there. She knew everything that went on in town and, besides, her oldest daughter was a classmate of Emma.

On the counter there were several ceramic knickknacks, probably from Oaxaca, and in the middle of them was the flying skirt of a scantily clad plastic dancing girl, but none of that was for sale. On the wall behind him were several shelves displaying different herbs and a huge picture of the Powerful Hand.

"Excuse me, do you have anything to drink?"

"What you see here," replied the girl, her fascination with the television uninterrupted.

There were some bottles of Jarritos brand tamarind and hibiscus soft drinks. Dante selected a tamarind and started to look for a bottle opener. At that moment, the owner of the store came in. The woman apologized, saying she had just gone out for a moment to have something to eat at home, and she scolded her daughter for not waiting on Dante.

"I was looking for the bottle opener," Dante began, but Mrs. Quintana decided to save him the trouble.

"You want to know about her. Isn't that right?"

"Pardon me?"

"Honey, turn off that TV now and wait on the customers," she said as she headed toward the back of the store.

"You, come in here."

Dante went in.

"Sit down."

He sat down.

"I had told you a long time ago, but of course maybe there was nothing you could do. Nothing. We parents are nobody in this country. And mothers are worth less than nothing."

Dante did not say so, but he did not agree with her last statement. He thought that if Beatriz had been alive, their daughter would not have run away. Mrs. Quintana was talking to him from the open door, and behind her there was a violent sunset. The sun was sinking and rising again in a distant sky that was redder than blood; perhaps blacker too.

"Are you listening to me?"

Dante Celestino nodded.

That's when he found out the name of the abductor. His name was Johnny Cabada, one of those young guys who join gangs and make a lot of money selling drugs.

"My daughter told me that they met him one night when they were coming back from choir practice at church. 'What a pretty voice you have. I thought Selena was singing,' she says he told Emmita, and that Emmita smiled because she'd always wanted to be a famous singer."

But Dante was not there to find out those kinds of details. He just wanted to know where the guy was.

"That's harder. What my daughter told me is that Johnny works in Las Vegas, at a place called Montecarlo. She says that he told them that's where he runs his business."

"In Las Vegas? In the casinos?"

"Exactly."

Dante asked nothing further. He had made a decision. He did not say good-bye or thank her for the information. Nor did he open the bottle of tamarind drink.

Dante went to see his boss and asked for permission to miss work for a few days. He went home and, when he got there, he was a different person. The poor, timid immigrant had disappeared, and in his place was a man ready to search the world over to get his daughter back. He found the donkey tied to a post next to his house and decided to find him a place in the yard. He thought to set up a shelter for him in case it rained, and while he was looking for a tarp, Dante talked to him, knowing that he would not understand but that he would listen without interrupting. He told him that he liked him because he seemed to be a good boy, and then he corrected himself and said a good donkey, and that he would have liked to keep him but that he had found out he already had an owner. He told him he would take him to the Salem police station the next day, and the animal flicked his ears, but Dante asked him not to worry and said to trust him, because he would not let anything bad happen to him.

Then Dante went to bed, but he didn't fall asleep. His gaze was fixed on the window where the Milky Way had not yet gone by, and he remembered that in the midst of that mass of stars, the souls of mothers wander. He thought about his mother and also about Beatriz and smiled a sad smile toward the place in the sky where he assumed they were.

3
Crying Without Laughing Is Bad for You

Perhaps the friendship between the donkey and the man began like the one that begins between a castaway and a tree on a desert island, or perhaps it began as Dante was driving toward Salem in a van, the vehicle that years earlier he had made run in the shop of the business where he worked. On the highway, he realized once and for all that he was alone on the planet and that the only person capable of listening to him was a donkey.

The van was an enormous vehicle with two beds, water and drainage service, a television, and a large space for carrying packages. His boss had abandoned it ten years earlier.

"Do you want the van? Take it. It takes up a lot of room in the shop."

With his mechanical abilities, Dante had managed to rebuild it the way he wanted and transform it into a vehicle capable of taking the family on pleasure trips on the weekends. Now there was no longer a family. There was only a man.

He had settled Virgilio in the back and was taking him to the police so that they could return him to his legitimate owners. Of course the first reason for his visit to the police station was to report his daughter's disappearance and demand the arrest of those who had taken her.

"What bad luck that we've met each other under these circumstances!" he said, playing with the donkey's ears. "You look like you would be a really good friend, but what can we do? I've been told that you have owners, and since I don't know where they live, these

men from the police will locate them. . . . You shouldn't worry about
the leg. The treatment I gave you will be sufficient, and soon you'll
be able to trot just fine.

"I've been told your name is Virgilio, that you escaped when you
were learning to read."

A huge, red-haired policeman met him at the door of the Salem
station and told him something that he was unable to understand
because in all the years he had lived there, Dante never learned to
speak English. He had had three bosses, and all three could make
themselves understood in Spanish, and when Dante himself had tried
to learn, he had been told that in order to harvest crops, take care of
animals, or repair trucks, it wasn't necessary to speak English.

After several useless attempts at communication, the officer
smiled and handed him some papers to fill out with his name,
address, age, marital status, ethnic origin, and a description of the
events that he was reporting.

"They're in Spanish . . . They're in Spanish," he kept saying in
English until he realized that Dante couldn't read or write very well
in any of the world's languages. So he had him come in and sit down
to wait for the interpreter, but Dante signaled to the officer to come
over to his vehicle and opened the back door so that he could take
the donkey too.

Still using gestures, the red-haired officer explained to him that
that wasn't necessary and that the police department did not accept
payments for its services.

"No, sir, what I want to do is to return him."

But the gringo insisted with his head, fingers, and words: "No,
no, no."

"This donkey isn't mine, and I want you to return him to his
family."

The policeman continued rejecting the "gift": "No, no, no.
Thank you . . . Thank you!!! . . . But it is not necessary."

An hour later the interpreter arrived. She was a tall, heavy,
blonde woman, dressed like a 19th-century pioneer in a floor-length
skirt and with her hair in a bun. She generously volunteered her serv-

ices to the police, but her knowledge of Spanish suffered from some very serious deficiencies. At any rate, she wrote down the information that Dante gave her and made mistakes on the numbers because she didn't know them, and when she asked him Emmita's age, instead of fifteen years, she wrote fifty on the form. After filling out the form, she realized her mistake and corrected it.

Height? Weight? Distinguishing features? At the end, she read him the statement of equal opportunity according to which everyone is equal under the law, and there is no sort of discrimination due to origin, beliefs, or race.

"Next, it asks here your daughter's race. Can you tell me your daughter's race?"

Dante was silent for a moment, amazed at the contradiction, but the woman did not allow him to respond.

"Colored. I'm going to put here 'colored' because all Hispanics are colored. And now the information about the plaintiff . . ."

"My name and my address? . . . Everyone in Mount Angel knows me. I'm a Celestino, of the Celestinos from Sahuayo, Michoacán. What do you mean you don't know where Sahuayo is? It's where that they make straw hats and also rubber ones. I'll give you an idea: if you go to Michoacán, ask how to get to Parangaricutirimícuaro. From there, it's just around the corner. Everybody there knows my last name, although only the older people know me because I came north more than twenty years ago."

"Your name, please. And here your address. And your Social Security number," repeated the woman who knew a little Spanish, but was not familiar with the communication styles of Spanish speakers.

When Dante told her, lowering his voice, that his papers were false, the woman didn't know what to say, but suddenly a light of intelligence appeared on her face: "The police take care of everyone regardless of immigration status," she said as if she were repeating a manual from memory. "But we don't kid around here. Don't tell me that after being here so long, you still don't have papers."

"And Virgilio?"

"Virgilio? Who's Virgilio?"

"Virgilio's the donkey, and he doesn't have any papers either. Well, I've been told his name is Virgilio and that the son of his owner tried to teach him to read."

The volunteer lost patience and told Dante to put his fingerprint on one of the papers and that the police would let him know when they found Emmita.

"And the donkey?"

The woman began to speak in English with one of the officers. They were probably talking about the story of the donkey because the officer began to laugh and laugh uncontrollably. The interpreter handed a pencil to Dante.

"The policeman says this is for your little donkey," the interpreter explained. "He says to put it above his ear. They'll let you know about your daughter. But you must understand that this is a free country and that a fifteen-year-old girl is a full-grown woman because the sexist, chauvinist taboos of backward countries don't apply here."

"Do you mean to say that I'll never see my daughter again?"

"Are you ever a typical Mexican, Dante! A fifteen-year-old woman needs her freedom. At that age, parents are almost a bother. At that age, a girl needs to get to know herself. She needs to find herself through different sexual experiences, and not through marriage to a man that will crush her and turn her into an object. That's for later, much later."

"And Emmita? Will I see her again?" repeated Dante, who had not completely understood the woman's speech.

"It's normal that she's run off with her boyfriend. And it's healthy. She has to enjoy her freedom before she gets married. She has to learn about dating, that is, get to know a lot of men, before society forces her to make a commitment as serious as marriage."

"Do you mean to tell me that Emmita's not coming back? That the police aren't going to help me find her?"

"It's obvious you're from a backward, patriarchal culture! If you want to stay here, you have to be modern. You can't be an old-fashioned *macho* man but a politically correct person. This is a free country in which we desire diversity but we don't want that kind of immigrant. . . . I'm warning you, Dante, if you try to impose permanent authority over your daughter, you'll become the sort of brutal *macho* that we don't want in this country," said the woman not hiding her anger.

When he left the police station, Dante decided to take a stroll in Bush Park while he decided what to do next. He parked the van, picked out a bench under a maple tree, and began to think what his life was going to be like from now on, as a warm, yellow sun was melting the world and turning it into an enormous drop of honey. Perhaps at that moment, Dante's luck was changing as fast as snakes do when they change skin.

He decided that this time he was going to head in the opposite direction from the way he had gone twenty-some years earlier when he came from Mexico. Johnny Cabada and his gang worked out of a Las Vegas casino, and that's where he would go. They had told him that the gang of young criminals was skilled at disappearing when the police were close to them. Therefore, they might go even further away, to San Francisco, Los Angeles, San Diego, maybe more. Dante had not left the state of Oregon in all the time he had lived there, or rather, he had done so just once, traveling as far as the border with the friends who were transporting his wife Beatriz's body to Sahuayo for burial. But now indeed, he would do it; he would go wherever he had to for his daughter and would return from the very end of the world with her.

Yes, of course, now he would travel south, and if the police didn't want to keep Virgilio, perhaps Dante would take care of him. He had found a very pleasant companion. Dante opened the back door of the van and got the big-eared one out so that together they could look at the grass, the skies, and their destiny. Then, sitting on the bench, Dante began to tell the endless story of his life to his new friend, and as the memories came, the leaves fell from the trees and went off along the pathways of air, transformed into birds and faded images of happiness.

"On the road that runs from Parangaricutirimícuaro to Sahuayo, there's a hermitage, and in it, there's a very miraculous saint whom we'll visit and ask for help if we don't find Emmita's trail."

He had begun to recall the roads of Michoacán, when from the door of a nearby house came an uncontainable explosion of laughter that made him think about leaving immediately in order to not pull it out of tune with his sadness, but his curiosity got the best of him, and he kept listening for maybe fifteen minutes to loud laughter of two voices, interrupted only briefly by short comments in Spanish. It was, as he would soon see, two Mexican women, mother and daughter; the latter was perhaps twenty years old and the mother twice that.

What were they laughing about? It was hard to know because their short phrases did not allow him to guess what was causing them such hilarity, and Dante moved to a closer bench to hear better. Soon, however, his curiosity was punished because the laughter of the two women began coming closer and closer until it spread to him like unbearable tickling that he could not resist, and he began to laugh too.

Ten, fifteen minutes, maybe half an hour, went by, and Dante, laughing so hard he was crying, had thrown himself off the bench onto the grass and was rolling around laughing constantly. He tried to go over to Virgilio to tell him something sad, but couldn't get up. He wanted to run back to the van, but his legs wouldn't hold him. He tried to think about the unhappiest events of his life, but that did no good, and when he finally managed to recall them they caused him to laugh even harder. He tried to cover his ears, but the wicked women were rehearsing increasingly higher-pitched laughter or using voices that made him laugh even more.

After perhaps an hour, they were quiet. It became silent in the park but, maybe from inertia, Dante was still laughing. The birds, the leaves, the paths they traced in the air, his own shadow, everything made him laugh, and he had the feeling that everyone in the universe was laughing. He managed to stop for a moment, but his tormentors had only taken a short break; immediately, one of them made a comment that he didn't understand, and they went back to the endless laughing.

Then, he realized what he should have done at the beginning: he stood up and, with tears in his eyes, went over to them to ask what they were laughing about.

A long time later, on the endless road, he would still be amazed at the strength he had to get up and walk to the yard of the house where Carmen Silva and Patricia León were laughing until they could laugh no more. What he would not be able to recall or imagine were the expressions on the faces of the two women when a man with uncontainable laughter and tears came over and asked "Please, tell me what we're laughing about."

"We're laughing," Carmen explained, "because my little Patricia lost her job."

Dante could not understand.

"The boss discovered that her Social Security papers are fake, they're falsified, and a couple hours ago he sent her home."

Seeing that he still did not understand, Patricia explained: "My mother and I are undocumented. She can't work because she has a health problem, and I just got fired from my job. Besides that, the landlord called to tell us we have one week to pay or get out."

He understood even less now, but he had to pretend that all of their misfortunes seemed very funny to him.

Then Carmen explained it to him: "We're laughing," she said, "because crying without laughing is bad for you." And she told him how despite everything that was happening to them as undocumented immigrants in the United States—they were alone, had no money and no jobs—they were choosing to laugh in order to feel better.

"We laugh at all the bad things, and we laugh until we cry. Patricia sometimes wants to go back to Guadalajara, but I tell her that if we're here it must be for a reason, and I tell her this laughing because, like I said, crying without laughing is very bad for you."

Hours later, Dante managed to return to the place where he had left the vehicle and the donkey. The van was there in the same place, but Virgilio was rolling on the grass and kicking the ground hard. Dante ran to help him, but there was nothing wrong with the donkey, except that tears were spilling from his eyes like when we're dying from sorrow or like when laughter is devouring us.

4
The Trees Whisper and the Whales Sing

The engine of the enormous vehicle snorted, crackled, started, and finally the man, the donkey, and the machine were becoming smaller and smaller as they disappeared down the Oregon roads heading south. The road that Dante had taken was not the fastest, but was the one that would present the least difficulties for his vehicle. There were no heights or very steep slopes, nor high-speed stretches, all of which made the noisy journey of the old rattletrap easier. He was sure they would reach Nevada, and his only thought was to search for his daughter casino by casino until he found Johnny Cabada.

As his van squeaked, buzzed, squealed, and creaked along, Dante had the impression that he was traveling toward the past, and he was astonished to notice that that time had a burnt color, perhaps that of an eclipse. And he remembered Beatriz. Twenty-five years ago, she had stayed behind in Mexico waiting for him until he was able to save enough money to send for her and form a new family.

Now he was traveling without her and that made him feel like the loneliest man in the world. What's more, the only friend accompanying him was a donkey. He looked in the rearview mirror and saw the ears of Virgilio, who was dozing. He looked a moment longer, and it seemed to him that some tiny doves were flying around the sleeping animal.

"He must be dreaming of doves."

The donkey twitched his ears and raised his head.

32

"No, sir. How great it would be if you could talk! The truth is that I never went to school either, and I'm as much a dumb animal as you. If I don't bray yet, it's just because I haven't picked up the right pitch."

The vehicle made its way along the Cascade Mountain range, which separates the forest and the desert in Oregon; nevertheless, Dante had the impression that he was traveling through his native Michoacán. Without taking his eyes off the U.S. superhighway, it seemed to him that he was arriving back in Sahuayo, his hometown, which in his memories was crowned with an eternal yellow air and filled with bees that never stopped buzzing. Or maybe he was driving through the sky, because suddenly he was aware of a taste of mint in his mouth, and everyone knows that is the flavor of love.

If he was driving through the sky, Beatriz must be very near, and yet, there was no one next to him.

"I didn't want you to travel alone in search of our daughter, and I asked for permission to keep you company even if only for a little while," said the voice of his wife.

Permission? Of whom did Beatriz have to ask permission? Were there permits, papers, and visas in Heaven too? As always happens to those who daydream, he had forgotten that Beatriz was dead and that perhaps the voice he was hearing was one of those echoes that last ten, twenty, or thirty years or more, like unattainable loves.

"And how did you get here? Can you tell me? Yes, how did you get here?"

"Dreaming," the voice said and repeated: "Dreaming," and perhaps it explained that everything up there is a permanent dream. Really, as much a dream as the one down here, the difference being that up there we can guide our dreams.

"But we're going to travel a very long way. Did you at least bring a suitcase?"

"All of that remained in the past."

"And what happened to the past?

"It was left back there."

From some place in the sky, a purple cloud emerged, like the color and flavor of hibiscus, the drink made from the reddest flowers in Mexico, and Dante realized that he had been daydreaming, and maybe it was then that it occurred to him that he would have to talk to Virgilio in order not to fall asleep.

It's not that Dante was trying to converse; it was enough for him to talk and be listened to. Besides, that's the way most people talk. When this story became news, *El Latino de Hoy* in Portland, Oregon published a collection of photos of donkeys in the western United States, but none of them seemed to speak. Every donkey on the published page was just a donkey, and looked toward one side, disinterested, neutral, expressionless, like diplomats, spies, and serious professors in this country, or women when they're ironing.

When Emma ran away, Dante had seen the great fiesta of his life ruined, had witnessed the breakup of what remained of his family, and had seen the world he knew fall to pieces. The overwhelming pain gave him a special sensibility to perceive everything that is strange in nature. So it is not strange at all that it would be enough for this man to be listened to by Virgilio and that he would even interpret his silence as a manner of speaking.

"If I just knew where my daughter was . . . I'm sure that when she sees me again, she'll run to my arms because she's a good girl. Certainly she has realized her mistake, but has no way to get out of the situation. The truth is that we're all in the same boat. Since I left my country, since I came to this place, I've never stopped feeling trapped, as if I had no way out."

"Make miracles happen," said "La Campeona," the radio station of all Hispanics, and then it began to play the jingle for a soft drink. Dante wondered if miracles existed.

Oh, if Beatriz were truly at his side to talk about those matters, or if at least Virgilio would speak, but, do animals talk?

"Animals talk, mountains converse, trees whisper, the earth sings, and whales listen to it and join in. The bad part is that they don't understand each other. All of them talk, but still there is no communication. See, sometimes there is not even communication among humans, who think they are the only ones who can talk. There are a lot of things that the Lord forgot at the time of Creation,

Dante, and communication is one of them. The universe is incomplete," said Beatriz.

"The universe would be incomplete without you, friend. So don't let us down this Friday at 6 p.m. at the great fiesta at 'Los compadres del universo,' the great restaurant and dance hall where all the Hispanics in Oregon gather. There'll be *quebraditas, corridos,* and Mexican *antojitos.* The first fifty ladies get in free."

Dante preferred to think that he was hearing his wife and not the radio.

"The world is incomplete, Dante. Those of us who are already walking those other valleys that exist up there know this well. There, it's enough to think about someone to be instantly connected; here on earth where you still live, Dante, that ability is destined for only distant, unattainable loves."

Perhaps at that moment, Dante had a different sensation of the road. Perhaps it seemed to him that he had begun to understand what a road is and therefore had the impression that neither he nor his vehicle were moving. Instead things were coming toward him one after another.

"All you have to do is put yourself on the road. Then you don't even have to move. All roads lead to 'Los dos amigos del universo,' where tonight the famous stars Marco Antonio Solís and Juan Pablo Seminario will appear, the two golden tenors of the new Mexican song."

The van followed the route of the great mountain, or rather the mountain was showing it the route. The heart of the Cascades, between Mount Hood and the Twins, was like an enormous snake lying in wait.

"Around here we leave the state. That way we get to Mount Jefferson. From there up it's enough to let ourselves be carried away a little to reach the line of the horizon. At any moment we'll pass under the horizon." Dante was saying this to Virgilio, certain that Virgilio would be interested in knowing their geographical location, and perhaps that was the case because the animal did not even yawn.

Virgilio moved his ears as if he were frightening flies or unlucky thoughts, and the man took this as a sign of worry.

"Well, it's nothing to worry so much about. Anyway, you and I will get where we're going."

Dante would have liked to talk more with Beatriz when she was alive because usually she was as quiet a conversation partner as Virgilio on trips. Generally it was Dante who spoke, telling stories, asking questions, and then the words would fall asleep in his mouth, and he didn't know what to do to awaken them.

It's impossible to know if it was really Beatriz who was talking to him with the same voice and the same taste of mint in her mouth that she had always had. It's impossible to know because nothing can be fully known about spirits. It is said that they are everywhere, here and there and behind you when you're reading an interesting book, but who knows. It's impossible to know because no one can see them so easily. Not even the old people who go about bumping into death every little while, not even *they* can see them. But animals can. That's why dogs bark and donkeys' ears stand up when a spirit makes its presence felt.

"I wish all of this were a dream."

He kept ruminating over that "don't come looking for me" and that "I'm an American girl" and finally that part about "if you go to the police, they'll pay no attention to you because here what you Mexicans think is abnormal is normal."

And bidi bidi bom bom. And bidi bidi bom bom. . . .

"Don't worry about what she wrote. When you find her, she'll already be regretting that. But you don't have to hurry to find her, it's enough that you're looking for her, and it's even enough that you're on the way and you'll find her when you're supposed to find her."

He could hear the voice, but he couldn't see the face of the one who was speaking.

"If it weren't for Virgilio, I'd become lost in dreams," said Dante sadly. "If Beatriz were here in the world with me, she would certainly have taken me to talk to Doctor Dolores. She would likely have said, 'Talk to her. Tell her to call our daughter on TV.'"

Besides soap operas, in recent years the Celestinos had never missed Doctor Dolores's show. On Thursdays about midnight, they watched the talk shows, and the last one was that program that was also broadcasted on the radio. Doctor Dolores, a dyed blonde with a very tight skirt, would interview her guests every night. Sometimes there were fights on stage, but most of the time the programs ended with a sweet reunion in which everyone shed tears, except the program host.

Adulterers and alcoholics, transvestites and prostitutes, orphans and adopted children looking for their real parents, all the misfortuned and the unfortunate came together on every talk show. It was always possible for the doctor to locate an unfortunate Hispanic in some corner of the United States. Her stiff eyelashes above the mascara and her scrutinizing alfalfa-green eyes pinpointed a tragic story in some town, and immediately the show's producers boarded the parties involved on a plane. There was no excuse for them, because the television network paid all their expenses, bought them new clothes, and even paid them a generous remuneration for declaring their miseries in public.

A neighbor of Beatriz and Dante in Mount Angel, Emmanuel Cordero, had participated in one of the programs. Emmanuel, who was twenty-eight years old at the time, was going through a tragedy. His beloved girlfriend Angelita was acting very indifferent, kind of slippery, and it seemed obvious that she was going out with another guy, whose identity Emmanuel didn't know, although some friends had told him that it was a handsome older man with a lot of money. Before two hundred million Spanish-speakers, the young man told how his great love had begun. For her part, Angelita declared that all of that was true, that she felt the same for the kind Emmanuel, and that she didn't understand why he had become so jealous lately.

"You mean you haven't been involved with anyone else? You've been faithful to this honest man who has given you his whole heart?"

"Yes," said Angelita.

"Would you swear it?"

"Yes, I swear."

"And if I told you that you're a liar?"

A curtain of music buried the final words of Doctor Dolores, and the camera zoomed in on Angelita's tear-filled eyes, but it was impossible to know right away what was going on because a very large woman appeared before the cameras to recommend the purchase of a medication that could solve a weight problem in two weeks. Then a man who had hair even in his ears said that he was a famous scientist who had discovered the cure for baldness. At that instant the station was flooded with phone calls, and the man had to admit that the remedy was not effective in all cases. "Perhaps in your case it won't make your hair grow back," he said, "but it will thicken the hair you have left."

"Would you repeat that you aren't a liar?" repeated Doctor Dolores, and before the girl could ratify her oath, not letting her say anything, she announced that within a few minutes a person able to reveal the whole truth would appear on stage.

"But I've been told," she insisted, "that you cheat on Emmanuel with the person with whom you should least do so. Marthita," she ordered a scantily clad woman who had been an attorney in Panama, "Please open that door and invite the man behind it to come on stage."

A gong sounded throughout the world as the indicated door opened, and from behind it emerged a very elegant older gentleman who looked a lot like Emmanuel.

"You know him, don't you, Emmanuel?"

Emmanuel couldn't respond. He couldn't believe it.

"You, Angelita, have betrayed the trust bestowed in you by this honest young man, and you will have to get down on your knees and beg him to forgive you. You, Don Raúl, have committed the most despicable act of your life. You've stolen your son's girlfriend. I think you too should ask his forgiveness. What do you think, distinguished, educated audience?"

That was as much as Dante remembered. He also remembered that Beatriz had been deeply affected by the program and didn't stop crying all weekend. He had tried to console her by reminding her that Emmanuel had never had a girlfriend and in fact didn't even have a father, but Beatriz had kept on crying and lamenting how inconsiderate certain men are and how wise, inflexible, and serene Doctor Dolores was.

"Oh, if she only knew about Emmita running away!" Dante said to himself now.

But another powerful, painful memory awaited him on the way to Las Vegas. The highway entered a three-mile-long tunnel and at the end of it he faced three black mountains.

"They're called the three skulls. I'm looking at them on the map," he said aloud, so that Virgilio would hear. "We're going to have to look at them for at least an hour."

Dante said no more, and he couldn't, because he was reminiscing about the first time he entered the United States. He had come through the desert with two young men he had met along the way. The three of them had managed to enter the cracked, yellow soil of Arizona and, for a week, saw nothing but a dry sandy wasteland and a jumble of mountains that sometimes looked yellow and at other times black like the wings of the birds of prey that ventured across those empty skies.

Walking became more and more difficult for them under an unrelenting sun, and when they were climbing a hill, the friend who was acting as the guide had made a macabre discovery: three dead bodies were lying there. The sand had probably covered them after they died, but later it had worn away, leaving them mummified. By their faces they could tell they were young men and that they had walked through those lands like they were doing now, led by a nightmare or holding the hand of a dream.

But that wasn't all. A little farther on, crossing the bend, they seemed to hear mariachi music, and if you pricked up your ears, you could tell that the violin was out of tune. His friends had told him to listen, and at first he didn't hear it, but after several attempts, he was able to hear the music and even understand the words of an endless ballad that mixed swallows with dark rain, and balconies with black eyes, and went on in another one that implored "*Beautiful, beloved*

Mexico, if I die far from you, let them say I'm only sleeping and let them bring me here."

The dead men were mariachis. Leaving their homeland, they headed toward the North, certain that some day their names would be heard on the great Hispanic stages in California, Arizona, and New Mexico. They had crossed the border and entered the desert thinking that they would be in green lands after a couple of days; but the time went on, each day they walked less, and when evening fell, they would camp and encourage each other by playing music. One night they heard some music more powerful than their own, perhaps more deafening than that of all the mariachis of Mexico together. It was coming from the north and the south, from the east and the west, fast and evil like a howl from the depths of hell. It was an accursed storm that buried their guitars and buried them, along with their songs, their "México, lindo y querido," their out-of-tune violin, and their dreams of making it in the United States. But maybe, from time to time, they awaken when travelers pass by, and then their dried-up bodies leave their bed of sand, and their hands, which haven't died, smooth their shiny, black mariachi uniforms and raise the guitar while their empty throats sing a tribute to the land and to life, to beautiful women and to eyes that are black as perdition, and thus awake until Judgment Day, they will keep playing day after day for all eternity for travelers who pass that way.

Suddenly Dante looked at his traveling companion and noticed that he was pricking up his ears. Then he slowed down, but could not leave his memories aside.

Generally, those who hear those mariachis in the desert remain with them in those regions of death. The sound of their music makes them forget the way and even lose sight of the differences that exist between this life and that of the deceased, and that could have happened to Dante and his companions because suddenly they realized that they were not advancing across the sand. More than twice they ended up back at the same hill they had left until, now lost, their eyes saw nobody other than the orange and purple body of the sun.

Then, they no longer knew where they were. They felt that they were eyes and ears, and that from outside and from increasingly higher above, they could see their bodies lying in the desert. They had gotten lost and possibly were already dead of sunstroke or buried in the sand. Perhaps they were already spirits moving away on their way toward the clouds. Dante would never forget that little plume of smoke that rose toward the sky from that man, who looked so much like him, lying face down with his legs and arms in the shape of a cross, as if trying to take possession of the land. He wondered, "Is that me? So that's what death is like?" and he was unable to answer himself. A while later he asked this of the angels when they were carrying him away, and they didn't know either because they had never died, but maybe he was being carried by chatty angels, and they were the ones who asked him:

"You say you're from Sahuayo. Can you tell us where that is?

"What's that, Mr. Angel?"

"What I said? That maybe Sahuayo doesn't exist and has never existed."

"What do you mean by that?"

"That maybe, what happens there, doesn't happen."

But they never finished taking him away, maybe because they had taken that day off. Or maybe they left him halfway between life and death, but a little this side of what is real death. What did happen is that Dante heard a noise approaching them that sounded more like the roar of an engine than the beating of angel wings.

"They have to thank God that we saw them."

They were immigration agents who saved them from remaining there entangled among death, the sands, the winds, and the mirages of the Arizona desert. They transported them in a land rover and had them in a prison on the border in order to question them before sending them back to Mexico. Dante then felt that he was Dante again, although he regained a body that was blackened and full of burning.

"I don't think we'll be able to question these guys. We might just start the interrogation, and they'll die on us," one of the agents said.

"And what would we have to interrogate them about anyway?" replied his companion, who was the other bilingual officer at the station. "It's obvious they weren't brought across by a *coyote*, and it's the *coyote*s that we're after. If they had had a guide, they wouldn't have gotten lost."

Lying on blankets, the three frustrated immigrants spent about three weeks in a cell. More dead than alive, they ate a soup that the officers served them; they couldn't eat solid foods and could barely move. Although at times they tried to converse among themselves, one of them would suddenly fall asleep or begin to talk nonsense. The man lying to Dante's right was named Gerardo, and he was the most talkative.

"The man from the *migra* is right. Besides, if the desert didn't kill us, the Patriots would have gotten us."

Gerardo had crossed the border several times and knew very well the dangers that lay in wait at the place they passed through. Some Arizona ranchers, according to what he explained, had organized in groups to eradicate the immigrants. Wearing red and white headbands and well armed, they stationed themselves at the exits to the desert to see if they could catch "illegals." If they saw a group of people coming out of the yellow lands, they shot at them. They did this in the name of the fatherland and the racial purity of the United States.

"Back home I've heard people say that *coyotes* never get lost because they know the Juan Diego map by heart," asserted the other man, whose name was Arredondo.

"What map was that?" Dante asked, and Arredondo explained to him that they were the stars that shine on the mantle where the Virgin of Guadalupe is painted.

"The main stars of the winter constellations appear on it. If you memorize them, there is no force in the universe that can make you lose your way. The Corona Boreal is above the head of the Virgin; Virgo, on her chest, even with her hands; Leo, on her abdomen. The Twins are at the level of her knees and Orion, where the angel is.

Anyone who remembers them and identifies them with those in the sky will never get lost."

They were talking without looking at each other in the darkness to which they had subjected them so that no heat would affect their condition. When Dante had recovered, the agents put him into a police van and left him in the first town across the Mexican border. The other two men had already been released, and he never heard from them again.

Dante remembered all this now that he was traveling in search of his daughter, and again the sounds of the land and the skies were mingling. For a long time he had felt that Beatriz was speaking to him from a very high place, but suddenly, her voice ceased being a voice and became a whisper or a resonance like that of wind bells, because that's what the voice of spirits is like when they are present. Perhaps it was not a resonance of bells nor a murmur of memory. Perhaps it was Beatriz alive forever in death and always with him, kissing him as randomly as the breeze kisses the sea.

"You'll find her, and remember that I'll always be with you." It occurred to Dante that Beatriz's voice was whispering next to him.

"Please, keep your eyes on the road. You'll have more time soon to talk at length with your memories," recommended Virgilio's ears, which spoke for him, long, cold, perhaps straight up from fear.

5
More Falsehoods about Virgilio

He was traveling very slowly down the right lane of the highway as if trying to let the sad memories pass him, but it wasn't for that reason he was doing it, but rather because he had realized that the engine was overheating. Several sputters and misses of the vehicle told him so. The needle on the temperature gauge was just about to the top. It was likely because it was a very old engine and maybe needed to be repaired or replaced. He thought it was strange that the problem would come on so suddenly, but then he realized that he had not driven the vehicle since Beatriz's death a year earlier. By then, their daughter preferred to spend the weekends visiting her girl-friends rather than taking little trips in her dad's car. "Dad, I don't want them to laugh at me and call me 'arrested development', can't you understand?" she had told him, and then she had explained that "arrested development" meant mental retardation and that's what fourteen-year-old girls who still went out with their parents were called.

In any case, Dante realized that he would have to stop and wait for the nighttime temperatures to cool down the engine, and he start-ed to look for a good place to stop, but the highway did not seem to want to give him that opportunity for more than ten miles of endless curves. Finally he found a turnoff and took it. It was a little country road with very little traffic, but in a few minutes it brought him to a clearing in the forest where he saw an abandoned gas station and, next to it, a dimly lit bar. He parked in the parking lot and decided to get Virgilio out and tie him to the bumper with a rope. It really wasn't necessary to tie him up that way, as he was a gentle creature that was not going to run away, but he did it more than anything so Virgilio wouldn't feel cooped up and would be able to enjoy the grass and the abundance of that clear, open night.

Dante found only the bartender, a very fat, very red, very friendly guy who spoke a little Spanish because he was born in Texas. He asked him how late his establishment was open, and the man said all night. Then he ordered a sandwich and a bottle of carbonated water and asked him if he could stay there a few hours, or if he preferred he would buy another sandwich. The gringo smiled and walked over to a huge clock to which he pointed with his right index finger motioning in circles to show him that he could stay all night and all day and as long as he liked.

Dante sat down at a wooden table facing a television, he didn't understand the football game that was on at the time. That position would let him doze from time to time with his head tilted back on the chair as if he were a fan of one of the two teams.

But, before falling asleep, he resolved not to worry too much about the van, because it would be sufficient to fill the radiator with water every once in a while and drive slowly to avoid trouble. Then, he decided not to think about his daughter anymore, and he ended up remembering Virgilio, whose image looked like it had been copied from a children's book. His ears were down, and his long black nose was always pointed to one side, as if he didn't care about looking at anyone. He imagined he possessed an enormous heart that caused him to be the companion of a sad man, finally, as Dante was nodding off, it seemed that he saw Virgilio on the television screen, replacing the burly football players.

The guy who had told him about the donkey had told him incredible stories. The time came when he became a man, or rather, an adult.

"When was that?" Dante had asked him.

"Umm. It was when he realized that he understood the drawings Manuelito brought him, and the bundle of papers turned into a notebook, and eventually into a book that told him what men did in this and other times, and how they managed to overcome the fleeting nature of life and the long evenings of death."

Virgilio hadn't thought about it before, and while he looked at the universe with his enormous eyes, he never saw it but had just found out that it existed and that it took people away in the evening and that the most beloved people sank one afternoon into the earth to never return. Generally they were seen in the sky flying toward the heights, rising beyond the clouds never to be seen again.

No, gosh, that was going to happen to Manuelito's parents and to Manuelito himself, and he would be left alone in the world. Virgilio had understood that death rode on his back and that it also rode upon the shoulders of people, but perhaps people can bear it because they're people and they live in families, protecting each other against pain, fear, and sadness, against the tireless eternity of the grass over their graves. Eternity was the other word that had become hung around his neck and tormented him. "He's going to be a year old, and that's like ten years for us. He's like an older brother to Manuel. And when he's two, it'll be as if he were twenty, and he'll turn into a dirty old donkey. We'll have to get rid of him then, drop him off along the road somewhere so he can go looking for female donkeys." Female donkeys and death are what I'll find along the road, Virgilio said to himself, and it frightened him a great deal to know so much, and maybe Mario José, Manuelito's father, was also becoming a little afraid such as when he said right in front of him as if he were talking in front of a wooden donkey: "This donkey knows a lot already. Maybe we'll have to let him go pretty soon."

That's why one Sunday, with great pain in his soul, he waited until very late at night, until Manuelito had fallen into a deep sleep, to leave the house and hit the road. He left ducking his head so that no one would see his enormous brown eyes hiding a tear, because donkeys don't cry.

Then he climbed and climbed and climbed, trying to reach the peak of Mount Hood, which he had seen from the home of the family that had him and from all the towns in Oregon he had visited with them; besides, he had heard conversations among the family that up there, on the rock at the peak, you had to urinate in the shape of a cross in order to truly be a man. He went all the way there, urinated in the shape of a cross, and didn't become a man, but did become a shrewd donkey. From the top, he sniffed north and south, east and west in search of meadows where he could lead the life of a wild donkey. If not for the fact that there was no pasture on the mountaintop, he would have stayed there to live because up there in the heights everything was beautiful: the wind moaned in his ears and became a chorus of angelic voices endlessly rising to the heavens.

"Have a cup of coffee!" proclaimed the fat bartender as his huge hand placed a fragrant, steaming cup in front of Dante. "Don't worry, it's on the house."

He had seen Dante nodding off and did not want him to fall completely asleep because sometimes drunks and thugs came into the bar. Dante opened his eyes, accepted the coffee, and drank it right down; then he lifted his gaze to watch the players moving down the field in their fierce uniforms. He watched them for a while until he closed his eyes again, and once again Virgilio was on the screen.

According to the old man, Virgilio had taken off like a shot toward McMinnville, Woodburn, Monmouth, and Corvallis, devouring around those towns the best grass in the world, which he had heard was cut and rolled up like carpet to be sent to Japan. He climbed to the top of Mary's Peak, the highest mountain on the coast of the far west, and urinated there too.

He was dying to conquer the most rugged peaks, especially Mount St. Helens, the volcano that had erupted twenty years earlier, turning the world into a valley of tears, destroying bridges, creating ashen forests, and diverting the Willamette and Columbia rivers. He set out toward it with the intention of urinating on a volcano, but on the way, when he was going through the town of Independence, despite the fact that it wasn't a mountain, he decided to urinate and did not do it in the shape of a cross, and that was what brought him bad luck.

He had not urinated for even twenty minutes when he heard police sirens behind him and discovered that he was surrounded by four patrol cars and two fire trucks. From one of the patrol cars someone was giving him orders in English, a language that Virgilio unfortunately didn't know for obvious reasons, and he continued to urinate. Then an officer got out of his car, opened a book, and began to read what Virgilio understood must be the rights contained in the Third Amendment to the Constitution. This, he understood, because he had watched a lot of police and outlaw movies with Manuelito.

The patrol cars kept their sirens going as the police cordoned off the area with yellow tape and used loudspeakers to order passing cars to take a detour off the highway. They were trying to prevent an overflow of the river Virgilio was causing from cutting the highway in two, and just two hours later, when the donkey seemed to have calmed his urinary furor, they put him into a police wagon to take him to jail, but they did not let him drink even one more swallow of water despite the fact that they were on the banks of the Willamette. At the Independence police station, Virgilio was forced to go through seven doors, and they covered one of his hooves with indelible, invisible ink, since this requirement was written in their manuals, or maybe to prevent another donkey from coming to visit him and taking the place of the incontinent prisoner.

Most of the men in Virgilio's cellblock were Mexican, and many were languishing there simply for not having their identity papers in order. But there, Virgilio and his companions were able to listen to the Spanish-language radio programs on La Campeona, which, besides sweetening their lives with music from the north of Mexico, offered them the advice of the Noble Pareja and the renowned cure-all medications from the Santo Remedio pharmacy. In addition, on the community call-in show, they heard the voice of Mr. Mario José Espino, who was offering a $200 reward to anyone with information on the whereabouts of a donkey named Virgilio who, among his many talents, knew how to read. The prisoners at the jail, following the common law that ruled among them, looked the other way and didn't turn him in. One of them even slapped him on the back and said: "So your name's Virgilio. What a guy you are. But don't worry because no one here is gonna turn you in, much less the gringos, because they don't understand a word of what's said on the radio."

Two weeks later, they set him free. A police officer walked him in the opposite direction, this time toward freedom through the seven doors, and explained to him that he was getting out of there because no one had filed any charge against him, but that one thing he recommended to him was that he always carry with him, perhaps tied around his neck, a little package containing his owner's identity documents, and he urged him to avoid drinking to excess and not to urinate in public.

Dante woke up when the television announcer interrupted the football game to appear on the frozen summit of Mount Hood with a bottle of extremely pure water that he was pouring one drop at a time over the spectators. At that moment, Dante felt the need to urinate, but he waited because he was suddenly overtaken by the fear of starting an unstoppable flow. Then he realized that he wasn't going to be able to wait much longer, and he looked over toward the side of the bar where the restroom should be, but didn't see it. Then, again, he raised his eyes toward the television, and, as his eyes closed, again it seemed to him that Virgilio was there.

The forced rest had given Virgilio more strength to continue his adventures, although his idea was to find a herd of wild donkeys and go live with them. Meanwhile, he jumped arroyos and fences, crossed highways as quickly and invisibly as a red devil or a black wind, and he looked for the gardens of the beautiful Victorian homes in order to savor there some delicious flowers and, sometimes, food set out on a tablecloth on a picnic table.

One night, about eleven o'clock, he trotted happily into the downtown streets of the city of Corvallis: clip-clop, clip-clop, clip-clop, he tapped his hooves as if calling people to wake up and come out to see him. This in fact happened because the residents of that town tend to go to bed early, and they had only heard that sound in television movies. Children and their parents, wearing pajamas and sleeping caps, peered out several windows, and the sight seemed impossible to them because Corvallis is the global center of a computer factory, and the only donkeys and mice ever seen there are cybernetic. Then they decided to believe that they were dreaming, and they went back to bed to avoid trouble, but there was trouble because that night most of the children wet their beds.

He was planning next to head toward the coast to see the ocean, and, after several days and plenty of pasture, he saw from a hill the blue, resplendent grandeur of the Pacific Ocean. It was his day for surprises because, just this side of the port of Lincoln City, he could make out several large, round tents. Not far from there, he saw what he had been looking for for so long, a herd of quadrupeds that, by their size, could be nothing other than donkeys. He couldn't believe it because he hadn't even reached the eastern part of the state.

Closing his eyes, he ran and flew toward the animals. When he was about a hundred meters from them and could hear them, he sensed that rather than braying, they were whinnying, but by now no one could stop him, and he had his eyes closed. Then, he opened them in order to jump over a fence that encircled the herd. Once inside, he felt next to him dozens of similar bodies. Happy because he had never before been among so many of his own kind, he opened his eyes but had to open them wider and wider, full of uncontainable astonishment because he was in the midst of miniature horses.

He thought of escaping, but it was too late. Inside the corral, there was not sufficient space to make a running jump over the fence; besides, he had been spotted, and a truck was racing toward him. Four hairy men surrounded him, and, before he knew it, his four legs were tied together, and he was placed upside down on the truck bed, and as the vehicle headed toward one of the tents, he heard someone say: "It's a donkey. The favorite meat of the most demanding, discriminating wild animals in the world."

A while later they untied him, put a rope around his neck, and led him toward the tent where the lion cages were. He walked between the cages of the lazy kings of the jungle, who did not even deign to turn their heads toward him, although he thought he noticed others salivating as they prepared for a leonine diet. Beyond the cages were the slaughterhouses, where some cows destined for slaughter were mooing. He was walking along so tamely and with such resignation that those who were leading him took the rope off from around his neck and just pushed him along gently down the path.

"Hey, hey, wait a minute," an old tamer's voice was heard. "Take him out of the slaughterhouse and take him to the corral. I want to have a look at him."

"The feeding chief said to bring him here."

"But I'm the head of tamers, and I'm the boss. That donkey is trained . . ."

Several weeks later, the Tiffany Circus was presenting the show: "A donkey, brought from India, where he listened to the lessons of the dervishes and Brahmans, will read your fortune." In fact, Virgilio, harnessed with a saddle and a cape designed to look like a Persian rug, walked toward the first rows of the audience. An older lady then asked him to read her fortune, and the quadruped, after looking at her closely, picked from a box a paper that told her future: "For a lady who still stops traffic." Then he went on doing different fortune readings according to the age and gender of the customers.

It is assumed that, during his time with the circus, Virgilio must have made friends with the other animals. The carrier pigeons were the most conversational. They told him stories of the trade that their breed had practiced from time immemorial, and how they had served the secret communications of spies, lovers, and warriors. Their trade had fallen on hard times in recent days with the invention of the telephone, the telegraph, and email, but the obsession to communicate had remained in their blood, and that's why they perched, all in a row and facing the same way, on telephone wires.

The elephants were people with a great sense of humor; they knew numerous jokes by heart and were always laughing, though courteous as they were, they didn't burst out into raucous laughter.

Virgilio had developed a very close relationship with an old horse; he would go to the corral to greet him and stand for hours at his side. Perhaps in their silence they shared an old sadness or a painful memory. For several years the horse had galloped at the head of ten equine acrobats, jumping obstacles, leaping through rings of fire, walking in circles on his hind legs, and performing several somersaults in which he was to turn in the air and land back on his feet to the applause of the crowd. When he got old, the circus owners wanted to retire him, but the other horses wouldn't jump at all if he wasn't leading them.

Finally one afternoon the horse fell on his side and broke a foot, and all the efforts to heal it were for naught. He was still lame, and one knee was so swollen it had formed a sort of bag. They had to retire him then, but they didn't put him down because he was very old and maybe the wild animals would refuse to eat him. Therefore, standing and ever imperturbable, moving only his ears, he remained in the corral. He rarely ate; he only accepted a few sugar cubes while he drank from the watering trough. This made Virgilio assume that his friend was waiting for death to arrive, but death was taking a long time to come, and if he didn't speak it was because he felt almost ashamed of still living.

One night when no one was looking, he collapsed, and that was the moment that Virgilio decided to end his chapter as a circus magician. It wasn't too hard for him because, being used to his tameness, the circus owners did not watch him at all, and one day when they were moving him from one town to another in a truck, he jumped out, fell on his belly onto the highway, got up, and began to run. He had hurt his entire right leg, but he kept walking in search of freedom. It must have been then when, lame, he arrived at the community center where Emma's fifteenth birthday party was being held.

Dante woke up again. Seven men had come into the bar, and six were very drunk and laughing loudly. He couldn't understand them because they spoke a Spanish that was mixed with a lot of English and were trying to look dangerous.

The man who wasn't drunk had sat down facing Dante, at the same table, but didn't seem very interested in him. He was wearing a leather vest with no shirt underneath. He had his hair in a ponytail and gave the impression of being very proud of his boots, because he would put them up on the chair and open and close his eyes, fascinated by the shine of the leather, as he played, tapping out different rhythms with the heels that were made of silver metal.

"Crocodile skin," he said and added: "Real crocodile skin."

Dante didn't know if he should congratulate him for that, but chose to refrain from making any comment, given that the man was bragging about his own boots without paying any attention to him. Then the man began to admire his huge belt buckle, then the two gold rings he was wearing on one hand, and finally a bracelet of the same metal that hung from his left wrist.

"How much does it cost?"

"Pardon . . . ?"

"How much! I'm asking you how much is that donkey you've got tied to your van."

Dante woke up completely and answered that he wasn't for sale.

"It's not for sale, huh? How interesting! And you? Can you tell me your name?"

"Dante, sir. Dante Celestino."

"Stand up when you talk to me. You were saying?"

Dante obeyed. "Dante Celestino."

But the man smiled, shaking his head. "That's not your name. What's your real name? . . . Don't sit down! I told you to stand up when I'm talking."

Dante stood back up.

"You know we're from the border patrol, and you have to tell us the truth. Understand?"

There was no response.

"Where'd you cross the border? What contraband did you bring in? What gang do you work with? Where are your weapons? How many men have you killed?"

Dante wanted to answer that he was an honest man, that he hadn't changed his name, that he didn't belong to any gang, that he had no weapons, that he hadn't killed anyone, and that all he was doing was traveling the world looking for his daughter Emmita, but the stranger kept repeating the questions without letting him speak.

"Take off your shirt."

He began to obey and as he was unbuttoning it, he noticed that the bartender was signaling at him. Maybe he was trying to tell him that the guys weren't immigration agents and that they were just trying to play with him.

"That's enough, guys, enough games. Come and have a drink on the house."

But the men did not accept the invitation. The most obnoxious one ordered: "Your pants too. Pull down your pants."

"Animals are branded. So are wetbacks. We want to see your brand."

Dante had finished taking off his shirt, obeying the man who had questioned him, but he couldn't decide whether to take off his pants. So far they had not forced him to do anything, but suddenly he felt the tip of a knife against the right side of his neck, and he thought that perhaps his time had come. All his life he had had the feeling that misfortune was prowling very nearby. He had almost seen its face when Beatriz died. He always knew when something was about to happen to him because he smelled it. Now it occurred to him that perhaps Misfortune had fallen in love with him because he hadn't smelled anything.

In response to another order, he agreed to take off his boots, but he was holding up his pants with both hands.

"What a weird wetback! He doesn't have a brand," the wise guy said, pointing to Dante's back with the tip of his knife as if he were teaching an anatomy class. The tip of the weapon returned to his neck and then rose to under his mouth and from there went to his left nipple. Suddenly, the knife went to his belt and cut it as if it were paper rather than leather. His pants fell to his feet.

There stood Dante, pale, almost naked, preparing to die. He made a supreme effort and began to see only the face of his daughter, then that of Beatriz, who was possibly reaching out her arms to him. One of the bullies went outside to pick on Virgilio.

Then the guys started laughing harder and harder as they pretended to divide up the shirt, pants, and boots of the silent man who was looking upward. One of them put his lit cigarette against Dante's right cheek, but Dante did not react.

This caught the attention of the one who seemed to be the leader. They were Chicano criminals, and they despised recent Mexican immigrants. In most of their experiences with them, it had been enough to put a knife against their throats for them to be scared to death, begging for pity and talking about their children, but this guy was very different.

The man who was not drunk began to look at him with respect.

The other guy moved the knife point from Dante's neck to his armpits, and finally let it rest beneath his left nipple, and there he sank it in, but Dante did not make a sound. Nor did the sharp weapon become covered with blood, but rather with a transparent liquid, as bitterness must be when it is about to overflow within us.

The respect became fear.

"Let's get out of here," ordered the man with the crocodile-skin boots. The bullies began to leave the bar single file. Outside, next to the van, lay the man who had gone out a moment earlier. Frightened, they did not even try to pick him up. They jumped into their pickup truck and drove away.

Inside the bar, the owner urged Dante to get dressed and leave right away. "It's best if you leave, because they'll be back. Take the main road and soon you'll come to an RV park. It's a park where retired people live on the road. There are hundreds of them. No one will find you there."

"But, the dead guy?"

"Dead guy? What dead guy? He's not dead; he's just drunk. Passed out. Your donkey must have kicked him for getting too close."

Dante and Virgilio headed toward the RV park, and, after parking, Dante didn't lie down on the mattress in the van. Man and donkey got out to rest under the stars, and Dante laid very close to the jaw of the animal eating the grass. As he listened to the wind that came from afar and contemplated the clouds that formed familiar faces, he observed the stars twinkling, and he thought that the stars were the souls of people flying toward the borders of a borderless universe. The cars and trees were blurred shadows lost in the night. The sky was still immense and white as if, up there, the sun always shone.

6

The Consolation of Wandering the World Is that You Become Tougher

He fell asleep next to the donkey beneath a sequoia, a few feet from the van that had brought them to the vast RV park. Lying like that, with so many stars spinning up there and his hat over his face, the problems disappeared. His arms formed the shape of a cross with his body, and his palms were turned upwards toward the sky. His hands did not look at the earth because perhaps he didn't want to stop the planet's ceaseless race. All he wanted to do was sleep and remember.

He remembered that Beatriz had been his sweetheart since they were eleven years old in Sahuayo, his only girlfriend, and it was when he turned twenty-one that he told her he was going to go north and he would work hard until he had enough money to ask her to join him and form a family.

"For us to have a home and a family here is nearly impossible. We'd have to live with relatives and impose on them, and you know full well that there's no room, nor can I get a job that allows me to contribute something. I have to leave Sahuayo and Michoacán and finally Mexico. I have to go to the United States.

His fiancée had understood and so had his mother. "Wandering the world is as normal as when birds get their feathers and start to fly. It's what is normal for men. For women, the normal thing is to wait. I was very young when your grandfather enlisted with the Villistas and went off to the revolution. He left with his eight brothers; the nine of them ended up scattered across other worlds."

At that point his mother would fall silent, and Dante knew why. The reason was that she was looking at the sky, and perhaps there she

56

was looking for her husband who also once took off to wander the world and never returned.

"I advise you, when you can, to take Beatriz with you because she's a good woman and she'll take care of you like I have. But make sure that when your time comes to die, tell her to bring you back here. The dead, like the plants, both have their land, son. And if you are planted here, just like the plants, you'll flourish . . . "

He was talking in his sleep. Virgilio heard him.

"I was the last man to leave town." Dante went on talking or perhaps dreaming. "The women, children, and elderly stayed behind, but not for long. It was as if a kite with a green tail had stopped above the town to force us to roam the world. I didn't even take a bus because I couldn't afford to. I hit the road and let the road move. And I think that either I made a mistake and took the wrong road, or the road made a mistake with me, because along the way I bumped into the Arizona border and I crossed over with a couple of guys who had become my friends, but I've already told you that's where immigration stopped us and sent us back. Back in Mexican territory, I realized that I couldn't go back to Sahuayo. I would have been really ashamed. Instead, I got used to living cross country. Wherever I went, I joined up with people like me wandering along the roads that go north. There were some that were leaving their towns with their wives and sometimes even children, but most of us were single men with just a little bag. It seems to me that I saw some who had even lost their own shadows. I met the infamous Facundo family. I joined them and walked with them for several weeks."

The Facundos had left Chiapas, in southern Mexico, and had already walked for several months when he joined them. They had become so accustomed to the roads that perhaps they no longer cared much about remembering where they were going, but where they had come from. The Facundos' father, whose name is remembered by few but whom Dante insists on calling Don Moisés and who had been working as a singer and *rezador* (prayer expert or prayer leader at a cemetery), used to tell that an angel had appeared to him saying: "Rise up. Awaken your wife and your children and take them north, because that is the will of the Almighty."

Because of all that, half-starved and exhausted, the Facundos emerged from the south during one rainy morning. They did not even have time to bring along any of their belongings, which were few, because nothing had gone well for Don Moisés for a long time. First he was a public schoolteacher, but he left that job when the government didn't have enough money to keep offering that service; then he was, successively, the owner of a small restaurant, a cook, a waiter, a lottery ticket salesman, and a taco street vendor, but in all these professions things went terribly for him because, according to him, it had occurred to the devil to tempt him like Job to renounce God.

Then, when they were already on the road, Doña Lupe de Facundo wanted to return to the house to get some belongings that she had forgotten in the rush, but the man shouted: "Don't do that, woman, you could be turned into a pillar of salt."

On the wretched back roads of Mexico, the Facundos had done everything they could to survive. Whenever they reached a town, people would offer them lodging, feed them, and give them used clothing, which Don Moisés was glad to accept because, as he said, "the little birds in the sky don't work and know only how to fly, and nevertheless the Lord feeds them." Perhaps Mrs. Facundo's facial features had been worn away, and that must be why no one remembers having seen her, and perhaps she was by then just eyes, black, shining eyes that glowed at night when her husband woke her again to tell her that the angel had appeared to him again, ordering him to change course.

Around that time, many people went with them, encouraged by the belief that Don Moisés performed miracles and that they would likely cross the Rio Grande without even getting wet and would enter the United States without being seen by immigration. About thirty people, which later reached ninety, came to follow them, but not for long, because Don Moisés had become very strict; he forbade them to stop in cities, drink tequila, or go into brothels, and in the end he forced them to pray, meditate, and fast for long periods of time.

Every so often they would leave the towns and orchards and enter the deserts. They hadn't yet reached the United States, but one fine day they found themselves in the middle of the Sonora Desert, with no supplies, destitute, malnourished, thirsty, and downtrodden. It was then that they all asked Don Moisés to pray.

"Oh, Lord. Oh, Lord . . ."

He repeated this about fifty times, until his mouth was almost too dry to go on, but he kept calling on the Lord, and when the Lord came close, he said to him: "Can't you see that we're in trouble? You probably have other more important things to do, and we do not wish to bother you, but please, we just ask you not to forget that you created us: with this tongue that needs others to talk to and at least a liter of water to drink every day and maybe some tortillas. Besides the fact that I am not even mentioning everything you gave the Israelites to eat in the wilderness. And if you are still present in this place in the world and haven't noticed, I want to let you know that all these people here are about to fall asleep, from hunger or in death, and are no longer going to be able to listen to me, nor will they be able to hear Your word.

"Lord, Lord, don't you see where you have left us! Don't you understand our needs? Don't you realize that you have given us a tongue and it is drying up on us?!"

"Amen," said ninety people, but not all at once, but rather one by one.

"Amen."

"Amen."

"Amen."

"Amen."

"Amen."

"Amen."

"Amen."

"Amen."

"Amen."

"Amen."

Some of the people just thought it. And before an hour had passed, the sky turned dark and it began to rain.

"Amen."

"Amen."

And all the rest was added unto them, that is, the plenty that they found in an abandoned tent with bottles of wine for everyone. And they drank so much that instead of celebrating the miracle, one man from

Jalisco was running from one group to another shouting "Cheers, bastards!" but the people corrected him:

"Amen."

"Amen."

"Amen."

They drank so much that the couples began to leave hurriedly for their respective tents and so did those who were not yet couples, but they began to leave from that moment to be just that.

"Amen."

"Amen."

"Amen."

They took their leave in order, they said, to go to bed early to give thanks for the miracle, but instead of prayers, what was heard in all the tents were moans, outcries, noisy shouts.

"Amen."

"Amen."

"Amen."

Then, Don Moisés Facundo, now a pastor, began to growl and said that this was not the will of the Lord. The following day he gathered the communal assembly and admonished those who were sinning in thought and in deed, those who were doing dirty little things, those who were in heat, those who mounted them, the procreators and the fornicators, and ordered that from then on the hot females and the stallion males sleep separately.

"Amen."

"Amen."

"Amen."

And perhaps that is why some time later, the Facundos acquired the reputation of being those chosen by the Lord to walk through the wilderness, but the people who had begun to follow them departed in other directions because, although they liked receiving water and manna from Heaven, they also loved to sob and moan in this vale of tears, Amen and Amen.

And had it not been for the menacing power exercised by Don Moisés, his own children would soon have moved away and each chosen their own path, but they stayed with him. So did Dante for a little longer, and all he remembers is that they camped in a deserted area or slept on a borrowed mattress, and when they were in the best part of their sleep, the old man invariably got them up and pushed them to walk, even if it was three or four o'clock in the morning. It was as if they had forgotten that they were traveling to the border and just walked hurriedly and at night, determined to erase their trail so that sadness couldn't follow them.

One night, when they were already close to the border and sleeping in tents, Dante awoke with a start to see the faces of old Moisés and two of his sons confronting him so that he would accept the Lord in his heart.

"I've already done so. I believe that I do so every day of my life," he wanted to say. But Don Moisés wasn't listening. He seemed content to give the order and not wait for an answer in order to make a decision later. Two days later, Dante fled and decided to walk alone the rest of the way to his destination.

He didn't hear anything more about the Facundos until many years later when he learned that they had crossed into the Arizona desert and that most of their followers had died of sunstroke. Others say that the Facundos, suffering sun glare, entered an enormous house and never came out again. It is said that at a certain moment, like any other person, their time came to die, but they didn't realize it. That's what a *corrido* says, but it's not true, because they weren't old enough to die yet.

The *corrido* says that the Facundo boys, after death, rebelled against their ghost father and took off on their own to travel the world that they had only known through their father's hypnotic eyes, and from there was born the story of the ghost Facundos who joined groups of travelers without being noticed. That's why sometimes among those who are walking north, it's not known who is alive or who is already dead. The bad thing is that they, the Facundos, don't know either. It happens with all of us that from so much walking in the lands on this side and the other side, at times we are overcome by the pain of not knowing who we are or where we're going.

There is no shortage of people who swear that in the middle of the desert they saw the face of old Moisés in a cloud, from which he is always threatening those who enter that he will turn them into pillars of salt if they leave the Lord and venerate the idols of the gringos. That's why people warn those who leave Mexico, saying "be careful not to run into old Facundo on the way."

Sometimes Dante would see them in his dreams, as happened last night when he clearly saw Don Moisés explaining how the world was created. According to him, all was darkness, and suddenly a voice was heard that was speaking as if in secret, saying "the light is being made," but suddenly that voice did not realize that it was talking alone and only to itself. Then it began to try to think what it could do to have someone to listen to it because there was no one else there. No sooner did the light appear than from somewhere came the idea of making beings in his image and likeness. It was not a bad idea, and he began the task. But since he had spent an infinite amount of time without doing anything, his designs didn't turn out very well. That's why before making people, he designed tigers, magpies, whales, eagles, sheep, cats, parrots, rivers, winds, elephants, and angels.

"In the end, he had filled the world with so many beings that there was no room left even for a pin," explained Don Moisés. "Then he created a nopal cactus and sat down in its shade to think calmly. That is where they say he invented a man and a woman, and that our first parents were born with wings, but God clipped them so they wouldn't run away from him at night. The population grew a lot and very quickly and was distributed in the north and the south. Those of the north turned out quiet, orderly, thrifty, and good with machines, blond and chaste, with their flesh a little raw as if the Creator were a bad cook and perhaps didn't season very well. But when he made those of the south, he put in too much salt and made them intense, somewhat toasted, fond of fusses and fiestas, intrepid, frenetic, and passionate, taking advantage of any moment that he left them alone to grow and multiply.

"Then, slightly annoyed, he realized that he had not done a good job of distributing the passion, the ardor, and the desires, and while those of the south were asleep, he made them vomit the flames they carried inside, and from there the stars were born. But even so our people were not satisfied. Instead, they stopped to eat the apples of good and evil until they choked.

"That was when the Lord had to allow the devil to come to bring us various tests and temptations. 'It's my turn now,'" said the devil according to Don Moisés. "'I suppose you will let me tempt them so that they will renounce you. Don't you think so?' That's why calamities, poverty, wars, tyrants, unemployment, hatred, disease, distrust, and hunger befell us, but the Lord couldn't free us from any of that because it wasn't his turn anymore.

"That's why the Lord began to appear in our dreams to advise us to exercise a little and walk toward the north. He didn't bring our dead back to life because that's not very attractive: one comes out of the earth all dirty, and the shine of the eyes cannot be restored. But, anyway, even though we may have to die, we will be left with the consolation of walking until the end of time and knowing that the stars came from us. That must be why many animals and some trees tend to cry but we don't, because even with all our sorrows and everything, we're still happy. The secret is not to cry when one remembers and to go along remembering everything as if one had his eyes turned around backwards and was looking for his memories."

That was what Dante heard him say and it's the honest truth, whatever the *corridos* may have said. Who knows where old Facundo ended up, or whether his children stayed with him, but what's for certain is that people began to spread the word that they had found a treasure and were incredibly rich, and maybe they had to hide so no one would kill them for their wealth.

"Whatever the case, the consolation of wandering the world is that one becomes tough, Virgilio. Once, I walked with a guy who was wandering the world just like the devil must wander when he is left with no soul and no hell, half angel, half devil, half animal, half living, half dead, half man, with long hair like a woman and a beard that hid his face. He ate hay, turning it over and over in his mouth for hours like cows do, and at night he seemed to sleep with his eyes open, and not to watch out for those of us who were next to him, but to watch out for his own memories, which were the memories of someone who will never again lie down on the soil of his homeland."

With this, Dante fell asleep again next to Virgilio under a sequoia, a few feet from the van that had brought them, his legs and arms in the shape of a cross and his hat over his face.

7
The Tallest, Oldest Gringo in the World

From time to time, Dante snored during his dreams, but he didn't want to stop dreaming. But now he was going to have to, because someone was knocking loudly on the door of the van to awaken him.

Lying on the grass, Dante moved his arms and legs and stretched. Then, he raised his eyelids very slowly because the brightness of the day did not let him do it any other way, and standing there next to him, he began to make out the tallest person he had ever seen in his life. Very high boots, extremely shiny even though they dug into the damp ground. Blue jeans, white shirt, his eyes took awhile to reach the head that he couldn't see completely because the man, or whatever it was, was standing against the light.

"Hey, you. You . . ." said the illuminated figure.

He looked as tall as the sequoia and wore his silver hair floating.

"Breakfast. Want breakfast?" the stranger said, bringing the fingers of his right hand to his mouth several times, but Dante didn't respond. Then he corrected himself: "Eat?" he said in Spanish. "You want breakfast? *Querer comer?*"

His name was Sean. In the conversation that followed, he said that he was ninety years old. He had lived for a few months in the RV next to where Dante had parked his vehicle. He spoke Spanish well because he had been married to a woman from Spain, but she had died some time ago.

"No, please, it's too much trouble," Dante replied.

But the old man had already spread out an embroidered white tablecloth on one of the tables in the park. Then, just as quickly he set out three cups and silverware.

"My friend Jane will come too. I'll call her as soon as you're ready."

He said all this so firmly that Dante didn't hesitate any longer and went to his van, got out the small bag that contained his toiletries, and headed toward the closest bathroom.

A half hour later, Dante was back with the gentleman who had received him so warmly. Together they finished setting the table, and finally Sean went over to his vehicle and knocked politely three times to tell his friend that she should come out.

A side door opened and from it extended out a platform bearing, as on a throne, seated in a wheelchair, the most elegant lady Dante had ever seen. Although it wasn't necessary, since the wheelchair was electric, Sean went behind it as if he were pushing it toward the breakfast table. Without further ceremony, once they were all at the table, the elderly lady said a prayer in English to which the men listened with their eyes closed and heads bowed. She asked God to remember those who had died, and her companion interpreted it into Spanish. Then she reminded God of those who have lost their families and prayed that He help them as soon as possible. Then she let Him know that there were many sick people who couldn't share that brunch, and she put in a good word for them.

She prayed for missionaries, seafarers, abandoned mothers, travelers, teachers, the poor, prisoners, the forgotten, sinners, foreigners, pilgrims, and she was going to go on praying when she realized that it was taking Sean a little while to interpret her words. Then, she reminded her table companions that the pine trees and the mountains grow by the will of God, and that without that will there is no air, nor love, nor crops, nor horses, nor cars, nor houses, but only a solitude with no air and no light, a nothing that is not nothingness but darkness.

Finally, Dante, who couldn't believe in so many happy images, found himself eating breakfast with two elderly people who, instead of staring at him, passed him the basket of bread, the pitcher of orange juice, the bowl of peaches in syrup, the bowl of scrambled eggs, the pats of butter, and a jar of homemade jam. Behind them, all that could be seen were the silhouettes of the trees and the donkey in the midst of a fog that hadn't yet lifted completely and that submerged the countryside in an intense violet color.

They didn't ask his name, but he gave it to them and told them that he was traveling to Nevada. Nor did it occur to them to inquire about the welts on his face.

"Jane says have some jam. She made it out of orange peel, you know?" Sean told him when Dante finished talking.

Sean Sutherland had fought in World War II and entered Europe on the beaches of Normandy. Back home, he worked in a real estate business and eventually became company president, and he had retired with a lot of money many years later. Jane Moynihan was his neighbor and was eighty-four years old. She was the widow of Bob Moynihan, who had also served in the war in Europe.

"Coincidence. *Ca-sua-li-dad*," Sean remarked. "Bob and I were together in the same battalion in France and Germany. We witnessed the death of Edward, Bob's brother, and back in Berlin, we stayed in Paris until we were discharged. We never saw each other again, and I had no news about his life until I moved to the south side in Salem, Oregon fifteen years ago. When I met Jane, I asked her if she might know anything about a man by the same last name who had served in the war, and she told me that he was her deceased husband. What a coincidence! . . . *Ca-sua-li-dad*."

Over time, the friendship between Jane and Sean had become firm and strong, indispensable for both of them. Every day, Sean took his friend the mail and the paper because, due to her disability, she couldn't go out to get them. He visited her every day, and they played cards and checkers. He often invited her to dinner and sometimes went to church with her at the Queen of Peace Catholic Church even though he belonged to the Episcopal Church.

"You really look like a traveler to me," Dante said to him. "Yes, sir, you have all the appearance of a traveler."

"Maybe you're right. I really am a traveler. I think I always have been. Since I was very young. I think I always go from east to west and from there back toward the east. "You're exactly right. I'm a traveler."

About six months earlier, the doctor who was treating him for the ailments of old age gave him the news that perhaps he had reached the point we all must reach someday. The doctor asked him to stay in the hospital because no one would be able to take care of him at home. It was impossible to combat the cancer that had invaded him. Thanks to the advances in pain medication, Sean would be able to spend his remaining days without great discomfort.

"And do you know what I did? I began to prepare myself for the trip. I reviewed my will with a lawyer. I made all the arrangements with the funeral home. I can't lie to you; I waited for death."

Since Jane couldn't visit him in the hospital, he would call her and keep her updated on what his doctor told him every morning.

"He says that perhaps death will surprise me in my sleep, and that saddens me because I would have liked to know what the final moment is like."

"You know?" he said to her on another occasion, "I'll look for Bob to tell him about you and your children and everything that's happening down here. Just imagine, I'll see the Moynihans and all the guys who died in the war when we were heading for Berlin. No, the truth is that we'll never stop laughing like we used to do in the trenches."

The lady said something at that moment, and Sean translated: "She says I'm not letting you eat with all my storytelling."

Without words, Jane was offering her guest another plate with hot roast beef and handing him a fork so he could help himself.

"I'm going to give you some good advice. Don't believe in doctors," Sean said and added: "Jane is asking me to tell you to try the corned beef with cabbage."

Sean became bothered by the doctor's inaccuracy. He had given him not more than two or three weeks to live, and he had already spent almost a month staying in a dull hospital room. At first he couldn't wait to die to go see his friends in the other world, but after four weeks passed he couldn't wait to leave because no one visited him. His only daughter was married and lived in Boston and called him only once to promise him that she would travel to Oregon for his funeral.

"After that time, it seems that the doctor grew tired of me. He told me that I could go back home because I had gotten better and could be on my own, but he recommended that I not get my hopes up.

"That was six months ago. That's when I got the idea of this trip, and Jane agreed to come with me. Her daughter Maureen applauded the idea because she had always liked me a lot. We didn't have a chance to get in touch with her son, Elmer, because he's a very busy attorney and hasn't visited Jane for a long time. The idea is to live on the road for awhile. If something were to happen to me, Jane would drive back home. She's an excellent driver."

"Say, Dante, by the way, Jane wants me to ask you about your wife."

Dante responded that she had been very beautiful and had blue eyes like Jane, but that he hadn't been able to go to her funeral in Mexico because he was undocumented. Then he fell silent.

Jane said something else to Sean, but he didn't interpret it, out of respect for their guest's silence. Later, he thought it good to ask: "And your donkey?"

Dante told everything he knew about him and ended by saying that he was a good friend.

"It doesn't surprise me. I know because I've lived to be very old, and in the midst of solitude I've become a very good friend of animals. Dogs delight me because they look at you while you're telling them stories. The bad thing is that it seems like after listening to us they're always laughing with their tongues hanging out."

A nearby murmur revealed the proximity of a stream. The sun grew brighter as if attempting to enter bodies and souls.

"Do you like accordion music?"

Dante couldn't believe his ears.

Sean Sutherland understood that silence and smiled. Then, with the agility of an adolescent, flew toward his mobile home, went in for a moment, and came back carrying the instrument.

Too—ra—loo—ra—loo—ra
Too—ra—loo—ra—lai
Too—ra—loo—ra—loo—ra
hush now don't you cry.
Too—ra—loo—ra—loo—ra
Too—ra—loo—ra—lai
Too—ra—loo—ra—loo—ra
that's an Irish lullaby.

He repeated the old Irish song so many times that Dante learned the *Too-ra-loo-ra-loo-ra. Too-ra-loo-ra-lai,* which he repeated along with Jane, while Sean made the instrument breathe.

Too—ra—loo—ra—loo—ra
Too—ra—loo—ra—lai
Over in Killarney many years ago
my mother sang a song to me
in tones so sweet and low.
Just a simple little ditty
in her good old Irish way.
Too—ra—loo—ra—loo—ra
Too—ra—loo—ra—lai.

Maybe Dante was in Heaven. Maybe he had already died and his Maker had brought him to this place so that he would be happy. Maybe it was all a dream, but he didn't want to wake up yet, and he took the instrument in his hands. The first thing he played was "María Bonita."

An hour later, with the accordion resting in the shade of a maple tree, Dante confessed: "I'm looking for my daughter Emmita."

Sean interpreted back and forth: "Jane wants to know what happened with Emmita."

"It's a long story."

"That's okay. We have time . . ."

When the guest finished telling his story, the old folks were silent and didn't look at him. Their sadness was apparent from afar. They sat a long time like that, until Jane spoke again and Sean again interpreted: "Jane says to keep looking for her because she must be a good girl, and by now she must be very sorry to have lost a father like you."

A while later, Jane said something in English that sounded like a good-bye. She turned her wheelchair and headed toward the RV home. There, again, a platform slowly descended to pick her up and again it went up, taking the chair and the elderly lady who wished to appear impassive, although the truth was that she wanted to cry.

"Now it's our turn," the old gringo said then, as he opened a huge toolbox. "You say it overheats. Maybe some gasket came loose and will have to be welded so it doesn't leak water."

Besides being a soldier, Sean had been a truck mechanic in World War II, and all he had to do was glance at an engine to make his diagnosis: "We're going to have to work a little. Two or three days, but don't worry, because I should have all the parts we'll need."

Sean put on his welding goggles and asked Dante to pick out a tube that would fit. Holding it on a metal surface, with the aid of the heat he cut it in half.

By the end of the week, the van was cured of all its ailments, but not completely because old age had it mortally wounded.

"Don't go too fast," Sean advised him as they said good-bye. "Put water in the radiator and stop often. There are a lot of camps like this one along the way."

Then, when Dante started the van and began to move his left arm to wave good-bye, Sean shouted something that he couldn't hear. He turned the car off, opened the window, and asked: "What's that?"

"Don't believe in doctors."

8
What We Think Is Air Isn't Air. It's Water.

"My grandmother used to say that what we think is air isn't air, it's water. 'Don't you see that when people are in a hurry they move their arms as if they were in the water?'"

They were back on the road, and now the engine seemed content. Nothing abnormal was heard, not a single noise or even a whistle. Dante kept talking to Virgilio, who was sitting on all fours and from time to time stuck his nose out the window as if he were smelling the grass and their destination.

"What I'm trying to say, Virgilio, is that in my country we're not people anymore. I think maybe we've started to turn into fish. I say that because no sooner are we born than we're on the road north. It's as if we began to swim in our mothers' wombs and, when we came out, we kept swimming but only north. I think that's how I got to San Luis."

He didn't remember how he had arrived in San Luis, Río Colorado, because those who have failed in their first attempt to enter the United States don't remember their subsequent attempts. But he reached that city and spent his last few pesos on a bus ticket to Tijuana. The reason for his trip was that he had a letter of recommendation for a *coyote* who had been born in his hometown. This gentleman had become very powerful in the profession in that important border city and would have no trouble helping him as he had done with others from back home.

On the bus, Dante was rehearsing the conversation he would have with the *coyote* and, at other times, what he would say to Beatriz several years later when he returned rich and triumphant to take her north. Perhaps his thoughts were similar to those of most of the people traveling with him, that they weren't thinking about failure either. In them a spirit was reflected whose first half was the hope of arriving soon in the country of dreams and opportunities, and the other half was a sadness capable of encompassing up to three halves of the soul.

When he reached Tijuana, there was no one in the bus because everyone had gotten off before reaching the station and had run to hide in a secret place. They did this out of fear of being in the terminal with the police who might interrogate them, and maybe beat them, and even steal their money.

"You must be Dante," said a middle-aged man as soon as he saw him come into the room that served as his office and his home. "There's no denying it. All the Celestinos look alike," and he didn't wait for the young man's response before introducing himself: "I'm Leonardo Ceja. I've been waiting for you for six months."

Dante tried to explain to him that he had spent that time with the Facundo family, but the *coyote* didn't let him say a thing.

"You weren't able to enter through the desert and now you come here. Maybe you died there and you don't remember. There's no denying it," he repeated. "Everybody in your family looks alike. I bet you got lost like your dad and your grandfather; you must have gone on following your dreams. But you're luckier, boy, because you found me."

Dante decided then to begin the speech he had prepared, but Ceja guessed that too: "Don't worry, I already know that you don't have any money left, but I'll put you to work for me a little and you'll pay for the trip that way. You'll represent me to the group of people before I get there. Also you'll help me cross a family that has two women in it. You have to be near them all the time to help them run when necessary. That is, you'll be my assistant, and maybe you'll even like the profession and come back with me."

The next night, Dante received directions to an abandoned cabin in the country, not too far out of town. He was to go alone and meet the group of passengers.

"You'll tell them that you represent me and for them to wait. Tell them not to worry because I'll get there precisely when we need to leave, but I can't tell them what time that'll be because I don't know myself. We have to wait till the *migra* is busy with other things. When that happens, there in front of the house you'll see a flashlight signaling three times. That'll be me, and at that moment you'll bring the people toward where you see the light. Understand? . . . Oh, be sure to ask about the Zegarra family, and when you find them, stay with them. They're a woman, her eleven-year-old daughter, and three older boys. Help them. Don't worry about the rest of the group because there aren't any more women in the group."

He had no trouble finding the place at 6:00 p.m. when it was already starting to get dark, but he had to deal with the questions and the growing fear of the travelers, who didn't feel safe without Leonardo Ceja. As it grew darker, more people arrived, and about eleven o'clock, there were about thirty people. Fortunately the weather was warm at that time of year, and also there were a couple of kerosene lamps, and all of that allowed them to gather in small groups to talk. There were four guys who looked like businessmen who were playing cards. Although it was after midnight, not even the children had fallen asleep.

Alongside the Zegarra family, Dante felt the hours passing. He was concerned that Don Leonardo was late, but he didn't say anything to anyone, much less to Mrs. Zegarra, who was sitting next to him. The only thing that seemed strange to him was that besides her and her daughter, there was another woman in the group.

He went over to her, but she had her back to the lamps, and the darkness did not allow him to see her face; nevertheless, he sensed that she was full of sweetness and peace. He wanted to talk to her but never even asked her name.

"Don't worry about me, son," was the only thing the woman told him. "Go ahead and talk to the others so they don't worry. I'll take care of your charges."

It seemed strange to Dante that the woman knew what his mission was, but he obeyed her and went to talk to some men from Guadalajara who seemed very nervous. As he was talking to them he kept an eye on the women, and it seemed to him that they were having a very pleasant conversation. Then he started talking about horses with the men from Guadalajara and hit the nail on the head, because that was their business and that was exactly what he had done most of his life. In Sahuayo, when things were still good, he used to be called to go take care of horses on the ranches, and there was no one like him for raising them from the time they were small, taming them, breaking them, and even helping the mares foal. Talking about horses, Dante was able to distract the travelers. According to what he was telling him, in the quadruped family, there was no animal as noble as the horse. The donkey, on the other hand, was a stupid, expressionless animal.

"They never move, and you can't tell what they're looking at. They're like drawings in the air. They're more ears than head. They seem destined to communicate with no one, not even with their own kind. It's a miracle they even bray."

About one o'clock in the morning, Dante saw the flashing signal and gave the order to leave. Everyone had to run, jump over a fence, and join the *coyote* who was calling them. Although it was a moonless night, there was a strange brightness over the land, and the travelers realized that they were in a true no-man's-land. There were no roads of any kind there, and the only thing they could see were hills and some gullies in which only garbage flowed.

"If the *migra* catches any of us, the whole family must go back to San Luis," Mrs. Zegarra said.

This worried Dante because, in the previous conversation, she had told him that she had sold everything she had to make the trip.

With the *coyote*, they had to wait another long hour until, now completely sure, Ceja gave the order to proceed. Then they all ran some stretches and walked when ordered to, amid hills and wheat fields. Several times they heard conversations of immigrant agents in English and even smelled the smoke from their tobacco, but thanks to the *coyote*'s skill, they were not detected.

Once in U.S. territory, one of the most difficult places was San Isidro, California. In order to get there, they had to cross a multilane highway where the vehicles were traveling at high speeds. As she ran, Mrs. Zegarra tripped and fell, but she got up immediately and, with knees bleeding, kept running.

In San Isidro, they still weren't safe. The *coyote* led them through ranches where the dogs miraculously didn't bark, until they reached a place where two vans were waiting for them. From there, they didn't stop until they reached San Diego, where Don Leonardo distributed his clients in two houses and wished them luck. When he said good-bye to Dante, he ordered him not to leave the Zegarra family until the woman's husband came to get them.

In the small apartment they had been assigned, about fourteen people were sheltered. Each of them had no food other than an egg taco made of two tortillas for the entire day. At night, they all slept on the floor and felt very irritated because often other people's feet were on top of them.

The next morning at eleven o'clock, Mrs. Zegarra's husband rang the bell of the apartment, which meant that the trip had come to an end for Dante. When the woman was saying good-bye and thanking him, Dante asked her what she knew about the lady that had accompanied them.

"What lady are you talking about?"

"Well, I can't tell you what she looks like because I never saw her face, but I left her talking with you."

"Talking to me? How strange, no! . . . Well, I don't remember."

"She sent me over to talk to the men from Guadalajara, and she said she'd take care of you."

"Oh . . . well, of course. So you're talking about the pretty lady that kept talking to me . . ."

"Well, yes. I suppose that's who I'm talking about. Do you know who she is? Do you know who she left with?"

"Well, no, I don't know."

"Could you at least tell me what you talked about?"

"What do you mean what was she talking to me about? What do women talk about when we're mothers! . . . She kept on talking about her young son who seems to be a really naughty child. I guess he's run away several times to go talk to some doctors. What I noticed most were her beautiful eyes and the fact that she wasn't even carrying a bag of any kind. All she was carrying was a little vase like the kind you carry flowers in."

๑ ๑ ๑

Swimming, flying, or perhaps just from so much dreaming, Dante crossed California, and it hadn't been difficult at all for him to get in because he was so thin that perhaps he couldn't even be noticed anymore. But his feet or maybe his hands were so used to heading north that he kept on walking and didn't stop until he reached Salem, the capital of Oregon. In the early days, he found work on a horse farm as a trainer and spent all day commenting to the horses about his plans, about how beautiful his fiancée was, and how many children they were going to have.

"Maybe that's where I got the ability to communicate with quadrupeds and that's why they say I have a way with animals . . ." Dante told Virgilio.

About forty men slept in the quarters as Dante; of them, twenty had come from Mexico. The rest were Salvadoran, Colombian, Ecuadorian, Peruvian, and Chilean, which, according to what a fellow countryman from Michoacán told him, was quite strange because immigrants from Central and South America go no farther than California and almost never to Oregon, and, also, they usually don't work in agriculture. "Time itself is wrong," Dante was saying, "because we used to come just for a season and as soon as we earned something, we went back. And the people from the south, they didn't even come up here. In my opinion, something is wrong in our countries. I think there's something that makes them accursed. Time is going backwards."

Dante had noticed that, during the night, one of the men screamed harshly and dreadfully. He appeared to be trying to say something in the midst of his dreams, but he said it with hoarse sobs and nasal words that no one could understand. As this occurred repeatedly, several workers complained to the manager that the guy's nightmares didn't let them sleep well. They asked that he be sent somewhere else, but there was no other barracks available, and they had to put up with the problem for two more months. The man with the nightmares was a tall, muscular Salvadoran, curt, hard, and silent, who didn't talk to anyone, not even his own fellow countrymen, whom he seemed to avoid. He was very strong and completed two tasks in the same amount of time that the others took to barely finish one, and this was the reason that the company didn't want to get rid of him. But they had to do something, and, finally, the manager ordered them to clean out a toolshed near the barracks and set up a bedroom for him there.

Nevertheless, the past is like certain birds that, even after they're dead, keep warbling. One morning that man didn't show up for work, and when they didn't see him in the field all day, his companions assumed that he had left without telling anyone. He had gone, but to the other world, because when the manager went in to check the room, he found him hanging by a rope from the ceiling. Next to the body, there was an envelope containing money and a letter. In it, the deceased begged the owner to send that money and his salary to a woman in El Salvador.

"Can you imagine, Virgilio? From then on, we didn't hear the nightmares, but from time to time, someone who had gone out to go to the bathroom said that he had seen him and that he was walking with a rope around his neck. The reason for all of this, I recently found out, a year later, when I got to know the four Salvadorans in the barracks. They had managed to find out who the hanged man was. Don't ask me his name because I prefer to keep calling him

Sánchez, but I'm telling you that he had belonged to a death squad that specialized in creating fear among those who opposed the government. They read me the newspaper clipping that told of the deeds of the group. A peasant farmer, who did not even have political ideas, came home one night and found his mother, his sister, and his three children sitting around a table; their severed heads lay facing their bodies and their hands had been placed on the heads so that it would look like they were patting them. The murderers had had a hard time getting the hands of the eighteen-month-old baby to stay in place, so they had nailed them to his head.

"The Salvadorans explained to me that the government wanted to instill fear to keep the peasants from joining the revolutionary movement. They told me that later democracy arrived, but that the civilian government wanted to avoid trouble with the armed forces, so they let all the murderers leave, and that's why Sánchez was here. The bad thing for him was that the memories crossed the border too. They came after him.

"The oldest guy in the barracks was a fellow named Jesús Díaz, whom we called Professor because he was more than forty years old and had studied to be a teacher in Ecuador, but he hadn't found work and had to come north. There were two engineers from Colombia and also two young men from Chile who probably had come for political reasons. They were both named Rodrigo. The taller Rodrigo, whom everyone called Rodrigo Grande, said he had been a painter back home, and the boss used him to paint the horses' fences white. Little Rodrigo or Romantic Rodrigo read letters for those of us who couldn't read. One day the owner found out that Little Rodrigo had studied medicine in his country and gave him the job of attending cows when they were giving birth."

❦ ❦ ❦

Although Dante took care of his earnings and sent most of his savings to Mexico, he always saved a little money to go with his friends to the Cielito Lindo bar in Salem, where most people spoke

Spanish. The truth is that, besides being a bar, it was also a sort of center for arranging marriages with gringas. At first he thought the enormous blondes were Spanish students. None of his companions could confirm this impression because they were in the same innocent situation as he was, but one day someone confirmed to them that the Cielito Lindo was a place to join the heart of a Hispanic with that of a gringa huntress.

"What's happening is that they're looking for boyfriends, and if, after living with them for awhile, things are going well, they get married and that changes your life completely. If you marry a gringa, a few months later, you have papers to work legally and you could even go to school."

That day, in the middle of the bar, there were two or three tables of Latinos who, it was easy to tell, were looking for love, because they had dressed in the way men tend to when they're desperate to find a woman. The women, you could almost call them shoppers, would go up to the bar, order a drink, and take their time choosing. Sometimes they stretched out one leg flirtatiously and winked mischievously at someone, but that wasn't enough. You had to wait until the gringa came over to the table and said to someone, "Want to come with me?"

But that took time because they seemed to study the hopefuls with a magnifying glass. Sometimes they asked the candidate to walk like a model on the runway, to show his biceps so they could feel how strong he was, or to open his mouth so they could check his teeth, but after a disdainful smile, they continued taking their time.

Dante explained to his friends that he wasn't interested in any of the giants and that never, not even for the queen of the world, would he break his promise to Beatriz. He resisted heroically for two years as his friends one by one joined the ranks of the married or engaged. Finally just Little Rodrigo and he were left living in the barracks.

Big Rodrigo had been one of the first to find a woman at the bar, but he still hadn't managed to get married. "We'll see how you behave," said the huge blonde who took him from the farm and set him up in her home. From time to time she repeated to him that if he behaved himself, they would get married in a year, and she'd request a work permit for him. But she seemed to be in no hurry because, in the small apartment in Salem where she had taken him, the woman slept almost all the time and lived on unemployment. For his part, given that the work was not very steady, Rodrigo had to take advantage of everything he found and at times had two or three jobs to cover the maximum amount of hours he could get. That's why he often returned home around midnight, but even then he couldn't be sure of getting rest.

The bed was narrow, and the woman would only accept him in it if he was willing to fulfill his marital obligations. If he came home very tired, she would send him to sleep in an old Ford with no engine that she had in the garage, while Barbie slept late because she was an alcoholic. But even so she was not the worst that Rodrigo could have found. The worst had selected a young man from Jalisco. She was a jealous woman who constantly asked him where he was going, with whom, and what he had done twenty-four hours a day. One night, as he slept, the man from Jalisco opened his eyes and saw that the woman was trying to listen to his dreams to hear if he mentioned any woman, and she had scissors ready to castrate him if she learned of a betrayal.

Big Rodrigo told this to Little Rodrigo, and the latter in turn to Dante, so both of them decided never again to leave the barracks or at least not go to the Cielito Lindo.

Sometimes Dante believed that Virgilio was asking him questions, and he felt obliged to answer them.

"Man to man, Virgilio, I never fell in love with another woman. But I can't lie to you, a man has needs, they call on you, they knock on your door every quarter hour. Once I couldn't stand it anymore and I went back to the Cielito Lindo. And do you know who liked me the most? . . . A woman who was enormous and fat like the rest, but she had a very sweet face identical to that of the cow that appeared on the cover of a very popular brand of cheese. 'I think the little laughing cow likes you,' one of the guys said to me, and it was true. The laughing cow took me home and, without hesitation, headed right for the bedroom and gestured to me that I should make love to her. Then I decided that if I was going to do dirty things with a woman who wasn't my wife, I would do it without kissing her on the lips, and therefore, sure that I was not cheating on Beatriz, I began to undress. The bad thing is that at the moment of truth I suffered an attack of laughter just looking at the face of the laughing little cow. But later, my needs were more powerful, and I threw myself on top of her and dived into the little cow with my eyes closed, and I think I did it well, very well, especially because, as I was doing the bad things, I was thinking that I wasn't breaking my promise to Beatriz, with no kisses and with my eyes closed.

"I've already told you that I wasn't looking for marriage but just to appease my hunger for a woman that was about to make me explode. The bad thing is that the gringa started to get fond of me, and, sure enough, she told me that we could get married whenever I wanted to and that she would ask the Immigration Service for a work permit for me, but I couldn't do that to Beatriz, nor to the gringa. Things had already gone too far. So I said good-bye to her and asked her if we could just be friends. She agreed, but some nights, I felt that desire was pulling me by the feet to go see her, but I resisted. When I couldn't stand it, I imagined how we looked when we made love, and I laughed thinking that in bed we certainly gave the image of an enormous woman giving birth, and I couldn't stand it anymore, I laughed and laughed until I cried."

Until that time, Dante and Little Rodrigo lived as recluses in the quarters with no desire to have affairs like their companions had, but one day, temptation came and found them there. Not all Americans had to be those huge huntresses, and the two little gringas who visited them on Saturday to read them the Bible certainly weren't. Slim, young, pretty, and very courteous, Heather and Jessica invited them to church and from then on began to take them to visit different places in the valley.

Heather and Jessica spoke Spanish because they had studied it in Chile and Peru where they had been missionaries, and back in their country they did evangelizing work among the Spanish-speaking population. Shortly after they met, Heather, who had begun a special relationship with Little Rodrigo, invited them to her home where she lived with her parents to celebrate Thanksgiving. There Little Rodrigo and Dante first met and got to know an American family, and they were received with a great deal of affection.

For her part, Jessica decided to teach Dante to read, but every class seemed to him a sort of betrayal of his absent girlfriend. As was to be expected, Little Rodrigo ended up marrying Heather and this allowed him to obtain a legal work permit. Although the relationship between him and his friend didn't disappear, their meetings became somewhat infrequent and sometimes several weeks would go by without Dante having anyone to read or write the letters he exchanged with the faraway Beatriz.

Did he love Jessica? Yes, he certainly did, as much as Beatriz, but in a different way. Nevertheless, his honesty was holding him back. But he continued, and Little Rodrigo was his confidant.

"It's like everything gets all misty when she appears. And when she starts showing me the cards with the letters on them, I learn them all really fast and then I forget them so she'll explain them to me again. Maybe that's why, through so many explanations that she gives me, I've learned all the letters and I know them even before I see them, but perhaps I've never wanted to stop learning."

"Maybe it would be best if you ended your relationship with Beatriz. Maybe she'd understand."

"Maybe she would, but I wouldn't because I'm very stupid."

Then one fine day, he talked to the *gringuita* and asked her not to see him anymore nor to go on teaching him to read. That same day he went to visit Little Rodrigo and asked him to write a letter to his girlfriend back in Sahuayo telling her everything that had happened.

"With everything Jessica has taught you, you could write that letter yourself now."

"Yes, but I've decided to learn to forget."

The letter had to tell her that he now felt economically secure enough to start a family and that he would travel to Mexico to help her cross the border. He was going to cross over to the other side near Tijuana, and very soon they would be together.

The letter arrived when Beatriz was already married and never reached her hands, but went directly into those of Don Gregorio Bernardino Palermo, her husband, who knew very well what to do. He ordered his men to find Dante Celestino in Tijuana, to capture him, and to take him on a little walk. When they asked what they were supposed to do with him then, Palermo just looked at his shiny black leather boots and muttered: "Do I have to spell it out for you?"

The men, fascinated by the shine of the boots, understood well, and they also understood what happens to those who misunderstand.

That day Dante and Virgilio had traveled almost two hundred miles. They had stopped four times for the engine to cool off, and, finally, night was falling upon them. Seeing as how there was no park or rest area nearby, Dante drove the van off the highway toward a flat area. From there they could see the Cascade Mountain range at one side and on the other a plain that seemed to float. There finally, night caught up with them, and since they couldn't light a fire, it was going to be a long, deep, and endless night.

The donkey was sitting down and Dante, who had finished eating, was getting ready to go to sleep, but before going to sleep he wondered what sleep is longer, this one that he sleeps during the day or the one of the night, that leads him always to Beatriz, like a phosphorescent light in a forest full of darkness.

9
Beatriz Was Nowhere to Be Found

Beatriz had been given orange blossom water mixed with drops of honey to help her learn to forget. Then they added rose petals, hibiscus flowers, and oregano roots in her breakfast, soup, and afternoon coffee. To all of this they added a prayer that they repeated in her name when she was away from home and whose text they stitched on a little cloth bag that was supposed to bring her good luck, but really it was so her eyes, her heart, and her very memory would be covered by a thick curtain of forgetting.

Nevertheless, they achieved nothing with all of this because great loves grow in the distance like vines that surround your house, your life, your hands, your feet, your mouth, your words, and your eyes so that the name of the person you love never leaves them. All of that was happening with Beatriz, who was so entangled in Dante's memory that she drank the vinegar in a single gulp, believing it to be camomile water.

Nor did she notice the changing flavor of the coffee that they served her mixed with honey, oregano roots, rose petals, hibiscus flowers, and even the letters of the paper containing the secret prayer against the spells of memory.

Beatriz received a salary from the city for administering the small town library, and she lived with her mother and her two aunts, who were still counseling her about the mistake she was making in waiting for her fiancé indefinitely.

"He's poor, he's very young," they would tell her. "As soon as he starts earning money in the north, he'll find a woman, if he hasn't

84

found one already. You, on the other hand, honey, look at yourself in the mirror. You're a teacher and a librarian, you're white, you're pretty, and you were born in San Marcos, Aguascalientes, birthplace of the most beautiful women in the world, the eternal perdition of men."

Then they would argue and never agree whether she looked more like María Félix or Silvia Pinal, whom they had seen on the screen in their best days. Around that time the television stations began to broadcast foreign films. They soon discovered that Beatriz looked exactly like Isabella Rossellini, pretty with a capital 'p,' as pretty or prettier than her mother Ingrid Bergman, with a prettiness that brought tears to those who watched her too closely on the screen.

"Lord, help us! My Lord, they look just alike! They're two peas in a pod!"

Perhaps Beatriz or Dante would find someone else and maybe they would die many times, but they were not going to be able to forget each other. She had read somewhere that great loves existed in the world before people arrived and even exist before those in whom they are incarnated are born. They form part of the universe, and their incidental shattering could cause an imbalance in the perfect, silent system where the suns travel in ellipses and the constellations are never-ending.

But was it logical for a librarian to fall in love with someone who was almost illiterate? He wasn't completely illiterate, Beatriz told herself, and she was sure that by her side Dante would not only read well but would also fall in love with the most marvelous apparatus that men had ever invented: the book. If he hadn't done so before, it was due to the overwhelming poverty that left him time for nothing but working the fields and working with horses.

Beatriz's mother was a sweet, quiet woman. She did not want to interfere in her daughter's decisions and all she did was tell her that she should always follow her heart because God would never allow her to take a misstep, as she was such a good girl and her whole family relied on her. Nevertheless, if Beatriz harbored any doubt, that doubt was based on her mother's situation. It pained her to think what would become of her and even of her two old aunts when she traveled to the United States to join Dánte. But in the long conversation she had with him before he left, he said that he would send money to the old women every month, or even take them to the north as well.

In her memories, she saw him standing there while she waved goodbye. She had no picture of him other than the one she kept in her heart. She was crying as he disappeared in the distance. She was thinking only that life is memory, and memory ends.

But the months passed and the communication was very irregular because Dante depended on very trusted friends to write his letters for him; then they made a long trip to Sahuayo, that is, if they weren't lost on the way or in the pockets of a postal employee. There was a phone office in town, but it was so primitive that one had to request that an operator make the connection and then wait in line to get a turn in the only public phone booth and finally shout into the phone in front of many curious ears. Thus passed twenty-seven months, two weeks, four days, and seven hours from Dante's departure in Beatriz's sad, exact calculation.

"Look at yourself in our mirror, honey. We never got married because we didn't choose in time. How long has it been since you heard from that man? . . . Go on, say it, how long? A year from now, or maybe less, you'll get the news that he's marrying a girl from over there. He won't have the guts to tell you by phone or in a letter, and he'll resort to using a wedding announcement so you find out that way and don't cause him any trouble. And meanwhile, what will have happened, Beatriz? . . . Beauty doesn't last forever, and suitors get tired of waiting. Just look at Don Gregorio Bernardino Palermo. He's a few years older than you, but he's tall, ruddy-complexioned, and from a good family, and he's always sending you flowers, even though you've rejected him so many times. He's a real gentleman. He has the richest ranch in Michoacán, a construction company in Uruapan, and several housing developments in Guadalajara. They

say he even does business with the United States. He says he wants
to marry you because he wants to have a trophy wife."

The younger aunt, although she looked like she was older
because she was very fat, added with a mischievous smile: "He's
alone, honey. All alone in the world. Like you."

Strangely, whenever this advice came out, there was always
some radio playing "The King": *With money or without, I always do
what I please and my word is law. I have no throne and no queen,
and no one to understand me, but still, I am the king . . .*

But Beatriz seemed unwilling to follow that advice. She wasn't
interested in phantom songs. When she looked at herself in the mirror, she didn't see herself. All she saw was the man who was so far
away: "Please, protect him, dear Virgin of Guadalupe, that all may
go well for him. Let him find a job and not have his false documents
discovered and be put in jail. Cover the eyes of the *migra* so they
cannot see him, or make him invisible. Here is my heart and here is
my life, and you know so well, Mother, that I would trade them for
Dante's. Please don't let anything happen to him, because he has
always been so noble and so innocent. Please allow me to receive a
letter from him because another day has passed with no news of
what is happening in his life. But, above all, when we see each other
again, please let us recognize each other immediately, because honestly, sometimes I think we won't even recognize each other."

When it had been exactly forty months since his departure and
more than a year without news of her boyfriend, Beatriz received
some bad news. After much insistence, she had convinced her mother to go to the hospital to be examined for some terrible pains that she
attributed to a *mal de aire* and preferred to wait for them to go away.
But at the health center, and after a careful investigation, the doctor
informed Beatriz that her mother had an incurable kidney disease.

"All that science can do is replace one of them with a transplant,
but that is very expensive, and it is necessary to find a donor. In addition, we cannot predict what would happen with the new kidney. The
alternative is to put her on periodic dialysis, once or twice a week,
that's the only way to keep her alive. But, I have to tell you that we

don't have that equipment at this office. Instead, you would have to
take her to Morelia, Uruapan, or Zamora. Something that also concerns me is that dialysis is very costly, and you've said that your
mother has no insurance."

"You know what you have to do, little girl," her aunts chorused
three days after the bad news began to fly around the house like a
green fly, the kind that foretells impending deaths.

"You know what you have to do if you truly love your mother
and want to save her life. Don Gregorio Bernardino would have no
trouble paying for dialysis in a good hospital in Morelia," the fatter
of the two aunts said.

"I happened to talk to him yesterday and again he told me of his
noble intentions."

>   *With money or without,*
>   *I always do what I please*
>   *and my word is the law.*

A month later, Beatriz became the wife of Palermo, who would
take her to Morelia to live in a beautiful home. He had rented an
apartment for her mother and her aunts nearby. The weekly dialysis
began immediately.

Beatriz, on the other hand, had not found a way to let the absent
Dante know of the decision she had made nor the motivations that
had forced her to take that step. All she had been able to do was to
send a hasty letter to one of the houses where he had lived some time
earlier, but she never got an answer.

She learned what it means to live like few people in Mexico live.
Mariachis, mansions, sunsets, love songs, León shoes, Taxco earrings, embroidered blouses sewn with gold thread, fireworks, silver
parrots from Veracruz, Querétaro puddings, silent thugs ready to do
the bidding of Don Gregorio, a bar with two pianos, two proud birds
in the window of each bedroom, a roof garden that could hold fourteen bands, several cars with dark, bulletproof windows, two cars
full of huge men with loudspeakers ordering people out of the way,

a lake that ran to the sky, a population of crickets predicting perpetual happiness, two Doric columns at the entrance to the house, two Ionic columns in the first patio, two Corinthian columns in the reception hall, a chandelier with crystal prisms and precious stones that told the story of the world, and, finally, she was given a white-gold ring that proclaimed the eternity of marriage joined in Heaven that no one here on earth can break asunder.

From the first moment, the Palermos had everything, and perhaps a little love too, and Don Gregorio was content with Beatriz's obedient acceptance, her sad smile, and her gaze that, as he well knew, looked not at him but at someone who was very far from there. *You'll say you didn't love me. But you're going to be very sad. And that's the way you'll stay.*

But Don Gregorio wasn't satisfied with that. He also wanted to be loved. He made up his mind to get what has no price.

"We're going to travel far so you can see my properties and all of Mexico. We'll be traveling alone for a whole year, and in all that time you won't be able to see all of my businesses. This will be our honeymoon."

Beatriz's resistance was not long in coming. She thought that if she hadn't died truly and completely it was because she had her mother and her aunts nearby and because in a way they connected her to the painful memory of Dante. If she left, she was going to have to actually live with that strange man who, no matter how much he tried, would never cease to be a stranger.

"You're worried about your mother's health? Beatriz, darling, that's why I've arranged for her to have servants around the clock and a nurse to care for her and take her to the dialysis center. I've paid the rent on the apartment a year ahead, and neither she nor your aunts will have any expenses or any need to work. Pack your bags because we're leaving this afternoon. You don't need to bring much because we'll buy whatever you need along the way."

That night they arrived at a hotel in Mexico City where a room had been reserved for them. Instead of a ceiling, there was a transparent dome that allowed one to spend the night observing the blazing path of the planets. Beatriz would fix her eyes on the sky as Don Gregorio's heavy body crushed her and traveled like a locomotive from her feet to her hair.

Then the locomotive traveled over Beatriz's ankles, knees, toenails, navel, eyelids, eyebrows, armpits, hills, caverns, curves, and paths. But she kept staring attentively at the stars reflected in her silent tears. The locomotive disappeared down the paths of that marvelous geography howling helplessly and not finding on any of the paths the wonder of love.

The next day, he took her on a boat ride at Xochimilco, and they walked together amid women with flowers growing on their heads and vendors selling the serpent and apples of paradise. They passed among men who devoured fire because they were vegetarians and among single women dressed in white. They strolled past blind men who made marimbas speak and old Indians attired in ponchos who stared at them intently as if they were psychics and the secret of their lack of love was revealed to them.

Beatriz imagined that the world had been painted white at the order of Don Gregorio, when he took her to inspect his cotton field in La Laguna. Then they painted it dark brown, almost black, in the Coatepec coffee plantations. Finally even the air had a freckled yellow color in the Tepanatepec mango orchards. In Yucatán they saw a cemetery with gravestones that looked like they were made of heavy gold. Don Gregorio made Beatriz pose and took her picture on one that looked like the virgin going down to purgatory to rescue sinners.

From there they skipped to Cuernavaca, and Don Gregorio bought some huge, fat candles, with peacocks painted on them, that gave off a pungent odor when lit and served, according to what he had been told, to kindle lovers' good and bad desires. But his wife seemed unaffected by that magic and chose to put the candles away to take them back to their home in Guadalajara, where they would go well with the furniture.

In the Cuernavaca hotel, Don Gregorio sat down and began to bounce with his huge behind on the bed to make it squeak and perhaps thus stimulate the sleeping desires of his spouse. But Beatriz's pretty face lost none of its seriousness or its sadness.

Later in the trip he showed her water beds, sand beds, narrow beds, fragrant beds, beds with mirrors, damp beds, musical beds, air beds, beds with no headboard, beds hot as hell, ascetic beds, beds on which the emperor of Mexico had rested, mystical beds, soft beds, and hard beds upon which he sat to sing to Beatriz's ear that *the bed must be made of stone, the headboard too, and the woman that will love me, must love me truly . . . Ay, ay, ay, must love me truly!*

When several weeks had passed, Beatriz informed him that she had tried many times to communicate with her mother, but that no one answered the phone. In response, Don Gregorio told her that he had the line disconnected so that mother and daughter could take a little break and get used to the idea that the Palermos were a separate family, with no contact with the rest of the world.

"It'll do you good too so that once and for all you can get rid of that stress that follows you everywhere and keeps you from enjoying the pleasures of life and of the flesh," he had said.

They spent months traveling. They were met at every airport by secretive men who gave the boss detailed reports on his businesses as a group of enormous men surrounded them, guns drawn, looking all around.

They went to Baja California and Chiapas and Monterrey and Tijuana. In this last city, Don Gregorio seemed worried. He left Beatriz at the hotel and had a ten-hour closed-door meeting with the administrators. When it was over, they all came out of the conclave with their faces lit up like someone who has spoken with the dead or won the lottery.

There in Tijuana, Don Gregorio purchased tiger balm and several Asian aphrodisiacal mixtures that he was to consume in order to become a potent, irresistible man. But all he achieved was that his eyes slanted a little and all the French lotions acquired the yellow odor and pungent scent of the Chinese mentholatum when they came into contact with his skin.

"We have to talk," he said to Beatriz and asked her to listen, which she did with the docility of a dead woman. He explained to her that the Mexicans who cross the border as illegal immigrants lose their memory as soon as they cross. They forget forever the girl-friends they left behind and immediately marry the women destined for them. Therefore, no intelligent woman should think more than ten minutes about the departed boyfriend, no matter how many promises and how many signs from Heaven she may have received.

Beatriz seemed not to get the hint, maybe because, as her husband was speaking, she was sleeping with her eyes open and dreaming of a transparent man whom perhaps she would never see again but whom she could never forget because he lived inside her.

They stayed in Tijuana for a week because the central office of one of Palermo's businesses was located there. But every night after the meeting with his managers ended, Don Gregorio took his wife to one of the best nightclubs in town, in which he also held stock, and ordered that the doors be locked and a show performed for them alone, and for the thugs who protected him.

Immediately, the place was transformed into a thousand places in Mexico: Guadalajara, with its innumerable mariachis and trumpets; Veracruz, where people tirelessly danced the *danzón* all night; Tepozotlán, where a man dressed in black appeared strumming a violin that had been manufactured through diabolical inspiration. But finally, whether there or in the hotel, Don Gregorio never stopped repeating the gibberish about the illegal immigrants who cross the border and never return *and tipitipití tipitín, tipitipití, tipitón, every morning, outside your window, I sing this song.*

The next day, as the limousine drove her to the nightclub where her husband was waiting for her, Beatriz ordered the driver to stop, because she thought she had seen a man who looked like Dante. The man had gone into a church. She went in and found the church empty. She imagined that she had seen a ghost and that perhaps Dante was dying at that moment.

But she had not seen a ghost, it was in fact Dante who, after four years away, had entered Mexico through the border city and was trying to get to Michoacán to rejoin his fiancée. He was going to tell her that he had a steady job in the United States and had come to get her. Neither of them saw the other in the church.

At the moment Dante entered the church, he felt himself strongly gripped by the arms and then everything went black. But it was not the devil, who sometimes plays these jokes at the door of God's house, but a couple of men who immediately put a bag over him, covering his head.

"Let's go, move it," they said. "What you feel against your ribs is a gun and it could go off. Do what we say, or a miracle could happen and you'll fly out of here to Heaven like the angels do."

They kept the bag on his head all the time, and then they put him into a big four-wheel-drive vehicle and drove away. They must have driven him to a building because they made him climb stairs and when they reached the roof they put him in one place and then pushed him so he would think they were throwing him off.

Then they left him in a cold, damp room. They turned on religious music so that he would believe he was entering the territory of death and was about to meet the twelve disciples.

Later they came back and beat him with huge sticks. Then they put him into the trunk of a car that kept traveling and bouncing over unpaved roads. The vehicle stopped, and the kidnappers threw him out onto the road. If it was daytime, it did not matter, because day and night have the same face when one's face is inside a bag and when perhaps one is already dead.

"Hey, he's not dead," one of the kidnappers noticed when he looked in the rearview mirror and saw their victim writhing on the road.

"It doesn't matter. I guarantee you he'll never come back to Mexico," his companion responded as the car sped away.

"That's what Don Gregorio ordered, remember?"

"No. I don't remember. What did he say?"

"Yeah, what did he order?" None of them knew how to decipher the order, but they certainly knew what would happen to them for not understanding.

"Maybe I'm already dead," Dante thought, because as he lay there he smelled white flowers, azaleas, carnations, tuberoses, and violets, like the world of the dead must smell.

But he was not a dead man yet. He realized this when he was able to get the hood off and found himself lying on the grass surrounded by buildings and stars in the middle of San Diego Central Park in the United States. He wouldn't be able to go back to Mexico because they had taken his money. When he got back to Oregon, the friend who got his mail told him that he had received a letter from Beatriz from a few months earlier. The letter erased his joy, his dreams, and his last guiding illusion.

That very night in the nightclub, Beatriz asked if the year-long honeymoon was over, and her husband replied that it was just beginning. Seeing her weakness and discouragement, he took her out to dance and, speaking into her ear, he repeated the stories about the people who never come back and *tipitipití tipitín, tipitipití, tipitón, every morning, outside your window, I sing this song.* But his metallic voice was silenced by the power of a Los Panchos imitator proclaiming *Goodbye, ungrateful little girl, don't cry no more for your Pancho, for if he leaves the ranch, he will return promptly.*

Then Don Gregorio dragged her through the Copper Canyon and made her look at the trees whose tops disappear into the sky and the fantastic waterfalls that work the miracle of silencing the world so that a couple can worship each other. But Beatriz looked the other way. Then they traveled through Comala and talked to a lot of people, but all of them were dead and only gossiped about Heaven.

From there they made a pilgrimage to the Zapopan sanctuary, where women sing until they die, and they entered a market that sold herbs that would rejuvenate husbands and tickle wives. They were offered bellflower that, when put under the pillow, makes you dream about the one who will return, and bark of the *cilulo* tree that purifies the blood and leaves it very red, free of evil thoughts. They were sold bracelets made of electrolyte steel that stimulate circulation and nutmeg that unleashes nightmares and Powerful Hand tea that attracts money. They wrapped up mandrake root for them, which dispels frigidity, and turtle shell, which makes impotent husbands' rumps firm and joyful. But there was nothing, nothing, absolutely nothing to kindle love, because that day the little there was had run out on them. Then they traveled through the Jalisco heights and the San Miguel de Allende tiles, and then they took a helicopter flight around the ice doors, walls, and windows of the Ixtaccíhuatl and Popocatépetl volcanoes and went everywhere like people who are looking for love and suddenly discover that love is not of this world.

Finally, Don Gregorio took her to Veracruz so she could breathe the phosphorous-laden air of the Gulf of Mexico, and also to Cancún and to Mazatlán so the oceans would give his wife their contagious, wild eyes and their howling of she-wolves in heat. As is well known, love comes from the sea, but it did not explode in her. In her, there was only submission and obedience, as they say happens when one purchases slaves and mermaids.

Then, Don Gregorio Palermo order that the honeymoon year was over suddenly because the moon did not work to heat up his inappetent wife, who had not learned to love the one she was supposed to love.

"Our honeymoon ends here. You'll have to figure out what to do to learn to love me," Don Gregorio stated.

The couple arrived one silent night at their Morelia home. Beatriz had to spend some days in seclusion, reflecting on how important it was to be a real Palermo and reflecting on how wise it was to give happiness to the man who had given her such an illustrious last name. Any visit to her mother was forbidden, as were romantic novels and songs of the type that know only how to bring back memories.

"In this house, as you well know, memory is expressly forbidden."

Therefore, Beatriz had to take refuge in her dreams, and in her dreams she saw her mother, who was coming toward her with a sad announcement: "Don't cry, honey, but I want you to know that you are no longer going to find me. I've come to thank you for everything you tried to do for me and also to tell you that I will be here in Heaven to help you, no matter what decision you make now. Don't cry. Don't let them see you cry."

She tried to believe that a dream was only a dream, but the next day, she found out the truth of her dreams. Don Gregorio told her that her mother had died several months earlier and that he had not wished to cause her pain by telling her what had happened and ruin the honeymoon for her.

"And my aunts? I want to go visit them."

"Unfortunately, I don't think you can. I don't know where they are. After your mother died, I didn't feel it was necessary to keep paying the rent of the apartment where they lived. Therefore I ordered that they be placed in a rest home for the poor run by the Sisters of Charity, but they did not agree and left without saying where they were going."

He sent her to take a rest, and in her dream she again saw her mother insisting: "Go on, honey, tell him you want to see the doctor. Tell him you want to know what my final hours were like."

When she did, he said, "Beatriz, it's not necessary for you to see the doctor. Besides, it's going to be difficult to locate him because now he must be working in some flea-ridden state hospital. Since you want to know, let's be frank, because it should be me, your husband, who tells you. Don't be surprised by the gossip. . . . What happened is that the great dialysis, besides costing me an arm and a leg, was no use. It kept the good lady healthy for three days or a week at the most, but then she had to have it again. My administrator called me urgently when you and I were in Tijuana and gave me an analysis of the costs and benefits of having your mother in that condition. Since I'm a generous man, I ordered them to continue with the dialysis for two more weeks, but after that, I had to end it."

He was silent for a moment, calculating the impact the revelation had caused.

"As you'll understand, I'm not just me. I'm the head of a business that provides work for hundreds of Mexicans and therefore, the business's finances must be protected. That doctor was way too insolent. He went to the hospital administration to ask for free dialysis, and when he didn't get it, he decided to go all the way to the federal police to accuse me and the hospital of murder. You can imagine how the police responded. They held him in custody for a good number of days until his communist, terrorist ideas subsided. When he got out, he found himself fired from his job at the hospital. Is there anything else you want to know?"

There was nothing more that she needed to know, because, from that moment on, she knew everything and what she didn't know, she guessed. At a wordless gesture from her husband, which she was to interpret as an order, she entered the residence assigned to her. She walked through the population of crickets announcing perpetual happiness and beneath the Doric columns of the entryway, the Ionic columns of the first patio, and the Corinthian columns of the reception hall. Finally she climbed a spiral staircase that took her to her room and fell exhausted onto the bed after leaving the white-gold band on the night-stand.

Then she submerged herself in a night of sleeping straight through and in a dream from which she could not come out and in which she was not a woman but a bird entering undulating jungles, gliding over plateaus, and following the courses of rivers of deafening torrents to then fly in through the window of a marvelous house that was at the same time her house and her cage, and where besides her, there was no one but the syrupy voice of a man singing into her ear that she was his queen, that she was his dove, and that she always would be.

Tipití tipitín, tipití tipitón, every morning outside your window, I sing this song, but there was no one next to her because all of this was happening on the seventh day of Creation, and next to her rested the huge shape of Don Gregorio Bernardino Palermo, but it was a shape and not a man because perhaps the Lord had fallen asleep and had left his creation incomplete, or perhaps he was just starting to think how to make men and what their purpose is.

10
The King Is Not the King Nor Is his Word the Law

Several weeks earlier, Dante and Virgilio had entered what seemed to be the skeletal frame of the United States. The van climbed slowly up outcrops of basalt and then entered a tunnel, meeting granite mountains of an intense purple color where everything seemed to end. Dante couldn't speak because the magnificence of the naked rock that predated men, the last thing that will someday remain of the planet, overcame him. Although he did not open his mouth, he felt an intense sound beginning to envelop him. There was a scent of dry oranges. Soon he would reach the luminous desert of Nevada.

> *Then a cattle driver told me*
> *that you don't have to get there first*
> *but you have to know how to get there . . .*

❦ ❦ ❦

Suddenly the air had been emptied of all the people she had ever loved. No longer were her mother, her aunts, much less Dante, with her. Without him, the world had lost all its water and corn, its salt and honey, and the sky was full of iguanas and vultures. Going back to Sahuayo was increasingly impossible. Morelia was her place now and also her destiny, although she wanted to leave.

"I don't know where you get these strange ideas of leaving this house which is your home and always will be because you're a Palermo now. What would a woman as pretty as you do in some remote town full of brown Indians? Remember once and for all that you're my wife and you represent me in society, and you would kill me with pain if you ever left. What could you find out there if you have everything here?"

Beatriz wandered through the whole house morning, noon, and night, with the sole consolation that her husband's business dealings forced him to be away at least three weeks every month. Sometimes he even stayed in other houses right in Morelia where, he told her, he held business meetings. He soon realized that the explanation was unnecessary because Beatriz didn't ask for one nor did she seem to care if he was gone. Perhaps two or three years or more went by, because time had already lost its scent for Beatriz. Curled up in her bed, silent, looking at the ceiling, her arms folded across her chest, dressed entirely in black, she asked him for a divorce when he got home after one of his absences.

"What? Divorce? And what are you going to live on? Have you not stopped to think about the mortal sin you are committing by even thinking about a divorce? Do you not realize that marriage has made us one single person in body and soul forever? No, Beatriz, you're wasting your time in even thinking about it because I will not accept it, and without my authorization no judge in Mexico will grant it. And should you decide to take off anyway, you know full well that I have people everywhere, sweetheart, and with that marvelous face of yours it would be very easy to find you."

☉ ☉ ☉

At the peak of the mountain, the van in which Dante and Virgilio were traveling was suddenly submerged in a cloud of smoke that had no beginning and no end. From a distance, it looked like multicolored sparks, but as they drew closer, it was as if the sky had begun to boil. Dante slowed down, but even so, the smoke did not allow him to see even what was right in front of him. He had to pull over to the side of the road and stop, and a glorious spectacle left him not knowing what to do.

Thousands of butterflies were flying together. They alternated between rising to the sky and descending sharply. They filled the immense plain and no longer fit in the sky. In the spaces it was not day or night but the color of the tribe of butterflies that surrounded the vehicle.

They were the monarch butterflies that leave Quebec and New England, crossing the United States and flying all the way to El Rosario, Michoacán. They follow a path of more than four thousand kilometers every winter when they leave their northern nests and take to the skies of the United States until they reach the warm mountains of Central Mexico, Michoacán to be precise, and there, specifically, the Immaculate Conception Church of Angangueo and then the towns and countryside of El Rosario. There are about 300 or 400 billion of them, and they fly as high as airplanes before diving down toward the yellow lands that are their destination. There they spend the hot season, and then they must find the winds that take them back. The generation that arrives will die during those months, and it will take three to five generations to again reach the land or the skies from which they came.

"So, if the grandparents and the grandparents' grandparents died at their destination, how do the children of the children of the children of the butterflies know that they must return to their homeland?"

He always talked out loud because he wanted to assume that he was talking to Virgilio, and he secretly wished that the donkey would raise his head toward him and answer.

❦ ❦ ❦

Beatriz was sitting in an easy chair when the parade of monarch butterflies began to pass across the skies. The small skylight in the music room allowed her to see the flight of one of the tribes, but did not allow her to observe them devouring the sky and the four horizons in all their splendor.

Beatriz went into the mansion, through the Doric, Ionic, and Corinthian columns. She entered the huge meeting hall like a sleep-walker. She saw her eyes replicated in the fantastic prisms of the chandelier. She climbed the fatal steps of the spiral staircase, and at the top, she curled up in a sitting room whose ceiling was the universe. From there she watched them pass by, and she understood that the butterflies were a signal that everything in the universe moves, including people.

This thought pushed her to go into her bedroom and take from one of the closets the small bag she had been packing for a year, which contained some jewelry and money to survive for some time.

"Don't even think about running away because no one in Mexico will give you shelter if they know you belong to me," Don Gregorio had told her many times, reminding her that no one would hire "a woman fleeing from her husband and breaking the laws of God that join us in Heaven and on earth and beyond the grave and when we are souls forever and ever, world without end, amen."

But she was not planning to stay in Mexico. Like the butterflies, she would fly toward the skies of the United States.

Though it seemed very strange to her, no one tried to stop her. She attributed this to the darkness. Neither the chauffeur nor the servants nor a single one of the bodyguards was there to keep her from leaving. The main door of the house was open wide, and that wind that tends to enter empty houses blew everywhere. It was as if the shadow of the butterflies had swallowed up all the people in the world. Her bag was light, and she moved along as if she were flying.

When she reached the border line between Mexico and the United States, she turned and looked back to remember eternally what she was leaving, and she saw nothing. It was as if her entire country had become invisible. The mountains, birds, people, roads—it had all disappeared, or rather was melting because she had begun to cry with happiness and had not even realized it.

She had been told that in order to cross it was necessary for all of one's bad memories to be left behind because they keep one from walking fast, and she decided to hurry her walk so her sorrows wouldn't catch up with her. She hurried along and got so far ahead in the line of travelers that she was just a few feet behind the *coyote*, but the man turned to look at her and signaled to her to slow down. The path on which he was leading them was infallible to reach the narrow, fordable part of the river, he had told them earlier, adding that for several months he had led many people along that path who were now well settled on the other side.

"See that blue mountain? That's the United States. It's not far at all. When the moon comes up, we'll have crossed the river and we'll see a different color on the land because even that changes when you get to the United States."

What Beatriz didn't know was that many feet above her, in a Mexicana de Aviación jet, Don Gregorio Bernardino Palermo was also traveling north. He had shaved off his moustache and had his eyebrows removed, trying to look like someone else. The bad news had reached him the day the butterflies arrived. Amid the darknesses and the colors, someone told him that the judicial police were looking for him, and he had no chance to appeal to the men he had paid off within the police because none of them would answer their phone.

"If I were you, Gregorio, I wouldn't wait any longer. Nobody here is going to want to help you," one of his most loyal men said, but he forgot to call him "don" and no longer called him "boss."

The news caught up with him at the home of one of his lovers, who begged him to leave immediately so as to not cause her trouble. Then he fired the chauffeur and climbed into the car. The important thing was to get out of town fast.

Soon the police would surround his house thinking that there were armed men inside, and when they would go in they would find only Beatriz. That didn't matter to him. He quickly headed north out of Morelia. His plan was to contact some influential friends in Mexico City to get him out of the jam, although maybe it was already too late, he thought. In the capital, he convinced himself that it was better to be satisfied with the money he had, buy a fake passport, and head for the United States.

This took him awhile, and it took even longer to run from one hiding place to another with the police on his tail looking to question him about certain suspicious business dealings and shipments of *the good stuff* that had been seized from several of his distributors. Three months later, he took the plane that would take him to San Francisco, requested a window seat, and distracted himself watching the silent movement of the rivers, the smoke of some volcano, the bitter green of the forest, the red lands, and the black roads. What he noticed most was the bitter taste of defeat in his mouth. Thousands of feet below, Beatriz was following the same path.

⑥ ⑥ ⑥

"And where do you plan to go when you get out of this?" the *coyote* asked.

Beatriz looked at the current of the water. The river ran to the horizon.

"Is there a bottom on this side of the river? Do you think we'll get out of this?"

"You haven't answered my question. I'm asking where you plan to go, if you don't mind telling me," the *coyote* insisted. Beatriz didn't respond, because no one other than she needed to know. What she was planning was that any place in the United States would be acceptable, except the place where she most would like to be, Oregon. She didn't want Dante to ever see her again. It was better if he believed she was dead.

As if dawn had broken, suddenly the waves of the river took on the light of a radiant sun, because there below, on the horizon, an enormous moon had begun to grow and move.

"It's time to cross," the *coyote* said and looked sadly at the woman.

He had warned her that this path was not for women, that perhaps she should look for another place to cross, not the river, but she had insisted with such determination that she seemed to have been born heading north.

"There's a crossing over here. I'll go first, and everybody hang on to the rope."

Again the water of the river lit up, and a ray of light fell upon them like a star diving into the water. Then they began to cross single file, gripping the rope as the *coyote* showed them. The water was calm and didn't even splash when heels, knees, waists, chests, and frightened hands began to sink into it. A moment later, they were on the other side.

As the travelers were jumping to dry off, the sound of police sirens was heard, and then a voice over a loudspeaker: "Listen, please. You're under arrest. Do not try to run. Do not resist or it'll be worse. We are officers of the U.S. Immigration Service."

She didn't understand how they had been spotted, because they had never seen a helicopter overhead. She dared to ask.

"By the reflection," a friendly guard answered.

"The reflection? What reflection?"

"We were very far from you, beyond those trees, but still we saw you just like we're seeing you now. I thought it was a mirage, but my boss told me that wasn't the case, that people who've eaten dreams generally give off reflections."

During the months that followed, she tried to enter through different places along the border and always failed. The last time she had managed to get to San Diego and from there was taken to Los Angeles in the trunk of a car along with a family. She thought then that the most difficult part of the journey was behind her, but that was not the case. The car stopped at an apparently empty building, its lights off. The *coyote*, suddenly giving orders, using obscenities, began to order the travelers to get out and hurry into the building.

Once inside, Beatriz and her group were put into a room where about twenty people had already been crowded for several days. Two armed men were guarding them. No one knew if their guns were to resist a possible attack by the police or to keep them from escaping.

Hounded by that doubt, all the travelers looked desperate, tired, irritable, and hopeless. One man said that being in Los Angeles was like having arrived in hell. It turned out that those people were there until their relatives living in the United States paid for them. The man who believed that he was in hell confessed that he had no way to pay for himself and his family. Beatriz realized that she was in a similar situation because, for security reasons, she had told the smuggler that her husband would be waiting for her.

All of them were overwhelmed by exhaustion, despair, and hunger. In three days of confinement they received food only twice, and both times it was a bean taco with chile. That was part of the strategy so the immigrants would pressure their relatives to go pick them up and pay the smugglers for bringing them across. For her part, Beatriz had the money in her suitcase and could pay, but she realized that she would be in even more danger if she did so because they might try to take it away from her or even kill her.

The two guards had started to look at her with too much interest, and the third night, one of them came over and told her that he had gotten her a better room. He ordered her to follow him. Realizing what the man was planning, Beatriz decided she would defend herself with an iron rod that she had found in the bedroom, but it wasn't necessary. At that moment, as had occurred on other occasions, police sirens were heard. A voice, speaking perfect Spanish, ordered the *coyote*s to give themselves up.

Back in Mexico, Beatriz tried to cross again. Without knowing it, she took the path that Dante had used many years earlier. Following a route she had been given, she traveled to Ciudad Juárez, but did not cross the international bridge that leads to El Paso because she knew that the men from immigration had her photograph and all her personal information as they did for all repeat offenders. She purchased clean clothes and stayed in a good hotel. Then, at night, she took a taxi to a house with elaborate architectural decorations in one of the city suburbs. Rather than going to the main door, she walked toward a narrow door to the left and, as agreed, rang the bell three times. She did not have to wait long because immediately a woman in a silk kimono opened the door and stared at her, astounded. Without letting her speak, she said: "Not a word, honey. You'll ruin the business."

Before Beatriz could reply, the woman had taken her by the arm and was closing the door.

"I'm letting you in so you won't be seen from outside, but the type of clients we have here are not for you. They can't pay as much, and, what's more, if the other girls see you, they'll take off running to another, less pretentious house."

She wouldn't let her sit down. She approached her and felt of her like she was trying to ascertain whether she was real.

"This isn't a brothel for luxury whores."

"I have to talk to Augusta," Beatriz managed to say.

"Augusta Robusta, that's me, but even if you had a letter of recommendation from the president, I wouldn't accept you."

"I'm looking for the Facundos. The Facundo family."

Finally at that moment, Augusta Robusta realized the mistake she had been making.

"Come this way," she said and led her to a small office. "Forgive my mistake."

Then she started to mutter about how bad the country was that even the richest, most beautiful ladies were trying to escape from it. "Don't tell me you don't have a passport or a visa," she added, but got no response.

⑥ ⑥ ⑥

With the passage of the years and their father dead, the young Facundos had set up a human smuggling system that was one of the best on the border. The religious conviction that they were obeying the Lord's command kept them together. According to them, their father had been a prophet, and the Lord had commended to him and his descendants to lead his people to the promised land. They had offices in unlikely places in the main border towns. From there, after paying an initial quantity, the future immigrants were led to a place in the middle of the desert. Though somewhat expensive, the service was the most advisable because it was in the hands of a religious group, and this offered everyone guarantees, especially women traveling alone. The Facundos were vegetarians and ascetics, but skilled in the handling of weapons and capable of confronting any eventuality, such as those that were occurring at that time. According to what Augusta Robusta told her, a paramilitary group of U.S. citizens, the Patriots, had declared war on illegals, and everywhere along the border there were armed groups ready to hunt them down. At times, the immigrants managed to cross the line and proceed dozens of kilometers without being detected, but almost always their path led them directly to the mouth of Hell.

"Do you know how to ride a horse?" one of the Facundos asked her.

With one jump, Beatriz was on the back of the horse that he was offering her.

They left from a place that she never could remember. Everything was so dark that the safest way to follow the one in front was to watch the sparks that the horseshoes made on the gravel. Once it was daylight they entered the sand, and the animals began to have trouble pulling their hooves out as they sank into the loose ground. Then the riders had to dismount and walk holding the reins. For an hour they couldn't see each other because the dunes raised some and hid others and because suddenly a tremendous flock of harpies and vultures began to fly so close to them that they had to take off their hats to shoo them away. Finally, the group reached a small, clear plain. However, to their surprise, there was no one from the Facundo family there.

There were about fifteen travelers, and Beatriz was the only woman in the group. When the light of the sun made its way in the world, they were able to discern that the guide was a woman too. Then one of them began to grumble that they had been tricked and that if he had known that they were going to be guided by a woman, he wouldn't have paid so much. The others began to protest as well, and one of them shouted that it didn't seem like a border crossing but a party to get a woman.

"After all, two for fourteen seems like a lot, but they're both really good and surely they'll be able to take it."

The man, trying to be a wise guy, approached the guide smiling, but the woman raised her rifle with one hand and placed the barrel against his forehead. She was extremely slim, and her eyes were the blackest eyes any of them had ever seen. When her rifle turned to aim at each of the rebels, one by one, they all became convinced that death is cold, passionate, and intense. After that there were no more problems.

The guide explained that they were going to ride west, and if anyone lost contact with the group, he should ride toward the sun. In fact they were already in U.S. territory, but the closest town was a hundred kilometers away.

"Anyway, if anything happens, don't ride north. The desert would devour you. In that case, the best thing would be to return to Mexico."

When someone asked the woman what the next step was, she told them that she would take them to the religious group's camp. The Facundos would be there with their faithful, and with their help, they could reach any U.S. city with no trouble.

"When you see them, then you can say you're safe."

But it wasn't so. During the course of the day, everything happened as the girl had told them, and they reached a small oasis born of springs in the middle of the desert. That was where the members of the group should be, and there they were, but they weren't going to be able to help them. In fact, there was not even a lookout to greet them, hold their saddle horns, and help them to dismount and go to greet the brothers. None of that. Only an intense odor of tragedy slithered along the path as a crowd of vultures overtook them from behind and flew on ahead, continuing to fly low to the ground.

Then, Beatriz saw the lookout and three other brothers. They lay face down on the ground on their blood. The guide jumped off her horse and took out her gun, but the murderers were no longer there.

Next to a rustic hut stood a cross. Some of the victims had been forced them to kneel and then were knifed by their attackers. Women and men lay gutted, and one of the Facundos had been beheaded.

Without getting off her horse, Beatriz followed the path that led to a small dwelling. There she saw a woman with her back to her, kneeling, eyes on the ground.

"*Madrecita*, what happened here?"

There was no response. Beatriz got off the horse, but when she tried to touch the elderly woman's back, she felt that she was touching only air. Beatriz had seen so many starving old women that she was not frighten by her. Beatriz kept rubbing her shoulder, telling her that she was from Michoacán, that she had suffered a lot, and that love and life sometimes seemed implacable. The woman's veil fell away, and beneath her thick black hair, turned toward the sky, was a cut-up potato.

The guide gave an order: "To the east. We have to go right away because the killers must be around here. The road between those two sand mountains is a faster route to Mexico."

But Beatriz could not free herself from the terrifying vision and seemed not to hear her. Around her, the dead gave the impression of having begun to be transformed into plants; their bodies and extremities had been devoured by the desert animals. All that remained of them were their heads like shiny watermelons just opened to the midday light. She raised her eyes to address a silent question to the guide, but the latter did not respond, and Beatriz had to say out loud what she wanted to know: "Why were they killed?"

"It could have been the Patriots; they're racists. But there are also drug smugglers who kill. Or some *coyote* who wanted to get the Facundos out of the business."

Beatriz tried to add something, but the guide silenced her.

"There's no time for anything. Those damn killers might come back."

As she rode at her side, the guide explained to her that in the coming days, the blood would turn into tar around which ants and scorpions would spring up by spontaneous generation. The desert winds would give Christian burial to the ghosts, and everything would again be as it was forever and ever, world without end.

"There's danger in these parts, you know, but I can tell you're brave," the guide's dark, solemn eyes said to her.

Beatriz didn't know if she was truly brave. All she knew was that she had to escape from Mexico and reach the United States.

After that experience, she failed so many times that one *coyote* refused to accept her in his group, because he was sure she was jinxed, but his wife took pity on Beatriz and decided to clear her of the curse. She rubbed an egg over her whole body as she prayed, and suddenly the egg exploded, which was a sign that Beatriz had suffered from witchcraft for many years and was now cured. Even so the smuggler refused to take her.

Although the overwhelming desire to go had not left her, the money with which she had escaped was starting to run out. She decided to travel to Sahuayo and stay there for a time, perhaps a few months, until she was sure that she was cured of any curse, especially of the curses of fear. Bus by bus, she traveled from a border town toward central Mexico. The last vehicle, the one that was finally taking her toward her town, entered the mountains as if it were trotting. Higher and higher it climbed as its axles groaned with each new slope. The vehicle leaned toward the edge of the precipice, but it climbed and climbed, and the more it climbed, the mountains grew even more.

As the bus entered the stony ground and plains of Michoacán, for the first time in a long time Beatriz had happy dreams. In one of them she was conversing with her mother: "What?"

"What do you mean what?" responded her mother, who loved to play with words.

"What did you come to tell me?"

"What do you mean what did I come to tell you? . . . How should I know? Can't a mother visit her daughter?"

After three days of travel, the vehicle passed a mountain range and went around a lake, and then Beatriz started to smile. The bus stopped at the main plaza in Sahuayo, and the woman was the last one to get off.

"Is that small suitcase all you have?" asked someone who was waiting for her.

She tried to see who was talking to her. When she looked toward the place where the voice was coming from, she saw a woman she knew well.

"I was asking about your suitcase. Don't worry, Beatriz. I knew you'd come back and I was waiting for you. I could almost say that your mother told me."

Beatriz was used to old folks in her town sometimes confusing dreams with waking, life with death.

It surprised her that Dante's mother was there waiting for her.

"No, what a face, honey! If you're worried about Palermo, don't give it another thought. His dirty dealings were discovered and he fled, before you did, I think. Now he'll have to live in hiding every-where because the police in this country and on the other side are following his steps."

The town was exactly the same as when she had left it. The pigeons flew over the low adobe walls, and their voices seemed to carry messages.

"I'm telling you not to worry, honey. You'll live with me for a few months. Maybe less and maybe more, and then you'll go to the United States. Dante knows everything that happened to you and he's waiting for you. I'm going to let him know that you're here with me now. Now, I'll help you wait."

11
Behind the Behind of the Man from Sinaloa

Dante stopped the car at a rest stop to look at the maps and find the best way to get to Las Vegas, but he couldn't find the map he was looking for.

"A friend gave me these maps," Dante said, "and he told me that one was for Nevada. I tell you it has to be here," he told Virgilio, who didn't respond.

"Politely . . . Politely," he insisted as if trying to make Virgilio see that he was being rude. "Maybe I brought the wrong maps."

There was no reply.

"I must have put the California maps in the glove compartment. I believe that in cases such as this, and always, the most important thing is to let the heart decide." He kept talking, and then he sat there thinking. He looked at Virgilio, looking him in the eye as if trying to hypnotize him.

"I'm going to give you an idea of what I'm going to do. At every intersection, I'll go in whatever direction my heart decides. Of course, I'm going to keep traveling on the side of the mountains and I won't change course toward the west. Don't you think?"

Virgilio's eyes remained fixed on the distance, but he twitched his ears. So, Dante smiled and continued on his way.

"I'm telling you Nevada is that way. When we reach the state line, we'll start seeing signs telling us how to get to Las Vegas."

For one long hour, Dante did not speak with his traveling companion. He drove along as though absorbed by mountains, as if the world outside were speaking to him. At the end of that time, it occurred to Dante to say: "Don't you think we're traveling in silence as if we were praying?"

A cloud of birds enveloped the van, the sky, the mountains, and the road, and Dante had to slow down almost to a stop.

"Beatriz used to say that when you pray correctly you become so absorbed by God that you forget you're praying. The truth is that I don't know what she meant."

The birds left, and everything returned to order. Then Dante decided to try a man-to-man conversation with Virgilio, like the kind you hear in bars, about women. He started talking, and then he forgot to talk and continued the memory in silence.

"I always remember when she managed to cross over to the North. We had been apart for ten years, and all kinds of things had happened to us, to the point that I had begun to believe we were cursed."

The van was overheating again, and Dante had to find a place to stop. He camped on the top of a headland. There they found coffee, restrooms, electricity, and even a pasture where Virgilio could rest. But Dante's memories did not rest because they had crossed an accursed territory of his life.

"When I tried to go back to Mexico to find her, Palermo's people caught me and brought me back here, nearly dead. Beatriz tried many times to enter the United States, but they caught her every time. On the last failed attempt she decided to go back to Sahuayo. There she stayed with my mother until I found a way to send for her. But during all of this, ten years had passed. . . . My grandmother told me that stories never end. They're passed to others. This that has happened to us will also happen to others but who knows what the outcome will be."

Dante fell asleep among his memories, and Virgilio lay down next to him and kept him company for a few hours. When Dante woke up, he poured water into the radiator and got back on the road. The landscape seemed to repeat itself every time they rounded a curve. Finally they came to a tollbooth. Dante took out three dollars and handed them to the attendant, who approached the van and scrutinized what was inside. Strangely, he didn't seem to notice Virgilio. Upon leaving the tollbooth, the landscape was the same again, and Dante picked up the thread of his memories again.

"Finally I got the name of a trustworthy smuggler, and I sent Beatriz enough money to pay for her and for my mother, but my mother refused to come.

"'Death is already calling me, honey,' she told Beatriz 'and I don't want it to have to go find me in the United States. I'll stay here,' she insisted, 'and I'll never tire of looking north. In the kingdom of Heaven, they'll give me a chair so I can keep watching over you.'

"After insisting for a long time on taking her along, Beatriz had to give up, and in an agreement with the smuggler, she decided to cross the border on July 4th of that year, because that day the gringos were busy with their Independence Day festivities, and the fireworks caused them to pay less attention to their border.

"Beatriz left Sahuayo along with twelve other families who had sold all their household goods to cross the border."

Dante spoke while looking straight ahead. It didn't matter if words actually came out of his mouth or not. What mattered was having someone next to him.

"Virgilio, you cannot imagine how poor those people were. They were so thin that it wasn't difficult to fit them all into the back seat of the truck which they loaded to avoid trouble at roadblocks. Beatriz's best friend, Adriana Herrera, was with her too. Imagine, they decided to travel together because Adriana was going to meet her boyfriend who was waiting for her on the other side of the border too.

"'Before we left, I had a mass said for San Jesús Malverde, and I prayed for us,' Adriana told Beatriz. 'Do you know who San Jesús Malverde is? He's really handsome. Look, this is his holy card. Have you ever seen a saint wearing cowboy clothes and carrying pistols? He kind of reminds me of Pedro Infante. Some say he looks like Jorge Negrete. I've been told that Juárez was his last name, not Malverde. Who knows! One thing's for sure: he was a very proper bandit. A real gentleman. He stole from the rich to help the poor, and the government was not able to catch him for many years because people hid him.'

"'He was from Culiacán. That's where men, not jerks, are born. And he was a man and a saint. The same thing that happened to Jesus Christ happened to him; a friend of his betrayed him. They laid an ambush for him and shot him forty times. They say that the governor, to please the rich people, ordered that he be hung from a tree and that anyone who got his body down would be killed.'

"'With all his wounds and everything, he got down from the tree, and a very poor family hid him in their home. But when he realized that he was going to die anyway, he asked the owner of the house to report him in order to get the reward and asked him to use that money to buy a ranch and help other poor people like himself.'

"'San Jesús Malverde is the angel of thieves and the saint of wetbacks. They say that he's the friend of smugglers too, but I'm not concerned about that. I ordered a mass for him and prayed to him to help us.'"

"When they arrived in Tecate, near Tijuana, they were told to get out, and they walked several kilometers down a dusty road on which their footprints were immediately erased by the wind. Beatriz told me that at times they walked holding hands for fear that the winds would drag them back to Mexico. After walking for three hours, they came to a hog farm with a fence next to which there was a cruel 'No Trespassing' sign. There they waited all day until at night another group of people arrived, likely from a more prosperous area of Mexico because they were better dressed and you could tell from far away that they ate well.

"Right then the *coyote* appeared, rough but a well-mannered type. 'I can almost welcome you to the United States, because when you leave this house you'll be in the land of the gringos,' the man began, and as the people did not show signs of having understood, he stomped on the ground several times. 'It's hollow,' he said. 'Can you hear? It's hollow. A tunnel runs under here that will take you directly to the United States. But be careful because there are rats in there, and at the other end there might be immigration officers. But this is a very good night because gringos will be staring at their fireworks on the sky like idiots. Ma'am, you there, next to the window. Open it and look at the sky. Look, those are the gringos' stars.'

"The departure had been prepared. There, on the other side, several people were responsible for receiving them and taking them to a safe place. 'We guarantee you mobility in the United States and also a change of clothes.' They were to leave in groups of four. 'It's not good for more people to go at one time because the tunnel is narrow and you wouldn't have enough air. Groups will leave every half hour. . . .'

"'The order of departures will be drawn by lot, because as you can see, we don't play favorites. This is a respectable, accredited business,' and luckily for her, Beatriz happened to be assigned to leave right after Adriana and a somewhat overweight gentleman from Sinaloa who would precede them.

"A few minutes later, the *coyote* was showing them the entrance to the tunnel, and it seemed incredible to Beatriz that that black hole could lead her to paradise. The narrowness of the tunnel, its lack of light, and the squeaking of rats scared her, but she knew that after an hour of suffering, I would embrace her. The gentleman from Sinaloa had bent down and was crawling into the hole with Adriana behind him as Beatriz looked toward the window through which you could see the sky and the Americans' stars.'

"'It's your turn now, ma'am,' Beatriz later recalled the *coyote* saying to Adriana. 'Remember that you have to crawl like little children do. . . . Did you hear me? . . . I told you to go into the tunnel. . . .'

"Like a robot, Adriana allowed herself to be led by the hand to the dark mouth of the tunnel, and there, without realizing it, her right hand crossed herself. A few minutes later, she was crawling. Despite the darkness, the *coyote* had given her dark glasses, although he hadn't said so, to avoid possible attacks to her face by the rats.

"Adriana crawled one meter, a meter and a half, two . . . The narrowness of the tunnel prevented her from going any faster, but in her mind time no longer existed, only an obsession. There, on the other side, in some house in San Diego, her boyfriend would be counting the minutes until they were reunited after so much time apart.

"These thoughts made her faster, and in a few more minutes, she couldn't say precisely how many, she caught up with the wobbly, corpulent behind of the man from Sinaloa, who was also crawling toward his American dreams.

"'Sir, sir . . . are you the man from Sinaloa?'

"It occurred to her that perhaps chatting would make the time go faster, but she got no response but instead something like a grunt.'

"'Sir . . .' she persisted, but she received no response. A short while later she realized that she would never hear one, because his enormous belly was blocking the path to freedom and preventing the passage of any sound.

"And if that was the case, where were those grunting sounds coming from? She didn't want to even imagine. Besides, she couldn't, because the bulky object in front of her was also taking away her oxygen. Soon she could barely breathe, but from time to time she kept hearing the grunts, and a moment later, she began to hallucinate. All she could see ahead of her were stars coming from the body of the man from Sinaloa, like the stars with which the gringos celebrated their independence.

"Adriana didn't hesitate a second longer. With her last bit of strength, she turned her body around and crawled back, with no obstacles in her path because Beatriz had not yet entered the tunnel. Soon she was emerging through the mouth where she had entered, along with two semi-asphyxiated women and a *coyote* who didn't know how to explain what had happened.

"'I love my husband and I'm dying to reach the United States, but I can't stand it anymore. I can't stand that fat man's behind,' said one woman.

"'Just a minute, just a minute, please, esteemed customers. Wait here for me, just a moment,' said the *coyote*, and he entered the tunnel, emerging a short time later pulling the man from Sinaloa by the seat of his pants.

"'The business,' he proclaimed, 'guaranteed all of them the right to arrive safe and sound in San Diego, with no sort of annoyances. Nor could the business afford the luxury of losing customers as frequent as those from Michoacán.' Immediately, he offered the solution: 'Like this, my Sinaloan friend. Like this,' he told the rotund customer who had triggered the crisis. 'Do what I'm doing, go backwards, that's right.'

"And he began to help him enter the tunnel in the position he had indicated.

"'That's right, that's right, with your head in this direction to remember your past, so you never forget your homeland. With your ass going first, because it brings good luck.'

"And this time, Virgilio, Beatriz *did* reach the United States."

12
Making the Puzzle with the Ferocity of Love

"And that's how it happened, Virgilio. As soon as Beatriz emerged from the tunnel, she got into a van that took her first to San Diego, the first city one comes to after crossing the California border from Mexico. Amid the jubilation and festivities of the Fourth of July, it was easy for the vehicle to pass unnoticed. They could not remain in San Diego because that was dangerous; recently, there had been many raids against immigrants, as the *migra* was on notice. The immigration agents had stepped up their vigilance in San Diego; this was obvious from the number of uniformed men present in the areas of high immigrant populations and also from the number of helicopters flying around the city.

"The van in which Beatriz was riding did not even take the main highway. It traveled down several country roads, and its occupants had to endure the whole trip with their heads bent down, so no one would notice their presence in the vehicle. Two men began to vomit. A woman was screaming at the driver to stop because she had to go to the bathroom. A very small child, who had escaped from his mother's arms, raced back and forth howling in fear.

"At any rate, despite all these problems, the van reached the south side of Los Angeles after several suspenseful hours. They arrived at a place where I, having crossed the entire state of California from north to south, was waiting for Beatriz." Dante fell silent, as if in another world.

At first they didn't see each other. Dante strained his eyes trying to pick her out of the group, but it seemed to him that she wasn't there. Maybe she was only in his heart. Maybe she was nothing more than a vision brought about by the long wait, or maybe she was no longer herself.

At first Beatriz could not pick Dante out among the group of people waiting for their relatives. So much time had gone by, and she had wondered for so long that she could no longer believe that they would ever actually see each other again. Maybe he was no longer himself.

What would happen if she had changed and was not that slim young woman looking at him with a startled expression, but instead that little woman walking with her eyes on the ground? What would happen if he had forgotten her face? What would happen if life had changed their feelings and now they were reuniting only out of a sense of obligation? They were not aware at what moment that long embrace, that lasting kiss, the uncertain hands, and closed eyes all began. Maybe they were already dead, as lovers usually are when they finally find each other again.

"We're together now. Nothing will ever separate us again," Dante declared with the certainty of one who knows that two people like them always end up becoming a single person, and he added: "Don't worry. You're in the United States now. This is freedom."

Ten years is ten years, and people change a great deal in that time, just as sheep change their wool every summer and take on a different tone. Black ones turn white or cream-colored or spotted, and it's likely that their souls change too, not just their wool; no one can know for sure. That is why Dante and Beatriz, for no reason other than fear, lowered their gazes to avoid confirming what changes had taken place.

At the hotel room, they sat down on the edge of the bed with their eyes down, Dante finally spoke: "A year ago, I dreamed that the moon was coming down to the earth and that you were standing on it, dressed in white, and you were begging me, 'Please, Dante, come for me soon.' But I had no way to do it because I didn't have enough money, and I begged you to keep waiting for me, but I couldn't speak, and meanwhile your face began to fade and your eyes were disappearing toward who knows where. The next morning I was in despair, thinking that maybe you had died. But that same morning I got a letter from you telling me that you were fine, and the friend who read me your letter told me that dreams where the moon comes down to the earth never have to do with death, but with luck and reunions."

Hours later, Dante and Beatriz forgot about their fear of seeing each other again and their fear of change. They no longer looked at the floor, but they still did not look at each other as they conversed as if each of them were searching for a distant object. Beatriz had also dreamt that Dante was flying above the world, riding a black horse, begging her to continue waiting for him, but the horse first turned into a lion, then an eagle, then a river, and, finally, a gentle donkey.

Then they continued to sit on the edge of the bed not knowing what to talk about. Dante was thinking that they had to talk about something, because when they were dating, they had not reached the point of having intimate relations and had done nothing more than talk. For a minute he thought it might have been best to get two separate rooms.

It was ten o'clock in the morning, but suddenly it became dark for them, and they stopped talking about dreams; they talked to each other with their eyes closed, as if they were asleep and were afraid to wake up. In that way, in the dark, they began to touch each other, and when they realized that they had not changed, they could no longer recognize themselves because each had begun to be the other, as if a puzzle had just been finished through the ferocity of love.

Ten years apart suddenly became a questionable memory, as they caressed each other, feeling, exploring, rubbing, smelling, tasting, absorbing, licking, nibbling, and devouring each other with the same curiosity as Adam and Eve in the time of Genesis. With the ferocity of two animals that cannot get enough of each other and fear disappearing again.

For Beatriz that was the first time, although she had been married to Don Gregorio Bernardino Palermo. When that man mounted her body, she was not herself; she was not there. While Don Gregorio's labored breathing, hairy shoulders, and large belly crushed her, drooled on her, and traveled like a fat locomotive along her body, she had never been there, and that is why her eyes had memorized the geometric lines of the room and the ceiling, the photographs on the wall, the frequency of the clouds, the birds, and the constellations that passed by her window.

Now everything was different. Hands against hands, hands against lips, lips against tongue, tongue against tongue, teeth against neck, breasts against teeth, tongue on fingers, tongue on nipples, tongue on legs, tongue on thighs, tongue on belly and again, tongue on tongue, belly against belly and knees against knees, and finally, war, occupation, and assault, the invasion of life, penetration and fever and surrender and rocking, storm and flood, and the infinite pain and the scream that lasts forever.

Perhaps an eclipse occurred, allowing Beatriz to now leave behind the timidity of a raped virgin and take advantage of the shadows to enjoy, for the first time, a man who was truly hers.

When they rested for the first time, they lay in an embrace, not moving for a long time, as if death had overtaken them in the midst of their happiness, but their breathing revealed that in that darkness there were two living animals who were becoming acquainted through smell. Later, Dante got out of bed and went over to the window. There he realized that night had fallen and that they had not left the room all day. Alone in the bed, Beatriz examined herself. Content, she looked at her firm breasts, flat stomach, and long legs, and the color of her pink and white skin that only the moon had bathed and that Dante took pleasure in licking. She caressed her belly and her navel and kept touching herself and then brought her fingers to her mouth. She felt that the moistness had formed a river that advanced toward her knees. Then she began to smell herself and the sounds of the sea and the flavor of clams came to her. Finally, she felt that the golden chain with its religious image was sinking between her two extremely swollen breasts, and she decided to take off the chain with the religious image so as not to offend them with the thoughts and words that were now coming irrepressibly to her, and then she could not tell if she was thinking or saying: "I'm the fucked one who has stopped being fucked in order to fuck." Facing the window, Dante watched the sea, and it seemed to him that the waters were phosphorescent and that the stars had melted, or perhaps they had not yet been created and were floating.

Water on water, drum on drum upon the roof of the hotel, it began to rain while Dante and Beatriz devoured each other again. Beatriz realized that she had had her eyes closed the whole time, because of her shyness. Then, she opened them, and when she did, a flock of wild ducks came out of the north and flew off toward the moon, a cloud came out of the south and became bigger than the sky, the sun came up again in the east and set again, but nothing could contain the invasion or the rocking. Then she let out a great cry, and another and another, and she realized that love is a cry and it is music and that lovesick animals snort, whine, grunt, screech, roar, howl, speak, shout, sing, groan, wail, and moan.

A loud knocking on the door reminded them that they had been heard. The manager of the hotel shouted something, but Dante went over to the door and slid a bill under it, and then he suggested that the occupants of the downstairs room move to another room. One night came and another night passed. When he remembers it, Dante is sure that was the moment when Emmita was conceived, and he believes it was such a night that perhaps his forty friends from the barracks, in their respective places in the Far West, or perhaps all the Latinos in the United States, were making love at the same time and generating new life, trembling and shining with the natural fervor of passion, which among us is twenty times hotter and more phosphorescent than that of the people of the cold regions of the world. Yes, at that moment Emmita and thousands of other children must have been conceived, all because of a global warming that on certain American nights falls upon a human group that is very hot and willing to propagate, eyes, hands, legs, feet, navels, breasts, voices, lips, desire, spirits that never stop seeking each other out and entwining on good days and on wolf days, in holy matrimony and difficult loves, day after day and hour, even in the distance, even after death.

Dante and Beatriz did not travel immediately to Oregon where he lived. On their way through California, Dante had met some people who told him about a way to achieve legal status in the United States. All one had to do was enroll in the groups of workers that did temporary labor in the vineyards, strawberry farms, apple orchards, or cotton fields of California. They could apply under what was called a *bracero* law, which would grant them temporary residence in the country and, according to their friends, could be extended every year and eventually become an indefinite work permit or a permanent visa.

"See, Beatriz? You brought me good luck."

They took a bus to the San Fernando Valley, near Los Angeles. That vehicle belonged to a contractor Dante had dealt with before, and he did not have to say much for the driver to take them to a camp. The *bracero* recruiter had convinced Dante that a new life was beginning for him. He would not have to worry about a place to stay, as the company provided it. Since they were newlyweds, they would be given a separate apartment rather than the large cabins that housed forty or fifty people. Beatriz could work in the cotton harvest too. That was not so odd: a strong young woman could certainly pick cotton; it would be an exciting experience for a young family just starting out. Of course Dante did not want his wife to work in the field. Instead, Beatriz suggested that if she was going to cook, she might as well cook for everyone and that she would sell tacos to anyone wanting them, and she insisted so much that the new husband accepted her proposal.

Nor was it necessary for Dante to be concerned about tools for work. The company would provide them, the contractor assured him, and handed him a cloth sack about five meters long in which Dante had to place the cotton flower. The Celestinos were ready to get to work the day after they arrived.

Beatriz found a rudimentary gas stove among the hundreds of objects stored in the warehouse. She rolled a wheat flour dough out on a wooden table. Then, with her hands, she turned it into a round, thin sheet. After cooking the tortillas, she spread the beans on them and gathered it all up in a basket and went with her husband to the fields. Both of them got on the bus that belonged to the contractor, who explained to them that they would receive their visas when the boss sent a letter to the Immigration Service stating that Dante was a new member of the *bracero* program, eligible for a temporary work permit.

Soon they reached the fields, an amazing sea of green and white in which the plants grew about a meter tall and had yellow and red flowers wrapped in green buds. Inside them was the invaluable treasure of the cotton. However, it was necessary to know just how to extract it, because the skins of the bud were like the claws of a tiger, and the wounds they produced were always a bloody baptism. Inexperienced workers generally had their hands and entire arms cut in long gouges as if they had been struck over and over with a knife.

On the first day, Dante, caught up in his enthusiasm, worked about ten hours. He did not realize that he was truly exhausted until the second day, and he walked like those people who have been struck by lightning and are still standing, not knowing that they are already dead. When night fell, Dante was unable to accept even a bean taco, and he fell exhausted onto the hard old bed he shared with Beatriz.

At the end of the week, for all his trouble, Dante received only $60.00, that is, a rate of $12.00 a day. The owner was paying between fifteen and twenty cents per pound of cotton, and that meant that Dante had been averaging about 500 pounds a day; he was left with a back that looked like that of a slave who has been lashed with a very thin whip and body pain from which he would not recover for a very long time. Nevertheless, Dante insisted that there would be a happy ending. His registration as a worker in the *bracero* program would take effect in the next two months, and he would continue working as long as the harvest lasted. Later, he would thank his boss, and, together with Beatriz, he would set out for Oregon to enjoy life and the freedom of the work permit.

The taco business had not worked either. The workers were too poor to buy them; they made their own or they simply didn't eat.

"Wouldn't it be a good idea, Dante, to just go ahead and talk to the contractor or the boss to find out when you'll get that paper you're killing yourself for?"

Beatriz's distrust was growing along with her sadness at seeing her husband turned into a beast of burden. Therefore she asked this question many times, but Dante did not even have time to listen to her other than in dreams.

When the fifth week arrived, Dante weighed about forty pounds less than when he started. He had never been a heavy man, but he had had an athletic build, and now he looked like he was about to lose even his shadow. One morning he was unable to get up, and despite his repeated efforts, his legs did not allow him to go to work. Around noon the contractor came to inform him that his production had been steadily decreasing and was not what the company expected of him. He told him that that year the boss was not going to sign him up for the *bracero* program; there were many other workers who deserved it a little more. Perhaps next year . . .

It was not easy to get Dante out of the living quarters where he had spent several weeks and stand him on his feet in order to take him to town and put him on the Greyhound bus, because he had just come out of a long fever and his whole body ached. But the contractor was impatient because he needed to give the bed to another worker. Therefore, after having given him 48 hours' notice, he sent two strong workers to get him up and put him into the vehicle that would take him to the bus depot.

Dante slept for almost the entire trip to Oregon, but from time to time he was able to admire the amazing windmills moved by the energy of the sun that gave strength and vitality to all the arable land in California. In his dreams, Dante felt that those windmills were watching him.

"You'll see. Soon we'll be all the way through California and we'll enter Oregon," said Dante.

In Oregon, death seemed to not exist. Trees conversed with other trees. Out of them came squirrels, hawks, swallows, eagles, wild geese, and *caballos de paso*. Their leaves changed color in autumn. Beneath the trees, a vast, generous land grew ceaselessly.

"You'll see. Oregon will be the best for starting our marriage," said Dante.

"Don't say anything more, please. It's not necessary."

Beatriz did not want her husband to waste his energy. She wanted him to continue resting. Maybe that way, not just the pain but also the disappointment would continue to evaporate. She did not have to insist because at the Paso Robles station stop, two women, a couple with a baby, and, behind them, two men wearing green uniforms all got on the bus.

Dante did not speak again.

13
His Heart Was Afraid, but He Wasn't

After some twenty forced stops due to engine trouble and other mechanical problems, Dante and Virgilio spotted the lights of Las Vegas, as bright as dreams usually are. Dante decided to stop. It was after midnight, and he decided to park in the next campground, a small clearing in the woods beneath an intense sky and a land with a ghostly glow. An enormous, yellow moon hung right over the old van.

The lights of the nearby city were real. What was an illusion was the city itself, because the van was parked not near Las Vegas but near Salt Lake City, Utah. Dante's intuition had not worked very well after all, and instead of heading south, he had crossed the Cascade Mountains toward the east and had continued on through mountainous lands that had confused him completely. The wavering lights that were visible in the distance did not belong to the lascivious casinos of Nevada but to the red apses of the cathedral and churches of the austere city of the Mormons. The traveler would not realize this until much later.

Meanwhile, it seemed that all the drivers in the world had decided to stop at the same park, and Dante was driving around and around looking for an available space. When he found one, he was very tired. Maybe he was already in the midst of dreams when he turned off the headlights.

"Listen, Virgilio. I might be mistaken, but that lake over there is where it isn't, or isn't where it should be."

It was already six o'clock in the morning, but the Moon, Mars, and Venus were still sailing in the intense blue of the eastern sky. They were floating in a line, which is generally ominous because it confuses travelers, causes shipwrecks, and difficult loves become impossible. Dante remembered that in his childhood one of his grandfathers taught him to guide himself by the stars of the Bear and advised him to beware of the treachery of the Moon, Mars, and Venus when he bumped into them, especially if they were aligned and gave the impression of being in cahoots.

"Virgilio, I have to tell you something. This lake isn't in Las Vegas. Or rather, we aren't in that city, and according to the map, we're probably near Lake Tahoe, where there's a lake like this. Therefore, we're going to leave this camp as soon as possible, and in a few minutes we'll be in the city."

But they traveled on and on and on without getting anywhere. As if they were on the Moon, the meadows became deserts and the rolling hills became dark brown crystal mountains. Several hours and a great deal of exhaustion signaled that they had arrived in Salt Lake City, Utah and that they had spent the night on the shores of the Great Salt Lake. From there, it was impossible to attempt a direct trip toward Las Vegas, because that would mean many more days of travel, and the van had barely made it this far.

"I think we have to go back to Mount Angel," Dante said after a long silence. He was embarrassed at having made several wrong turns and gotten lost along the way. "We're going back, Virgilio," he added.

He was talking to himself like people do when they make the toughest decisions of their lives. He turned the key, but the vehicle refused to respond. He tried again and heard only a sad melody of a dying engine. He got out of the van, opened the hood, and began to clean the battery terminals. He returned to his seat, but this time only clicks were heard.

That was not going to upset him at all. He took out his toolbox and began to work on the engine. After two hours of work, it was unchanged. Then a blue jay that had emerged from some distant tree perched on a branch just above the vehicle as if it were interested in mechanics. It seemed unafraid of the man. Dante looked up and remembered that birds with blue crests are the closest to God, because their silence and their call are the echo of a very great silence and the resonance of a very deep thought.

That gave him more confidence. When he got back into the van, he stepped on the accelerator with the certainty that everything was going to be fine, and so it was. Then he looked up again to find the bird, but no longer saw it. So he turned around to see how his traveling companion was. This time, Virgilio deigned to look at him, but did so as if asking, "Is the search for your daughter over?"

"I'm going back to Mount Angel, but just to put a new engine in the car. Then we'll be back on the road, Virgilio."

The return trip began quickly and happily. Rather than returning with an attitude of defeat, Dante seemed to have the spirit of someone who has conquered the most difficult stage of a very long trip. After one day of travel, the van glided along parallel to the lazy waves of the Willamette River, in the very heart of Oregon, as an Indian summer spread over the valley and colored the forest. Red and hot was the land, and the air was full of birds. Life gave the impression that God had ordered that for at least a week no one should die. The highway dipped and climbed, going in and out through small towns where the houses and the people were trivial. It was as if, on the road, Dante, Virgilio, and the van had agreed to be happy, or as if the three of them had finally been cured of an endless spell.

Suddenly, the vehicle's radio turned on, allowing the entry of "the friendly airwaves of La Campeona, the radio station of all Hispanics," which precisely at that moment was broadcasting a live program of the Noble Couple. Dante turned the volume up all the way.

The highway became a thread that would at some point end in Mount Angel. Dante tried to imagine what would become of him if the forest didn't exist, or if he couldn't see it. He wondered what would become of him without the endless memory of Beatriz and of their distant town, and he thought that he was a lucky man. As he proceeded toward his destination, he played at trying to think of all his possessions, and he could not think of them all. He gave thanks for the red prickly pears and for fragrant, warm tamales, for the grinding stone used to make tortillas and spicy salsas, for *churipo* made with red chile and vegetables, for the copper kettles for cooking *carnitas*, for the strong smell of *pozole* and *chilaquiles*, for the prickly pear cacti pads that are trimmed of their thorns and are excellent in salad, for the shape of clovers and the aroma of mint that flood the memory, for papayas and quinces, for *guanábanas* and *tejococos*, for pineapples, mandarin oranges, and plantains, for the smell of limes and the taste of oranges in the middle of the day.

As Virgilio half-closed his eyes, Dante recalled the names of the horses he had known in his profession, and he disentangled from his memory the purebreds that he had treated, fed, broken in, and accompanied in rodeos where everyone drank and danced. But he did not finish thinking of them because the radio program that gave advice to people began.

Gong!

Gong!

That was the characteristic sound announcing the astrology program.

So, nothing was lost. Nothing, really, because now his memory turned red and embarked on warmth, giving thanks for his wife, for passion, for beds, for knees, for eyes, for tenderness, for desire, for enchantment, for secret love, and, again, for the roads he had traveled when he allowed them to take him over the hills of Taxco, past the Colina volcano, through the Tapalpa forest where there is a labyrinth and anyone who enters it is lost forever and has to be born again to be found, for Lady Death who seeks us out and brings us greetings from those who have gone before and memories of those who will never return, and also for the law of life that joins laughing and crying in a single basket in the same way that it joins man and woman and Jalisco and Michoacán, and, finally, for the bass guitar and the trumpet whose eternal howl will be the first thing we hear as soon as this world ends for us.

Gong!

Gong!

The gong he was hearing was coming not from a mystical oriental temple nor even from the radio special effects department, as he had believed. It was parts of the engine and frame of the car that had been falling off on the highway and, fortunately, had rolled off the road. When he heard the last gong, he was rolling along with Virgilio at his side in the front seat.

As he emerged from the cab, Dante began to think what he could do to get to Mount Angel under these circumstances. On U.S. highways, it is absolutely necessary to have a map because there are no people walking along them. Besides, at gas stations you can't find anyone willing to give directions because the employees are only familiar with the area twenty blocks around. Anyway, familiar with the landscape he had seen for years, Dante realized that he was in the central valley of the Willamette River and very close to the city of Eugene, about 80 kilometers from his destination. He decided to abandon what remained of "the powerful van." There was not much to remove from the cab. He just put on Virgilio's back a bag containing some photos and the few groceries he had left. He left Highway 5 and headed toward 99 because the former was a high-speed highway, while along the other there was a bike path. He walked there alongside Virgilio.

The highway seemed too narrow as it entered the forests, and at times from a high point they could see perfectly the zigzag it made as it descended. So, man and donkey left the main road and walked down the hills, taking shortcuts. But 80 kilometers is 80 kilometers, or more, when one is walking along loaded down with so many concerns. When night fell, Dante found a hay field and pushed Virgilio toward it so he could eat. Dante devoured the two tamales he had in his knapsack. Afterward, they camped in a pine grove sheltered only by the thin trunks against a coldness that was increasing at that hour.

Very early, they stopped at a railroad track because an endless train of the kind that hauls wood and supplies was passing. Not a single human face looked out to see them, and that eased Dante's mind, since he did not know how he was going to explain his situation to anyone who asked. But there were hundreds of cars, and the train, besides going very slowly, stopped frequently. So, the traveler decided to leave the highway perpendicular to the railroad tracks and instead follow a path next to the tracks. In this way they walked about ten kilometers. The only bad part of this matter was that the road crossed properties with threatening signs reading: PRIVATE PROPERTY. NO TRESPASSING, and there was no longer any way to return to the highway.

Next to a small bridge, there was a dreadful, poor-looking little house. A filthy, sad dog came limping out and came over to Dante and began to sniff him.

"Good dog, good dog!" Dante said.

"Sic him, Sultan," a voice shouted in Spanish from behind the little house. The animal leapt and managed to scratch Dante's face.

"*Mieeeerda!*" Dante screamed.

"Damn thief! Sic him! Eat him alive!" the voice kept shouting, and dogs began to appear everywhere. Then, the voice could no longer be heard because the barking drowned it out.

Virgilio, carrying Dante's bag, was stopped and showed no reaction. He didn't run away and didn't fight back.

"Looks like there's two of 'em. Finish 'em off, bastards," the voice said again. It was an old man's voice, but a moment later he reflected: "*Mierda?* Did you say *mierda?*"

Dante didn't respond.

"I asked you if you said *mierda.*"

"Forgive me. I'm sorry. It was because of the dogs . . ."

"Forgive you? What do I have to forgive? Sultan, Duke, Damnit, come. Come, these are good people. And will you tell me where you're from, my friend?"

The old man was the caretaker of a house where tools were stored. His job consisted of living in the house with the dogs and keeping strangers from trespassing.

"From Sahuayo, Michoacán."

"I didn't hear you. What was that?"

"Sahuayo, Michoacán. Mi-choa-cán."

"Not so loud, I'm not deaf."

When he finally understood that Dante was from Michoacán, he apologized and asked him in.

"Well, what a coincidence! I'm from there too. What town did you say you were from?"

But before Dante could say the name of his town again, the old man went off into the kitchen. The house smelled like rotten corn tortillas.

"Would you like something to eat?" he said, but got no response. Then he went over closer to Dante and saw that he had nothing more than the clothes on his back and that the donkey's little saddlebag seemed to be carrying only some photographs.

Again he went into the kitchen that was visible from the small living room. He began to hum a song by José Alfredo Jiménez. He went back and forth without finding anything. The old man opened the door of a yellowish refrigerator, took out a plate of old enchiladas, and put them into a microwave to heat them up.

"There's a horse corral very close by. We can leave your animal there at the manger for awhile. He'll have his fill of hay."

The old man talked about Michoacán, about the time when he left there, about his dead wife and his two children, but he didn't ask what a man and a donkey were doing walking near a U.S. freeway. Maybe he assumed he was a fugitive, but he respected brave men, and he had learned when he was a child that it is never good to know more than what's necessary and that snitches are wretched bastards.

He was a caretaker because, now that he was old, that was all he was good for. His left arm had gone numb, but with the pistol in his right hand he could do wonders, or so he said. He had a harsh voice and an emaciated appearance; he wore an enormous sombrero and shot into the air every time he heard footsteps or when the dogs barked.

"Help yourself. There's some beans too," he said to Dante as he put the hot plate on the table.

"I can't pay you."

"Pay me? And for what may I ask?" the old man asked. He picked up an enchilada and brought it to his mouth.

The sad, dirty dog that had greeted Dante was there with them.

"His name is Sultan," he said, offering the animal a piece of enchilada.

Sultan, his chin resting on the floor, raised his eyes and looked excited. He jumped up, stood on his hind legs, and took the food.

"I had taken you for one of those martyrs, and that's why I didn't shoot."

Dante asked who the martyrs were.

The dog raised his nose and inspected the visitor with his sad eyes. He sniffed him for a few seconds and finally seemed to accept him.

"The martyrs are good people. You know? A little crazy, but good people."

"So, they're not outlaws?"

"I shot into the air. Just to scare them."

"I don't understand. Why'd you shoot at them?"

"I just told you I shot into the air. Outlaws? The martyrs aren't outlaws at all!"

The martyrs traveled the rural roads one by one or in small caravans. They carried their water in pigskin canteens. They were unshaven and had very long hair. Rather than conventional clothing, they wore robes like the people in the Bible. They used goat skins as coats. They stopped at houses in rural areas to read the Bible to the occupants, but they were not very well received because they stank. They didn't bother to convert Mexicans to their faith because their prophets only spoke English, but they didn't hide their interest in making them know the new faith someday. They very kindly welcomed those who were already bilingual. They were vegetarians and enemies of all the evils of civilization. In their opinion, Satan personally had invented the television and the microwave. Nevertheless, they sent email messages and had a web page. The sun and life in the elements had turned them dark and reddish like onions when they're left in a jar of vinegar. They swore that the second flood was about to come, and that's why they had left their houses and the cities and everything that smelled like sin, gasoline, and DDT.

"They wanted to take me with them because I speak English well and because I told them that in my better days I had been a livestock tamer."

"Really? Like me. But, what good are tamers to them?"

"It's for when the end comes. First, the earth is going to turn very red. That's what they told me. Look at the print you leave; don't you see that it's a little redder than yesterday? According to them, that's a sign that the cauldron is heating up, and when it boils, the sky is going to fall. And all that will happen because of the sins of people, because of insecticides, gasoline, artificial fertilizer, and the lack of love with which we've been treating the earth. The truth of this is that it will rain for forty days and forty nights, and all the plains in the world will be flooded. That's why they're taking the livestock to the mountains."

"I was asking you about the tamers. . . ."

"I was getting there. After the flood, the animals will become very nervous, and that's where we come in. It will be necessary to redomesticate them, feed them sugar, speak softly to them, whistle to them. We who have a way with animals will be essential; we'll be worth our weight in gold."

"But I don't think there'll be enough animals by then."

"Neither animals nor people, sir. But they say the rainbow will come out, and behind it, the Lord will appear to make a new covenant with humanity and call upon the people and the animals to multiply. In my humble opinion, the Lord is going to get hoarse shouting because you know that the gringos are a little lazy in those duties. 'Don't wait til Saturday or til nighttime,' the Lord will shout, 'grow and multiply,' and the gringos will have to get undressed, brush their teeth, take a shower, and at times even resort to certain medications, in addition to asking their wifes' permission to lift up the blanket and get into her twin bed. No, sir, I think that at that moment, we Hispanics will be more than useful."

The martyrs passed by the ranch frequently because they had a camp in a nearby woods. They were putting up corrals, and from time to time they took a tool without asking because, according to them, those were the Lord's orders, but the old man wasn't willing to let them rob him.

"Some families are building the ark with measurements taken from the Bible. The last ones that went through here were single men. When I asked them about their families, they told me that the women and children were going to get into the ark and remain there until the waters subsided. The men will be in the high places taking care of the herds, but some will travel in the ark as crew. The birds, dogs, and cats will be in there, too."

When Dante wanted to know more, the old man began to become irritated because he didn't like to be disloyal, but he told him that in California, Oregon, and Washington there were people building arks, although they were doing it very secretly because the police didn't understand.

"I think I'm taking too much of your time," Dante said, thinking about his own time. The enchiladas had made him feel better, but he was anxious to get back on the road and to Mount Angel as soon as possible.

"You said you've worked as an animal tamer, too?" the caretaker asked, his eyes shining.

"Yes, sir."

"Might I ask what purebreds you've known?"

"Known, really known, no, but I've heard people talk about some really good ones, and I know who their parents were."

This was a favorite topic for both guest and host. Dante forgot he was in a hurry. The two men reviewed and described all the animals they had known and those they had heard of. They could not agree on the origin of the Paso horses, and this matter took them more time and some bean tacos.

The old man conceived of human society as an enormous horse corral. His language was full of equine terms. To him, Adam had been a stud and Eve a fine mare. He thought that Noah was also really something. Before setting out, he had spoken with two angels (probably breeders) who gave him instructions to speed the species' reproduction.

Latinos, according to him, were a beautiful breed but their corrals were a little untidy.

"The gringos don't know what they're missing. They should accept everybody who wants to come in. Not just that. They should invite them to come and improve these cold northern breeds."

Dante had never thought about that, but it seemed very wise to him. That was the moment Dante chose to recall Beatriz and Emmita. He was anxious to get the old man's advice. Maybe he knew how to get the young girl back. He reached into the knapsack and took out pictures of both. He spread them out on the table. But before he said who they were, the old man made his comments.

"What a beautiful mare!" he exclaimed when he saw the picture of Beatriz. "This is the best offspring I've seen in a long time," he commented about Emmita's picture.

Hours passed as they conversed. They had started to eat breakfast at seven in the morning, and it was already noon when a huge, dusty black pickup truck parked in front of the house.

"Old man, what's going on here?" someone asked in English from inside the vehicle.

And the old man replied in English: "Nothing. Want enchiladas?"

The two men in the truck worked for the same business as the old man. They said they didn't want any enchiladas because they had already eaten, and they gave him some instructions. They didn't even look at Dante.

An hour later, other men arrived. One was American, the other Chicano and he spoke half English, half Spanish.

"Is there a problem?" the old man asked.

"The donkey."

"Oh, the donkey. He's over there in the corral. The poor thing was hungry."

"The donkey didn't come alone. Who brought him?"

"Do you want to take some enchiladas for the road?"

"Quit kidding around. Hey, who you are?"

"I have *huevos rancheros* and *pimentos morrones,* too."

"Who are you?"

Just then Dante realized that they were referring to him. He wasn't used to talking to Chicanos because it seemed to him that they spoke with a heavy accent. He went to the door and saw that the men had Virgilio. When they discovered him at the manger, they had put a rope around his neck and had gotten him to climb into the back of their vehicle.

The dust raised by the pickup when it entered the corral was still floating slowly in the air. The Anglo man was at the wheel and the Chicano was waiting for him with a shotgun leaning vertically on his thigh.

"I asked who you are," the Chicano put the barrel of the shotgun against Virgilio's left ear, but Dante was frozen and did not know how to respond.

"Or would you rather I break his foot first?" said the Chicano, aiming at Virgilio's hoof as the Anglo smiled. He whispered something into his ear.

"The *güero* says get in back."

Dante obeyed, without saying a word.

"I don't know why I asked who you are. You ain't nothing, stupid bastard."

Before taking off, the driver began to use a cell phone. He was moving his arms as he was talking, and that seemed strange to Dante because Anglos rarely gesture. From time to time, he pointed at him with his finger and then returned to the conversation. In the end he burst out laughing and said something to his assistant, who laughed too.

"Hold on. Don't fall," shouted the Chicano, whose laughter was muffling his words. "Don't fall . . . "

The pickup sped off. It was heading north, and Dante believed that they were taking him to his destination, but then it turned west and headed toward the highest mountain on the Oregon coast,

Mary's Peak. There it took one of the entrance roads and began to climb curve after curve for more than two hours. In that short time, the landscape changed completely. The peaceful forest disappeared behind them, and in its place a black mountain gave the pickup truck quick access. The curves climbed, as if marching vertically but forming "N" shapes toward the peak. It must have been only about four in the afternoon, but the sun was left behind, forgotten down below.

The truck finally stopped on a frozen esplanade that must have been the summit, but the driver didn't turn off the engine, perhaps for fear that the cold would paralyze it. Two knocks on the window by the Chicano from the cab alerted Dante: "Get out now. Hey, you, get your ass out!"

He shouted it again because Dante had not understood.

"My friend says that if we find you trespassing again, you won't live to tell about it. Not you or your donkey."

Thus Dante arrived in the world of darkness, but he couldn't stay there because it was very cold. He took Virgilio's rope and began to look for the way back. When he found it, it occurred to him that he was entering a funnel in which there were only moaning trees and black rocks. Maybe it was a stormy night and perhaps the sky was torn by lightning, but he couldn't see the sky. He left the funnel after midnight, and the road led him through a white valley. The moon, which was just now visible, allowed him to make out a pale lake and an abandoned hut where they could spend the night. It was still far away, and as he headed toward it with the animal behind him, everything seemed like a dream.

They slept in the hut until late the next day, because the day didn't completely enter that place. It was probably nine or ten in the morning when Dante shook Virgilio's reins and guided him toward the road. They were still in a very high place and would have to walk for hours before they reached level ground where they would find the main highway.

"Hurry up, Virgilio, we don't have any food left," Dante urged as he loosened the reins so that the animal could go ahead a little way and show him the path. They walked like this for almost an hour

when suddenly Dante heard something like the explosion of a light-
bulb. He took off running, but didn't find Virgilio, who had been
about fifty meters ahead of him. He went over to the cornice of the
mountain and saw that Virgilio had slid down the side of the cliff and
had gone flying into space until he disappeared into the whitish
abyss where perhaps death awaited him.

To reach that point, Dante had to walk another hour. He ran,
flew, slipped several times, jumped, walked, and ran again to reach
the place where his friend had fallen as soon as possible, and as he
did so, he wondered if donkeys have souls. He told himself that they
must have one and that God could not be so unjust as to put such
heavy loads on their backs and deny them a soul. Finally he saw Virgilio and was astonished to see that his body was in one piece. When
he reached him, he couldn't believe it. Virgilio was alive and resting
in a sand pit. This was one of the few times that Virgilio stopped
looking toward one side. This time, he raised his head, twitched his
ears, and looked at Dante.

An initial inspection convinced him of how incredible it was.
Virgilio was all in one piece and had not even hit the rocks as he fell.
He had landed on a sandy slope and had slid down it like he was on
a toboggan. Dante touched his nose and it was moist; he felt his ribs
and they were intact. Before Dante gave the word, Virgilio got up
and began to follow him as if nothing had happened. A short time
later they were on the highway by Mary's Peak.

Down below, there was a group of men gathered next to a fleet
of trucks. By their appearance, which was very similar to his, beards,
robes, long dirty hair, he assumed he had come upon a martyrs'
camp.

They didn't ask any questions because they believed he was one
of them.

"Want a ride to Salem? . . . Get in, man," they said in English.

From the back of one of the trucks, a man held out his hand:
"Get in, brother."

Although Dante didn't understand English, he did understand
that they were offering to take him to Salem, where he would then

be very near his destination. Nevertheless, he gripped the reins that held Virgilio and did not hold out his hand to the man who was offering to help him. He wouldn't go anywhere in the world without his friend.

The driver exchanged glances with another who was next to him. At first it was one of confusion, then of joy. They realized that it was an excellent idea to take the animal to the demonstration.

"Of course, no problem. Get in, man. Get in with your donkey."

Dante enjoyed a pleasant ride. The martyrs didn't ask questions. They offered him oranges and patted him on the back. They were going to hold a peaceful demonstration in front of the capitol in Salem. It was to protest the indiscriminate use of pesticides that was spoiling the quality of life of wild animals. They entered the city and headed toward the complex of government buildings downtown. Then, they lowered the tailgate of the truck as a platform for Virgilio, and they found a place for him and his owner very near the capitol. A fat, red-faced man handed Dante a sign and, using gestures, told him to hold it up when the governor went by and also when reporters and photographers looked at him.

A reporter came over to them, and Dante posed beside Virgilio for a picture. That photo was published a year later by a paper that called Dante an ecological fanatic and "martyr of the Ark."

When the demonstration ended an hour later, Dante led Virgilio down State and Center, the main streets of the city, and turned on Church. No one noticed him. A police car sped by beside him, but the officers did not even look at him.

At the intersection of Church and Chemeketa, without thinking he headed toward St. Joseph Church. That was the way to go to begin leaving the city, but there he was indeed noticed because there had been a Mexican wedding and all the people were out along the street congratulating the bride and groom and their parents.

Dante walked through them without daring to ask for a ride, and that was the first time I saw him. I had been invited to Hortensia Sierra's wedding. I asked another guest: "Hey, what's going on with that guy?"

I felt like going over and asking him what he was doing in that strange outfit, but I never did because someone asked me if he was a friend of the bride or the groom. I never guessed that one year later I would be writing about him and his donkey.

They didn't make fun of them, but they also didn't go over to ask what they were doing. At that time everyone was busy deciding who was riding with whom and in what car to the reception. Someone said that Father Victoriano Pérez must be preparing a dramatization for Palm Sunday and that the man and his donkey would play Jesus entering Jerusalem.

A little later, Dante and Virgilio crossed the campus of Willamette University, went down Lancaster Avenue, and turned onto Silverton, the road that would take them to Mount Angel. It took them about four hours to walk through the Oregon state capital and get to Mount Angel, but in all that time, misty, almost unreal, other than those attending the wedding, no one saw them. Perhaps the same thing happened with the Redeemer of the world when they stopped cheering him upon his entry into Jerusalem.

By sunset, Dante and Virgilio reached Mount Angel. While Virgilio was taking over a warm backyard, Dante fell asleep in his room. He dreamed that he was crossing borders with an enormous human group that no one would ever be able to stop. Footprints on the ground, heels, knees, chests, shoulders, napes, necks, elbows, hands, faces, eyes, souls, shadows, all walking. No one had prevented them from entering. No one would be able to prevent them from achieving what they set out to do. No one was going to keep him from preserving his family. He dreamed that the next morning he would get another vehicle ready, in which he would set out in search of Emmita. He asked himself if he was afraid of what might happen, and he knew that although his heart was afraid, he was not.

14
The Heart, Aprons, and Pants of the Engine

The next day was another one of feverish activity for Dante. It consisted of constructing a vehicle, but he had to do it with love, which was not difficult for him because he had always treated cars and animals that way. About ten years earlier, the owner of the farm had given him the van when it was a confusion of rusty parts. "If you want it, take it, see what you can do. I think the engine runs, but you'll have to put a lot of work into it," he had told him.

Patting the hood a few times, Dante had said to it: "Poor thing, don't worry, I'm going to put you together."

He had worked hard looking for the parts that were missing or inventing them and putting them together in his free time. When he had finished fixing it, he painted the colors of the Mexican flag on the van's exterior. With it, the small family took weekly trips to various nearby places.

But the van had been left abandoned on the highway. Luckily for him, the boss, astonished at the work he had done with the van, had given him another old truck. "When you need parts for the van, you can take any parts you need off this truck." Now the vehicle needed everything, but he had to put a lot of love into the new work.

Although Dante had plenty of love; it was money that he was lacking. Prudently, upon his return from his failed expedition, Dante went back to the job from which he had been absent since the fifteenth birthday party. Every afternoon when he got home, he threw himself down on the ground to work on the van, while Virgilio came over to sniff around. First, he pulled out the old engine and marveled at its condition. The brass bushings showed many years of use, the yellow coloration made it obvious that it was extremely rusted, but it seemed to have the desire to run again as in long-ago youth. Then Dante connected it to a hose that he squeezed as if measuring its blood pressure.

"No, there's no denying it. These machines have souls, Virgilio."

Day after day, he pulled out part after part from the engine to determine which ones he would have to replace. After two weeks of work, he realized that the necessary parts were going to cost him a fortune, but the problem didn't scare him because he knew that he would find a solution for it, too.

Antonio Nole, a Peruvian mechanic friend of his, gave him the head and valves of a discarded engine. Dante then had the task of finding the heart and putting it together with the right pistons, fittings, rings, hoses, valves, pants, and aprons.

Week after week, he purchased each one of the parts, and he would spend every evening in the yard. The neighborhood children would look on, fascinated by the splendor of lights he created with the welder. It seemed to his neighbors, however, that he was working in vain, but they never said this to him because they either thought very highly of him or they assumed that, deprived of the slippery hope, Dante would cease to exist.

The children and their parents kept him company until a little after eight every night. While the strangers were there, Virgilio would stand next to the engine pretending to be an indifferent donkey, but when they would leave, he would walk over to Dante and sniff the construction.

One afternoon, Dante was driving home in a borrowed truck when he noticed that he was being followed. The distance of the car behind him, and the fact that it was against the sun's last lights, prevented him from identifying it. He slowed down and the car did the same. Dante thought he must be mistaken and continued on his way home, which was interpreted as an order for the car to accelerate.

When he was a block from home, he saw in his mirrors the flashing red and blue lights of a police car. He was starting to pull over when he heard the bullhorn: "Stop, you're surrounded."

It had to be a mistake; he was surrounded by three patrol cars that had joined the one that was following him.

"The weapon! Throw down your weapon. Now!" a voice was shouting in Spanish. Dante didn't know what to do because he had never used a weapon.

"Throw the weapon out the left window."

"No, weapons, no," was the only thing that Dante managed to stammer.

"Put your arms against the window. . . . Good. . . . Now with your right hand, open the door and get out."

"Now, hands on your head . . ."

He got out of the car and moved forward in the position they had told him.

"Careful! . . . Don't come any closer."

It was not necessary to tell him this because before he could take a step, a policeman grabbed him from behind and handcuffed him.

Then the officer led him toward one of the patrol cars that had one of its back doors open and forced him to get in, pushing him by the head.

"No, no, get him out of there and put him in his house. We're going to have a very instructive conversation with him," shouted the voice of the one that was probably the sheriff.

They took him into his own house and out again through the back door. There Dante contemplated a disastrous scene. The vehicle he was building had been taken apart piece by piece. They had been unable to lift the old engine, but they had dropped it and it had cracked. More than a year of work was lost and had to be sought among the pistons, fittings, rings, hoses, valves, pants, and aprons that he had laboriously put together during all that time. The head and the valves lay on the ground, wet with black oil like bloody decapitated heads.

"The sheriff wants to know where's your Bible?"

Dante had no words, nor did he understand why they were asking him that question.

"Your Bible!"

More silence.

"And he's also asking about your cult ID card . . ."

"Cult? What cult?"

"You destroyed it. You destroyed the card?"

Dante was unable to respond.

"How do you respond?"

There was no response.

"You mean to say we're falsely accusing you? Are you saying the sheriff is lying?"

Dante looked again at the panorama of his destroyed work and got up from the seat. He didn't say a word; he just shrugged his shoulders.

"The sheriff wants to know how many sheep you've killed."

"How many what?"

"Don't play dumb. How many sheep have you burned in the sacrifices?"

There were two police officers who spoke Spanish. One of them tried to help him: "Sheep, sheep, for the martyrs' sacrifices. You'd better answer, because you're making your situation worse."

"How many children have you killed?"

Dante didn't know what to say. His gaze traveled back and forth over the scattered remains of the van as if with his eyes he could put them back together. He was opening and closing his eyes to convince himself that he was dreaming.

Then the sheriff took out a bilingual pamphlet that had been found near the capitol when the martyrs were holding their demonstration.

"The sheriff wants me to read it to you and wants to know what you think. It's a quote from the Bible."

The policeman who appeared to be sympathetic to Dante read it slowly: "At that time the Lord spoke to Noah and told him: 'Within six months I will cause it to rain for forty days and forty nights, until all the earth is covered with water and all the bad people are destroyed. But I want to save the good people and two creatures of every living species on the planet. I order you to build an ark. And amid lightning bolts and sparks he gave the instructions of what he was to do while, trembling, Noah could only manage to say: Yes, sir.'"

"Understand?"

Dante was looking at them without saying anything.

"I'm asking you if you understand."

"Yes, sir."

The policeman continued reading: "'Within six months the flood will begin! the Lord roared. When the six months had passed, the sky suddenly clouded and the flood began. The Lord looked out from among the black storm clouds and saw Noah crying in the yard of his house, and he did not see any ark. 'Where is the ark, Noah?' God asked.

"We aren't going to ask you where the ark is, Dante, because we already know you're building it, but we want you to tell us other things."

"Yes, sir . . ."

"Because that's what you're trying to make with that mess, isn't it? An ark? We've already seen that you've started gathering animals."

Dante saw clearly what the police's mistake was and tried to tell them that he was going to use the truck to go look for Emmita. But they interrupted him.

"We aren't going to arrest you. But you have to help us," he added and, after taking off Dante's handcuffs, went over to the patrol car to see the sheriff, who hadn't come out of there at all during the interrogation. He said something to him, and the man returned.

"The sheriff wants you to know there's freedom of speech and worship in this country. That we're not persecuting the martyrs, but preventing them from committing criminal acts. You must tell us right now on what mountain they perform the sacrifices of animals and children. Tell us and we'll leave you alone."

Given that Dante continued to be silent, the policeman used stronger arguments: "Do you have a building permit? Have you paid for the patent? Will the ark have a fire safety system? And do the animals have their vaccination certificates? . . . And lastly, are you sure you aren't carrying drugs on that vehicle?"

His words were interpreted back to the sheriff, who seemed very pleased with the interrogation. But, suddenly, the Sheriff realized that something was missing. He called the policeman again, and the latter came running with another question: "The sheriff says that in this country we respect diversity, and he wants to know if all ethnic groups and sexual minorities will be represented on the ark. . . . We don't discriminate against anyone here."

As the questioning went on, a police technician checked the parts and the destroyed structure of the vehicle under Virgilio's watchful eye. After the inspection, he shook his head and went over to the sheriff's car to tell him that what Dante had been building was not an ark. It appeared instead to be a truck.

"Shit. Impossible!"

The Sheriff picked up his cell phone and began to shout at the person on the other end. All they could hear him say was "Impossible, impossible!" Then he called the officer over again and gave him more questions for Dante.

"The Sheriff wants to know if you're Dante Celestino. And if you're the man who more than a year ago reported the disappearance of your daughter."

When he heard the answer, he relayed it to the Sheriff.

"What? What are you saying? His daughter? Is he crazy?" The sheriff added a few more phrases and then burst into raucous laughter. He gave the order, and the officers got back into their patrol cars.

When the police left, Dante turned on a light and began to look for the parts of the engine one by one, from the head through the shirt to the heart. It was going to take him another twenty months to fix it, but he would do it. The memory of his arrival in Oregon hand in hand with Beatriz began to take shape in his mind as he searched the yard looking for more parts.

❦ ❦ ❦

When Dante and Beatriz arrived in Mount Angel fleeing the pain and agony they had suffered in the San Fernando Valley, Dante had not yet recovered from his back pain and was not able to lift his wife into his arms to carry her over the threshold. He barely managed to open the door for her. Then he went in, lay down on the bed, and remained there like a dead man until the next day.

"This is going to be our home," he had told Beatriz, showing her a small duplex that was part of a complex that contained a park, a gym, garbage collection, a small post office, and a community social center that were shared with all the other apartments. After living in multiple workers' quarters, it was the best he had achieved now that he was beginning his married life. Along with Beatriz, everyone else would come in, too: a family of squirrels, a toucan, a falcon, a dog, a stray cat, and a cardinal bird with a blue crest, the type that announces with a screech that they are seeing the other world.

The squirrels moved into the tree in the front yard. The dog sought out a warm corner in the kitchen and occupied it as if that were his right. The toucan muttered curses against the enemies of the house's owners. The falcon flew around to let the world know that it was protecting the Celestinos. The cat never came into the house, but it emerged from the woods at seven o'clock in the morning to be fed by the lady of the house. The cardinal was invisible, but it sang constantly, flooding the new family's space with its trills.

Years later, Beatriz would leave there dead and all those animals would go silently away, which to Dante would be proof that domestic animals are often guardian angels. A week after she died, Dante thought that he was going to disappear too, that there could be no force on the planet capable of keeping him on his feet. The animals and the angels had become air; the ground was turning into air, too. The front window was the only stable thing; through it could be seen the constant sky and the eternal forests of Oregon. Perhaps from there came to him the resignation that life has a limited number of dreams, that they are spent one after another, and that it makes no sense to cling to one of them.

⑥ ⑥ ⑥

As he prepared for the trip, Dante began to feel the throbbing that indicated that his old back pain was returning, but this time he did not have Beatriz to help him recover.

To distract himself from the pain, he reviewed what he was going to do so as not to get lost on the way. Doubts assailed him. He did not know what his words to Emmita would be when he would finally face her, nor what her reaction might be.

At other times, he could not believe the story he was living because he did not understand how the girl, whom he remembered as a sweet little girl, could have become so hard as to go off and push him out of her heart. Whenever he arrived home, he looked without success for the loving letter that he waited for throughout his work day, which never arrived. At night as he worked, he noticed the vehicles that went by from time to time, thinking that the girl, suddenly regretting what she had done, was going to alight from one of them. Since he had returned to Mount Angel, he went to the Salem police station every weekend to ask if they had had any word of her. The news was always the same, that every year millions of young people disappeared in the United States and not to worry because most of them did so of their own choice and sometimes to start a lovely family. When he responded that his daughter was not a young woman but still a girl, the policeman, holding back laughter, would ask him up to what age children were children in his country.

After more than twenty months of work, an enormous silver vehicle stuck its head out the gate of Dante's yard. The builder could feel happy that, not only had he finished the job, but his boss had given him permission to miss work to go look for his daughter again.

"I couldn't find another person like you, so don't worry, you can leave with the assurance that your job will be waiting for you," he told him and added, "at least for a month or two."

The next day, when Dante tried to become a driver, he couldn't even begin to do so. In the act of getting into the driver's seat, a convulsion invaded his body. It was the old pain that had attacked him many years earlier and it was now back with a vengeance. It was a torture that came from hell. It grabbed his arms and held him, gripped him by the hands and played with them, took him by the feet and prevented him from walking, twisting his neck so that he could only look toward the north.

It was eleven in the morning, the exact time when the Noble Couple show started. Dante layed back on the seat and turned on the radio. An instant later the typical gong and musical chords were heard, and Virgilio perked up his long, furry ears.

"Ladies and gentlemen: A new chapter in your lives begins here. Josefino and Mariana, the Noble Couple, are with you now to guide you and light your way toward the future, to wipe away those hateful body pains that have been tormenting you for so many years, so that your luck may change from this moment on. Welcome to this advice from the ether world with Josefino and Mariana, the Noble Couple, from the friendly waves of the most listened-to Spanish radio station in the Far West.

"Ladies and gentlemen, during the month of March when we were absent from this point on your dial, Josefino and I traveled to the Holy Land to bring you two gifts, which many of you are already familiar with. The first is the Cristo Afortunado and the second is the Miraculous Amulet of the Three Wishes," said Mariana, who then paused for Josefino to speak.

"We don't have to remind you that the Cristo Afortunado and the Miraculous Amulet of the Three Wishes are true reflections of health, and, thanks to them, you will possess positive energy and the majestic ultraviolet rays that they emit, since, speaking within the laws of parapsychology, those are the true and only sensorial rays against a person's bad luck and against unrelenting pain that may have been caused by someone envious of your happiness," Josefino asserted.

No matter how much Dante searched among his memories, he could not find anyone who envied his happiness. Of course he had been very happy with a wonderful wife and daughter, but he did not consider that type of happiness to be interchangeable. Besides, he did not believe that his lack of papers, his vulnerable illegal status, or the impossibility of visiting Sahuayo were facts that anyone would envy.

Dante decided that when he recovered, he would visit the Noble Couple. He was certain that Beatriz would approve of his decision if she were alive.

Strains of the ballad "The Sparrowhawks Depart," interrupted through the speakers.

❦ ❦ ❦

On Friday night, Dante joined a group of people seeking help at the apartment of the Noble Couple. A thirty-five-year-old woman wanted a cure for her arthritis; her misshapen hands looked like those of an old woman. A carpenter confessed that his saw slipped due to intense joint pain. Two women were there because the husband of one of them was cheating on her, and that's why she had gone there with her mother. A pale woman in her forties found the love of her life, but the love of her life did not want to marry her.

The Virgin of Guadalupe, glorious and beautiful, next to a crucifix of the Cristo Afortunado and the Amulet of the Three Wishes conferred respectability upon the place. The apartment was full of knickknacks, yellowed newspapers, and diplomas conferred upon the Noble Couple.

The apartment was in a building for immigrants that had achieved something in life. Across the street lay the immense campus of Hewlett Packard, which had made Corvallis one of its global centers.

Dante's treatment was one of the acts scheduled for the end of the session. At about nine o'clock at night, they had the client who was in love without hope of marriage go in. Dante heard them tell her to inhale tobacco soup through her left nostril as she contemplated with inexorable love the picture of the man she sought.

"Repeat after me: 'I'll have you at my feet.'"

"I'll have you at my feet."

"You will come."

"You will come."

"You will cry to me."

"You will cry to me."

"You will beg me."

"You will beg me."

"You will tell me that I am the love of your life."

"You will tell me that I am the love of your life."

"You will tell me that you seek me desperately in your nights and in your dreams."

"You will tell me that you seek me desperately in your nights and in your dreams."

"You will seek me to the point of insanity."

"You will seek me . . ." the woman began to say, and she interrupted herself: "Dios mío," she lapsed into Spanish, "that's not what I want, I don't want him to go crazy . . ."

"Of course not, but you interrupted me. Repeat, but more carefully please: "You will seek me until you go crazy with love over me and even ask me to accompany you to the altar."

As this was happening, Dante saw through the door, which was ajar, that Josefino, a tall, bald man with very thick glasses, was goose-stepping around the woman.

When it was Dante's turn, the masters informed him that his body pains were going to require several sessions to obtain a cure. They made him inhale tobacco soup, and drink hibiscus tea mixed with Genciana perfume. The mixture of all that caused him nausea and diarrhea. In addition, an intense sleepiness left him prostrate in bed for the entire weekend, but on Monday morning he felt much better.

Free of his pains, Dante found himself free and healthy. Like when his health and happiness returned earlier when Beatriz would sweetly, cover his eyes with her hands, and call to him "Dante, Dante," when he fell sick.

Dante tried to convince himself that he was at peace, like the nights when, following a wondrous battle of love, he and Beatriz would lay with their eyes looking at the sky and listening to the ballads of their faraway Michoacán.

Healthy, but without Beatriz and Emmita, he thought that, all the stars would go out one after another. All that would remain would be the light of the moon, but it would be useless to him because the moon only protects couples and tightknit families. The pain was making him wise and helped him realize that there is no greater happiness than that which comes from that puzzle of bodies, moans, and dreams that is love. His understanding became more subtle. That same day he started his second trip with Virgilio as his copilot.

15
Emmita Came to the World Through a Tunnel

From Mount Angel, Dante and Virgilio were to travel to downtown Salem and from there take Church Street, turn right on Center,
and right again on 12. Go as far as Mission and from there go east to
I-5. Take I-5 south, stop in Sacramento, California. With this vehicle, they would make the trip in about twenty hours.

He memorized the route during the long months of rebuilding
the vehicle. In Sacramento they would stay one day and one night at
the home of Che Maldonado, who had invited him some time earlier and had introduced him to *mate.*

After that came streets with names as beautiful as River City
Way, Millcreek Drive, and El Camino to reach I-5 again, where they
would travel 400 kilometers to Route CA 46, which would take them
to CA 99, then to CA 58, to CA 14, and again CA 58 until I-15,
which would take them to Las Vegas.

Dante repeated the directions to himself like a song, in order not
to forget it, as Virgilio stuck his nose out the window. They left in the
early morning and rolled down highways that went through endless
pastures. The van creaked at times, but Dante chalked it up to the
cold. He set the engine at moderate speed so as not to force it too
much, and it was as if it were trotting at a half-gallop. The road rose
suddenly, almost vertically, to the peak of a mountain that seemed to
be very near the stars. At three in the morning, the constellations
gave the impression of finally being in their correct places, and
Dante thought that the fortunes of men had also begun to be straightened out. Then there were only stars and silence, but from some

place in the universe the tolling of a bell began to reach him, and it did not stop vibrating no matter how far away they got.

Dante and Virgilio reached the home of Maldonado, and Che was astonished to see the vehicle in which Dante had arrived and to know that, after almost two years, he was still persisting in such a difficult search.

"But nothing surprises me anymore, you know? By the way, what's with that animal?"

"Are you talking about Virgilio?"

"The ass, dude," Che said as he stoked the fire of the barbecue he was preparing. The coals glowed red in the heart of the fire, but he could not get the charcoal to light. Suddenly, the charcoal shone like stars, and the happy Argentine forgot the question he had asked.

The next morning, Dante and Virgilio drove down River City Way, Millcreek Drive, El Camino Avenue, and finally I-5, one after another, but after driving nearly 300 kilometers, Dante did not find Route CA 46 and had to exit toward a gas station where he filled the tank and tried to find someone to help him. He did not find anyone, because in California, unlike Oregon, the gas stations are self-serve and drivers don't pay in a store. There was no one there who spoke Spanish. There was no need to panic, however, because a couple of blocks later Dante saw a sign that read: "Restaurante Cheverón."

Dante sounded it out: Che-ve-rón.

It sounded even funnier: "Puerto Rican, and proud of it," said a friendly voice from inside and added: "Does it seem incredible to you to find a Puerto Rican in these parts of the country?"

The voice belonged to a hairy man with a big moustache as anxious to help as he was to converse with someone.

"How to get to Las Vegas? Of course I know because I work right there? *Chévere*. But, first, allow me to serve you a coffee so I can explain it to you."

Dante could not turn down the invitation because he did not want to upset the man, but he wanted to tell him that he was in a hurry.

"Do you take your coffee black or with cream?" the man with the moustache interrupted Dante's thoughts. "By the way, you say that you're going to Las Vegas . . . and does it seem okay to you to go to those places?"

Dante didn't want to share Emmita's story with everyone and decided to give an explanation, but his host was already telling him that coffee should always be accompanied with a well-conversed sandwich.

"I have something very important to tell you, you know? I have a lot of things to tell you."

Dante started to get up, but the man got up first, patted him on the back of the neck, and asked him to kneel. But Dante seemed not to understand him.

"I already know who you are. You're one of those people who go through life alternating gambling with drinking and women. Someone who has not yet known the Word as I have known it."

"I thank you very much for everything, but I think I'd better be on my way."

"I'm going to explain it more slowly for you. I'm proposing that you accept the Savior in your heart."

Then he took out a photo and showed it to Dante.

"This was me five years ago. Do you see the difference?"

Dante couldn't find any difference at all. Somewhat more pale and skinny, perhaps, but just as hairy and with the same big moustache.

"Look at me," said the restaurant owner. He stood up and spun all the way around on his right heel. He posed for Dante with the photo next to his face. "I'm a new man. I've changed. I don't deny it. I don't deny that I was like you. The casino was my life. Beer and women. One day I was so wasted that even my shoes were stolen. Luckily they gave me a little job to get by, but I lost it too."

Dante examined the two photographs more carefully. If there were differences, they played in favor of the guy when he was a splendid sinner. He thought that it was going to be really difficult for him to find any more differences.

"It cost me God and his help. Cold turkey. One day Pastor Juan Paredes Carbonell arrived. I'll never forget his name. He read to me from the book. He demanded that I accept the Lord."

The man remained silent.

"And what do you think happened? Nothing. I accepted Him."

He closed his eyes and acted as if he were snoring.

"A devil and an angel were fighting in my heart. Cold turkey, yes sir, cold turkey. I see that the same thing is happening in yours. But finally the Lord spoke to me. Man to man."

Dante was waiting for a pause from his kind host in order to leave. The man opened his eyes, raised his head, and started to look at the sky.

"Kneel! I ask you, I beg you! I demand it!"

He closed his eyes, and Dante pushed the cup of steaming coffee aside.

"Don't run away. Please, don't run away from this opportunity that comes along only once in your life. Kneel and renounce your passion for gambling! Renounce Satan, his vanities, and his splendor! Do penitence for your sins and go away to the mountain to pray. Listen to what I'm telling you. It's not my voice that's speaking to you, and you know it. Now, get up from the table and come with me."

Dante had to obey him, but he stood up and fled. He ran as fast as he could from the friendly, hairy man with the big moustache. As he started the van, he could still hear the man shouting at him from the door of the restaurant: "To the mountain! Go to the mountain!"

One lane of the road they were on went toward the coast; the other, toward the mountains. Dante and Virgilio proceeded in the direction proposed by the friendly man. Dante commented to Virgilio that he was not going to be bothered by small obstacles. He smiled, looked steadily at the horizon toward which he was moving, and, with his eyes in that direction, returned toward the tireless memory of his happy years with Beatriz.

❀ ❀ ❀

Mount Angel has no more than three thousand inhabitants, most of whom are of German descent. The signs for the businesses are written in Gothic letters and 90 percent of the population considers itself Catholic. In the small space of the county, descendants of three nations as distant and dissimilar as Germany, Russia, and Mexico coexist. Those of German ancestry are owners of the modern farms and the livestock industries. The Russians, who still wear old-fashioned clothing, have small farms. The Mexicans do the manual labor for both groups. What the three groups have in common are large families and devotion to the Catholic faith, although the traditions expressed within it may be different.

Oktoberfest is celebrated in September. The Germans dress up as Germans and toast with overflowing "chops" of beer that they've made themselves. Since the town is small, all one has to do to see it in a very short time is to drive along the main street. This street, with its uneven design and abrupt ups and downs, passes the convent and a church of Gothic reminiscences, St. Mary's, and then climbs a steep trail toward an abbey in which time stops and so does the road.

The Mount Angel Abbey was built in 1879 on the model of the European religious constructions of the Gothic centuries. Every day Benedictine monks repeat an ancient ritual in which prayers alternate with songs in Latin and German intoned by a choir that would seem to have been singing there for a thousand years and an eternal morning.

If after the tour the traveler descends and takes the wrong street, they'll miss the delicious chalets where the Bavarians live and, without stopping at the Russians' farms, will end up in front of the small apartments where the Spanish-speaking families live. That is where Dante and Beatriz went to live when they first arrived. It was a special concession by the boss who gave them the apartment because, besides being the owner of the entire condominium, he lived nearby and wanted to have Dante at his service at any hour of the day.

Mount Angel, like Salem, Portland, Corvallis, Eugene, and other Oregon cities, exists in a green world divided into green mountains on which the tops of the trees hide the houses, erase the people, and allow only the smoke from a chimney and the flight of migratory birds to be seen.

Perhaps it was not because of the boss' decision that the Celestinos lived there, but because God so ordered Dante in his dreams. Perhaps God said to him: "Behold, son, the life and the world meant for you. It will not be like Sahuayo, but you will not complain. You will not find the reddest prickly pears nor the fragrance of hot chile peppers, but one thing is certain, in the cosmos you will not find trees like these because this is where I practiced making them when I invented pines and maples. This is where you will live and work.

"I will not order you to multiply, because you will have only one daughter, but you won't complain either—as you know I too had just one child.

"Remember what I'm going to say to you: this is your land and the land of your daughter's children and your daughter's children's children. Do not ask me if you will be able to return to Michoacán because I do not want to tell you that." God fell silent for a moment as if trying to decide whether to say anything about returning to Michoacán, and afterward, he did an *Ang Ang* to clear his throat and decided to tell him. "No, in life, you will never again smell the fragrance of the hot chile peppers or look upon the reddest prickly pears in the universe.

"Listen well to what I'm telling you and don't pretend to be asleep because I know you. You will eat bread with the sweat of your brow and the pain of your soul and the nostalgia for your homeland, and at times it will be hard bread, very different from the tamales of Michoacán, and you will be happy with the companion I've given you but you will hate having been so happy when you lose her and when you take her body back to Michoacán, and you will even want to forget what she taught you of the art of reading and writing. Yes, although you may not believe me, she is going to teach you that because she's a librarian, but when you lose her, you will forget what you learned.

"You will be happy with the daughter you're going to have, but you will bite the salt of tragedy when she leaves you, too, and when you go out on the road looking for her."

Perhaps God made another long pause and did not tell him if he would find his daughter.

On his shoulder, Dante felt the arm of an elderly, fatherly man who complained, "This business of inventing destinies is not that easy." Then Dante felt that a spirit like a light was spreading through the entire van, illuminating Virgilio. It kept spreading through the north and south, east and west, and all around the planet.

Dante remembered what Beatriz had told him about her experience in the tunnel, and suddenly it occurred to him that their daughter, Emmita, had entered the United States through a tunnel also.

Up there in the highest part of the heavens, he had been told, is a great door where the souls of those who are going to be born look out, and there, they choose the woman who is going to be their mother. Surely Emmita glimpsed at Beatriz cooking in a small house in the middle of the forest and, without thinking about it for an instant, jumped onto the celestial toboggan that passes by the moon and descends into a forest in which a woman is waiting.

In those days, Beatriz started preparing dishes from Michoacán: beef *churipo* with red chile and roasted pork; red, green, and pink tamales; *atole* with sweet corn and anise, green anise from the country; and wheat flour *uchepos* and *corundas* that were round like tortillas. All of it was served with tomato salsa, sour cream, and hot chile. It was an infallible secret for attracting the soul of a marvelous child. It's difficult to say what attracted Emmita's soul more: the fire-roasted tamales and the cream with eggnog; or the splendor of the garlic and the fragrance of the hot chile peppers; or the intense aroma of nostalgia and memories, of mint and treasured hopes that rose to Heaven from our house.

Dante was on his way home from work when he made out a light-blue cloud perched above his house and filtering in through the kitchen window, and it was then that he looked at his watch and said to himself: "My mother used to say that this is the time of day that the souls come down."

When Dante opened the door to his house he felt that both he and his wife were in the midst of an intense light, but he did not comment on that to her because he had something more important to tell her. The boss had offered to get him his green card.

"Dante," Patrick McWhorer had said to him, "I've consulted with the company attorney and he thinks you qualify for legal status. For my part, I can't complain. You've worked very well with me, and I'm going to fill out the papers to request you."

"Really, boss? And if you request me now, when will I get my papers?"

"It's a matter of months. Maybe a year or two."

"That's what he told me, do you realize what this means, Beatriz? In a year or two I'll be legal and then I can petition for you. That means we'll be able to go to Michoacán again and return there as many times as we want."

His wife's silence made him think that perhaps it was a bad time to mention it, that he had made her recall her entry into the United States.

"Don't be afraid. We'll travel like the gringos do, like normal people. We'll take a plane in Portland and we'll fly over the border, and no one will ever bother us again."

He walked toward the kitchen because Beatriz had not moved from there at all, as she always did when the dish she was preparing was about done.

"I'm telling you we'll fly . . ."

But he did not repeat the sentence because at that moment he saw Beatriz clearly and noticed that her eyes were half-closed, and she started sinking down onto the floor.

Beatriz then opened her eyes and with a luminous gaze looked out the window. Some say that the clouds that bring the souls have a touch of indecision. They accelerate, stop, change direction, as if they didn't know what they wanted, but the cloud that reached them knew perfectly what it wanted. On its way, it had submerged itself in a lake of yellow, orange, and red stars, like ripe plums, and then it went around the Moon, aimed toward the Earth, and when the Earth was an enormous globe, it chose America, it chose the north, it chose Oregon, it followed the course of the Willamette River, it chose the brown-roofed house of the Celestinos, it chose a marvelous smell of sweet peppers and entered the womb and the life of Beatriz.

"I think I'm pregnant, Dante, and I think it's a girl. We have to start saving for when she turns fifteen. The *quinceañera* will have mariachis brought directly from Michoacán. . . ."

16
Stones in his Pockets Kept him from Flying

"You have to take River City Way and turn right, and then Mill-creek Drive, and finally El Camino Avenue to get back onto I-5, Virgilio."

Dante repeated the route as his memory dictated to him. He could swear he had taken the correct roads and had turned right or left according to the planned route. Nevertheless, nothing seemed to indicate that I-5 was nearby. Now, instead, he had gotten on a cheerful trail along a brook and then climbed toward a mountain that looked familiar to him. Suddenly he had the impression that he had just been going around in circles. The trail narrowed and ended abruptly at a restaurant he knew well.

Resigned, Dante got out of the van and opened the back door so Virgilio could get out and rest too.

He let himself be carried away by the view. Tall, slim flocks of birds plunged into the whirlwinds and then continued on their way south. The trees changed color quickly, and their red and yellow leaves flooded the world. He turned his head toward the mountains and looked to the west where a long cloud was tracing amazing shapes on the blue firmament. Then it got dark, and from one side of the universe arose a ball of fire and a tail with millions of colors. Suddenly, a healthy peace filled him.

Dante began to think about the comet that appeared at different stages in his life to announce some big event. He remembered that in the days prior to Emmita's birth, the wandering meteor had been circling the skies and shaking its tail as if it had lost its way. As he slept, in his dreams he saw the one who would be his daughter, equipped with a pair of wings, looking like angels must look.

"Stop flying, dear daughter, it's time for you to come into the world," he said to her.

"I don't want to," replied the little girl.

"But you have to be born," Dante told her with loving, fatherly authority.

"No."

"Why not?"

"Because I'll make my mother suffer a lot. Probably you, too."

"But those are the rules of life."

"Why?"

Dante hadn't known what to say.

Emmita was born on Christmas Day no less. On the night of the 24th, Dante drove his wife to the Salem hospital. The strange thing about it all is that, despite the fact that in the winter daylight arrives at nine or ten in the morning, on the 25th the sun came out at five in the morning, wrapped in a bright blue dawn that invaded the skies and the forests and awoke many of the inhabitants, Dante among them.

"That must be a sign of good luck," he said to himself, and nevertheless it wasn't so. At that time the labor had already begun, but Beatriz was not doing well.

The pains were intense and almost unbearable, but still the baby struggled to stay in the womb, and several hours passed before she was born. At eight in the morning Dante was allowed into the hospital. At that same hour, his wife was stifling the howls of pain but could not contain the silent flow of tears.

Unaware of what was happening, in the hospital hallway next to a big window, Dante was thinking that it was a very beautiful day, a spring morning right on Christmas. At the moment when the doctor was likely operating on his wife, Dante heard a series of explosions in the sky. The explosions grew completely dark and began to split in blackness and dreadful bolts of lightning. It was as if a great final war had broken out up there and as if ten, twenty, or thirty solar stars had collided. Astonished by the sky that was vomiting flames and thunderclaps, Dante didn't know what world he was in because, during the ten years he had spent working and observing the skies of the place where he lived, he had never seen anything like that.

Although the state of Oregon is located on the same parallel as New York, rarely is it too cold; there are only one or two snowfalls a year and never are there storms as frightful as the one he was witnessing. Suddenly a terrifying lightning bolt began to look for a place to land on the earth, and it went up and down in different parts of the city of Salem until it landed on the hospital grounds on an enormous sequoia that split in two.

But that was not the strangest nor the most worrisome part of it. A doctor, looking tired, emerged from the operating room. Dante went over to him to ask about Beatriz. The physician's only response was to lower his eyes sadly, as if telling him that his wife had not withstood the birth.

"Your wife is fine, although she may not be able to have any more children. The problem is her blood sugar. . . . Your daughter is beautiful. But you'll have to be patient, because you're going to have to wait a few hours before you can see them. Your wife's in intensive care, she's very weak."

All Dante could do was look out the window, where he saw that the storm was no longer there, and, in its place, a sun, perhaps the largest he had ever seen, had come to rest over half the Salem sky. He looked all around and did not see a trace of the lightning bolts that had been battling. Additionally, the skies were sparkling, people walked on the street as though they were levitating, and the trees trembled with joy.

6 6 6

A few days before Emmita's second birthday, Dante thought that perhaps the time had come to talk to his boss about getting a work permit. Dante went to the office several times, but Mr. McWhorer was always extremely busy.

One morning, a Salvadoran who worked in the firm's accounting office approached him: "Dante, don't take this wrong if it's none of my business, but I think I have to tell you the truth. The boss isn't going to make good on the offer he made you. He changed his mind. Yesterday I heard him say that if you get the work permit, anybody would hire you for a lot more than they pay you here. It's best that I let you know."

The same day that Emmita was turning two years old, a neighbor came to tell Dante that he had received a phone call from Mexico, but that they hadn't been able to find him because the Celestino family had gone out to celebrate their little girl's birthday.

"A man who said he was your uncle called you."

"There's no phone in Sahuayo, and besides, all my uncles are dead."

"It sounded like they were calling from very far away. He told me to tell you that your mother died."

In the days that followed, Dante and his wife didn't talk any more than necessary, but one night while they were having dinner, they heard Emmita shouting joyously from the next room: "Nana, Nana."

Dante and Beatriz referred to his mother as Nana. The little girl waved her hands as children do when they've lost something. "Nana? Nana?"

Dante could not answer, but his wife pointed to the sky: "She's up there. Now she's a star." Beatriz took the little girl in her arms and carried her to the dining room, repeating to her that Nana was a star.

"No, Mamá, Nana there," the little girl said, pointing to a nearby chair. "Nana!"

Dante chose not to wonder if children can speak with deceased loved ones; he got up from the table, opened the door, and looked up to the sky. The stars were moving from north to south as the birds do at the arrival of winter. Dante feared that the sadness he felt would send him back south with the birds, toward Mexico, and he had to put stones into his pockets in order not to fly away.

❦ ❦ ❦

More alone than ever, immobile, without tears, resentful at the time it had been his lot to live, Dante chose to remain silent. But there came Emmita's memory again. That girl was like a star from birth. Perhaps she was going to go through the worst crises in life, but she would always come out unscathed.

After the pregnancy, Beatriz was very weak since her blood sugar was uncontrolled and caused her some shocks and sometimes convulsions. But Beatriz did not want to feel useless, and she kept taking care of Dante like she had before. Sometimes she and Emmita went out in the van, like the day they went to Salem to visit Rosina, Emmita's godmother, and buy a birthday gift for Dante. He had told her many times that he didn't care much for birthday parties. Besides, he was concerned about Beatriz going out alone because the doctors forbade it. When she gave birth, her diabetic episodes had grown more severe, and the doctors had told her that she suffered from a condition called hypoglycemia and that at times her blood lost its sugar content. Therefore, she was to always carry candy with her, or when the shock occurred, she was to go to the nearest medical center to be given insulin, but so far she had been feeling well, too well, and her body had allowed her to produce plenty of milk to nurse her daughter. So Beatriz was completely sure the she could make that short trip for Rosina to see her goddaughter.

Mount Angel is twenty kilometers from Salem, and to get to her friend's house, Beatriz should not have taken more than half an hour. But what should have been a short ride turned into a several-hour nightmare. Without Beatriz realizing it, the diabetic episode was already occurring from the moment she got into the van, and a few minutes later, on the highway, she began to travel aimlessly.

Although her hands were gripping the wheel and her eyes were fixed on the distance, her soul was traveling through spaces of amazing happiness and allowing her to drive asleep. In the midst of her unconsciousness, she depressed the accelerator or the brake, skillfully turned the wheel when necessary, and dreamed that she had gone out for a walk. Sleeping, she saw herself flying over the golden fields of Michoacán; the days became immense and the nights quivered with lights and stars. On the huge, endless moon, she tried to guess what paths her mother and grandparents were on.

When she reached the Independence Bridge, instead of taking the curve to go on to the bridge, the vehicle went straight toward the river, hit a small rock, and, due to its initial speed, flipped over and began to sink upside down in the brown waters of the Willamette River. At that moment she woke up and, through her instinct of self-preservation, took deep breaths until she became fully aware that the van was about to sink and that behind her, belted into her car seat, was Emmita who was not crying.

Dante said later that at the stable where he was working, he had the sudden impression that his little daughter was walking toward him. Emmita had not yet learned to stand, but Dante swore that he saw her walk with her arms stretched out toward him, and he felt that something bad was happening. Everything else transpired in a time that Dante did not feel as time. He climbed into an old truck that someone lent him, started the engine, and the fields, the streets, the birds, the other vehicles, and the trees began to go by. He thought he was going to his house, so he did not understand why he took Highway I-5 without intending to and why he was driving so fast.

Maureen Dolan, a professor at Western Oregon University, who was driving to the Portland airport would say she experienced something similar. She would state later to the *Statesman Journal* reporter that she felt an irresistible need to stop her car to look out from one of those scenic overlooks that offer travelers panoramic views of the valley. Although she was in somewhat of a hurry to get to the airport, she pulled over and got out to look toward the river. There, she is sure that she heard the voice of a little girl calling her: "Maureen, Maureen."

When her eyes made out the river, she saw that a vehicle was sinking. She looked all around. There was no one who could help. She put on her hazard lights and ran down toward the river. Wading in the current, she made her way through the brush and fallen branches until she reached the van; the engine was running and throwing off steam. Immediately she went to the driver's side and tried to open the door, but she couldn't. She went underwater to see how many people were inside and was able to see Beatriz and Emmita. She broke the window of one of the back doors and got the little girl out. She had noticed that the woman at the wheel was breathing, but she thought that the priority was to get the baby out and put her on the bank. Luckily, several drivers had been alerted by her car's emergency hazard lights and some were already on the bank when she got there with Emmita. A policeman managed to tear off the seat belt that was holding Beatriz, get her out of the water, and turn her over to the paramedics. The firemen began to see about pulling the vehicle out of the river.

For his part, Dante, like a robot, had driven to the Salem emergency room, and something seemed to tell him to be patient and wait.

Inside the ambulance, a policeman concerned with statistics was trying to ask Beatriz for her personal information. Since he couldn't awaken her, he didn't know if she was "white or Hispanic," "married or single." Maureen Dolan came over and offered to interpret when Beatriz showed signs of coming to.

"Ask her if she's taken drugs or drunk alcohol."

Maureen believed that those questions were ridiculous, but found herself obligated to repeat them in Spanish.

"No, no," Beatriz responded several times. "And my daughter? How's my daughter?"

"What's your name?" Maureen asked her. "Was there anyone with you? What's your husband's name?"

"I don't know, I don't know," said Beatriz's frightened eyes as one of the policemen came over and gave her a piece of candy. When Beatriz ate it, she finally began to come out of the diabetic shock and was able to say that her name was Beatriz, that her daughter was Emmita, that her husband was Dante Celestino, and that they lived in Mount Angel.

They got to the emergency room and there was Dante, who was beginning to believe that whenever Emmita was in trouble a guardian angel would always come to save her.

⑥ ⑥ ⑥

Remembering Emmita made him feel optimistic, and he understood that nothing bad could happen to her or to him. The light of the moon then broke through a splendid open hole among the clouds and enlarged the shadow of Virgilio, whose ears were standing up as they felt the scene in front of them turning ghostly.

⑥ ⑥ ⑥

It was obvious that Emmita had a destiny as stubborn and determined to carry itself out as the character that she herself showed from the time she was little. Before she turned six, her parents took her to John Kennedy School, which was the closest to their home. When she was tested to determine what grade level she was at, the teachers were astonished at her maturity and wisdom, and they gave her a place in a class for advanced students. The class was taught in English. Emmita studied for three years without the slightest problem and was always considered the top student.

Nevertheless, Mr. Flint, a state education reform commissioner, came to the school to do research on the subject and focused his work on the section where Emmita was studying.

"What is the meaning of this?" he asked. "There's a girl by the last name of Celestino in the class. She's Hispanic. She can't be in a section where only English is spoken."

They explained to him that Emmita spoke the language perfectly, but Mr. Flint replied that a Hispanic girl should be in a bilingual class in order to learn English gradually. Although the bilingual classes were at a lower level, the commissioner insisted: "She's Hispanic, and we have to give her special treatment to protect her under the Equal Opportunity law."

He asked to talk to the girl, and they sent for her. When Emmita arrived, he looked at her and said, "Sorry, I believe someone made a mistake," and asked her to leave.

"I asked you to bring me the Hispanic girl," he insisted, angry at the teachers. They told him that Emmita *was* the Hispanic girl. The commissioner knew Hispanics only through a stereotype in which Emmita's white skin and green eyes did not fit.

"Okay, okay, this is an order: switch her and send her to the classroom she belongs to. A Hispanic is a person of color, and we're obligated to protect them," Mr. Flint, who prided himself on being a person of progressive ideas, stressed vehemently.

Being moved to a level much lower than the one appropriate for her was something that Emma Celestino never understood. Nor did she like for teachers to explain to her, in Spanish, concepts that she had learned two years earlier. She began to experience an anger toward those decisions and also against the language of her own people. With her mother dead, Emmita believed there was no possibility of anyone understanding her. Although her father loved her immensely, she knew that he couldn't understand her problem or go to the school to protest, because the administrators would laugh at him or ask him to sign a thousand papers even knowing that he was almost illiterate.

For his part, Dante never understood why Emmita kept quiet when she was alone with him, or changed the TV to English channels and yawned when Mexican boys came to visit.

⑥ ⑥ ⑥

Dante also knew that Emmita had secret powers. One day, she and her classmates were taken on a field trip to an arboretum to study the different varieties of pines and maples in the area. The forest contained several thousand trees, and all of them were covered with a moss that glowed in the dark. The branches intertwined with the fondness of old friends and only allowed the sun through in rays that contained the density of gold and light. The children were gathered around the teacher listening to the explanations about plant life in one of the small clearings in the forest. Emmita, however, stood separate from the rest and appeared engrossed in the contemplation of the little bit of sky that could be seen from there. Suddenly, it seemed to her that the air was disappearing as a deathly silence overtook the place and perhaps the whole world. She had had that sensation before, and she knew what it was. It was as if the whole forest was calling her.

"Surely the soul of the world is talking to you," her mother explained when she told her about it. "When that happens to you, listen to it respectfully."

Emmita looked at her teacher and her classmates, and it gave her the impression that their faces had lost their clarity. She looked at her feet, and they appeared to be suspended about ten centimeters above the ground. She felt that something terrible was about to occur, and she shouted to the teacher to get the group out of the forest right away.

"But we've just begun the presentation, Emma. You must learn to be more patient."

Emmita understood that telling him of her strange perception would accomplish nothing. So, she invented the pretext of a terrible pain in her chest and asked to be taken back to town. Only then and reluctantly, the teacher headed back with the children.

"Let's go, hurry up," he ordered.

The small caravan was a kilometer away from where they had been listening to the lesson when an enormous blaze emerged from amid the trees, rose to the heavens, and fell back into the forest. The teacher and several students later swore that the fire was accompanied by music like a military march. Others insisted that it was not a march but a very sad ballad. The students agreed that Emmita had saved their lives.

17
Rosina Was Not Rosina

In Salem, Dante and Beatriz met the person who would become their best friend, Doña Rosina Rivero Ayllón. Rosina had been born with a different name in Venezuela, but when she arrived in Mexico, determined to cross the border, she found a *coyote* who was somewhat expensive but more efficient than most.

He told her that she did not need to crawl through a tunnel or walk through the mountains, much less run from immigration officers. For a reasonable sum of money, he offered her legal papers and the name, Social Security number, and even the memories of a deceased woman who had been born at the same time as she.

Rosina accepted the deal and spent several weeks in Tijuana memorizing the other Rosina's memories. She learned that the other Rosina's husband had left her when she was living in Berkeley and about to give birth to a son. She learned that she had wanted to return to the hospital where she used to work, but it had been difficult for her, and she had spent the last year of her life doing odd jobs sewing and mending and taking care of the elderly and mentally retarded. Her death had come when her son was only a year old.

She also found out that Rosina had belonged to an evangelical church and that she met with her brothers and sisters in worship every Wednesday and Sunday until it was her time to die. Finally, Rosina learned the intonation of the Spanish spoken by the real Doña Rosina.

The friendship between Beatriz and Rosina began at the Chemeketa Community College library, when the two of them discovered that they had the same profession.

"Did you just arrive from Mexico?"

"No," Beatriz responded immediately, as she had been taught to always reply to strangers to hide her illegal status. "No," she explained, "I've lived here for a long time."

But Rosina was familiar with those responses because she too had rehearsed them in her day. It was obvious that Beatriz was undocumented because she was looking at books on the shelves without asking to check them out.

"I didn't want to be any bother, ma'am."

"Bother? None at all. What bothers me is you're being too formal with me."

"The problem is I don't have a library card."

"That's why I'm here. So you can get one," Rosina replied and gave her some forms to fill out.

Beatriz stared at her. Although Rosina inspired her trust, she couldn't reveal to her that she was undocumented.

"Don't worry. I'm going to give you a card without you having to show me anything. That way you can check out as many books as you want."

Soon Rosina became the couple's best friend, and when Emmita was born they asked her to be her godmother.

More than once, Rosina tried to convince the Celestinos to do the same thing she had done and purchase false documents. She still had the name of the man who had sold them to her and knew how to get in touch with him. But Dante and Beatriz had already made a life for themselves in Oregon, and they didn't want to leave Mount Angel, moving from one end of the country to the other and going to live in a city where no one would recognize them. They would have to die as Dante and Beatriz in order to become the owners of new names and new destinies, and they didn't much like that idea. Therefore, they did not accept her advice, but they always considered her an excellent friend. Rosina often took care of Emmita so the couple could take a break or go to the beach on the weekend. For her part, Emmita called her "Madrina Rosina" and said that when she grew up, she wanted to be as kind and beautiful as she was.

Neither the immigration service nor the U.S. Treasury ever questioned the woman's papers. So she settled easily in Salem and made a life for herself like any other U.S. citizen. The truth is that she had a law degree from Caracas and, therefore, with her papers in order and her university training, it was not difficult for her to find a suitable job.

During all the years she had lived in Oregon, she had worked as a librarian at Chemeteka Community College and planned to retire from there. She sometimes felt nostalgia over her lost identity, and it was difficult for her to talk to her friends about her memories.

Nevertheless, sometimes in her dreams memories of Caracas emerged angrily, and she felt that her soul had been left behind entangled like a long howl in the tunnel that connects the capital of Venezuela to the port of La Guaira. Then she would console herself thinking that when she retired she would go to Caracas and seek out friends and relatives to whom she had not written for all those years in order to keep secret her former identity.

Not only did her memories of Caracas besiege her, her false identity seemed to confront her as well. Sometimes the dead Rosina appeared to her in dreams to demand the return of her name and her personal description. At times she would come to her in nightmares, howling in pain, to confide to her how much it hurt when her husband abandoned her. One whole night, the spirit of Rosina chased her all around the house with a cup of blood in her hands, telling her "you haven't suffered as I have, and you dare to carry my name."

Rosina talked about this harassment with Dante and Beatriz, and they knew that she slept with the light on for fear that the darkness would cause the ghost to materialize. Sometimes Emmita went to stay with her, and she got the ghost of Rosina to pass by without knocking on the door of the house.

It was logical, then, that the relationship between Rosina and Emmita was as close as that of mother and daughter, and the little

girl felt happy to have two mothers. Rosina would leave her the lega-
cy of the endless conversations about the geography of South America, the love of books, and the multitude of conversations about
ghosts.

Emmita knew by heart the face, voice, and walk of the man who
had left the real Rosina; she had the impression that if she ever ran
into him, she would say: "You're Leonidas García. You were born in
Guadalajara. The Santamarías, your enemies, swore they would
hang you and that's why you fled to San Diego. There you met Rosina Rivero Ayllón, who was nicknamed La Venezolana. You made her
your wife and at times you treated her like a princess, but when you
received that shipment that made you rich, things changed and you
got yourself not one but several replacements for Rosina. She was
pregnant with your child when you left her."

But Rosina's past materialized as a young man's pleading voice
on the phone. He begged her to give him the chance to see her. Rosina delicately declined. The young man told her that he was passing
through Salem and that it would be enough to be able to greet her to
feel satisfied. Rosina, now a little frightened at his insistence, replied
that she was just leaving the house and would not be back all weekend and to please not call again.

"Don't you think you should call the police?" Dante suggested.
"He might be a criminal, maybe a drug addict."

"And tell them what? That the man is after me, but he's not after
me, but the true owner of my name? . . . Tell them that I exist, but
that I am not Rosina Rivero Ayllón and that that's not my name?
Reveal to them that I'm undocumented? I'm not going to give them
the chance to call immigration to destroy fifteen years of labor,
working decently and saving for my retirement."

That weekend, the young man who had called showed up. Stum-
bling over his words, he tried to speak to Rosina in Spanish, but she
understood that English would help him more to unburden himself
and reveal what he wanted from her.

He told her that he had turned eighteen and was considered an
adult. That he could talk to adults face to face, that all he wanted was

to know the truth, even if it hurt him. He told her all of this all at once, without stopping, as if it were a speech he had been rehearsing all his life.

Rosina did not understand, but the young man inspired her trust. She asked him to come in and rest a moment to catch his breath.

"Is that your motorcycle?"

"Yes, ma'am."

"Have you come from very far away?"

"Yes, to see you."

"Don't you think you might be making a mistake? Are you sure I'm the person you're looking for?"

"No."

The young man was dressed in black from head to foot. He had a black cap on but took it off when he realized that it made the woman uncomfortable.

"A cup of coffee would do you good."

The invitation made the boy suddenly feel happy, and he went over to the table to which Rosina was inviting him.

"Would you like some toast?"

"No, thank you. I came to see you . . ."

Rosina was already anticipating what the young man was going to tell her, but she didn't know what she could say in response, and she was trying to buy time to think. She couldn't tell him that the name she was using wasn't hers. That would be dangerous.

The boy poured his cup of coffee slowly, as if to give himself courage. He took a sip and placed the steaming cup carefully on the table before speaking. "I'm Leonidas García's son. Eighteen years ago you and my father brought me into the world. If you don't want to, don't kiss me or hug me. Say that you don't recognize me and that I don't look like my father. I'm not asking you for anything because I'm not accustomed to asking. I just want to know two things. I want to know if my father is alive and under what name I should look for him, and I want to know why the two of you abandoned me. Why did you give me to the Cabada family? They told me that you did it because you were dying, but one day I found out that you were alive, and that's why I've come to see you."

When Rosina told him that he had her confused with someone else, the young man stared at her, incredulous. Rosina did not want to hurt him.

"You may be talking about a woman who had the same name I do."

"And the same age as you? With the same life story?"

There was silence.

"Why don't you tell me that you don't want to see me? . . . Don't worry, I won't bother you again. I'm going to leave you alone."

More silence.

"Thank you very much," said the boy, as he got up and left the house.

The young man kept his word because he never again knocked on her door or called her, although sometimes he would park his motorcycle in front of her house and stare at the door. Once when Emmita was visiting her godmother, she happened to see him, and she thought he was handsome and very mysterious.

18
When You Die in the United States, You Die Twice

The moon is nothing. It's nothing with a yellowish ring. Nothing more than a ring. It has no light. The light it has is borrowed from the sun. Therefore all we can get from it are mouthfuls of cold air, memories, and omens. Dante was thinking about this as he recalled the green moon in the skies the night of the *quinceañera*. Dante must have sensed that nothing good was going to happen, but he went ahead because he and Beatriz had been preparing for the celebration for fifteen years. He was not prepared, however, for the cutting words of his daughter's goodbye letter or the idea that he would never see her again.

The moon had been green one year earlier as well, the day he was working overtime, and one of his coworkers came running to the farm to give him the news: "I have to take you with me, Dante."

"Take me?"

"Yes."

"Where?"

"To your house."

"I'm not finished yet, and Beatriz already knows I'm going to be late."

"It's about her. No one knows what awaits us in this world."

They were both quiet. Dante got into the car and thought of asking something, but held back. All the way, he sat with his head down.

"Nobody knows . . . nobody knows . . ." his friend kept repeating, but he forgot the rest of the sentence and said no more during the entire trip.

When they got to the house, the neighbor's wife was trying to fan Beatriz, who lay in an armchair. But no one could offer her air in this world anymore. Her wide, astonished eyes had remained fixed on the window, and her soul was escaping.

Dante wanted to ask what had happened, but he could not speak. He stood there with his hat in his hands. Then he threw aside his hat, went over to his spouse, and spoke into her ear, like someone telling a secret.

"Beatriz, Beatriz." He was able to call her, but she was no longer within that name, she was no longer in this world.

Dante looked at his friends as if asking for an explanation of why death exists, but they lowered their eyes. It seemed that no one wanted to meet the eyes of the sad man or meet Saint Death, la Santa Muerte, who was probably still fluttering around the room.

Beatriz had managed to call her neighbor before she stopped breathing.

"She asked me to tell you, Dante, not to ever forget about the fifteenth birthday party."

Emmita's fifteenth birthday was still a year away.

"Don't cry too much for her. She told me that. That you shouldn't cry too much for her. Don't make her look back."

Suddenly, the light of the day turned dark and cloudy. Dante was looking out the window to try to see Beatriz's soul, and she, flying far away, already close to a star, looked back toward him, and they looked at each other with their mouths, they looked at each other with their entire bodies. But it was too late, and fate was being fulfilled.

Dante dropped into a chair and looked at the floor. No one saw him cry. An hour later, when he stood up, he was a different man.

Dante discovered that when a Mexican dies in the United States, he or she dies several times. It is necessary to hold the funeral in this land which is not theirs as the papers are being prepared to take the body back to its homeland.

Dante would forever remember the friends who embraced him and murmured comforting phrases to make him feel better, although he did not feel consoled by any of what they said. The glacial cold that filled his body deepened with every Ave María of the Rosary they were all praying, until he felt that there was nothing inside his body; there was not even space in it for pain because everything within him was a shadow.

There was no time to lose. He telephoned and visited funeral homes and airlines. In the offices of the latter, they very courteously informed him that they did not ship cadavers unless they were accompanied by someone, but Dante could not travel to Mexico.

"It's best if you bury her in the United States because you won't find an airline that'll take her."

But Dante couldn't listen nor did he want to listen to anyone, and he insisted that his wife would travel, by plane and in the sky, the path she had previously traveled through the darkness of a tunnel.

The sky ended up falling on Dante when they demanded thirty thousand dollars from him to transport the body. In the years he and Beatriz had lived together, they had barely managed to save half that much for the *quinceañera*, but even if he had had all the money together, there was another problem.

"You have to give us the deceased's documents. We need papers that prove she is a person born in Mexico and a legal resident of the United States. What did you say her name was?"

"Beatriz. Isn't that enough?"

"I'm sorry, sir, but so far we do not even have proof that she exists or that she existed. Were the two of you married? Do you have proof of your marriage? Do you have her passport or her visa? Her Social Security number? I need to verify that you and your wife exist, or rather, that you exist and that she ceased to exist . . ."

Dante could not keep listening to the interpreter from the airline because, at that moment, he had begun to seriously doubt his own existence.

The problem had a solution. It was provided by their neighbor William Gil, who, with his wife Edila, decided to accompany Beatriz's body to Mexico. They had legal papers and a more or less comfortable economic position, so they were happy to offer to help him.

"Who says that hardships defeat us? We always have a way to overcome them. What would you think if we took her all the way to Michoacán?"

"To Sahuayo?"

"All the way to Sahuayo, by way of Parangaricutimícuaro. They just put in a highway that's really nice."

They got to work. In just one day of calling Dante's friends, William Gil collected $1,700 and got several fellow countrymen from Michoacán to join the funeral procession with their cars. In a matter of hours, fourteen vehicles full of people from Mount Angel and Woodburn began the funeral procession to the California border with Oregon. From there, the enormous RV that the Gils had borrowed would travel alone. It was necessary to avoid arousing the suspicions of immigration officers, who, if they did stop them, wouldn't know what to do, whether to jail the deceased or deport her from the country. There was nothing else they could do because in order to be buried it is also necessary to have papers that prove the previous existence of the decedent. As the hours passed, the collection grew and grew and became enough to get to San Diego and from there to cross the border toward Mesa de Otay and then continue the trip toward the heart of Mexico. There would also be enough money to hold a mass in the Sahuayo church. For his part, the widower would have to remain at the border, because if he entered Mexico he couldn't return to the United States.

Father Victoriano Pérez gave them an altarpiece that used to hold a life-size Virgin of Guadalupe, and since it was not being used, he sent it so that they could place the deceased inside and take her back to her country.

Then, as time was passing, they rushed to get on the road immediately, and they camouflaged the altarpiece with the body inside it beneath a mound of roses and daisies. A man from Sinaloa who was a medical expert had prepared the body to preserve it for the length of the trip. Although he did not reveal what his procedures were, it was suspected that he had caused the dead woman to ingest a kilo of salt, several liters of water of the Perpetual Aid, and a preparation of his own invention. Then he had placed beneath her, inside the altar-piece, a little mattress of mint leaves and peach blossoms, all of which would give them about five days before decomposition began. They calculated that they would reach their destination in a little less than four days.

The friends said goodbye at the California border, and from there the RV drove at top speed. In Los Angeles, it began to lose power and slow down. At one point, they could not go more than 30 miles an hour.

It was Sunday, and it was going to be difficult to find a mechanic shop, but not even that could stop them. They exited the high-speed freeway, and Gil, always optimistic, told the widower not to worry. They went into the big city directly to a neighborhood populated exclusively by people from Michoacán.

On the huge map of Los Angeles, they emerged near Olvera Plaza, near the old mission. No sooner had they arrived there than they began to meet people with the last names Gil, Carrasco, Fonseca, Céspedes, the most common last names in Michoacán. All they had to do was enter a small church to bump face to face into the pastor, a man named Carrasco from Sahuayo, with whom they had common acquaintances. The other church members introduced themselves one after another and offered to help them. The pastor took them to the mechanic shop of a church member who would be glad to take care of them, but not until the next day because he was gone on a trip.

The pastor informed them that they could not leave the coffin in the church because, at other times of the day, it was used by the dear Anglo brothers and sisters. They had to spend the night in the mechanic's yard. In light of the fact that there was no other solution, Dante's friends stayed there with him, holding a wake for the deceased. They made themselves comfortable in the office, which was quiet, sheltered, and well furnished. They began to tell the stories that people usually tell at a wake. The stories soon became jokes and the jokes turned racy, to the point that the pastor, laughing his head off, begged them not to go on.

In the early morning, when almost everyone else was asleep, Dante thought he heard the buzzing of bees. "They must be attracted by the flowers," he said to himself, but at about five in the morning he realized that bees don't buzz at night. Then he remembered that the souls of the dead change into butterflies and bees. He commented on this to the Gils, who were also awake.

"Maybe you're right. They must be her ancestors and all the people who died in Sahuayo during these years. They've probably come to greet her and to keep us company in our mourning."

Later that morning, the RV was repaired, and they started off on their way again, much faster than before. But no matter how much they hurried, Dante had the sensation that they were flying along within a cloud of bees, and he told himself that must be the reason that in times of misfortune people feel their ears buzzing.

When they were about to reach San Diego, a patrol car began to follow them and signaled to them to stop. As Mr. Gil was pulling over to the side of the highway and beginning to look for his documents, Dante thought that all was lost just when they were beginning to make out the first blue hills of Mexico. Maybe they would make them open the side doors, and there inside they would find the casket. Where would they take her? In what dark morgue would she be abandoned forever?

When the officer came over to the window, he asked the driver for his documents and began to look curiously around in the cab. Then he seemed to remember something.

"Romero, Romero, come here," he shouted in English.

Another officer, with Indian-like features, got out of the police car. He said something to him, whispering in secret, and Romero came over to them to inform them in Spanish that, according to city regulations, he had to be the one to question them in their own language.

"All the papers are in order, but why were you going so fast? Was someone chasing you?"

"It's just because I was afraid that the darkness was going to overtake us," Gil began to say and went on in a very long explanation that Dante couldn't hear because he was surrounded by the echos of his own memories. All he heard was the word darkness, and it seemed to him that the darkness was not outside but rather had been entering all the corners of his body and his life.

As the two men conversed, the gringo policeman began to inspect the vehicle's contents through the window. It seemed strange to him to see so many flowers. Farther on, he located a pair of angels and next to them the stubs of the candles burned the night before. Again he whispered to Romero.

"Where are you coming from? Please open the side door so we can inspect what's inside."

Mr. Gil had no choice but to obey. Without moving from his place, he pressed a button that automatically opened the door. As the blond policeman was getting in to investigate, Romero chatted with the driver about vehicles and engines, a conversation Dante could not participate in because he was feeling very bad. A rearview mirror allowed Mr. Gil to follow the movements of the policeman, and soon he realized that, after pushing aside the roses and daisies, he had found the door of the altarpiece and was starting to open it.

"How many cylinders did you say this engine is? What kind of mileage does it get? . . . I won't ask you how fast it can go because I've already seen that. If you had gone a little faster, you'd have left us behind, and my partner was getting ready to call the helicopter."

"Romero. Romero. Come here, immediately!"

The blond policeman had managed to open the door of the altarpiece and was frozen in amazement. All he could do was call Romero again and talk to him privately. Then he picked up his cell phone and began to call someone.

For Dante, this meant the destruction of another dream, and he didn't know what to do. All he could do was stomp his foot against the floor of the vehicle.

"I don't want you to think this is a bribe, but my partner just started going out with a girl, and, well, um, he asked me to ask you, as if it were my idea, if you could give him some of the roses, because he wants to take them to the girl he's dating. He says that for now we aren't going to give you a ticket, but that you shouldn't drive so fast and to go ahead and take your dear Virgin of Guadalupe wherever you want."

The officers took the flowers, and the RV finally reached the border, and there, right on the border, before reaching Tijuana, on the last hill that belongs to the United States, Dante was left waving goodbye to his friends and to the woman who had accompanied him in his life. He looked toward the south and thought that there it was always day. It occurred to him that he had always lived in the night.

Then he began to retrace his steps. From the point on the border that runs from Mesa de Otay to San Diego, he had to walk for at least an hour, and, with his wretched appearance, red eyes, dry lips, hands like those of a dead man, he feared that he might appear suspicious to any police officer. Dante decided to stop to eat at the AmPm restaurant.

He wasn't hungry, but it was best to order something and kill time. Something strange began to happen then. He had to choose one of the selections from a blackboard on the counter, but he couldn't read what it said there. The letters were moving or disappearing and ended up saying nothing to him. In the years they were together, Beatriz had managed, on evenings and weekends, to teach him to read, but now he seemed to have forgotten everything.

He thought he was having trouble with his eyes or that perhaps a tear had remained hidden in them, but it wasn't that. It was as if Beatriz's death had taken care of erasing everything he had learned from her. He tried again to read the blackboard. The letters all looked alike now, like sorrows, or said nothing to him, like clouds.

"Can I help you, my friend?"

"No, thank you."

"It's okay. Let me help you. In this place in the world, we all need each other. It's that way everywhere, but nowhere is it more present than here."

The man next to him was dressed all in black. He had furrows in his face, which was red as a tomato, and he spoke with great authority. His old age gave him the wisdom to speak and take over as he did.

"By the way, do you like chicken enchiladas?"

There was no response.

"How about some roasted pork tacos?"

Dante still said nothing.

"The gentleman would like some *huevos rancheros*. The same for me," he ordered.

"And after the meal? A soda or coffee?"

"I said I don't need help," Dante insisted.

"Two coffees."

The man chose a table, and there they ate in silence and without looking at each other, like blind men.

"If I had known how they prepare *huevos rancheros* here, we'd have gone to the restaurant across the street," the stranger said as he straightened his necktie, which he had loosened before eating.

Then the two of them explored their respective plates to see if they could find anything edible besides the restaurant's dreadful eggs. At precisely that moment, they looked at each other and smiled.

Finally, the waitress brought coffee for both of them. Perhaps, then, Dante began to speak. He was talking not to the old man, but to himself, and he said many things, so many that the man went back to looking at his plate purely out of politeness.

"What sense does the world make if death exists? My God, and now what am I going to do without her?"

The old man did not want to interrupt him.

"Tell me, did it get dark or is it sorrow?"

"No, it hasn't gotten dark."

"I'm telling you everything looks dark to me."

"No, it's not darkness. It must be sorrow."

Just at that moment, Dante decided to ask him who he was.

"That's not the most important thing. Our names are not the most important thing, but rather why we are here and why we suddenly appear in a person's life."

"Are you an angel?"

The old man laughed heartily and took a deck of cards from his jacket pocket.

"I don't think they allow this up there," he said.

"Then you're the devil. Are you the devil?"

The man laughed again. He started laughing so hard he was crying. He would have thrown himself onto the floor laughing, but he didn't want to wrinkle his black suit.

"I don't think I said anything so funny."

"One of the demons, perhaps. The one that accompanies travelers and unhappy people."

Then the man in black put his fingers on his forehead in the shape of horns.

"Do I really look like a devil?" He laughed again. Then he composed himself and straightened his tie again. Finally, he informed him that he was from Veracruz and reminded him that he was waiting for him to cut the deck.

"I don't know how to play. And even if I did, I wouldn't play cards. I don't feel like it."

"And who said we were going to play cards?"

The stranger began to straighten the cards and shuffle them in different ways, and all Dante could do was watch. He had to kill time in a place like that because he had been told that the buses didn't leave until much later.

"Maybe I'm seeing in these cards many stories that you haven't told me."

"Oh . . . really?"

"The truth is that I'm a retired gambler. Now I devote myself to reading the cards for people who ask me to."

"And what do you see?"

"The country. Pastures. Some animals. Hmmm . . . this is the sword of justice. It's been above you for many years. Are you a fugitive or a wetback?"

"You don't have to look at cards to know that."

"Maybe so. Hmmm . . . here is death dancing a *danzón.*"

Then he shuffled again and asked Dante to cut the deck.

"What do you want to ask?"

"Nothing."

"What do you mean nothing?"

"Nothing. With Beatriz dead, I have nothing left."

"Are you sure?"

Dante remembered that their daughter had remained behind in Doña Rosina's care. He decided not to ask about her destiny. It seemed wrong to do so.

Then the old man handed him the deck of cards and asked him to pick one.

"And what have you seen?" asked Dante.

"Nothing."

"Nothing?"

"Nothing, just what you said, that you have nothing left. Two children."

"One, a girl."

"It says two here. Maybe she'll be getting married soon."

"She's too young."

"All the more reason . . . Hey, cut again. Go ahead."

Dante obeyed.

"Now, start picking cards one at a time. What do you see?"

He got the king. He got the queen. He got death. He got a sword. He got justice with her eyes blindfolded. He got a guitar. He got a road. He got a crown. He got a coffin. He got the sun. He got the moon. He got a wolf, and the wolf ate up the sun, the moon, the coffin, the crown, the guitar, justice, the sword, death, the queen, and the king. All that was left was the road.

The man told him not to worry about the darkness. He reminded him that all the lights in the world are hidden in the hearts of men. He told him that sometimes all you have to do is find the switch and flip it for the lights to go back on.

"The earth is a flat, cloudy globe spinning through the blackness, and the blackness is its true nature. We are the ones who give it light," he asserted, sure of what he was saying as he walked with him to the Greyhound station, where Dante bought a ticket for Salem, Oregon, and the old man gave him a hug and said goodbye.

Settled in a seat next to the window, Dante tried to read what the ticket said, but the letters did not speak to him and said nothing to him. He looked out the window and saw the boundless solitude that awaited him in the United States.

19
Dolores Huerta's Glowing Eyes

Drip, drip, drip . . .The drops falling upon the earth knock at the door of the newly deceased. Maybe Beatriz, tired of so much dying and of having traveled the entire length of the United States and half of Mexico, would like to sleep, but, *drip, drip, drip,* they pound and dance on the ground and force her to awaken. All her friends have already left, and the sun is flying away. The wind is trying to carry away the garlands placed on the graves throughout the cemetery. Several tablecloths are threatening to fly off and spill the meals left for those returning from the other side. It just so happens that she was buried in her hometown cemetery the evening before the Day of the Dead, and the people are carrying guitars and bottles of tequila back and forth.

> *I'm going to sing you a ballad,*
> *saint of wetbacks*
> *true child of prisoners,*
> *blessed one of smugglers,*
> *True child. True child.*
> *My dear Saint Death.*
> *Love me silently*
> *and don't snatch me away* . . .

Some prayers are still heard, some laughter, and the voice of that *charro* singing a ballad about his loves with Saint Death. Meanwhile, the dead Beatriz awakens, opens and closes her eyes in order

191

to remember the last days, months, and years of her life. Then she walks, glides, and even flies through the whole cemetery until she tires and goes to sit down on the stone covering some stranger.

Her face is suddenly moist because it has begun to rain more intensely. The rain gives way to the storm. *Little hill of Tijuana, you who have seen me go by, please greet Saint Death when she stops there from time to time.* The mariachis have stopped singing, and they're hurrying away because they're afraid the rain will soak their guitars. The bottles of tequila sit obediently in front of the graves, and the plates of tripe, tamales, and *mole* are still steaming under the awnings placed over them. Beatriz then wonders how far the dead can see and whether it is possible for her to see her husband on the other side of the border. She angrily remembers that her friends had to go find a gravedigger in the neighboring town because the one from Sahuayo had left for the United States.

Beatriz sees herself arriving in Oregon with her husband, who could hardly walk due to his work in the California cotton harvest and remembers that it hurt him even to talk. She asked him to allow her to work in the fields even if just for a short time. Of course he opposed this, insisting that her body was not made for those tasks, and they had the first argument of their married life.

"Times have changed, love," she told him. "Life isn't the way you left it when you came here, nowhere, not here or in Mexico. What happens is that you never finished learning, and you didn't see that women are now equal to men and that we can work. If you don't let me, I'll feel you aren't capable of loving me as much as you said."

Dante would then remind her that he had spent ten years breaking his back so she could cross the tunnel and come to live with him without having to work.

"Let me work a few months in the cherry harvest, and I promise I'll stop working really soon, when I'm about to give you a child."

As he looked at the ceiling, he dreamed of the child that would come, the skills he would teach him, and the name they would give him.

Beatriz found work in the strawberry harvest that was demanding hundreds of workers, as many as it could find.

"You want to pick strawberries?" they asked her in English.

She accepted immediately and found herself in the midst of a red sea of strawberries that later turned into cherries and finally into grapes, raspberries, and blackberries, where she labored even when her husband had recovered and despite his weak protests, she always won out and convinced him with her woman's reasoning.

On many posters placed in the fields, she read: GREEN REVOLUTION and did not understand the meaning of those words that nevertheless announced a fearsome season. One day, worried by the shadows, and the incessant roar of the planes, she asked the foreman if they were being watched from the air to check their efficiency.

"What we're doing is rationalizing production," answered the man, who was not the owner of the land, but might have thought he was, and who also talked to himself and went on and on reciting a long speech about the productivity of the land and the people. He was of Mexican ancestry, but spoke Spanish with difficulty and repeated a speech that was common at that time. According to him, certain chemical products were going to do wonders in the field: the squash would be two or three times their normal size, the land would give six crops per year, plagues would disappear from the United States, and most importantly, the workers would harvest double or triple what they did at present.

Fearsome rumors started circulatin that in Oregon and California, dozens of agricultural workers had fallen victim to mysterious illnesses. A woman born in New Mexico named Dolores Huerta was constantly organizing unions, assemblies, and boycotts to improve living conditions for immigrant farmworkers and to demand that they be granted the same rights as all workers in the United States.

Beatriz only saw her once, but would never forget those shining, black eyes or that flowing black hair. Nor could she forget her inspiring words that traveled through the fields, denouncing pesticides for endangering the health of the farmworkers and consumers and poisoning the environment. When Dante was starting to recover, Beatriz convinced him to go with her to Salem, where the famous leader was going to speak.

They listened to Dolores Huerta speak, but Beatriz didn't approach her out of shyness. Some time later, in Saint Mary's Church parish hall, Beatriz looked around for her and didn't see her. She said to herself that perhaps the greatest charm of that admirable woman was that she looked so much like any one of us that it was impossible to pick her out.

"And you, my dear? It's obvious that you haven't been here long, and I would even guess that you're from Michoacán. Do you pick grapes? You have to take good care of yourself and never let that light in your eyes go out."

Beatriz and Dante were so fascinated that at first they didn't know where Dolores Huerta's voice was coming from until they saw her standing next to Beatriz. Later they bid her farewell waving a white handkerchief. The next week, in his Sunday homily, Father Victoriano Pérez asked them to pray for César Chávez, the other farmworkers' rights leader. His health was in danger because he had done a prolonged fast, demanding that Mexican laborers be paid the same salary as U.S. workers.

A very slim woman and a sickly man who was fasting were teaching farmworkers a lesson of great strength. Because of them, people realized that they should stand up and not give in. In order to be heard, they went on strike. Rumors circulated that Chávez had died, and farmworkers and their supporters were advised to give up once and for all. Finally, mediation specialists arrived. A pretentious Latino who smoked a pipe and made them call him "Doctor" tried to make them see that they were going to gain nothing through those movements. Then he accused them of being encouraged by anti-American communists, but the farmworkers did not back down. As they did not have trucks to block traffic, they went out arm in arm and closed some roads with human resistance, and they succeeded.

The memory comes and goes. Meanwhile, completely soaked by the rain, Beatriz walks through the cemetery and discovers that everyone has left. Even the storm is about to end and has left intact the bread of the dead and tortillas placed next to her grave. A newly opened bottle of tequila invites her to experience delirium, forgetting, and the joys of the agave.

"Ah! If only Dante were here, we would drink together, but God sentenced us from before we were born to walk blindly, drinking sadness and dirty water as we made our way north. All we'll have in the end will be a few yards of earth and the consolation that there is eternal life. The silent light will return to our eyes when we return to the light of the world on the glorious day of resurrection. But oh, dear God, what shall we do until then to appease these memories!"

Meanwhile, she raises the bottle to her lips. Beatriz felt happy to be Mexican and to have been taken to her hometown to be buried. Once, in Oregon, she witnessed an American burial, and it saddened her greatly to find out that after crying for a few hours, the mourners left the dead alone forever, immediately auctioned off all the furniture from their houses, and didn't leave them even so much as a *quesadilla* next to their graves, much less a marvelous bottle of tequila like the one she was enjoying now.

The tequila made the bad memories disappear and brought her those in which a young Dante, sitting next to her one autumn night, was pointing at a shooting star. "Quick. Let's get on it, and whatever happens, we'll always be together." They had spent most of their lives apart, and now a rumbling eternity was coming, but they would live forever in the shelter and protection of the shooting star.

She thought about teaching Dante to read. She would borrow several novels at the local library, and as soon as he would get home, she would read to him aloud until she managed to delight him with the river of stories that flowed from the books.

In any case, she had not hurried much because she had plenty of time ahead of her; at least, that's what she thought. Nor did she use any certain method to teach him, instead, she improvised as she went along. The two of them lived happily, very happily, and she felt that it was like leading her husband by the arm through the darkness. One day she realized that he could come and go alone from the darkness of the letters and the river of the stories whenever he pleased.

"I can't thank you enough," he had said. "You have no idea how much I like reading stories. Now I can hear the people in the book. Sometimes, I even feel like a character in the book."

"And what do you know about our story?"

"That it ends happily."

"That it ends?"

"I don't think I said it ends."

Beatriz remained silent.

"Dante, I want you to promise me something. I don't know why I'm asking you this, but after I die, I want you to read and read a lot. Don't ever forget to do it."

Dante did not promise her that. He was very interested in telling her that their story would never end.

"The story never ends, Beatriz, because the telling of it has no end."

Beatriz's soul remembered. Beyond death, she realized that Dante was right, their story had no end. She took another sip of tequila.

"You were right, Dante. This will never end."

Then an ill-fated memory came to her. It was the time when Palermo reappeared. Those were times of happiness, and hope filled the house because once more Dante had been told that he was about to obtain his resident visa. Emmita had turned nine and was a very diligent student when Beatriz received that telephone call. She put the phone to her ear, but all she heard was a sound like the one that misfortune sometimes makes.

"Hello."

She was about to hang up because no one was talking, but her curiosity got the better of her.

"Hello. Who's calling?"

At the other end there were murmurs and electrical noises. Beatriz thought it was a call from Mexico and the connection was bad. It was right before Christmas, and she thought that some friend or relative was trying to call them.

She identified herself.

"This is Beatriz. This is Mrs. Celestino. With whom do you wish to speak?"

"So now your name is Mrs. Celestino. No, sweetheart, you are legally my wife, and if I don't agree, no one will divorce us. Remember that I'm your husband and that there is nowhere in the world that I can't find you."

He hung up.

Dante got home that night and found her looking drawn.

"Is something wrong?"

Beatriz preferred to keep the calls to herself and not worry him, although the calls went on for several months.

"I wanted to tell you that I'll be going to see you, and I want you to come with me. If you refuse, something bad will happen to that poor devil that lives with you. And you know it."

She didn't know why she didn't hang up on him. Fear froze her and forced her to listen.

The calls were calculated and always occurred at the moment Dante left for work.

"The truth is that one of these days I'd like to have a little chat with your husband. Maybe I'll tell him a few things. Maybe he'll get angry with you. After I talk to him, he'll never be the same."

Beatriz wanted to disconnect the phone, but was afraid that if she did, Palermo would show up. A year after the first call, he said he was ready to come for her. "Prepare yourself, I'll be getting out of here in a couple of weeks. I'll be there on Thursday. Speak. Say something. Say that you love me and that you've been waiting for me. Tell me that I'm the fire."

Beatriz, frightened, called Rosina.

"You should have told your husband."

"I didn't want to worry him. I didn't want to push him into doing something crazy. I always thought Don Gregorio would get tired of calling me."

"Don't stay home alone. Take Emmita out of school and stay with me for a few weeks."

"And Dante? You don't know what Don Gregorio could do to him. He's a tyrant."

"And if that's the case, why hasn't he shown up before?"

A phrase had slipped out of Gregorio Bernardino Palermo: "I'll be getting out of here in a couple of weeks."

As a librarian, Rosina had access to a lot of information. She called different prisons in the neighboring states, but did not find out what she wanted to know. She wrote letters to the national prison administration and resolved to await their response.

But the days of misfortune were not going to return so soon. On Thursday nothing happened. Nor on Friday or on the weekend. The following Tuesday, the phone rang at Beatriz's house. It was Rosina calling.

"He's in Florida. In the federal penitentiary, and he should have been released last week."

That did not reassure Beatriz.

"I just received a letter from the Florida prison administration. In fact, he was going to get out, but something very strange happened."

One of his former partners was waiting for him at the prison gate in a fabulous, brand-new Mercedes Benz. "It's the least they could do," Gregorio may have thought when one of the bodyguards opened the back door for him. He got in smiling, but was a little surprised that his friend didn't sit down next to him, but instead sat next to the driver. For his part, he had to make do between the bodyguards.

"I see you haven't lost your good taste . . ."

Perhaps his partner didn't hear him because he did not respond.

"It might be a good idea for you to take me to a hotel near the airport."

There was no reply.

"I want to be there because tomorrow very early I'm leaving for Portland, Oregon."

The man in the front seat had been his representative in Florida. He had been under his orders all the time and had always been obedient to the point of servility. His silence confused Palermo.

"Are your deaf?"

Just then the man turned to look toward the back seat but looked not at Gregorio but at one of the bodyguards.

"Fire."

"I said, are you deaf?"

The thug took awhile to get a pistol out of his bag and put the silencer on it. But Gregorio didn't see him:

"I told you to take me to a hotel near the airport."

"Fuck you, quit giving orders. And you, kill that bastard once and for all," said his former assistant.

The executioner was taking his time. He took a pistol out of an impeccable case and wiped it with a rag as if to shine it. Very slowly, he studied his victim's skull and chose the most appropriate spot. Finally, he placed the barrel against Gregorio Bernardino Palermo's right temple.

"Fuck him once and for all."

The man seemed to make a gesture with his finger and then a small spark was seen. The noise of the bullet, like that of a key opening a door, mixed with the voices on the Spanish radio station the driver was listening to.

With the silencer, the pistol was long. It jerked several times when it fired, and a whole handful of Palermo's brains emerged from the hole opened in his head and dirtied the impeccable shirt of the man who was firing the gun. Beatriz's former owner sat with his head up, as if he had decided to take a nap with just one eye open.

"Quick, let's get out of here. I have to burn my shirt. We have to get rid of this creep before he starts to stink."

They drove to a safe place where they poured gasoline over Palermo, and the assistant lit him on fire with his cigarette. Palermo's body shook until the fire left it transformed into a burned tree trunk with its roots in the air.

In the newspaper photos kept in the files from that time, there is mention of a possible argument between drug traffickers. The reporter describes the stain left on the earth as "one of those pits that connect this world to hell" and added "there will be no burial because the man disappeared in the fire."

❻ ❻ ❻

Sitting on her grave, Beatriz feels Dante's hands traveling over her body, her lips meeting his, his words swearing to her by God and all the saints that he will never leave her, that life and death have no reason to be for them. The next time that she raises the bottle it seems to her that someone clicks theirs against it.

20

To Be Born in Sahuayo Is to Be Born Walking

Dante and Virgilio had been on I-210, CA-30, I-15 north, and after 320 kilometers on I-15, they were approaching Las Vegas. But Dante's memories were as fast as the marvelous van he had built in his backyard and which Father Victoriano had blessed before they left.

"Speaking of guitars, everybody knows that the best ones are made in Sahuayo, and that's also where they play the accordion in the purest Michoacán style," he said, but the donkey's only comment was to sniff the window.

Dante wanted to keep talking about accordions and about his talent for pulling melodies and memories from them, but he didn't dare. He feared that the animal would turn its enormous head scornfully toward the roads they were leaving behind. Therefore, he kept talking about his land.

"In Sahuayo, the lands of Michoacán, as if to say the world, end. That's why you can hear the music of Heaven, which is not as audible in other places."

This did not attract the attention of his co-pilot either, although he knew that even if he was listening, he would keep looking at the wind.

"I think we're almost there," he said to get Virgilio's attention and to persist in making conversation.

"I'm referring to the fact that being born in Sahuayo is like being born walking, toward the north, of course. At night, even if there's no one there, the church bell never stops ringing, as if it were still calling those who've gone away. And we are the only ones who hear it wherever we may be."

Dante spoke of his hometown as if everyone were familiar with Sahuayo. More than once, another Mexican asked him: "Sahuayo, where's that? Where did you say?" Others, when they heard him talking, thought about their own towns, which were very similar to the community he was describing, and then each town was transformed into a ghost or grief.

"Sometimes in my dreams I see myself in Sahuayo, Virgilio. I see myself walking toward the little farm where my father told me that I was going to learn to be a man. In those dreams I hear the chicks, but the hens don't appear because we've already eaten all of them, and I see some fierce, green winds tearing off the roofs and the trees, the windows and the doors, the church and the school. They carry them off toward yesterday, toward a time of no return."

Dante stopped the car at one of those highway rest stops to drink a coffee and so Virgilio could relieve himself. When he was about to get back on his way, a man asked him for a ride.

"Give me a ride," he said in English, without adding *please*. But when he noticed Dante's startled expression, he thought it was because he didn't understand English.

"I told you I want you to give me a ride. Or rather, give us a ride," he said in Spanish.

He wasn't talking, he was ordering.

"What was that?"

"Open the door now, and let us get in."

The man was old, nearsighted, and perhaps arthritic. He moved slowly, carrying only a bag like the ones that mechanics and small-town doctors use. He assumed that his age gave him the right to talk the way he was talking. Dante could do nothing but open the door and conclude that he was predestined to converse with every strange guy on the road. A thin, young man, nicely dressed, with a face like a fox, got in next to him.

"Go back near the dog," the old man ordered his companion. The young man put Dante's accordion on the floor and sat in the seat next to Virgilio.

"Where are you from, sir?"

"I'm the one who asks the questions. Are you a criminal? A fugitive?" He stopped to look at Dante who, overcome by incredulity, could not respond, could not even utter a word.

"I'm from El Paso, Texas, if you want to know, although I was raised in Los Angeles. The truth is that my parents probably made me in Mexico and my mother had me in El Paso when they crossed the border. It's really something being the child of illegals. I've spent almost all my life in Los Angeles."

"What are you doing so far from home?"

The man did not respond. Dante persisted. The old man kept his arms crossed over his chest like people who haven't embraced anyone for a long time do. The young man who was with him, who seemed to be his guide, did nothing but obey him.

"I don't have a home."

"I thought I heard you say that you were born in El Paso and raised in Los Angeles. Neither one of those places is your home?"

"They were. That's what you say when one has nowhere to go."

"And if you have nowhere to go, why are you asking me for a ride? Do you know where I'm going?"

"It's obvious that you're going to Las Vegas, although you don't have the appearance of the people who go to casinos."

"I've never gone to one."

"But now you're going, isn't that right?"

Dante did not respond.

"In any case, take me to Las Vegas. Take us there."

Again the old man was ordering instead of asking.

"And the dog you have in the back? Pretty big for a dog, isn't he? Those huge dogs are the stupidest ones. This one looks like it. Yes, sir, it's a stupid dog. . . ."

Dante wanted to defend Virgilio, and perhaps he thought it, or maybe he said: "You, Virgilio, you know very well you aren't a dog."

"Who are you talking to?"

There was no response.

"Who are you talking to, I said! Don't tell me you're talking to the dog . . . although the truth is that it wouldn't be strange if you were talking to your dog. It's obvious that he's all you have in this world."

Astonished that the old man knew so much, Dante asked him how he figured it out.

"Because I'm going to die."

"Who told you you're going to die?"

"I don't remember anymore, but no one has told me anything to the contrary either."

"Who did you say told you?" Dante asked again, a little hard of hearing because his vehicle's engine sounded like an explosion.

"The doctor told me that my heart is as strong as a horse's, but horses have to die too. One day their knees give out, and then they remember their whole life." He paused and asked: "Do you know who I am?"

"No," Dante responded. "Looking back, I realize that's where we should have begun. The polite thing is for you to introduce yourself."

"I already told you where I was born and where I was raised. I assume that all I have to do is tell you that I *am* heading to the casino. . . .

"And you? May I ask who you are? Are you sure you're not a crook? . . . Have you ever killed anyone? It's not uncommon to encounter criminals on this highway, and the most suspicious ones are those traveling in vehicles with a foul-smelling, ugly dog in the back."

The old man turned to look toward the back of the vehicle.

"What a weird dog! I've never seen one that big." He lowered his thick glasses, but not even then did he see Virgilio clearly.

"Or is it a mule? Juan Pablo, do not play with that dirty dog."

Juan Pablo was stroking the donkey's ears, and he chose not to provide any explanation.

Dante changed the subject: "And you, sir, have you ever killed someone?"

"Have I killed someone? I've killed many times," the old man confessed, laughing. "Killed, really killed. I don't think I ever have. I haven't. But they sent me to the Korean war, you know?"

There was silence again, and the van drove by a large corral in which there were enormous cattle, which nonetheless looked malnourished and almost transparent because the sadness that invades the world at certain times in the afternoon was seeping into them.

"Now I see that you're my kind of guy. Although I was born in this country and I've never had the kinds of problems you have, I understand you, man. You drive with your hands gripping the wheel as if you were going in search of an enemy."

Dante thought about the boy who had taken away his daughter but didn't consider him an enemy.

"I can help you, you know?"

The road brightened for an instant and then darkened and brightened again due to the wandering clouds that flew above them.

"I said I can help you," the old man proclaimed, and he lifted the bag from the floor and slowly opened it. "You know?"

Dante couldn't know anything because he was driving and keeping his eyes on the road. It did not seem very courteous to him to examine what he assumed was the briefcase of the man he had allowed into his car.

The old man closed his briefcase.

"Where'd you say you were from?"

Dante smiled, looked at the man riding next to him, and cast a friendly glance his way. He liked what he had asked him because he enjoyed talking about Sahuayo. "Now I'm liking the old man," he may have thought, but his enthusiasm did not last long because the stranger was one of those people who ask a question to answer it themselves.

"I myself don't know where I'm from. Sometimes I'm from here. Sometimes from there," began the old man, who had not taken his hat off.

"But you said you were born in El Paso."

He was wearing a vibrant, light cowboy hat of the kind that some tilt toward the side of the right eye to appear distinguished.

"My parents were Mexican, but my mother had me on American soil and I speak English as my first language, but I usually dream in Spanish. When I was young I always spoke, thought, and ate in Gringo. Now I live more on memories and dreams, and everything comes to me in Spanish."

He pushed up his hat, revealing his whole forehead. He was probably getting hot.

"The truth is that I don't know what I am anymore. Sometimes I take out my memories and stir them around to put them in order, but I don't think that's possible."

"And where do you live?"

"I don't know."

Dante began to think that the man might be pulling his leg, or maybe he was a saint of the kind you meet on the highways that don't know where they are.

"What day is today?"

"Saturday."

"I mean what day of the month?"

"I don't know."

"So how do you know it's Saturday?"

"Because there are seven days in a week. . . ."

The old man tilted his hat down again, but this time over his left eye like people do to inspire fear.

"Are you trying to find out if I'm a soft old man with these questions?"

There was no response.

"Since you want to know my story, my parents were carried away by their dreams. They returned to Mexico so we could have our very own farm. It belonged to us because we were poor and descendants of Pancho Villa. My last name is Villa, you know? . . . And there they died more from sorrow than from hunger because the supposedly wonderful land we were given had no water rights. At that time, I came back and what has always helped me is having been born here and being a U.S. citizen.

"And that's why they sent me to the war too, and when I got back, I went to Los Angeles. I got married, had three children, got fed up with my old lady, and we separated. She died about fifteen years ago." He was quiet for awhile and then went on. "You want to know more? One of my children I have no contact with each other. The other one died of something. His widow found me two years ago and begged me to take charge of my grandson, Juan Pablo." He pointed at the young man. "He's great at computers, but he doesn't have money to go to college, and I'm planning to get it for him."

It seemed rude to Dante to ask him how he was going to do it. Instead he asked if the young man could speak.

"Can he talk? Yes, but he doesn't speak Spanish. Or at least not very well."

The young man didn't bat an eye. He didn't seem to know they were talking about him.

"My other son lives in Florida and from time to time manages to locate me wherever I'm living and sends me a letter. The last time he did was five years ago. He's an electrical engineer and I'm a Mormon. Or rather, I was. I converted when I was in jail, but when I got out I forgot about the whole thing."

Dante was astonished at receiving such a flood of information all at once. "Are you a fugitive?" he asked. "Are you fleeing from justice?"

"No. I was put in jail over a business deal. For some smuggling I helped do. They didn't pay me much, you know? But I got a couple years because I couldn't afford to pay a lawyer. The lawyer appointed for me by the government didn't take any interest in my case. Of course the owners of the merchandise never went to jail. After that, I've had jobs here and there."

"Are you going to look for work in Las Vegas?" Dante was wondering what kind of work an old man like the one next to him could do.

"Well, something like that," the old man repeated several times, and he stared into the distance.

Dante felt his sadness and began to share his own memories. He knew that when memories aren't shared, they wear out. He talked about Beatriz. He talked about his daughter. He talked about the party. During the hour of his monologue, the hat covered the old man's face. The man had slept through it all.

"Don't take it wrong, but I tried to put your memories into my dreams. And I think I succeded. I listened to your story, and I'm not going to keep on telling you mine because from here on I no longer have one. At this time in my life I've been left alone, with no family, no money, no retirement. And with a grandson I want to send to college. This is the only way I have to live."

As he spoke, he slowly opened his briefcase, revealing an old-fashioned, somewhat rusty revolver upon a lining of red velvet.

"Are you a collector?"

The old man didn't answer.

"But, you can earn a living with that? Being a collector?"

"I never said I was."

The old man seemed startled and added: "Man, like living, living, no. You know how times are."

"Excuse me, why you have that pistol?"

"I'm going to tell you, although the truth is that I don't like it that you talk to me without hardly moving your mouth. I'm taking it to Las Vegas, and I plan to rob a casino."

The van proceeded several miles in silence as if, like the people, the engine had also decided to be quiet.

"I'm not a specialist in this business, you know? But in jail I heard the guys talk about certain tricks."

He was serious, and Dante wanted to warn him that that kind of work wasn't for people his age.

"I already know what you're going to tell me. Yes, I'm kind of old, and it's possible that they might arrest me, but I have no alternative. If the robbery is successful, I'll have enough money to live out my remaining years. If I don't get it, they'll take me to jail, and

I won't have to worry about finding a place to live. Besides, I know people there, you know? And sometimes, it's a really fun place."

Finally they went over a bridge and entered Las Vegas, and the first thing that caught the their attention was an enormous pyramid.

"It's an Egyptian pyramid, friend. Later we'll go next door to the Eiffel Tower and you'll realize you don't have to travel far to see the world."

Dante thought about Emmita's letter. She said that she was leaving with Johnny Cabada and that the first thing they would do would be to settle down in Las Vegas. She had always dreamed of becoming a famous singer like Selena, and she knew that Las Vegas was one of those places where great talents are born.

"Just a minute. Stop. Pull over, please," the old man said.

Astonishment made Dante stop the vehicle immediately. In their entire conversation, it was the first time he had heard him say "please."

"Let's go!" the old man ordered Juan Pablo. "Thank you, thank you very much!" he said to Dante. "It's not a good idea for us to be seen together."

A few blocks later, Dante found himself inside the immense hotel-casino where it was easy to find a parking place immediately. He got Virgilio out of the van and tied him to a post next to the yard so he could graze.

Then he went into the most spectacular building he had ever seen in his life. At first he didn't know how he was going to find his way to the manager's office in that palace full of rooms and noises and screams and disguises and people and gamblers who were elegant and nervous and black and white and yellow and pink and beautiful women and roulette wheels and music and laughter and the sounds of coins falling endlessly. Miraculously, he managed to find the place he was looking for, and, even more luckily for him, he was waited on by a girl who spoke Spanish.

"Morning."

"Morning."

"Morning?"

"Morning," Dante repeated.

"Are you looking for someone?"

That was what he had been doing for the last two years. Finally he had arrived at the place where he was going to find the necessary information. But he hadn't practiced this. He didn't know what he should ask the girl at the desk.

"It might be good if you sat down. You look tired."

Dante sat down while the girl tried to guess the reason for his visit.

"I can ask them to bring you a drink."

"Thanks," he said.

"Thanks for what?"

"Thanks."

"Yes, thanks or no, thanks?"

Just at that moment, Dante realized that he couldn't say anything. The girl facing him was looking at him as if he were the most important man in the world, but Dante didn't know how to start.

He looked at her from the chair, he observed her. He steeled himself and began to speak. First he told her that he wanted to talk to her about a fifteen-year-old girl, and she didn't know what to say.

She was Argentinean and very pretty. She had studied psychology, and her mission at the casino was to talk to customers who were suffering from stress and calm them down. Therefore, she had all the time in the world to listen to Dante.

She let him talk. Dante, who had been holding back his words for so long, let them out in an uncontrollable flood. He talked about everything: Beatriz, Sahuayo, his entry into the United States, Emmita's birth, her disappearance, the twenty months that had passed since then, the friendship of Virgilio, the vehicles he had traveled in, the stubbornness of his hope.

The young woman, meanwhile, seemed to be writing down some notes on a piece of paper.

"Where do you live?" she asked.

But the Dante did not hear her.

"Where do you live?" she repeated.

Dante misunderstood. He thought that the she was asking him where Beatriz and Emmita lived. He stood up. He put his hand to his heart and said that they lived in his soul.

"Miss."

"Call me Andrea." On her vest she wore a pin over the casino logo with that name on it.

"Okay, miss. What I want to tell you is that I've traveled for two years in search of my daughter, and I will keep on doing this for the rest of my life if necessary. But I know you can help me. Help me, please, and I will work here for nothing as long as you want. Help me find her because I want to talk to her for a little while."

Then it was the young woman's turn to explain to him that it was very difficult to find someone with the small amount of information that he was providing. She was trying to say it gently, carefully choosing her words so as not to hurt the man whose innocence touched her. But finally she asked him why he had associated the casino with his daughter.

The question sounded strange to Dante because over those two years he had become so accustomed to thinking that as soon as he reached the Montecarlo Casino he would find out about Emmita.

"You don't know her?"

"How would I know her?"

Dante began to explain the story of the boyfriend, but Andrea interrupted him: "You said her name is Emmita. Emma Celestino. I've been working at this casino for seven years, and I've never heard that name. What's more, I've worked in the personnel department, and no, I've never heard it."

"Have you heard of Johnny Cabada?"

That name did in fact say a lot to Andrea.

"Please don't repeat that name. Don't say it here."

At that moment, someone from management called Andrea on the office phone and asked her why she was taking so long with Dante. She responded that he was a man with anxiety and that she was going to give him tickets and coupons for some shows to settle him down.

"I advise you not to repeat that name. Don't do it, please. Why don't look around the casino?"

Dante felt stunned. He had spent those two years traveling toward an illusion. That had prevented the sadness from coming down from the sky and swallowing him up. He obeyed. He let himself be carried away. A courteous waitress took him on a guided tour around the inside of the casino: "Come in, sir. Come in, this way. I'm going to take you to the bingo hall. It's the largest one in the world, and I'm sure you'll love it. By the way, would you like a drink?"

On the way, Dante saw different masked characters taking turns entertaining the visitors. Then he sat down at a table and picked up a card at the waitress' insistence. He took it, but didn't know what he was going to do with it.

His guide explained it to him, and he understood immediately. Even though he forgot how to read from time to time, he was very aware of numbers.

Both Dante and the waitress were amazed: she because it was the first time she had seen a man who had never gambled, and Dante because the game proved to be fun and he had never participated in that kind of leisurely activity. The girl who was calling the numbers had a very pretty voice and, listening to her entranced, distracted him several times and he forgot to record the numbers on his card.

He was so concentrated on her that he did not notice the presence of the old man and Juan Pablo accross the room. The old man had taken off his glasses and was using them as binoculars to find Dante.

"Come. Come right away," he waived to Dante.

"What's happening, partner," Dante managed to say, somewhat annoyed because he wanted to stay at the bingo section and listen to the girl call the numbers.

"Come with me now, and don't call me partner."

Before he could decide whether to obey, Juan Pablo came over next to him and took him by the arm. Dante couldn't resist and went with him to a roulette wheel where the customers were playing with bills rather than chips.

"Point to the 41," Juan Pablo whispered into his ear, and as Dante hesitated, the boy put his hand into Dante's shirt pocket and found a one-hundred-dollar bill folded in fourths.

The old man put that bill and another just like it onto the space of a chosen number as the operator started the roulette wheel. Then colors, images, and numbers started passing before the amazed eyes of Dante, who had never bet in his life. There was only one chance in very many of winning, and there was no way to get the bill back. At that precise moment, Dante realized that not only was he betting that money, the last he had left, but he had bet his entire life on a hope that had just been erased.

The roulette wheel's initial impulse was slowing, and it was about to stop when strangely it sped up again. Then it again allowed its colors, its images, and its numbers to pass before a sad man whose closed eyes saw only the black holes in the universe.

The wheel landed on the number 41. As everyone watched in amazement, the operator gathered the bills from the table and had to take many more from the cash register in order to pay one hundred times the bet of the two crazy guys.

"And now?"

"41 again."

At that moment, they began to hear the clinking of coins falling steadily from the slot machines. None of the gamblers knew where to put the coins that were falling uncontrollably into their pockets.

A dozen enormous, apelike men dressed in impeccable navy blue began to run through the casino. It was casino security in action. But no one knew what was happening nor could the men in navy blue force the customers to leave the machines. While the bingo game was awarding prizes on the first plays, in the hallways, instead of music, a clinking sound was heard as if all the coins in the United States were falling on their sides and rolling across the world.

From its operations center, the manager of the Montecarlo could not explain what was happening. The computers seemed to have failed; everything was programmed so the slot machines would give one grand prize per night, so no one would ever win at roulette, and the grand prize in bingo would fall to a single privileged card. But the machines had gone crazy.

⑥ ⑥ ⑥

Marlene Quincot, the manager of the Montecarlo, was a red-head, and the color of her eyes varied from a glacial blue to a fierce green. She spoke to the head of security and ordered him to find the responsible parties. If he didn't find them, he would have to take responsibility of the chaos. Later they brought her the computer engineer, a man who claimed to have worked in Seattle with Bill Gates, but he was not able to provide a satisfactory explanation. Nor did he know why they had found him in his underwear locked in the disk storage area next to the computer room.

Nothing he was able to tell them made sense. An old, near-sighted man, armed with a pistol from the frontier era, had threatened him as he was working in the computer center. He thought it was a joke.

"Something wrong, grandpa?"

The barrel of the pistol moved and stopped against his jugular. It began to press on it.

"I asked if something's wrong."

"But you said 'grandpa.' I'd rather you call me 'boss,'" said the old man and made him get off his chair.

A young nicely dressed man with a sly face had replaced him in at the computer. He was a boy of few words. He ordered: "The password!"

The barrel of the pistol dug into the engineer's neck.

"Talk!"

"You're crazy!"

The old man cocked the trigger of the old pistol. Then the engineer typed on the keyboard in front of him and a woman welcoming him to the secret program of the Montecarlo Casino appeared on the screen .

"The second password!"

The pistol seemed to be piercing the engineer's neck.

"Don't be nervous."

"Excuse me?"

"Don't be nervous, boss."

When the old man felt satisfied, he withdrew the weapon from the man's neck and put it into its ostentatious case with the red velvet interior. Then he remembered that it was necessary to lock up his victim, and he took the weapon out again.

"That door, where does it lead?"

It didn't go anywhere but guarded a disk depository. Only a very thin man could fit in there.

"Oh no! No, please," said the computer engineer, who was somewhat heavy.

They had taken away his cell phone. He couldn't scream because no one would hear him. He had managed to open a small window like a porthole that looked out at the sky and the Nevada landscape. The mountains and the forest stretched out in the distance. For the first time in a long time, he was looking at them. It even seemed to him that he was hearing the flapping of many birds. Up above, the sky had turned maroon and the stars began to spin. The engineer realized that the universe was extremely beautiful and that he would now have all the time to look at it when they fired him.

⑥ ⑥ ⑥

As the guards ran, the customers celebrated, and the coins rolled, the old man, Dante, and Juan Pablo headed to the parking garage. There the traveler from Oregon untied Virgilio and put him into the van. The old man and his grandson sat in the same places where they had been before.

They entered the city and came to a neighborhood where it was difficult to drive due to the number of vehicles. It was a bohemian area full of bars and people coming in and out of them.

"Is it here? Are you sure you want us to go here?" Dante asked.

This time the old man looked at him over his glasses: "We have to celebrate this, wouldn't you say?"

The search for the right bar took them more than half an hour. Finally, they parked behind the Los Libres de Jalisco Bar. Open Mic. Dante got Virgilio out and tied him to the bumper.

"We have to celebrate this. Besides, I want to hear that accordion."

"But, now, are we criminals? Aren't the police going to come after us?"

"Are you crazy? The casino owners would have to confess that they cheat with the computers. They'd have to turn themselves in first. You think they'd do that? Would *you*?!"

They went into the Los Libres de Jalisco. The old man explained that Open Mic meant that the microphone was open to amateurs. Then he ordered three margaritas without bothering to ask Dante if he liked them. Juan Pablo had to show his ID card because he didn't look old enough to drink.

"Of course, boss. Of course!" The waiter, who was Mexican and dressed as a cowboy, made his metal-heeled boots click and ran to bring them three drinks decorated with lemon slices. In response to a question from the old man, he said that the microphone would be available within an hour and that everyone was invited to participate.

"The clock should be an ahead."

"Pardon me?"

"I said the clock should be an hour ahead," the old man repeated as he placed a bill in the waiter's hand.

The waiter looked at the number printed on the bill and couldn't believe it. He was so amazed that he didn't speak or move.

"What do you say?"

"Nothing, boss. You're right, the clock is wrong."

"In addition, the mic will be available for Dante for the rest of the evening . . . Dante, what's your last name? . . . Oh, okay. As I was saying, the mic will be available for Dante Celestino, the Solitario de Michoacán. Here are two other small reminders. They're for the manager and the announcer who will introduce the Solitario."

A few minutes later, the waiter informed the esteemed guests of the surprise of the evening. By special request, they were hosting

Dante Celestino, the accordion player, whose fame had crossed borders, and whom the Los Libres de Jalisco Bar had the honor of presenting exclusively.

The Los Libres de Jalisco was a bar for U.S. citizens or Mexicans who had made it, and among them predominated people in their forties, fifties, and in some cases, older. That's why when the accordion suddenly arrived with old songs the lyrics immediately incited the best memories.

> *Four roads there are in my life,*
> *which of the four is my way?*
> *You who saw me cry in anguish,*
> *tell me, dove, which one I should take . . .*

A Mexican with bushy eyebrows and slanted blue eyes decided to sing out loud, and everyone began to sing along. Each time the Solitario de Michoacán began a piece, they joined in. For Dante, it was as if he had finally reached Heaven. He had played like this only in his hometown or for small groups of friends, but he had never been applauded as he was at that moment. They were requesting old songs, and his marvelous accordion was bringing them back from the corners of memory where they had been hidden all that time.

> *Life is not worth a thing,*
> *life is not worth a thing,*
> *it often begins with tears*
> *and crying too it ends.*
> *That's why in this world*
> *life is not worth a thing*

A man loudly proclaimed that men didn't cry and begged him, almost in tears, to sing "Carta a Eufemia."

"Let's see if I remember it."

> *Cuando recibas esta carta sin razón*
> *Uuuuuuuuufemia*
> *ya sabrás que entre nosotros todo terminó*

y no le des en recebida por traición
Uuuuuuuuuuufemia
te devuelvo tu palabra
te la vuelvo sin usarla
y que conste en esta carta
que acabamos de un jalón
No me escrebites (iiiites)
y mis cartas anteriores no se si
las recebites (iiiites)
tú me olvidates
y mataron mis amores
el silencio que les dites

A ver si a ésta si le das contestación
Uuuuuuuuuuufemia
del amor pa´qué te escribo
y aquí queda como amigo
tu afectísimo y atento y muy
seguro servidor

"Good-bye, pretty Mariquita" was followed by *My life, if I had four lives, four lives I would live for you*, and then by "I awoke in your arms." Someone was asking for Dante to play "Help me, my God. Help me forget her," but Dante wasn't forgetting because immediately he was playing it, and he continued with "When you live with me," "Open book," "Night of serenade," "La llorona," and "María Elena."

> *This is the ballad of the white horse*
> *that one Sunday set out happily*
> *with the plan of reaching the north,*
> *having left from Guadalajara . . .*

When Dante finally managed to make his way through the crowd of admirers back to his seat, it was after midnight. As Juan Pablo dozed with his head and arms on the table, old Villa ordered the last two margaritas and told Dante that there was a hotel nearby where they would all spend the night. The next morning each would go his own way.

"And then, where am I going to look for her?"

"Don't worry. Now you have enough money to continue on your way. Leave Las Vegas as if you were coming back, but the road won't let you come back," the old man said and explained that roads are alive, and they lead people to their destinies.

In the morning, Dante's van was passed by two lowriders and a heavy motorcycle leaving Las Vegas toward California. It was Johnny Cabada and his gang who, without knowing it, crossed Dante's path again. What Dante did not know was that the vehicle behind him was following him.

21
The Ballad of Los Peregrinos

At the Greyhound station, Juan Pablo jumped out and waited to help his grandfather.

"And where are you planning to go now?" Dante asked them.

The man did not respond because he was very busy putting the pistol case into the bag in which he was carrying the money. As if following a ritual, he opened it, took out the weapon, and blew several times across the barrel. Then he placed it upon the red velvet and carefully wrapped it up, but he had to repeat the action because he hadn't wrapped it up right, and the weapon wouldn't fit into the case that way.

"You were saying?"

"Where are you planning to go?"

The old man pushed away the hand of his grandson, who was trying to help him out, and got out by himself, but with difficulty, due to his arthritis and the height of the van. Dante had gotten out too, to say goodbye to his friends. The old man wiped his boots on his pants and went over to the ticket window.

"The boy's staying in San Francisco, where he'll be going to school. I might go to Berkeley."

"Do you know anyone there?"

The elderly man looked at him in amazement: "Not everyone needs a good reason to go somewhere."

۞ ۞ ۞

Dante was again alone with Virgilio. Dante knew that feeling by heart, as well as that of returning without having achieved his objective. He sped up and got on the freeway.

He didn't get far when he noticed that he needed gas and got off the road to fill up. Before reaching the gas station, the vehicle that was following him passed him and pulled him over. A man approached him and, speaking Spanish, asked him to get out of the vehicle.

"What?"

"Get out with your hands up."

Dante obeyed.

There were two men. One could pass for the other because both wore their hair long, to their shoulders.

"Police," Dante thought, and without intending to, he said it.

"Something like that."

Dante and Virgilio had left the Pacific Coast and were now almost in the heart of the United States. Dante was surprised to find so many people everywhere that looked and spoke like he did.

"He's clean."

"No way, man! He came prepared."

"Prepared? No!"

"What do you mean 'no'?!"

"He didn't bring it."

"Where do you think he'd have it? In his pocket? . . ."

"No, but . . ."

"Look in the van, stupid."

"I already looked."

"Listen."

"Listen," he repeated, shaking Dante.

"What's going on? What's the charge?"

"Charge?"

The men exchanged surprised glances. Finally, one of them stated: "The chief will tell you that later."

"What do you want?"

"Don't ask so many questions, idiot. I'm the one who asks the questions here. Where's your accordion?"

Dante pointed to a metal case in the back of the van. One of his two captors headed in that direction.

"It's true. Here it is."

"Okay, leave it there. Let's go."

One of the men took the wheel of the van. The other, who had a huge, round head, nodded courteously at Dante, pushed him into a blue car with tinted windows, got into the back seat with him, and ordered the driver to take off.

"Don't worry about your van or your donkey. Chango's going to drive it and he'll follow us."

They took a back road that followed every little bend in the river. They went by a cornfield, a field of tulips, and an area of pasture for animals. The curves kept coming one after another, and the cars went up and down little hills with a speed and bouncing similar to those of a trotting horse. One of the bumps caused them to hit their heads on the ceiling, and that made Dante laugh. The man laughed too, but with his eyes, and didn't say a word.

At the next bump Dante laughed again and looked at his companion, but the latter did not accompany him again in his laughter because he seemed to be forbidden from establishing any communication.

"Where are you taking me?"

There was no response.

"Where are we going, if I may ask?"

"You'll find that out when you get there."

"I'm asking."

"When you were born, did you know where you were going to end up?" his companion asked and sank back into the silence only to say half an hour later: "Damn job!"

"Damn life!" said Dante, surprised to find himself cursing life. It was the first time he had ever done so, although he had had reason to. He didn't like having cursed or thinking about all the time he was wasting. He resolved to calm down, not ask questions, not attempt to converse, let them take him anywhere, let his bones rest.

They arrived. You couldn't see it from the road, but after passing by the gate and going through some bushes that surrounded it, one could see that it was an ugly but ostentatious house. It stood in the suburbs of some Nevada town, was two stories high, and surrounded by a dozen short trees. The barred gate at the entrance gave it the appearance of a Mexican ranch; an enormous satellite dish pointed toward the skies. The cars proceeded almost two hundred meters to the garage.

"We're going to go up that stairway inside the garage. You go first."

On the second floor they found a hallway and walked to what looked like a radio recording studio. There was no way this was a police station, Dante thought, but he did not say it aloud. They went into a small living room and told him to wait there.

"Someone will be with you in a moment. Wait," the guy who had ridden with him whispered politely and then left him alone.

"If it takes a little while, I beg you to understand. Business, you know . . ."

Dante didn't think that the police would apologize like that.

"Don't get nervous, man. Amuse yourself. Walk down the hall. Okay, see you later. I'm sorry for any inconvenience you may have experienced. Excuse me."

So Dante found himself sitting in what in a town in Mexico would have been a dentist's waiting room. On the walls hung images of Saint Judas Thadeus and the Virgin of Guadalupe, and on a small center table was a pile of dozens of yellowed newspapers and magazines. As the time passed without anyone coming out to see him, he fiddled with the metallic chair, taking it apart, and putting it back together. Then he decided to walk down the hall and, finally, discovered an open door that led to a recording studio. The man and woman who were working there saw him come in but showed no reaction. Perhaps they took him for someone who also worked at the business.

The man was the blackest Mexican Dante had seen in his whole life. Almost blue. He was sitting next to a microphone and read his part of the script in a pompous voice. His head and ears were encased in thick brown headphones. The woman was very slim and wrinkled, looked to be over sixty, and was dressed entirely in sequined, electric blue.

"How do you feel when you get up? Tired, right? Exhausted, friend. Exhausted and for no reason, because you've gotten enough sleep. And your breath? How's your breath? Stand in front of the mirror and do this . . . ahhhhh . . . ahhhhhh."

As he spoke, the announcer blew against the glass window of the booth, and his breath formed thick, steamy maps.

"Bad breath, my friend. Very bad breath. How disgusting! And if you took a look at your tongue, you'd see that it's white, milky."

The man was putting his right index finger into his mouth and verifying what he was saying: "How disgusting, my friend. I bet you can't even make it to the corner! Bad breath, headache, stomach discomfort, here, right up here, in the upper left-hand part of your stomach, it hurts there. You come home tired, ready for bed, and can't fall asleep because your blood tingles, your arms and legs hurt, and you feel like your back is broken. And then, swollen feet, back pain, burning when you urinate, constipated for two or three days, neck pain, eye pain, headache. And look at the color of your urine. Oh, what a color it has!"

The announcer was touching the body parts he was referring to, and Dante was suddenly afraid that he was going to urinate there at the microphone, but he didn't. Then the woman made the telephone ring and started reading.

"Doctor. Doctor. I'm calling because I don't know what's wrong with me," she complained, using a young voice. "I got married two years ago, and I haven't been able to get pregnant."

The alleged doctor did not seem to take an interest in the caller's problems.

"First thing in the morning, are your eyes red and you don't feel like going to work because you haven't been able to sleep all night?

Are you a newlywed unable to perform your marital duties like a gentleman? Do you have bags under your eyes? Do you have greasy skin, black lungs, yellow teeth, and brittle hair? Do you get up to urinate five times a night? By the way, do you wet the bed?"

"Doctor. Doctor. I'm not getting my period," the woman squealed.

"What have the doctors told you about your inability to fulfill your obligations in bed? What have they told you? Nothing, absolutely nothing, because these days medicine is nothing but a business. And do you know what's wrong? I'm going to tell you once and for all. You have dirty blood, and it is necessary to purify it. You don't wear the same clothes every day. You have to wash them, don't you? Well, in the same way, you must purify your blood. There is a natural remedy known since the Paracelsus and Aztec era, but doctors hide it in order to have more business. Happily, Holy Nature Pharmacy, with the aid of science and technological advances, has managed to synthesize for you lizard lard, shark fin, bull testicle, and salamander heart. One tablet every morning, and you're all set!

"All set! Understand?" the announcer repeated. "Understand? You'll be ready to make the woman beside you feel like a princess and a prostitute all at the same time. Understand?" His eyes gleamed wickedly like red stars in a blue-black sky. "And do you know how much this miraculous remedy costs you? . . ."

"Doctor, doctor, I'm telling you that I'm not getting my period," insisted the teenage voice, but the announcer, after gesturing to her several times to be quiet, disconnected her microphone, and the woman went on shouting things that Dante couldn't hear, but which he could imagine based on the woman's gestures.

"It's you. What are you doing here? My gosh, don't tell me they haven't taken care of you."

A kindly but powerful voice interrupted Dante's observation of the announcers recording a Holy Nature commercial.

"Come with me," repeated the voice behind him. The person who owned the voice took Dante by the arm and led him down the hallway to the interior of a house full of surprises. From the recording studio, they proceeded to another hallway that led to an elegant area. The living room was filled with white horse statues of all sizes, all in different positions. There were only two statues that were different from the rest. They were of Saint Jesus Malverde and Saint Death, placed in wall niches like those in old churches.

"Would you like a drink?" The man, whom he still couldn't see, said again.

He made him out sitting facing him in a black leather recliner. His body began in ostrich-skin boots and continued in jeans. Then you couldn't see anything until you got to the precise, metallic blue that shone in his slanted eyes. After looking at him for a moment, Dante realized that he was the fan who had applauded him the most the previous evening in the Los Libres de Jalisco.

It was clear that the man was sad and impatient because, before Dante could say "No, thank you," that he didn't want anything to drink, the man had already forgotten about the invitation and was starting to talk business, his eyes on the floor.

"I'm not going to argue price. No, definitely not."

Dante did not understand. At first he had believed that he was being taken to a police station, but suddenly he found himself in the presence of a gaunt, elegant man with the appearance of a mild-mannered murderer, who was talking business with him.

"I had thought about offering you an amount, but I think it's best if you set it. Don't worry, I've already talked to the Peregrino, and I've accepted his price."

He laughed mischievously.

"And someday, you'll write a song telling how I kidnapped you to compose a *corrido* for my son."

The silent laugh became a sad grimace.

"The Peregrino, you know. The Peregrino, the best composer in Texas."

Dante shared neither his laughter nor his grimace.

"I can't deny that at first he refused. I offered him all the money he wanted, and he wouldn't take it. 'It's not the money,' he said. What do you think of that?"

Dante did not respond, although he felt like saying that he wasn't understanding any of it and to please let him be on his way because he had to keep looking for his daughter Emmita.

"It's not the money! It's not the money! . . . What else is there besides money?"

Dante had given up on understanding.

"'You're stepping on quicksand, Peregrino,'" I told him. "And you know what he said?"

"Could . . .?" Dante was going to ask him to explain it to him from the beginning.

"That's right. When I said to him, 'You're stepping on quicksand, Peregrino,' he said 'Could be.' What a load of crap!

"He forced me to kidnap him, rather, detain him. I had him locked up here for two weeks before he began to give in. And he had to give in. Every man has his price, my friend. I said to him: 'I want you to compose a ballad for my son Juan Miguel, whose nickname was San Miguel. Understand?' And he understood. Shit, maybe he didn't understand my money. Maybe he understood my love as a father."

"Am I kidnapped, too?"

"Don't say that word; it's so ugly. Let's say you're being held here to accompany the Peregrino on your accordion. Understand me, my friend. Understand that I'm doing all this out of my love as a father."

Perhaps that last sentence was sufficient for Dante to agree, without completely understanding what he was asking him to do. He began to make wordless, affirmative gestures to everything the man was saying to him. The recording studio was his, as was the Holy Nature Pharmacy, the will of many men, and the property of a series of businesses that he enumerated to him during his monologue.

"The Peregrino explained to me that he writes ballads about friendship, but never about drugs. He told me to my face that he knew me well and didn't want any deals with me. You, of course, do you know who I am? I won't deny that people talk about me, but so far no one has proven anything against me, and the proof of all of this is that the U.S. police have never arrested me. If they did, I'd have to show them the articles of incorporation of these businesses from which I live honestly."

No, Dante didn't know his name. He just imagined him to be a man with power and an enormous sadness.

"All I am asking for is a *corrido* for my only son. Do you understand that? Maybe that is all I'm asking of life."

He fell silent. Then he looked the other way. Dante did the same to avoid invading his pain.

"Finally, the Peregrino agreed, but on the condition that I would place at his side a man who played the accordion in true Michoacán style. Artists have their whims, you know? That's why I believe that seeing you in Las Vegas and hearing you play your instrument at the Los Libres de Jalisco was as if Divine Providence had put us face to face."

Finally, the man in the ostrich-skin boots decided it was time to put Dante in touch with the Peregrino.

Dante then understood what power was and imagined what men who had it were like. They were like turtles, because only their bodies were vulnerable. The rest of the world could feel and see their shells.

As they were bringing the Peregrino, the man explained that Juan Miguel had brought a load of marijuana from Mexico and had managed to get it into California, and even be paid for it, without being caught by the police.

"Even if they had seen him, they wouldn't have believed it because he was slim, kind, decent. He looked like a young priest and always dressed in black."

He touched his heart.

"Pure soul, you know? . . . Pure soul. Who would believe he was involved in that business? Juan Miguel was caught because of his love for horses."

"Here, on the ranch, you will find magnificent breeds of horses. I can tell you like animals too. It's something that shows on a person's face. When you're working with the Peregrino, I advise you to go into the corrals. You'll see the horses there, restless, nervous, about to go crazy, agile as knives, and black as hell, with their long, wavy manes and their eyes that are always a threat.

"Juan Miguel would pay any price for a good horse. And, that day, after making the deal, he headed to Paso Robles to buy a Peruvian Paso horse that he had been looking for for a long time. You know what a Paso horse is, don't you? More than four hundred years ago, in Peru, the most extraordinary breeds of horses in the world were mixed. Breeders crossed the Andalucian breeds, the Berbers and the Spanish ponies. This horse is the heir of the one that crossed the Strait of Gibraltar to conquer Spain. It is also the one ridden by Cortés, Pizarro, and the rest of the *conquistadors*. It has crossed the tallest mountains and the deepest canyons. It has forded rivers and crossed the Andes with San Martín through Uspallata and Los Patos to attain America's freedom."

He paused, looked at the ceiling as if the horse were there.

"Horse, horse. The only horse that is truly a horse is that horse. Only that horse."

He looked at Dante again.

"When Juan Miguel was almost back to the ranch, the police started to follow him because he had driven in the high-speed lane of the superhighway in an animal transport vehicle. Just for that. Juan Miguel decided to flee, and the police began to call other patrols that immediately appeared from all freeway exits to trap him. . . . 'Give up!' they say they shouted to him once he was stopped. Maybe he was going to give himself up, because he did not have the least evidence of the deal with him and to the police he was just a suspect. 'Give up!' they shouted again, but maybe they didn't even wait to let him give up. I don't know if they machine-gunned the trailer or threw a grenade into it. Who knows! What happened is that the trailer exploded and the horse flew through the air, a black Paso, engulfed in flames. They explained later that my boy went crazy and started shooting and killing policemen to avenge his horse's death. They say they had to kill him when he ran toward them shooting. I don't know why they had to shoot him forty times, though."

Suddenly the Peregrino appeared. He was wearing a shiny velvet shirt that was open from the navel to the neck, so one conversing with him could enjoy looking at a heavy gold chain upon an unrestrained belly. The man with the ostrich boots excused himself and left. His businesses, which were many, were demanding his attention. As he was leaving them, he dialed his cell phone, mumbled something, and two men appeared at his side to accompany him.

"What did you say your name was?" the Peregrino asked Dante, but didn't let him respond. "I'm sorry, I'm so rude. I'm asking your name without introducing myself first."

He pulled a wallet from one of his back pockets and opened it like someone opening a book to read. He took out a pack of faded, dirty cards but did not find his own.

"I can't complain. He's offered me a brand new Cheyenne and as much money as I want. When I explained to him that I could not compose the *corrido* without an accordionist from Michoacán, I don't know what he did, because there aren't many around these parts, but he found you. Who did you say you play with?"

Finally at that moment, Dante had a chance to explain that alghough he played the accordion, he was not a professional. Additionally, he begged him to do everything possible for him to be freed. This entire matter, he assured him, frightened him, and he did not understand it at all. He told him that he worked in Mount Angel and confessed to him that he was in the area looking for his daughter.

"We'll talk about your daughter later. I may be able to help you, because I know the Las Vegas casinos. But right now we have to get out of this problem. And don't worry about not being a professional, that doesn't matter to me. I just need you to give me the rhythm, and I'll write the song. It'll take us two weeks at most. And we'll do it well, because, paid or not, I don't do things halfway."

Dante's accordion had been left in the waiting room. The Peregrino invited Dante to accompany him with the rhythm of a very familiar song.

"Sing, sing, I don't do it professionally either," the Peregrino explained, "but I want to see how we sound together."

The accordion began with the chords of "María Bonita": *Pretty María, my dear María.* Then the world took on a violet coloration and the rain began to enthusiastically penetrate the earth, a flock of geese was suspended in the sky, and a mysterious bolt of lightning shot down into the middle of the forest. Then everything turned calm again and the birds flooded the sky. The moon that had been watching them for awhile pretended not to look. *Remember Acapulco, those nights, pretty María, my dear María. Remember that on the beach, with your pretty hands you rinsed the little stars.* By the time they had finished repeating the song dedicated to the woman with the most beautiful name in the world, it seemed like the two guys had been friends for many years, and the woman that lived in death or in a memory, like Beatriz or like María Bonita, were inviting them to sing and to exchange secrets.

"Writing a ballad is easy. At the beginning, the salutation. At the end, the closing. Because, in all of this, one must be courteous and polite with the audience that is going to listen to him. And then in the middle, there you have to tell what the character in the song wants to be known about him. Where were you born? Who were your parents? Why is your town famous? Are you a cockfighter? What women have you loved? . . . And that's where the men cut loose and start giving names, until they suddenly shut up because they don't want their current wife to get jealous."

The Peregrino was pacing as he spoke: "But, let's see, what do you want me to talk about? What important thing have you done in your life? How many men have you killed? How much time have you spent in jail? . . . People have to have done something in life to deserve a ballad. I can make up the rest. It's interesting that so many people want to be immortalized in a ballad without having done anything to deserve it."

He was walking back and forth from one side to the other, his eyes on the floor as if searching there for ideas. He came back with another opinion.

"No, the truth is that we are all to be respected. We risk it all. And when it's our turn to lose, we accept in silence, with our eyes downcast, but with our heads held high, without making faces. Life is life, you know. God gave the trees the power to grow without confronting anyone. But it's different with us, we can't live life without fighting for it. There's no way to avoid this game. They put us at this table, and they dealt us the cards. And you can't deal the cards or move the board. That's why you have to learn the rules of the game."

Then, whispering his words, the Peregrino stated: "Yes, I believe that San Miguel deserves the ballad, and his whole family too. I imagine that Güero already told you."

"Güero?"

"Güero Palacios. The one who was talking to you. He's the one that . . . ," he searched for a word other than "kidnapped," "He's the one who hired us."

"Güero Palacios? Doesn't he have a name?"

"He has one, but it's not good for you to know it, my friend. Death has quite an appetite around these parts."

There was a long silence as if an angel had passed by, or as if death had come in to have tea.

"Güero Palacios is from Guerrero, and nothing but tough people come from there. Come on, let's get to work."

The Peregrino and Dante kept singing and playing the accordion as they waited for inspiration to write San Miguel's ballad.

From love ballads they moved to classic *corridos* that the amazing memories of both of them held as if they were the only thing they had ever listened to in their lives.

> *They came from San Isidro*
> *all the way from Tijuana*
> *the tires of their car*
> *full of marijuana,*
> *it was Emilio Varela*

and Camelia the Tejana.
They went through San Clemente
were stopped by immigration,
asked for their documents,
asked . . . "Where are you from?"
She was from San Antonio
a good-hearted woman.

As if the story, already a classic, pained them, the accordion and the singer fell silent there.
"But it doesn't end there."

When a woman loves a man
she can give her life for him
but you'd better be careful
if that woman feels hurt
betrayal and contraband
are unshared things.

They arrived in Los Angeles
and went on to Hollywood,
and in a dark alleyway
they changed the four tires.

There they delivered the weed
and there too they were paid.
Emilio says to Camelia,
"Consider yourself fired,
with your part of the money
you can make a new life,
I'm heading for San Francisco
with the owner of my heart."

Seven shots were heard.
Camelia killed Emilio
all the police found
was a pistol lying there.
Nothing was ever heard
of the money or of Camelia.
Nothing at all . . .

"And do you know this one?"

I started selling champagne,
Tequila and Havana wine,
but this I did not know
what a prisoner suffers.

Very soon I bought a car,   *For selling cocaine,*
property with a residence,   *morphine and marijuana,*
not knowing that very shortly   *I was taken prisoner*
I'd go to the penitentiary.   *at two o'clock in the morning.*

Suddenly, the Peregrino asked Dante for a solemn accompaniment in order to recite: "I ask permission, ladies and gentlemen, to sing a ballad."

He had it. His eyes, his body, his hands, his entire being was flooded by the ballad.

"We'll talk about fate and about the respect we owe each other. I repeat that we are all to be respected."

That was how Dante understood it. He also understood that fate exists and that it had marked him to be a wanderer.

"We need to put horses in the ballad, lots of horses."

At the request of the Peregrino, Dante began to tell him about all the horses he had known. With the aid of his accordion, he talked endlessly about steeds, Pasos, percherons, so that their hooves could be heard, their trot felt, and even their breath perceived.

"Clip-clop, clip-clop, clip-clop . . ."

The ballad was beginning to take shape as Dante slapped his knees with his hands in order to describe the gait and tremendous elegance of the equines. He slapped his left knee with his right hand and his right with his left, *clip-clop, clip-clop*, so that the singer would understand the dance and the quick trot, the majesty and the speed, the dream and the reality of the horse.

Then they turned to thinking about Juan Miguel. Güero Palacios had supplied them with many photos taken in school, church, with friends, and next to a very beautiful young woman. But the scene of the coffin had to be lasting for anyone who had been there. Amid a sea of lights in the form of candles, the silver coffin was barely visible because flowers of every color flooded the room. In their midst was etched the ashen face of the young man, his jaw jutting out with the arrogance of one who has always prepared himself to die very young and to demonstrate that he accepts his fate. In the background were men with dark glasses and women wearing gold bracelets. His father looked like a stone statue. Dante acknowledged that sometimes one has to turn to stone in order to remain on earth and not allow his soul to fly off in pursuit of the loved one.

"One thing," Güero had asked them, "in the ballad don't call him San Miguel. Just plain Juan Miguel. He'll be made a saint when the Pope feels it's appropriate," he had added.

Juan Miguel's huge eyes had opened several times during the wake, and on one of those occasions his picture was taken. The Peregrino imagined him riding horseback across the sky and sang the story in that way. Only the face and the feet of the horse stood out in the blackness that invaded Juan Miguel. He was riding away from the world and sinking arrogantly into the meadows of the universe. In the ballad, they sang of a horse and a man amid the stars, galloping down the sleepy trails invented by God.

The second week, they started recording with the announcer's professional assistance. From his soundproof booth, the man would signal to them with his fingers: "One, two, three, ready?"

But Dante would not stretch his accordion until the Peregrino sang, and the Peregrino did not always obey the pompous black man in the booth.

"One, two, three, ready?"

"Go to hell," the Peregrino told the announcer.

"What was that?"

"Go to . . . Let us do it our way."

The composer exaggerated a little on the shootout with the police and added ten patrol cars and several armed helicopters. Juan Miguel had had to shoot in all directions and even toward the sky. At the end, the ballad had too many verses, and they had to cut some out because no commercial radio station would accept a song that lasted more than three and a half minutes. Therefore the Peregrino left out Juan Miguel's childhood in Baja California and certain shady dealings. Mention of his father and his girlfriend, the death scene, and the names of the stars near where the dead man and his horse entered were left behind. After three weeks, to Güero Palacio's fascination,

the ballad was finished, and the duo had established a great friendship with the man in the sound booth.

I'm going to sing the corrido
of the brave Juan Miguel.
I'm not lying when I tell you:
there'll never be another like him.

He took a load of the good stuff
as far as California,
but before going back home
he bought a Paso horse.

An amazing black
with eyes like hell
as agile as a knife
as speedy as Miguel.

As soon as they saw his truck
fifty güeros followed him.
They said to ask him questions
but I think it was for a bribe.

He could have turned himself in
but that's not what his daddy
*   taught him.*
He put the pedal to the metal
and left the police behind.

Machine-gun fire is heard
a grenade is thrown at him
and the horse riding in the trailer
flies straight to Heaven.

Ten patrol cars follow him
he annihilates eight of them.
Finally, a treacherous grenade
turned him into stardust.

The sky goes round and round,
the stars spin even more.
They seek your blood, Miguel,
to carry it to the sky.

Tell him, little dove, tell him,
tell Juan Miguel right away,
with your eyes on the heavens,
that there'll be no other like him.

Fly, fly, Juan Miguel
with the bloody star,
with the planets spinning,
the lightning, the fire, and your steed.

The soundman's name was Alex; he was from a country he never
mentioned, but he spoke with a Mexican accent because it was easy
for him to imitate people's voices or because he preferred to disguise
his origin. From his neck hung a white gold chain with an effigy of
Saint Death, and he was always commending himself to her protection, because she had been the one who had helped him cross into
the United States with no problems. He called her the Lady of the

Night and also Flaquita and *"mi dueña Blanca,"* and he advised
Dante to talk to her and to pray to her for his daughter.

It was Alex who suggested that the three of them form a band:
"Come on, Peregrino, I think that if rocks had loves or sorrows, you
would give them a voice and a song. And you, Dante, you would
make them speak through that accordion. The truth is that you guys,
or rather, we, should start a band and tour the country."

That was the last thing that Dante could think about, as all he wanted was to regain his freedom and continue his search for Emmita.

"We'll look for her together," the Peregrino told him. "At every
venue we play, we'll try to find information about her. We'll write
songs to look for her. The public will help us find her."

Güero, who had already sent the recording to several radio stations, gladly allowed the musicians to take Alex along.

"Thanks to you guys, Juan Miguel is with me again. At night, I
feel him galloping across the sky. If any manager is hesitant or does
not want to help you, Alex will take care of reminding him that
you're my friends and that you represent me."

They wasted no time, and the next morning, they set out in two
vehicles. The sound equipment and Alex traveled in the Peregrino's
brand new Cheyenne. The Peregrino and Dante rode in the van with
Virgilio, who was also part of the band. Since *corrido* bands tend to
take photos of themselves with huge pickup trucks and machine
guns, Virgilio appeared in the photos as a reminder of listener's
homelands.

Alex, who would also be the host, announcer, promoter, and
manager, gave them their name. "Ladies and gentlemen, I present to
you Los Peregrinos de la Santa Muerte!"

22
Selena Got Up

Selena got up, dressed all in gray. Went down to the Days Inn and never came back.

Like Selena, Emmita dressed in gray. She was eating breakfast next to Johnny in Las Vegas. All Johnny had had to do was ask her to go off with him for her to abandon her father. She had made no attempt to find out what her life would be like. For her, there was no one but Johnny Cabada in her life, and she would follow him to the end of the world. She thought the same thing about her career as a singer and about Selena, whom she admired so much. Selena was the beginning. Selena was the end. She was the origin of music. She was the music of the origin. Selena was the river. Selena was the night. Selena was love. Selena was love at midnight. The night could not exist without Selena. But Selena too had an end, and even so, Emmita also liked Selena's end. She wanted to live and die like her. Dressed in gray.

A shot rang out throughout the empty lot, and she won't be singing for us anymore.

Selena, we miss you. I wish you were here.

"Sometimes I don't understand why you're here," said Johnny Cabada, looking into his coffee cup.

"Yes, you do. You know I'm here for you."

There was no response.

"What are you thinking?"

"About what?"

"About anything."

The young man shook his head and shifted his feet. He had taken off two very long boots and was wiggling his toes.

"Are you mad at me?"

"It's not that."

"Then tell me what you're thinking about?"

"Why'd you follow me? Why'd you come with me?"

"You know why?"

"Why?"

"Because."

Almost a child, Emmita had left everything for Johnny. Because of him, she had become an adult and left school and her home, renouncing her father's authority. Deep down, she didn't want her girlfriends to make fun of her when she couldn't go out at night or stay over at other people's houses like they all did. Leaving meant, above all, that she could be like Selena, a great singer.

Johnny had tried his hand at musical activities. But the rock group he led failed. In fact, it was never very important; it was more a cover up for his illegal activities. The methamphetamine sales in the casinos were somewhat profitable for him, though from time to time he had to move to avoid attacks from rival gangs. He was not the king of the world he had promised Emmita he would be, nor could he get her everything she wanted.

He took her to a couple of radio auditions where he had friends, and she had even had some tryouts, but they told her that she was still very young, that she should wait a little longer.

"And you, why are you here?"

"Don't you know?"

"No."

"You don't?"

The young man poured himself another cup of coffee and looked attentively at the shine that its blackness gave off.

"There's a man I've been looking for for a long time. I know that his businesses are here, but I don't know where he lives. In fact, no one knows."

He continued talking to his coffee cup as if Emmita weren't there. He said he believed that man was his father and that he had abandoned him when he was still in his mother's womb. Emmita stood up, reached out, and covered the eyes of the man she loved, not wanting to let him go on speaking. She didn't want him to suffer.

Nevertheless, Johnny Cabada continued his story. He was in Las Vegas working the casinos that belonged to that guy, especially the Montecarlo, trying to provoke him. The important thing for that man was the considerable amount of money he acquired manipulating the machines with the aid of computers installed in them, but he definitely did not want anyone selling drugs in his casino. Any action of that nature could cause him to lose his permit or trigger a very thorough police investigation.

"It's probably time for us to go our separate ways," Johnny said without looking up.

Love, love, I love you so much, you're my dream, you're my passion.
That's how I like it, you're my life, you're my everything.
Bamba, bamba, hey you, come over here.
Bidi bidi bom bom. Bidi bidi bom bom.

Every time, every time I see him go by
(A phone rings) Hello? It's me, Love,
before you hang up on me . . . (dial tone)
Every day is the same in my hallway . . .

"What are you saying?"

Abandoned heart, what are you doing there with that sorrow?
Dear little heart, dear little heart, never fall in love again.
When the evening falls and daylight is fading,
when no one loves you, when they all forget you.

"What are you saying?"

After January comes April, maybe I'm mistaken.
Tell me, what's happened
since you left my side.
He has gone away, and I'm left with my sadness.
Time goes by, and you're not here
(In love with you . . .) I feel a thrill
deep in my heart

"You're joking."

That little smile that comes with no reason and no explanation.
This heart, which still loves you,
is dying, day by day.
This pain that I have so deep inside.
I'm with you for eternity,
there's nothing that can separate.
Photographs and memories . . .
I have a picture of you . . .
I could lose my heart tonight, if you don't turn and walk away.
I know you've taken my lead, am I so easy to read?
I said a no, no no no no, no no no no, no no no no
no no, no no no.
I see him walking, I sense the danger, I hear
his voice and my heart stops.
I see the distant lights ahead, another hour or
so, and I'll be back in bed.
If only I could hear your voice
your words
I'm sorry. For the things that I have
done to you. So sorry.
The door closed; you can't come in again.
Last chance, last chance for love.
Late at night when all the world is sleeping I
stay up and think of you.
What good is my life if I no longer have you.
It looks like it's going to rain, the sky is clouding.
I swear to you that my intentions were good
I, I have a love, a love that makes me happy.
You will always be . . . always mine. All my
friends say that I'm a fool
You're always on my mind,
day and night.

"You should go to Oregon. It might be good for you to go back to your father." Johnny explained slowly, between sips of coffee. There would be danger when he could confront his father, and he warned her that, if she stayed with him, she too would be in danger.

Then it was Emmita who began to look at her own cup of coffee, and she told him the story of her parents. The ten years that they were separated, the searches that both of them undertook until they were reunited. She acknowledged that her father was a good man, and that perhaps in time she could have convinced him of her feelings for Johnny, but that was in the past. She swore that what united her with Johnny was indestructible, and therefore she had given up everything else. If he left her, she would become a memory that would fill him completely forever. She thought that the souls of human beings are their memory. The soul is memory or it's nothing.

While Emmita was remembering her parents, Johnny was searching his own recollections too. He recalled nothing, no family images. Just streets and music and drunks and motorcycles and beer bottles. No light, not the light of God, nor the light of the world.

"I wish I could talk about my family like that."

He repeated to her that it would be a good idea for her to go back to her father. He said it sadly, as if he were going to cry, but he spoke looking right through her, as if he were a blind man, and the blind cannot cry.

"He wouldn't take me back anymore."

Johnny realized that he was looking weak and, as usual, turned to giving orders.

"Then we have to go. We'll go together. We'll go to California. But we'll come back," he added. "I promise you we'll come back." Johnny said and checked his phone that signaled an incoming message.

The message that the young man received was extremely clear: "If you're a real man, I'll be waiting for you to settle up in San Francisco, Sunday the seventh, at nine at night at the place the messenger tells you. We can get things straight, set new borders, put things in order. I repeat, if you're a real man . . ."

A few hours later, it was not the earth that was trembling, not even the sky. It was the engines of many motorcycles shaking the air and the skies near Las Vegas. At the head of them, dressed in black, Johnny Cabada was helping Emmita get on his motorcycle.

"Don't go. Why can't we just stay here? Why don't you forget about that man?"

Without intending to, Emmita imitated the sound of her mother's voice when she begged Dante not to work so much overtime because what he earned was enough and more, and there was even money left for the future fifteenth birthday party fund.

"I have to go. I want to find out what he's like."

"And after you meet him, will we come back to Las Vegas? Will you help me get started in my singing career?"

Johnny answered something that Emma never heard, she was clinging to his back on the motorcycle. She also said something that he did not hear either: "It doesn't matter if we don't come back. You know I'll follow you anywhere."

As they proceeded toward San Francisco, the air turned white and milky as if suddenly the planet had entered the deepest part of the Milky Way. The motorcycles roared as they sank into regions of luminous smoke and tiny stars spinning around all of them. The motorcyclists were evaporating, and Emmita had the sensation that all of it, rather than a road, was a dream.

Johnny dreamed of the man who was waiting for him in San Francisco. In his delirium, he saw him dressed in black corduroys, mariachi boots, a sequined shirt, a black felt hat reaching halfway over his eyes, and a gold chain with the image of the Virgin of Guadalupe. It seemed to him that all was a repetition of past events, and he thought that it was strange that he had never investigated Leonidas García.

23
Leonidas García Ordered the Universe

Leonidas García was from Veracruz, and he had studied medicine there, but when he received his degree, he went from one hospital to another without finding work. He did not have enough money to open a private office and wait to establish a clientele. He had to get work as a sales representative for drug companies, but the businesses would hire him for awhile and then let him go in order to cut down on their expenses. He soon discovered that he was not destined to be an important man in his homeland. One winter day, which he would remember for the rest of his life, he got up when it was still dark and said, "Dear God, what am I doing here?"

He picked up his pants that were draped over a chair and put them on. He examined his nearly empty closet, discarded the suits and ties he wore to visit doctors, and with his fingers picked out a very thick wool shirt. He held his boots up to the weak early morning light in order to distinguish the right from the left and put them on. Then over his shirt he put on a heavy jacket that looked like it was lined with wool and, without having breakfast, closed the door to the rented room to which he would never return.

The winter he crossed the border was extremely cold. The *coyotes* had stopped working because they were afraid to go through the tunnels, for fear they or their clients would freeze beneath the earth. Leonidas García was delighted to hear that news, because he had no money with which to pay them. All he had to do was talk one of them into telling him the route. He found the man, but he ran into a problem. Each *coyote* had his own tunnel and never shared it.

"The tunnel?"

"Yes, the tunnel."

"What tunnel?"

"The tunnel, man. Where did you say the tunnel was?"

"I didn't say anything."

"I know you can't use them during this time of year . Where'd you say it was?"

"I repeat: I didn't say anything. And I'm not going to tell you because it would be dangerous for you to try to go through it."

"If it's dangerous, that's my business."

"You aren't from the competition, are you?"

"From the competition? No, but I could be from the Judicial Police, and it would be good for you to have friends there."

Once in the United States, he chose San Francisco because he had friends and relatives working there. They helped him as much as they could, but he was not able to realize his dream of working in a hospital. Without papers, that was impossible.

Then he bought false documents and worked as a paramedic for a year and a half. When they discovered that he was undocumented they fired him. They warned him that he had committed a federal offense and that the next time they saw him, they would call the police.

He was stubborn and obtained false papers again. He got a Social Security number that, incredibly, was not detected as irregular by the officials at the Oakland hospital where he began to work in the pharmacy. Years later when he remembered those days, he felt it was the craziest, most beautiful time of his life in the United States. Although he didn't earn much because he couldn't get credit for his degree, he enjoyed a pleasant, moderately comfortable economic position, drove a European car purchased at a low price, and met Rosina Rivero Ayllón, a girl who worked at the same hospital and had the darkest eyes on the planet. Rosina was mysterious, slim, beautiful, crazy, and when she looked at him in the darkness, her gaze seemed to attract eternal damnation. They got to know each other and immediately started living together because living together was the most important thing that could happen on the planet. Leonidas was sure of it when they walked along the streets of Berkeley holding hands and sometimes flung themselves down on the sidewalk to kiss.

After two years of doing the same thing, Leonidas spent one night thinking that he had not yet achieved any of his goals. His dreams of being an important doctor were not going to come true carrying packages in the pharmacy and throwing out expired medications. Without waking Rosina, he got up and got dressed because the night had offered him some infallible advice for making money and being important.

He got to the pharmacy long before his co-workers and left an hour after than they did. He kept his pockets empty in case someone searched him, although that had never happened, but under his thick raincoat he hid a bag full of discarded medications. From Oakland he went to the Mission District of San Francisco, entered a building with peeling walls, and knocked on the door of an apartment whose address he had memorized.

"Yes?"

"Do you remember me?"

"What do you want?"

"I asked if you remember me."

"I know a lot of people. I have no reason to remember all of them."

"I work at the Oakland hospital."

The man didn't invite him in, but did look at him with greater attention.

"You spoke to me some time ago. You told me you were interested in certain substances."

"I don't remember."

"They're substances I can get at the pharmacy. I work there, you know?"

"Maybe it's best you leave."

"Take a close look at me. You'll remember my name. I'm Leonidas."

"Leonidas? Leonidas . . . okay, come in. Come on in."

The man opened the door wide and burst out laughing.

"Sooner or later you had to show up," he said, still laughing.

At that moment, Leonidas' prosperity began. Rosina noticed the difference when her partner had them move to a more elegant apartment. Then he showered her with gifts and dresses and left her large sums of money to buy anything she wanted. She knew there was something strange about all that but she preferred to believe the stories he told her.

Finally, he began to take her on trips to different cities until Rosina told him that she couldn't get off work so often because she would end up being fired.

"You don't have to wait for them to fire you. Resign. With my job at the pharmacy and the little business deals I make, we have more than enough to live on."

He told her this many times until finally he convinced her. She was not aware of anything, but at times imagined that her partner was working in something dangerous. Perhaps that's why she was so affectionate with him, to protect him from his own conscience and fears.

Not long after, everything became a race against time and fate. Leonidas went from being a methamphetamine dealer to owning the business that marketed it. He left his job at the hospital, but got dozens of suppliers throughout the area. He rented an apartment in San Francisco and left Rosina in Berkeley in order to protect her from possible danger from the police. Little by little his business became more diversified, and he became the man he had always wanted to be.

Rosina and he lived together a little longer and were very happy, especially the times when he spent a week without leaving home in order to hide from his enemies and his remorse. But at a certain moment, he freed himself completely from both, and he began to need less from the woman he had loved. He often left on endless trips that he justified with business and was out of touch for months.

On top of the world and a powerful central California dealer, one day he pretended that the police were looking for him, and he told Rosina that he would have to be gone for awhile until things cleared up. He never returned. Rosina never got to tell him that she was pregnant.

Two years later, someone gave him the news that Rosina had died, but no one told him that she had left a son who was a few months old and that she had had to entrust him to the protection of a family.

"Dead? Really, she's dead?"

"I swear to God."

Perhaps at that moment he realized that the line between holiness and disgrace is very fine. All he had to do was close his eyes to see Rosina's eyes, dark black, like hell. It seemed to him that he was seeing those eyes that were looking at him for the last time, begging him not to leave her. And when he opened his eyes, he knew he belonged to the kingdom of villains.

More than twenty years had passed since then, and now he was powerful and legendary. In addition to his wealth, his glorious deeds were spoken of. Certain storytellers who exaggerate tell about him. It is said that, on one occasion, pursued by the police, he dug a deep hole and went into it with a few boxes of crackers and two drums of water. A friend put a lot of branches on top of the hole and dirt on top of them. It is not known how long he stayed there, perhaps weeks or months; but it's true that he came out of there to freedom with that flavor of chocolate that the earth has, a flavor that never leaves you.

Others tell the story in a different way and say that he was buried alive by the people of a rival gang and that he had despaired underground for a week, but that he had emerged unscathed, with a certain fear of the light. They add that perhaps he came out of death without knowing he had been in it.

Aside from the photograph that would be published later in the newspapers, there are many more legends about Leonidas than there is objective information. The San Francisco police department has no record of him.

When leaders of the two most powerful drug gangs had died in an all-out, hopeless war. Leonidas, experienced in that business, easily acquired power amid the chaos. Nothing had prevented him from achieving it. It is said that he even resorted to black magic in order to get rid of rivals as powerful as Peter González and Harry Malásquez.

The first was hung by his own men who had been bribed by Leonidas. Malásquez awoke insane one day, and no one was able to cure him.

They say that was when Leonidas took over the entire region between San Francisco and Las Vegas that his rivals had dominated up to that time. His business extended to gambling. Leonidas bought the Montecarlo Casino, which he managed over a complex cybernetic network.

The roulette wheels spun a winning number only once every evening, and often the winner was someone who worked for Leonidas. The rest of the time, the roulette wheels and bingo games gave consolation prizes to soften up the gamblers and encourage them to continue betting. Only once had a man with extremely good luck managed to defeat the computers and win a million dollars. Nevertheless, the man and his entire family crashed on the highway on their way home and died in the accident.

Now something similar had just happened: an old man and a boy had come into the casino and, apparently, had put a virus on the computers.

"Don Leonidas, we lost control, and all the machines started giving prizes. It was as if the computers were under a spell."

But no one was going to convince *him* of witchcraft.

"Do you know if Johnny Cabada is working in that area?"

He didn't know Johnny Cabada, but he had begun to recognize his methods of working. They were the same ones that he had used when he was still a young man weakened by dreams.

Immediately he suspected Johnny Cabada, who was involved in the methamphetamine business and whose territory included the region from Oregon to Las Vegas.

"He's coming into my territory, but I'm not going to allow it."

"It wasn't him, Don Leonidas. The people say they saw an old man."

"They saw what?"

"An old man, Don Leonidas, yes, an old man and a farmworker. They say they escaped in an old van and that they had a donkey with them."

"A what? . . . I want you to bring me Johnny dead or alive. No, wait. People like you aren't going to catch him. It's better if he comes willingly. Catch him through his pride. Send him a message from me."

"But where will we find him?"

"Don't worry about that."

In this regard, the accounts also differ. Some say that police officers were bribed to give him the address, but it is at least interesting to hear what they have to say. According to them, he called Filemón, El Maldito, and ordered him to look for his enemy. In an endless session, the witch doctor drank brandy, swished it around in his mouth, and spit toward the four directions so that the illusive air would become air of death, and then he began to look. He tracked Johnny Cabada in the flight of the birds, in the worn-away tracks on the road, in abandoned houses in Portland, across the plains and through the mountains of that immense territory, but it was all in vain.

Nevertheless, when he was shown a photograph of the young man, the search became easier, and soon he managed to find him in a Las Vegas house where he was spending the night with a very young girl. There was something strange in all of that. Filemón looked back and forth between the man in the photograph and Leonidas.

Whatever the case may be, what happened is that Leonidas found him and would soon meet him. The boy was not so innocent as to be unaware of the danger that this brought with it, but he indeed was conceited enough to accept the challenge.

"Tell him that Leonidas García is summoning him urgently to once and for all resolve the problems between the two of us and to establish new business borders, if necessary . . ."

"Is that all, Don Leonidas?"

"And that if he considers himself as much of a man as they say he is, he'll come and see me."

24
The Ballad and the Tour

"The *corrido* of Juan Miguel Palacios" was a hit. First, the Spanish radio stations in Nevada picked it up, and later those of Texas, New Mexico, Arizona, and California received a noncommercial cassette with the "request" that they broadcast it. The request was extremely persuasive, because the administrators received personal phone calls from Güero Palacios, whose promise of friendship or veiled threat no one could resist. The story of the young man who traveled across the sky riding a flaming steed was heard at all hours and on all the programs, and people called their local stations to ask how they could get the cassette.

> *I'm going to sing the corrido*
> *of the brave Juan Miguel.*
> *I'm not lying when I tell you:*
> *there'll never be another like him . . .*

Holy Nature Pharmacy began to sell the ballad over the radio along with its miraculous prescriptions. The recording contained, additionally, other ballads by Los Peregrinos de la Santa Muerte, who appeared on the cover photo next to a donkey that brought back memories of the beautiful days back home in their villages for many of the possible purchasers. Later, the CD entered the regular market and could be found in any establishment that carried music in Spanish. Finally, Los Peregrinos began to receive invitations to appear at restaurants, theaters, and coliseums in different cities. Before leaving for them, Alex designed a tour that would take eight months and could be extended for a longer period, depending on public demand.

For Dante those were surprising, magical, and miraculous times, after so many bad days. He looked toward the sky and said to himself that the sky was ripening. So many stars had been born and had grown that there was no longer any open space up there. Many of them ended up becoming wandering stars like those that showered them the night they began their trip to their first show in Fresno, California.

"Wanderers. They're wandering stars, like us," the Peregrino said to Dante and Virgilio, both of whom were looking out their respective windows at the scenery.

"Yes."

"Yes. Migrants. Like you and me," repeated the Peregrino, who felt obligated to talk about himself a little.

Before devoting himself to composing ballads in the United States, the Peregrino had crossed the border many times and had always done so through tunnels. On one occasion, pursued by the *migra*, he remained hidden for three days in an open grave in a border town cemetery. Maybe that's why he smelled like dead man's land, although that had happened many years earlier. If he had crossed the border so many times it was because he suffered from uncontrollable homesickness and could not remain in the United States for long without leaving for a few days to see his loved ones. On the way back, he had to sneak in, and he knew no better way than walking underground and hiding in cemeteries. Now he had papers and could even fly in a plane over the borders, but he still felt a certain love for the darkness and the earth.

"I don't remember who told me that I looked like a dead man or a wanderer, and I liked it. That's why I became a *peregrino*, a pilgrim, and a troubadour. It comes naturally."

He had lived in many cities in the United States, but was attracted most to those near the border.

"El Paso, Texas, was where Güero's people kidnapped me. I think that's where I've lived the longest. Counting all the times I've lived there, it is. If you ask me why I like the border, I can give you a lot of reasons, but the main ones are these two: the first is that I can go to the other side whenever I want to. From El Paso, I cross the bridge and I'm already in Ciudad Juárez. The second is that they are cities for very malicious people. You have to be brave to live in them as well as to die in them, of course. Violence is like a moonlit night. Violence is one hundred percent of what inspires a serious, spiritual composer.

"I have four children, but I've never married. Of course I fulfill my obligations with the kids, and I'm always sending their mothers money. But being alone allows me to live the life that I like and not expose my family to the dangers that sometimes lie in wait for us. Can you imagine what would happen to us if one of Güero's competitors didn't like us?"

Dante did not imagine that. He did not have any space in his heart to dedicate to that fear.

"Now that I think about it, they wouldn't do anything to us because everyone knows I'm a professional, and they respect me. But economic ups and downs are not something to impose on one's family. For example, I'm fine right now, and there's more than enough money to send to the kids, but sometimes I have to go to Mexico and sing on the buses."

Just like Alex, the Peregrino was a devotee of Saint Death, and he was a firm believer that she helped him cross the border and had sheltered him in the cemeteries.

"I believe she was at the side of the immigration officer who signed my passport. She guided his hand. Saint Death, my friend, is very miraculous, but she always asks you for something in return."

"And what did she ask you for?"

"When I started to compose by special request, most of my clients talked to me about her, but they did not agree in their descriptions of her. Some said that instead of a face she had a skull, and others described her as young and seductive. I always imagined her to be languid and lovely."

The Peregrino began to go on about the miracles of Saint Death. According to him, she had helped people cross the border, had gotten others out of jail, and she helped many recover lost loves.

"The last night of every month you have to light candles for her, leave her an apple, and a bottle of tequila on the dresser."

"Do you light a candle for her?"

"Sometimes, when I remember. But, what was it you asked me first? Oh, I remember now. You want to know what she asked me for. Do you really want to know?"

Dante did not reply because he was driving and they were approaching Fresno. He did not want to make a mistake in the many turns he had to take.

"I'm going to compose a *corrido* for her, Dante."

He was silent for a few minutes.

"I haven't done it yet, but we'll do it soon. We have to start somewhere, and I believe we made a good start when we agreed to be called Los Peregrinos de la Santa Muerte. Maybe Saint Death herself whispered it into Alex's ear."

When they were entering La Perla de Fresno, the Peregrino slapped Dante on the back: "Come on, man, cheer up. I know you're still wondering what you're doing here and why you're not on the road looking for your daughter. But if you can't look for her, we'll give her a way to find you. You'll see, we'll be famous, and it won't be long before she finds us."

The hall was packed, and the people applauded even before each song began. Those in attendance were a very diverse audience. There were farmworkers, but more numerous were businesspeople and bureaucrats. One table was full of teachers from a local school who cheered throughout the show. There were also several Americans who were whistling, and this mortified Dante at first until he was told that in the United States whistling is a sign of approval. Age and taste were the only thing the large number of people had in common; generally they were people in their forties or older, and they loved romantic oldies and *corridos*.

After the first hour of the show, the musicians were led to a table where their Fresno sponsor, the owner of a local radio station, was sitting. He had also invited two reporters and two academics: a professor and a Ph.D. candidate who was writing his thesis on Latin American immigration. It was an informal press conference and the questions began. The Peregrino was in charge of answering them.

"Will you be doing any shows with Los Tigres del Norte?"

"God only knows."

"What record label do you work with?"

"None. We put out this first CD."

"You yourselves?"

"Yes, just us."

"Didn't a well-known businessman help you?"

"Bullshit!"

"One with kind of shady dealings, you know what I mean? I'm talking about smuggling."

"Bullshit! Are you asking or accusing?"

"Shall we say someone they call Güero?"

"That's nothing but bullshit."

"They say your songs are macho, patriarchal."

"More bullshit."

"How much do they pay you for writing a *corrido*?"

"It depends."

"On what?"

"On whether the interested party is a real man or a fuckin' faggot pretending to be a journalist."

The reporter who was asking the questions got up from the table, not because he felt indignant but because he was scared to death. In a leap, he headed for the exit. The other man from the press was nicer. Laughing hysterically at his colleague's escape, he began to congratulate them for their compositions. He spoke so fast and omitted so many "s's" that with so much noise in the room they couldn't understand him. He realized it and explained that he was Chilean and that's why he spoke like that.

"Is it true that you travel with a donkey and that his name is Virgilio?" He asked.

"Very true."

"Would you mind if I took your picture with Virgilio?"

"Well, just say the word. That's what we're here for, my friend! Come to our hotel tomorrow morning at seven."

"So early?"

"And what time do you think donkeys get up? You, what time do you get up?"

Dante was glad to hear that they would take his picture with his quadruped friend. Maybe Emmita would read the news in the paper. The only thing that worried him was whether Virgilio would agree to pose, if he would look toward the camera or stretch his disdainful neck to sniff other airs.

For his part, the doctoral candidate asked the Peregrino if he agreed with postmodern aesthetics.

"Post what?"

"What is your opinion on Octavio Paz's poetry?"

"I haven't read it."

"You mean that one shouldn't read Paz?"

"Listen, that's not what I said."

"Why aren't you interested in Paz?

"What band does he write for? No, my friend, don't make me say anything against any colleague. We all have the right to compose *corridos*."

The man from the radio station had to intervene because he had run into academics before, and he knew full well that they didn't understand popular singers and perhaps didn't understand Octavio Paz either.

"What he wants to know is whether you consider yourself a poet."

"And you too, right?"

The doctoral candidate then excused himself to go to the restroom and didn't return. Then the professor who was with him pretended to wave to someone in the audience and left also.

> *Two souls that in the world*
> *God had joined together*
> *two souls that loved each other*
> *that was you and me.*

The second night there were hundreds of people because, besides the fans of the endless repertoire of Los Peregrinos, a group of Saint Death devotees had also arrived. The show was dedicated to render homage to Javier Solís. At the request of the audience, Los Peregrinos would then perform some of their own songs.

Because of the bloody wound
of our immense love
we gave our lives to each other
as was never seen before.

One day, on the path
which our souls were crossing,
a shadow of hatred arose
that separated you and me.
And from that moment on
it would have been better to die
neither near nor far away
can we any longer go on.

Other songs followed: "I awoke in your arms," "Ashes," "Desperately," and finally "Bésame mucho," which everyone sang over and over. The Peregrino started each song, and the people would repeat it. Many then begged them to sing it again. At the end of the show, the manager of La Perla de Fresno announced that he did not have permission to keep the establishment open after two o'clock in the morning and that, in a few more minutes, he would have to close. He added that, at his insistence, Los Peregrinos had agreed to stay through Saturday and do one more show, in which their original compositions would be performed. Again, as the lights blinked on and off to urge the crowd to leave, people kept on singing Javier Solís' song:

Bésame, bésame mucho
as if this night were the last time.
Kiss me, kiss me a lot,
for I'm afraid I'll lose you, lose you tonight.

On Saturday, the man from the radio station and the manager of La Perla de Fresno got together to urge Los Peregrinos to stay for a several-week engagement. Their success was so great that it allowed them to guarantee them a lucrative contract for all of that time. But Alex courteously declined the offer and assured them that they would consider the invitation for next year. For now, that very Sunday morning, they would leave to fulfill commitments in San Bernardino, Los Angeles, and San Diego, and that was only California. After that, they were to continue on to Arizona, New Mexico, and Texas, and after finishing their show at the El Patio Hotel in El Paso, Texas, they would have to leave immediately for Berkeley and San Francisco.

The last show began with a nostalgic trip through the ballad that the Peregrino had written in homage to several acquaintances, a soccer team, and some Mexican politicians, and on the occasion of the race riots in Los Angeles, the hurricane that devastated Miami, and an earthquake that had leveled Mexico City. His favorite topic was the men and women who walk beneath the river or the land and cross the border to invade a land that they also consider theirs. At the end, however, people insisted that the band repeat two songs: "The *corrido* of Juan Miguel" and "Angélica the Courtesan," which made many of them cry. There were men, young and old, dressed like the horseman of the skies. *Fly, fly, Juan Miguel . . .*

Angélica's story was very unfortunate. When she was just a little girl, her stepfather had sold her to a white slave trader. But since she was just skin and bones, she had no clients. So the pimp had to feed her for six months before reselling her to a Guadalajara brothel. From there the girl escaped and took refuge in a convent. However, the pimp paid a few more pesos and got her back. Finally, Angélica asked the police for help, but they raped her and sold her to the prisoners in the jail. The head of the damned pimp rolled in the closing verses while the radiant young woman flew above misfortune and across borders in the maternal arms of Saint Death.

"Blessing, blessing!"

They had finished the recital and were getting ready to leave with Alex and the radio station manager, when a woman threw herself into Dante's arms loudly asking him to bless her. She had dyed blond hair and very long eyelashes and was about forty years old.

"Blessing! God in Heaven, don't deny it to me, please."

The woman was kneeling. "Don't deny me your blessing. Tell God to forgive me."

Seeing as how Dante was frozen and did not know what to do next, the Peregrino came over and put his right hand on the head of the crying woman. He whispered something inaudible into her ear. It is not known whether he prayed or cried with her. When the pleading woman left, everything about her had changed. Her face was transfigured as if some ancient joy had been returned to her, as if she were learning how to be happy again.

The following day, as he was driving toward San Bernardino, Dante looked at his companion with greater curiosity and wondered what heavenly power he had exercised to calm the woman. He didn't see where those gifts could have come from to a man with the vulgar appearance, loud hats, exuberant belly, and loud horse's voice.

"No. It's not what you're thinking?"

"It isn't?"

"No."

"And how did you know what I was thinking?"

"I knew, that's all."

Dante thought that his companion was trying to silence him, but that wasn't it either.

"I want to tell you that I'm not a witch doctor or a saint. I'm a singer of the people, that's all."

He was going to stay quiet, but he couldn't contain himself.

"The world, this whole globe that we call the world, doesn't have its own light. It's darker than what it is. Those who live here could be lost, but we, the singers, are like guides that remind everyone of their life and their paths. It's through us that people take strength to go on living, to keep giving it their all. Those who suffer know that, like that woman you saw last night."

"Did she say anything to you?" Dante asked and did so just to ask. He had been present, and he knew that the woman had not opened her mouth except to ask for a blessing.

"Nothing."

"Then?"

"It was written on her forehead."

"On her forehead?"

"Yes, she had her story there. Her whole story. It's normal. We all carry it there. Both you and I and anyone who is listening to us at this moment."

The Peregrino took off his belt with its enormous silver buckle. Then he unbuttoned the top button of his pants to free his magnificent belly. He reclined his seat and rested his head on the headrest, but he didn't fall asleep. Virgilio had to move so he wouldn't squash him.

"She went to La Perla de Fresno to have fun. Rather, she went to hear us, to sing our songs, and to say goodbye. Yes, she went to say goodbye because it's her time to die."

"Is she sick?"

"The fact is, she's going to die."

"I asked you if she's sick."

"I don't know, but it's already predetermined that she's going to die."

"What could she die of?"

The Peregrino stretched like a cat. Then he started talking, not allowing interruptions: "Let's assume that when she was a very little girl, she entered this country with her parents and they died, leaving her alone. What did they die of? Anybody's guess. But that's not what we're talking about. What we want to know is who took her in. Let's assume that it was a family from here that took her as a goddaughter, but in fact used her like a little servant, and at suppertime, they made her eat under the table. What does that girl do? Well! Once she's an adolescent she runs away and goes back to Mexico. There she gets together with a good young man, and they have two children, but some time later, he comes to the United States as a *bracero*. And what happens then? Well! Every month, he writes her and sends her money to feed the children and also his mother who has remained under her care. But time passes, and nothing further is heard from him. Either he's found another woman or he's died, and there is no one to report a Mexican who dies under those circumstances. Time passes again, and she comes here to work with her children and her mother-in-law. Let's assume that here she finds another companion, but not a good one, a son-of-a-bitch who fathers two more children by her and abandons her. What does that woman do to support her family? She works all day and all night. In what? Don't ask me because I'm not a psychic. Let's think that this happens for many years and that Saint Death takes pity on her and comes down to get her. Let's think about that. So, what does the woman do? Well, when she feels old and useless, she goes one night to La Perla de Fresno to say goodbye and ask for a blessing. No, sir, none of this is true. You invent another story, or let the Lord keep inventing them. . . . Every story is the same."

Dante wondered if the heat of the desert was making his companion delirious and asked him a question to change the subject but got no response. So, he took his eyes off the road for an instant and turned toward him to see what was wrong. He discovered that the musician's belly was rising and falling rhythmically; he was already in the deepest, most peaceful sleep, and was snoring like a singer or a poet does when he's sure of what he is. He noted that Virgilio too had allowed himself to be carried away by sleep and was sleeping with the tranquility that only a donkey can have.

Dante stepped on the accelerator and proceeded all the way to San Bernardino; their next show would be in San Diego. In both places, dozens of their fans, interested in the stories of bad guys but also in talking about Saint Death and the Virgin of Migration as well as other inhabitants of heaven who protect those who cross the border, were anxiously awaiting them.

In the El Chalán Peruano restaurant in Los Angeles, many of those gathered belonged to that nationality, as well as Ecuadorians, Colombians, Chileans, and Bolivians who filled the tables and spoke of a Peruvian saint named Sarita Colonia who had made many people invisible to the eyes of the immigration officers.

In response to Dante's question, they recounted Sarita's poor childhood in Lima and gave him holy cards in which the young woman, dark, small, and homely, appeared against a pink background surrounded by innocent flowers. When he asked where she had been born and how she had died, the devotees did not have an exact answer nor could they agree.

"I never saw a saint like that in any church."

"No, of course not. In heaven, she still hasn't been recognized. They still have to have a trial in Rome and go through some formalities."

"How can you know if Sarita is close to you?" Dante asked.

They told him that the spirit of Sarita Colonia is present when a pungent scent of white lilies reaches us. At that moment, the person who breathes it realizes once and for all what life is: dust, smoke, nothing and wind, emptiness, darkness, oblivion, absence, dream, solitude, illusion, and death. Suddenly, while they were talking about the saint, Dante began to smell the pungent scent of the white lilies.

"And it is possible to ask her questions?"

"Like what?"

"Like where to find someone you're looking for . . ."

They all fell silent, but a Chilean woman advised Dante to commend himself to Saint Rita, patron saint of the impossible.

Someone else told that at a Venezuelan restaurant in Houston, Texas, he was shown the photograph of a naked woman who performed miracles, but she was a witch not a saint. He was told that her monument stood in the middle of a Caracas freeway, in the middle of the city with her private parts showing.

"Naked. That's right, naked. With some relentless legs around the neck of an enormous jaguar."

"Has she done a miracle for you?" Dante asked.

"You know it, man! Of course. María Lionza helped me at the Miami airport. My passport and visa were fake, and the damn officer was looking at them with a magnifying glass. He was taking forever. An eternity, man. So, I started praying to my fellow countrywoman, and I promised her that I was going to have three masses said for her if she helped me cross. Suddenly, the guy picked up the stamp, put it on my document, and told me in Spanish that I could be in the United States for six months. What do you think that is? A miracle, man. The immigration guy, a real specialist, didn't realize the passport was fake, even though he looked at it for a long time. I believe that he didn't see my face, but María Lionza's legs."

"I'd do the same thing!" another Venezuelan chimed in. "Don't look at the guy's face."

"And did you keep your promise of having the masses said for her?"

"I feel guilty when I think about it. No, man, I forgot, but one of these days . . ."

"Has she appeared to you? Have you ever seen her?"

As the Venezuelan was starting to respond, Dante was already thinking of his next question. What he really wanted was to get to the one he considered most important: what to do to call María Lionza.

"I don't know. Seeing her, actually seeing her, I don't think so. Let's say I felt her presence. Let's say that her yellow odor, her sticky warmth, reached me. Nothing can be known of her, but she does indeed help us. Ask her for anything you want, and she will grant it to you."

"Anything I want?"

"Anything you want. But come here. What do you want, man? Do you want me to tell you what to do to call her? . . . Call her with your accordion, because she loves music."

María Lionza
pagan goddess,
I'm singing to you,
I'm falling for you,
I can see you
because I want to
what you've shown us:
the border without officers,
the world without borders,
the moon in the background and the jaguar at
*   your feet.*
And I want to see
the moon above
the sun below,
María Lionza,
pagan goddess,
the world without borders.
María Lionza, my dear.
Your amazing legs that no one can see.

Dante thought that perhaps María Lionza was not the most appropriate person to give him information about his daughter. Besides, he felt shy. He thought he wasn't going to know what to do nor where to look if the lady with the relentless legs presented herself to him. But a few days later, desperate, he began to call her with his accordion, while the Peregrino improvised the words to a future song.

Another month went by with no news of Emmita. In Santa Fe, New Mexico, Los Peregrinos de la Santa Muerte became friends with other Venezuelans who also spoke of María Lionza. They acknowledged her merits, but they were not her devotees. Rather, they had another saint that performed miracles. It was an entire family. The father had suffered from an incurable disease, and he had to leave his job in a government office. Unemployed, he had no way to support his small children, but he commended himself to José Gregorio Hernández, a doctor from Caracas who has lived in heaven for eighty years, and thanks to him, he regained his health. Additionally, in the lottery that the U.S. Embassy holds every year, he got a visa to enter the United States.

The story seemed remarkable to him, but the only bad thing for Dante was that Doctor Hernández's specialty was not looking for young women who had run away from home.

In San Antonio, Texas, a captivated audience did not want to let them leave the restaurant where they were performing until they repeated many times the "*Corrido* of the Ghost Guitar" that the Peregrino had composed. The ballad told the story of when Dante found himself in the desert with the bodies of three mariachis who had crossed the border to become famous. In the song, the wind covered and uncovered the bodies, from time to time, but the guitar was forever heard upon the shining plain forever and ever, time without end.

The ballads triggered conversations about crossing the border. Some people spoke up and told how they had crossed the Rio Grande thanks to the intercession of María Sabina, a sorceress from Tlaxcala Lake, who sounded her enchanted timbrel and the waters parted to allow the people through.

They told Dante that María Sabina was the best expert on mushrooms and that among them, there were children and elderly, dwarves and giants, hateful and in love, and also those of love and forgetting; she had domesticated all the species. But Dante was not interested in mushrooms but in his daughter's whereabouts.

In El Paso, Texas, after an extraordinary performance, they rested for a couple of days in the El Patio Hotel. In the hotel restaurant, there was an enormous mural showing Pancho Villa who, according to what they told him, had stayed there when he invaded the United States.

During the day, Alex invited them to lunch in Ciudad Juárez. All they had to do was walk over the bridge to get to Mexico.

"You all go without me. If I go, I might not be able to come back."

The manager, who prided himself on being able to buy any one in the world, advised him not to worry because, if necessary, he would pay the bribe.

"The gringos accept them too; you just have to know how to talk to them."

"It's not that. I don't know if my feet would let me come back. I don't know what would happen if they touched Mexican soil again," Dante said.

❦ ❦ ❦

Their path was being made by leaps and bounds due to Alex's skills as an amazing negotiator. Wherever they went, he got additional contracts. In this way they went through all the states in the South and West of the United States. The plan was that the tour would end in El Paso, but Alex received an invitation to do two shows one weekend in Miami, and they accepted. They left Virgilio boarded at a stable in El Paso, and the great Florida city was the only place to which they traveled by plane.

The Moros y Cristianos restaurant scheduled Los Peregrinos de la Santa Muerte for two nights of "Latin Nostalgia," a Friday and Saturday when they performed music and songs by Agustín Lara, Jorge Negrete, Pedro Infante, and Javier Solís, among others. Iván Ganoza, the owner of the restaurant, had a few drinks and began to sing with them until Pilar, his wife, discretely managed to get him off the stage.

The Ganozas were Cuban, and this was their second business. Their first one had been destroyed in 1992 by Hurricane Floyd, a monster that came down from the sky to destroy 76,000 homes and left many lands changed into something like the crater of a volcano. Their present establishment included a more spacious locale and was in a more prestigious area north of Miami Beach.

"In 1999 we were about to lose this one. Hurricane Bonita almost destroyed it. But Saint Barbara saved us."

"Saint Barbara?"

"My mother brought her from Cuba. My mother came here from Cuba on a raft, just to bring us a Saint Barbara. She always said we needed a Saint Barbara, and that because we didn't have one, we had lost our previous business."

Among the stories that the Peregrinos had heard, there were few like this one. The Ganozas told them that in September of that year, Bonita was bearing down on Miami at more than ninety kilometers an hour; she would stop at an island, rest for a few days, and be back on the attack. People began to evacuate to states to the north. Those who stayed in the city boarded up windows and doors and were expecting the worst.

The tension lasted for more than a week. Nevertheless, when Bonita was just a hundred meters from Miami, she suddenly stopped. There she stayed for an hour, roaring and howling. Then a wave formed whose height surpassed all those that have been seen since the continent was formed. It covered the sky. From that wave came wind, black doves, silence, cold, death, nightmares, oblivion, and the oblivion of oblivion. Suddenly, Bonita disappeared.

"Bonita sat there looking at Miami, and then as if she were scorning us, she turned north and from there toward the north of north, and she flew off until she disappeared," Iván Ganoza said and then sat there thinking.

"You say that Saint Barbara saved you?"

"That's what I say."

"And that your mother brought her?"

"That's right."

"Is your mother the elderly woman in the photograph? She came alone in a raft? But, how could that be? When did she bring her?"

"I'm telling you she brought her, and that's all. Would you like a *mojito*?"

When they were about to leave El Paso, they were joined by a man they had met at the stable where Virgilio had stayed. People smuggler Curcio Fernández Arce asked them for a ride. Curcio was no longer a *coyote* because he was quite old and had begun to lose his vision. He had smuggled people across the border for more than twenty years, but he felt that his time to retire was approaching, and he was going to San Jose, California, where he had bought a house. With his son, he planned to open a taco stand and live in the Golden State for the rest of his life.

He was fat and almond-eyed, with straight hair and quite dark skin. His father had been a Mexican and his mother a Nez Perce Indian from Oregon.

"The strange part of all this is that they call me *coyote*. I'm a *coyote* by profession, but I've also been a coyote since I was a child, because my mother raised me as an Indian and commended me to the care of the coyotes since before I was born. Everyone else in my family has been crows; I'm the only coyote."

The Peregrino and Dante were used to stories that didn't make sense. They let him talk and didn't interrupt him, and Curcio took advantage of the opportunity to tell them the story of the world as his mother had told it to him.

"In the beginning, there was no one. A very soft darkness spun around all sides of the void. Then, the crow beat and beat the darkness with his wings until he got it to compress and turn into solid ground. But all that came from that was a frozen black ocean and a thin coast. When people came, they bumped into each other because everything was very dark. What's more, they had nothing to eat.

"Noticing this, the crow pulled some branches off an alder tree and dropped them onto the ocean. Soon the leaves were absorbed, and the water began to bubble. The leaves returned to the surface, or rather, they jumped, transformed into fishes, and so now people could eat and fish.

"The people became so happy that they forgot that the world was a dark globe, and to this day, they act as if that were not the case. There are enormous nights that last for years and centuries, and the wicked take advantage and steal from us. Our world is very disorderly because, in the darkness, our lands have dried up, and when you try to leave them, you find yourself crossing borders.

"In order to solve this problem, *coyotes* were created. *Coyotes* are born with the mission of leading people, becoming their guides, and taking them to where they can be happy. In the former times, when the Indians were the owners of the land, the coyotes were trackers of game. Now, the *coyotes* are just coyotes. They have eyes to see behind the mountains, the water, and the night. They can change shape and transform themselves into trees, birds, or snakes. Therefore, immigration agents can do nothing against them."

"Do you transform yourself?"

"Don't you?"

Curcio wore very thick glasses and perhaps heard more than he saw, but he turned his head and acted as though he was looking at his questioners.

"Who's there? Who's in the back with us?"

The Peregrino explained to him that it was Virgilio, the mascot that had brought them great luck.

Curcio looked toward the sky as blind people do and said that the donkey was an animal close to God, that the weak, solitary, sustained braying was like a bell ringing. He said it with a great deal of certainty and kept looking toward the sky.

Then Dante dared to ask him if he could track a very beloved person that he was looking for.

"You'll do it yourself. You yourself are tracking her, and you are about to find her because you carry her deep in your heart."

❀ ❀ ❀

The road from El Paso to San Francisco was interrupted by many invitations to perform, all of which would make a total of eighty-four shows on the tour. Besides that, they met thousands of people who told them, in addition to joys and tribulations, the odyssey of their passage toward this other side of the world.

Curcio stayed in San Jose. He asked them to drop him off on a corner, and Dante parked his vehicle to help the old man in case he didn't know where he was. Through the rearview mirror, he observed that the man, finally on land, breathed deeply three or four mouthfuls of fresh air and moved his lips from one side to the other as if he were tasting the air or brushing his teeth. Then he turned his face toward the streets that met at the corner. He discovered that he did not need to look at the city to orient himself. He raised his nose and began to sniff the wind. Perhaps he noticed that he was being watched, and he quickly took one of the streets. It seemed to Dante that the last thing he saw of him was a coyote's tail moving quickly back and forth.

Four eagles, huddled on a power pole along the road, shook their wings at the headlights. It was as if they had been waiting for them. Then they took silent, serious flight toward the black depths of the universe.

"Eagles," Dante said.

"Crows."

"Eagles."

"Crows."

"Yes, they must be crows."

❀ ❀ ❀

Back on the road to San Francisco, the duo was silent for half an hour. Dante broke the silence to comment that the people in heaven were very busy helping their people walk. The Peregrino then wondered: "Could Saint Death be another name for the Virgin Mary?"

"Perhaps."

"My God! What is that woman doing with so many names?"

Then they began to remember the mysterious forms with which a slim, pretty blue woman helped travelers who commended themselves to her. They tried to remember some of the names they had heard along the way.

"Virgin of Guadalupe."

"Virgin of Carmen."

"Virgin of la Soledad."

"Virgin of Bethany."

"Virgin of Chiquinquirá."

"Virgin of Tears."

"Virgin of Coromoto."

"Divine Pastor."

"Virgin of Copacabana."

"Virgin of the Door."

"Beheaded Virgin."

"Virgin of Dolores."

"Virgin of the Rose."

"Virgin of the Rosary."

"Virgin of Mercy."

"Mystical Rose."

"Ark of the Covenant."

"Tower of David."

"Virgin of Charity of el Cobre."

"Virgin of Perpetual Help."

"Virgin of the Immaculate Conception."

"Virgin of Light."

"Virgin of Consolation."

"Virgin of Lourdes."

"Virgin of Pilar."

"Virgin of Fátima."

When they stopped to rest on the way, Dante took out his accordion and began to play a melody that he did not remember where he had learned. Then the Peregrino sang:

If the sea that spills over the world
had as much love as it has cold water,
out of love, its name would be called María,
and not just sea, as we call it now.

Night fell. Alex joined them. The crickets and the frogs were singing. A scent of eucalyptus was running through the world.

The Peregrino stopped singing. Dante slowly opened and closed the bellows of the accordion and produced a wordless melody that sounded like the saddest music on the planet.

It was already very dark, but they resumed their trip. They had to follow the Cheyenne driven by Alex. The manager's instructions were clear: they should arrive in San Francisco as soon as possible. They were scheduled for La Grande, where they had an interview very early in the morning. This would greatly help publicize their shows. At dawn, an intense odor of sea let them know that they were nearing the coast, and then, all the rest was a succession of signs announcing cities, one after the other. Very soon, the road signs indicated to them that they were entering San Francisco.

In San Francisco, an applauding crowd followed them all the way through the Mission District, and they were showered with gifts from all sides. The children wanted their pictures taken with Virgilio, and reporters from the Spanish-language media wanted photos for their front pages. They invited them into their homes and served them everything from modest tamales to healthy dinners in exchange for the simple pleasure of their company. They did not want to force them to sing at their homes. They did not wish to take advantage of their friendship, although deep down there was a certain degree of self-interest in all of that. They weren't aspiring to be characters in a *corrido*; that was beyond their expectations. However, they felt that a singer is a refuge against the sorrows of this world, and so they told them their troubles in great detail. The death of a relative over there, on the other side, the unjust incarceration of a friend, the betrayal by a lover, everything was included in the story, and the Peregrino and Dante never asked them to be quiet. But no one, anywhere, was able to tell Dante anything about his daughter or the young man she was with. It was as if they had never even been born. It was as if she lived only in a dream or an illusion of Dante's. When people replied that they didn't know anything about them, the world was again the dark dream that it was before it was created.

Finally, one night at a Salvadoran friend's restaurant, the Peregrino said that he was inspired to write a song. He asked for a guitar accompaniment and began to sing the story of his friend Dante, "Dante's Ballad."

> *This is the corrido that sings the sorrow*
> *of wandering minstrel Dante Celestino.*
> *In the south and in the north, he lost his way*
> *wandering pilgrim in a foreign land.*
>
> *Feeding on dreams, he crossed the border,*
> *spent ten years without his love.*
> *Finally they were together, her name was Beatriz,*
> *they united in sweet, crazy springtime.*
>
> *Beatriz went to Heaven on a star,*
> *their dear daughter fled into the distance.*
> *Their fate was cursed, their joy had died,*
> *wandering troubador, treacherous world.*
>
> *The clouds and wind told nothing,*
> *his wounded heart fell toward Hell,*
> *he felt Hell spilling into his blood,*
> *his broken soul filled with trembling.*
>
> *His guide Virgilio, the good little donkey,*
> *listened to him all along the way,*
> *Dante Celestino sang and cried,*
> *nothing was a stranger to his grief.*

Speak to Emmita, sing at her window,
fly little dove, go 'round the world again,
to the north and the south, the heights and the depths,
tell her her father will be there tomorrow.

Speak to Emmita, sing at her window,
tell her her father will be there tomorrow.

That night, Emmita, if she was somewhere in the universe, was turning eighteen. Her father had by now traveled three-quarters of the United States at Virgilio's side. His dreams did not weigh him down, but his eyelids were heavy as if he wanted to cry or ask himself questions with his eyes closed.

25
Death Is Impossible when You're Used to Living

Interior: short shift knob, black embossed leather seats, and steering wheel. Exterior: Icon wheels, silver wing, tinted windows, carbon-fiber hood, and 360-degree power mirrors. Performance: air intake, super suspension, and combustion gas products that explode when cruising speed is reached. The lowrider destined to impress and stun.

It was a Daimler Chrysler that was not born that way but that a mechanic friend of Johnny's had painstakingly modified. The red, aerodynamic body was mounted over three-quarters of the wheels, and the tires were barely visible. The car proceeded silently, as if dragging its feet, until the moment when its driver decided that it should resonate like a combat tank.

The muffler was very low, and when the lowrider bounced, it hit the ground and produced blue, red, and yellow sparks. This time it was being driven by Johnny's best friend and right-hand man, the Águila Azteca, the Aztec Eagle, who was traveling in the company of three serious, silent young men with their shiny hair slicked back, as if it had been licked by a loving cow.

Two kilometers behind them, Johnny Cabada's huge motorcycle roared. He had decided to keep that distance for security reasons, but they planned to meet at a motel along the way. They were coming down out of the Nevada mountains toward San Francisco Bay. They took advantage of the narrow country roads because they were safer. The zigzag route led them through a thick forest of pine trees that were more black than green. There, only God would witness their trip, along with the moon that peered out and then disappeared again among the pointed treetops.

Dressed in gray, with black boots and helmet, on the back of the motorcycle, Emmita had her arms around Johnny. The men in the lowrider did not think that was a good idea, and they were convinced that love is always blind to danger.

All of them wore headphones; Emmita listened to Selena through hers. Behind the motorcycle a cold wind whistled.

When they got on the freeway, it occurred to Johnny to check the rearview mirror, and he discovered that two enormous vans had turned suddenly as if they were following him. He pulled into the passing lane in order to make sure, and the vehicles did the same.

Since they were much more powerful than the motorcycle, one of them passed him, leaving them trapped between the two. Therefore, without intending to, Johnny was forced to turn off, but thanks to a daring maneuver, he was able to get back on the highway. Suddenly he found himself in a no-passing zone, but he could see a stretch of highway ahead that would allow him to escape. He pulled into the left lane and passed the truck in front of him. Then he accelerated quickly toward the lanes of oncoming traffic. Heading in the other direction, he felt that he was finally free of the pursuers. He saw them continuing on in the other direction. He managed to pull in behind a beat-up truck from which garden tools protruded.

"They'll switch over to this lane, but I don't think they'll catch us now," he thought as he pressed the motorcycle to a speed that was unusual and impossible on any other occasion, especially on a highway with so many curves. Nevertheless, despite all his efforts, ten minutes later he was in the same situation again. This time he made visual contact and was able to make out, next to the driver, a man dressed in green. The man shouted something when they passed him, but the only thing Johnny was able to see was the flashing of his mirror sunglasses.

At any rate, he was determined not to be defeated so easily.

"Hang on!" he shouted to Emmita, as he stepped on the brake with all his remaining strength.

The vehicle threw off sparks and stopped in the middle of the freeway. To avoid hitting him, the truck behind him went off the road, skidded, and overshot him. Suddenly, Johnny slid off to one side of the road to allow other vehicles to pass him and so his pursuers would continue on.

But the night became a storm. The sky filled with trees of fire that extended their branches and roots north and south, east and west. At that moment, the motorcycle slid slowly down the shoulder and glided smoothly over to a huge sequoia.

Without turning off the motorcycle, Johnny kept going, trying to hide in the blackness of the forest, where the croaking of toads was heard. Suddenly, one of the vans was on him like a damned sun. The head-on collision totaled the motorcycle and threw its passengers through the air.

The occupants of the van stopped the vehicle, but left it with its lights on and then went to check on the couple.

"Are they dead?"

"I imagine so."

"It's better if they are."

They hadn't died. Two of the men tied the motorcyclist's hands behind his back. They tied a rope around Emmita's neck and pulled her toward the van. The leader went over to Johnny and with an iron rod that he carried in his left hand knocked Johnny to the ground. In his right hand he carried a pistol.

"Bingo!"

"Son of a bitch!"

"Let's see if I can guess. You're Johnny!"

He kicked the fallen man in the face with his boot and shouted again: "Bingo!"

Then he put his foot on top of him and made a theatrical gesture to inform his people that the most important task was accomplished.

"Ladies and gentlemen," he shouted and he was going to go on, but he realized that Johnny was trying to stand up.

"Shit!"

He hit him in the knees several times with the iron rod until it was impossible for Johnny to make any move toward getting up.

"Yes, gentlemen. Here we have none other than Johnny Cabada . . . And he is in very good company!"

"Leave her alone!"

The man took off his sunglasses to take a closer look at the girl.

"In *very* good company!"

"Leave her alone . . . I'm the one you want!"

A bird sang. Despite the night, the leader of the assailants put his dark glasses back on. They were off the highway, but the light from the passing cars made his gloved fingers shine.

"I told you to leave her alone!"

"You're in no position to be giving orders, Johnny. Oh, Johnny!" he exclaimed in an ambiguous tone as he struck the young man's back again and again with the iron rod.

They were in a clearing in the forest, and the highway ran nearby, but no one could observe the scene from the asphalt strip. If anyone did see the vans and an overturned motorcycle, they perhaps thought it was the police making an arrest.

Then another vehicle arrived. It pulled off the road, entered the lit clearing, and parked. Someone opened a door from inside and pushed two of Johnny's men out.

One of them, near death, fell at the feet of the man with the iron rod. The latter pushed him aside with his boot. He approached the one that was unharmed.

"Are you Águila Azteca?"

Johnny looked up and recognized his closest friend.

Águila Azteca looked at him and knew that it was all over. Then he turned to look at the man with the iron rod, he held the pistol. There was neither defiance nor sadness in his young eyes. The man pointed the iron rod off in the distance.

Águila looked the way he pointed. The man put the pistol against Águila's neck and fired.

The shot bounced from mountain to mountain, and the young man's head exploded.

When the shot stopped echoing, Águila Azteca's body collapsed completely next to the young man who had arrived with him. Then, as if death had held out her arms, an almost absolute silence followed, broken only by the voice of the dying man who, rather than moaning, was making a sound like gargling.

On a maple branch, a crow was watching. It had its head tucked between its wings. It began to cry out.

Then the assailants looked at Captain Colina, their boss, waiting for him to come up with another way of killing Johnny. Emmita's fate was also easy to predict. He would use her to satisfy his fantasies, and then he would sell her at a brothel or find another way to get rid of her.

The men made Johnny stand up, and Johnny again asked them to let Emma go, but the leader hit him in the mouth with the pistol, and blood gushed out.

"Do you want me to break your teeth one by one? It's obvious you were born here. You have all the gringos' tricks, but I'm from South America, and I've served in my country's glorious army. That's where men learn to be men."

The dying man stopped singing. He didn't do so because his soul had left him, but because, at the captain's order, the men picked him up and stood him against a tree as if he were drunk.

"I've never liked singers," Captain Colina informed him.

The young man raised his cloudy eyes toward him as if wanting to ask him how he was going to kill him, but he no longer had any voice left except to make the gargling sound again. The man did not raise the gun again. Instead, he went to him and, like one drunk with another, embraced him. With his free hand, he put the weapon away in one of the large pockets of his army jacket and pretended to take his time looking for something else in the same pocket, from which he finally pulled a hunting knife.

"No, sir. I've never liked singers," he repeated, and with the hand he was holding him with, he took his face and forced him to look up toward the sky. At that instant, as if the ritual had already been performed, he took hold of the knife with the professionalism of a barber and cut off his head.

The blood came flying out of the dead man's neck as if instead of blood it were a flock of black butterflies.

"It's Coca Cola, bastard! Doesn't it look like Coca Cola?"

The dying man was still standing, leaning against the tree as he had been before, like a drunk, but without a head. Perhaps the cloudy eyes in the rolling head remained in life much longer than the body, or perhaps it was just the opposite because the body trembled. No one can know.

"There are two of your men, Johnny. We'll have to see what we do with them," said Captain Colina.

Between the clouds, the moon showed dark red. The crow stopped cawing and flew toward it.

Leonidas García's head of security was a South American soldier who had specialized in torture and murder of civilians in his country. He was part of a unit that murdered persecuted politicians, their families, and their lawyers. The techniques of torture, mutilation, and rape were part of the "intelligence" training he had received in order to intimidate the population that did not believe in the government's democratic, Christian principles. Among the feats that he remembered and bragged about was that of having kidnapped ten college students and their professor and having burned them alive. He had buried their burned bodies and clothing, leaving them "disappeared."

"They were terrorists. They may have gone off to join the guerrillas," the country's president said with a strong Asian accent when foreign journalists asked about the students' whereabouts.

On another occasion, a group of very young guerrillas occupied a foreign embassy to demand the freedom of other members of their group. Captain Colina was one of those charged with removing them from the embassy, and when he found out that some of the rebels were still alive, he put his gun to their heads, forced them to kneel, and shot them between the eyes.

When the dictatorship ended in that republic, the democratic government, eager to establish good relations with the army, awarded him a medal for his actions at the embassy and declared him a national hero, but at the same time arranged for him to go to the United States so that the ghosts would not pursue him. There, he was to live with a passport and legal immigrant visa that bore another name to prevent international human rights commissions from having him arrested for torture and genocide. But Colina did not try to keep his secret; on the contrary, he had always gotten security jobs by boasting of his bloodthirsty talents, and he had let word of them spread among his subordinates to inspire fear in them.

Before working in San Francisco, he was well paid in a border job. The Patriots paid him for helping them rid the country of undesirables. According to the arrangement, he was to frighten the illegal immigrants or chase them back across the border, but sometimes he went too far. Then the Patriots scolded him or pretended not to know, but they made it clear to him that their attorneys would not defend him nor would they acknowledge knowing him if anything happened. In general, they were happy with his skills and his lack of scruples. For his part, he told them that he did it not only for the money but also for the pleasure, because, like them, he did not care for those filthy, disgusting, half-breed, savage, stupid, brown, black, dark, monkeys, Indians, who were coming to ruin the American race. He said it with pleasure, but when he spewed out the string of racist epithets, the Patriots were a little surprised because they didn't see much physical difference between him and the rest of the immigrants.

But, unlike the Patriots, there were also generous gringos who left food and drink along the immigrants' routes. That was where Captain Colina slipped up. They were paying him a lot of money, and he thought they would reward him even more for the head of one of those terrorist gringos. One day he presented his boss with a container full of alcohol that held the pale face, yellow hair, and blue eyes of one of the alleged enemies. That was when the Patriots got scared and gave him one hour to leave or they would report him to the police.

Far from there, in San Francisco, Leonidas García hired him to head his security force. Their work relationship had gone well for several years. Leonidas was not unaware of the captain's dark specialties nor had he failed to recognize that many years earlier he could have been one of his victims, but he was impressed with his efficiency and his military discipline.

With Johnny tied to the same tree as his dead companions, the Captain Colina decided to have a little more fun.

"What's your name, honey?"

There was no response.

"You're quiet, but very pretty."

The men were watching the scene with curiosity, waiting to see what entertainment Colina had in store for them.

Finally, Colina stopped being nice and ordered: "Turn around!"

As he was saying this, he punched Johnny in the face.

Emmita obeyed. "You look really good. Now, come here."

Colina moved forward, embraced her, and began to caress the long hair that reached to her waist. Then he took her by her hair, pulled her head back as if to make her look at the sky. Then he started to look with delight at the length of her throat and the blue line of her veins. Suddenly he pulled harder on her hair until Emma fell to her knees.

"I like you better like that."

Emmita started to say something quietly. It was impossible to determine whether she was saying words or trying to inhale the odor that forms on the earth after a rain.

"Do you want to fly to heaven?"

She started crying. Her tears were flowing, but she was no longer making a sound.

"It's really easy, you know?"

In the midst of the night, the sky got brighter than ever.

"You can choose any heaven there is."

A north wind started blowing.

"But there's no one up there, you know? . . . No one."

Captain Colina ordered his men to put the two men's bodies into one of the vans, and to everyone's surprise, he didn't put his gun to Johnny's neck nor did he take Emmita yet.

"Don Leonidas is going to want to meet you," he said to Johnny.

"As for you, if you behave yourself, I might take you to my house," he promised Emmita.

Finally, the car, followed by the vans, proceeded down a road that Emmita and Johnny, although they didn't see it, guessed was gravel and barely even a road. Many hours later, they reached a house.

"Get out! Hurry up!" the captain shouted. As Johnny tried with great difficulty to get up, one of the men opened what looked like a garage and pushed them toward it. Inside, all that was visible was a metal door and a corrugated tin roof.

"Let her go! I told you to let her go!" Johnny screamed.

"If it were up to me, I'd cut out your tongue, but I can't because the boss is gonna want you to talk," Captain Colina said.

Then they closed the thick metal door and put two locks on it.

"Yell and scream all you want. No one will hear you. Scream and call the dear souls from purgatory. Don't they say that Mexicans and their children talk to the dead and to the Virgin of Guadalupe?"

"Are we going to leave them without any water, boss?"

"What do you think? By the way, would you like us to leave them a TV, too?"

They left, and the hours began to pass very slowly. Emmita and Johnny lay side by side in the garage. Emmita, who had been badly injured in the fall from the motorcycle, awoke from time to time, not knowing if it was day or night, but she knew that death was close by. She tried to talk to Johnny, but he was just a mess of flesh and blood, and he didn't respond. It was unbearably hot. The corrugated tin roof intensified the heat to the point that a deathly thirst reached her much sooner than she would have dreamed. Finally, as if death were lulling her, she fell asleep.

Emmita dreamt that she was dead and her parents were holding her wake. In the midst of the dream, she thought that she couldn't be dead because she didn't see a shining tunnel like they say is at the gate to Heaven, but instead felt the dreadful desire to die as soon as possible. From one moment to the next she thought she saw sparks in the garage, she thought it was the angels coming for her. She began to fear that the angels wouldn't be able to get into that very airtight morgue to accomplish their task.

For his part, during the moments when he regained consciousness, Johnny felt guilty for the deaths of his friends and for what might happen to Emmita. Dying didn't upset him too much. But sometimes death seemed impossible to him because he was too used to living. Suddenly, he felt, more than heard, a sweet voice calling him, "Now, Johnny, now," and he began to know what heaven was even before having set foot on those lands up there.

A slow bolt of lightning stretched across the cosmos. The thunder boomed so loudly that it seemed to come not just from the sky but also from the earth. It was as if heaven and earth were departing and separating forever. Two long lightning bolts entered the darkness until there was no longer enough space for them. He felt a light going through the back of his neck into his soul. Then the sky was no longer the sky but a pack of winds, and he was no longer Johnny either, but the wind and the lightning. That sweet voice was calling him again: "Johnny, don't give up, dear son." Then all the craziness up above ceased, and he began to think about how wonderful it would have been to live with his mother.

Emmita, meanwhile, was trying to look toward the place where God must be, but she could not find him, and all she could remember were her childhood days in catechism. There God was like an impetuous river that had not been a river during an infinite past and that suddenly had broken loose to split mountains, wash away roads, and roar beneath bridges. She was also told that God slept before time, motionless forever and ever, until suddenly he decided to create, in seven days, everything that exists; on the seventh, he created life. Then she understood that the shapeless, silent God had become a tumultuous person in love, a creator of puzzles that are tirelessly put together, eyes with eyes, lips with lips, shadow with shadow, during dawn, morning, midday, evening, night, forever.

Later, in her dreams, a man appeared, his hat covering his entire face. She guessed that it was her father and she tried to ask his forgiveness, but he walked away sadly.

Finally, she also saw the face of Rosina Rivero Ayllón, her godmother, and it seemed that she was trying to tell her something. If any hope remained, it soon left her because in the distance music began to be heard, and it was coming closer and seemed extremely familiar to her.

❻ ❻ ❻

They must have awakened a day or a night later. Although the place was airtight, they could hear the wind moaning as it landed on the mountains, howling and trying to awaken them.

Emma awoke first, raised her right hand, and held it in front of her face as if trying to determine whether she could still see. She made out her fingers, and her thumb and index finger seemed to form the letter "D." She wondered if that meant death.

Then she heard her companion moaning, and she felt bad to know that Johnny was still feeling pain even though he was dead.

She managed to take his hand in hers.

"Do you think we're dead?"

"Aren't we?"

"I think so. Do you believe there's something up there?"

"What do you believe?"

"I don't know. It seems like all this is a dream. How long do you think we slept?"

"Thousands of years. Go to sleep."

"Don't let go of my hand. I'm afraid to sleep."

26
What if this Burro Could Talk?

They were barefoot, but they wore elegant black leather clothing as if they were on their way to a very important meeting. Their faces looked toward the sun of the bay, but not their eyes because they were already closed, empty. They were three young men, and each of them had a black hole in his temple from which black blood had ceased flowing. They must be gang members, said one of the men who discovered them. We'd better not move them until the police come.

The police cars arrived with sirens blaring when the cool, blue fog had not yet lifted from San Francisco. Then another body was found and next to it a box containing its head. They're very young, one of the policemen said. It must have been a revenge killing. They were transported from some other place and placed here so they would be found together. Their faces showed red cheeks, a gentle rouge on the lips, shadows of lavendar on the eyelids, and their eyebrows had been accentuated with eyebrow pencil and India ink. The soft rouge on their lips concealed the fact that their teeth had been smashed before the coup de grace. The only thing that moved was the long, disheveled hair of one of them. It must be the work of a professional, said an experienced policeman.

❻ ❻ ❻

"What did you say? You left the couple in a garage? In one of my garages? Are you crazy? Were those my instructions? It's so

285

obvious that you're from the place you're from! What country did you say you were from? In those countries you can buy the police, you can buy the government, you can buy the army, you can buy everybody. And the ones on TV? Are they Johnny's whole gang?

"They're the ones that were with him."

"All of them?"

"All of them."

"All of them, what?"

"All of them, boss."

"You're sure you got all of them?"

"All of them, boss."

"You're a perfectionist. You shaved them and made them up so they'd look presentable. They really look nice in the paper."

The captain didn't respond. He knew that Leonidas García's rage was uncontrollable and that he, personally, did not like to get blood on his hands nor did he like to admit that he had ordered what he had just led them to understand.

"Not a single one was left alive, boss."

"I didn't ask you anything."

"But not a . . ." Captain Colina insisted.

"Yes, there is one, and he's the main one, imbecile. I didn't give you any orders about killing them. I have nothing to do with that business. What I told you is to bring Johnny here because I wanted to see him, and you disobeyed me. You dare to speak to me as an equal, you damn bastard! Didn't you tell me you were a captain back home? In your country, you may have gotten a medal for killing people that had already surrendered, but you're in the United States now, and you're dealing with a Mexican. Mexico is the land of real men, and real men kill face to face. We don't kill people who surrender, you coward. What's that? The same story as always? That your security business has nothing to do with mine? That your methods are your methods? . . . I won't kill you, because I need you to bring Johnny to me. Maybe he already got away. How long have they been there?"

"Not long."

"Not long, how long?"

"About a day."

"About a day, what?"

"About a day, boss."

"About a day bleeding. And the girl, why'd you bring her? What does she have to do with this business? Get going and bring them to me, or bring me what's left of them because I want to talk to Johnny. And you'll be sorry if they're dead! I need that boy alive, and you'd better find a way to make it happen. If you find him dead, go down to hell and find him, and use your connections to get him out of there any way you can, but bring him here to me because I need to see him right away!"

It was not necessary to repeat the orders for Captain Colina. He knew that even if he was humiliated and trampled on in public, he should click his heels and bow his head, because obedience was a virtue in every army in the world. Nevertheless, there were times when he felt tired of being publicly embarrassed. Then he lowered his head, swallowed his pride, closed his eyes, and walked slowly as if he were walking with a shroud on, as if he had no body or soul, as if he were nourished only by bitterness and the desire for revenge.

Therefore, after he swallowed his pride, he climbed into the van that had brought him and ordered the driver to leave San Francisco immediately and go back the way they had come. The driver complained that he had been working without a break and was hungry. He added that he wanted to get out of the car to get a taco.

"You dare disobey my orders? You think you're my equal?! Start this car up now, you damn bastard!"

Leonidas García had always been very careful, and up until that time, he had not had any problems in any of his businesses. He feared the competition, but after prevailing over the mafiosos, he had established excellent relations with the other businessmen, and he operated his casino and other businesses completely legally. The drug dealing was done through small distributors who did not have the slightest idea who was in charge. Nor did Leonidas have the slightest idea about that unknown young man operating from Oregon to Nevada who at that moment had just gotten the best of him in a big way, with the help of an old man, an idiot, and a donkey, no less.

❧ ❧ ❧

ANNOUNCER: Yes, friends of La Grande, the radio station of all Hispanics in the Bay Area, as we told you, after two weeks of great shows, we have with us again today Los Peregrinos de la Santa Muerte. This was the station that welcomed them when they first arrived, and on this station they are saying goodbye to their fans. At our request, they just sang "Dante's Ballad."

Commercial

ANNOUNCER: By special request of our esteemed audience, we are going to take calls for our guests.

Phone rings

ANNOUNCER: Yes? Yes? . . . This call is from San Jose and is for our friend, the Peregrino.

More questions

Commercial

ANNOUNCER: Yes? . . . I can't hear you, ma'am. Turn off your radio. That's better, of course . . . Hello.

LISTENER: Off the air, please. It's for Mr. Celestino.

Commercials

As the announcer reads the first series of commercials, a man knocks on the glass window and tells Dante to come out of the booth to take the call.

"Yes? Hello . . ."

"Dante, it's Rosina . . ."

"Rosina!"

Dante remembered that Rosina had been unable to attend the *quinceañera* because she had moved to Berkeley. Among the papers he had in the van, he had a postcard of the Bay Area where Rosina, apologizing for missing the party, had written her address in case he was ever in the area.

He remembered that when she found out about Emmita's disappearance, she called him and told him to come to see her if he didn't find her in Las Vegas. "Don't forget, Dante. Maybe I can locate my goddaughter. There's something I know and there's something I suspect. Please, be sure to come see me."

That was three years ago. He had heard nothing from her in all that time. Or had he? Yes, Rosina had called him when he returned from his first trip. She called to ask about Emmita. Dante, out of embarrassment, told her not to worry anymore. He lied and told her that Emma was living with some relatives in Nevada. What relatives were those? Dante didn't know what to say, and Rosina realized she shouldn't keep asking questions.

What had happened after that? The trees lost their leaves and got them back again. The leaves changed color and flew to the sky. Autumn, winter, and spring passed. And then summer. And again fall and winter. His neighbors tried to conceal their pity. The welder threw sparks at night as he built the new van. Virgilio's face had not changed expression as Dante confided every thought to him. And then what? The confused road to Las Vegas first, and then disappointment. And then? "Ladies and gentlemen, Los Peregrinos de la Santa Muerte." In Nevada, in Texas, in Arizona, in New Mexico, even in Florida, and now in California. He had looked everywhere, but it had not occurred to him to talk to Rosina.

"Are you listening to me, Dante? I think I have something to tell you about Emmita. Or have you given up?"

Dante shook his head.

"No. I'm not made to give up. I'm stubborn like a donkey."

He didn't wait for the radio interview to end. He signaled to the announcer through the glass that he was leaving, and he moved his index finger in a circle to tell the Peregrino that he'd see him later, but before he put on his jacket, the singer came out of the soundproof booth and walked over to him.

"Let's let Alex answer the questions. I think I should go with you."

ANNOUNCER: Los Peregrinos de la Santa Muerte are leaving us for a few moments, but their manager, Alex, is still here with us. *Phone rings*
ANNOUNCER: Yes? Yes, of course. We'll hand the phone to the manager when the quartz clock in our studio says exactly eleven o'clock in the morning.
ALEX: Hello? Hello, yes? . . . Speak now, or forever hold your peace.

A few minutes later, the van was crossing the Bay Bridge toward Berkeley. It traveled as if suspended above the blue vapor. It was speeding along, as if flying through the air.

The first thing they saw was a tower.

"Take that exit. That must be the Campanile, the university tower, and it's right in the center of Berkeley. What street is she on?"

"I have to get to a street called Telegraph. From there, it's twelve blocks to Russell Street."

They didn't make any wrong turns. It had been less than an hour since the phone call when Dante, followed by his friend, rang the bell at Rosina's house. It all happened as if time had not passed. The door opened by itself and led to a stairway.

"I knew you'd get here in time, Dante. Really, I've been waiting for you. Come in, please," said Rosina from the second floor as she invited them to go up to her apartment.

Although her words sounded strange to him, it was not the time to ask questions. Everything was happening as if he were dreaming, and one does not ask questions of dreams or of the people who appear in them. The only thing Dante wanted to know was why Rosina was so sure that she could help him find Emmita.

"Remember when I told you and my *comadre* Beatriz that I'm not Rosina Rivero and that in order to have identity documents I had to use the name of a dead woman?"

Dante remembered all that, but he had only recently learned that the Leonidas García in the story was a real person who lived in San Francisco and owned a lot of businesses, among them some Las

Vegas casinos. Had Rosina seen him? . . . Only in the newspapers, but she had found a way to get his direct phone number.

"And what good does that do me?"

"Remember I also told you about a young man who used to call me and who came to see me one day and told me his parents had abandoned him? His name is Johnny Cabada."

Little by little the story was becoming clear, and Dante couldn't believe it. He had been swimming upstream all this time. The police, first, and then almost all his friends had tried to convince him to abandon his search for Emmita because he didn't even have a good reason to travel to Las Vegas and then halfway across the country, and also because every year in the United States, there are hundreds of thousands of disappearances of young people who go off to live with their partners long before they are legally of age to do so. Now, however, from one moment to the next, the woman facing him was giving him a complete description of the young man who had taken his daughter.

"I started thinking about it later when I heard that Johnny was involved in some shady business. It seems he was invading his father's territory. The thing is that Leonidas García did not even suspect the identity of his rival. Do you know what I mean?"

Dante understood most of it, but not everything, because maybe all of this was nothing more than a dream. He wiped his hand over his face to see if he could wake up once and for all, but Rosina kept talking to him without stopping. Dante didn't know how that information would help him to find the exact place where Emmita was. Besides, he knew that the young man was no longer in Las Vegas. He told her about his experience at the casino.

Rosina showed him a copy of the *San Francisco Chronicle*.

"Look at these pictures. Do you recognize anyone?"

Dante took the newspaper and looked at the page indicated. He didn't know the faces, but they looked familiar to him.

"The young men you're looking at belong to a gang whose leader is Johnny Cabada."

At that moment, Dante recognized them. They were the guys who had entered the community center the night of the party to take Emmita away.

"The newspaper says they were assasinated and that makeup was put on them and they were thrown into the San Francisco Bay."

The reporter speculated about a revenge killing between rival gangs. All of the deceased were young men, none of them looked to be more than twenty-three years old, and they had been murdered in a very cruel manner.

"Johnny and Emmita aren't there."

"No, they're not."

A very fine but noisy rain began to fall over Berkeley. Through the window, Dante tried to see the water but couldn't.

"We have to do something right away," said Rosina, and she began to dial a phone number with the expression of someone carrying out the wishes of a dead person.

"Yes . . . I want to speak with Leonidas García. No, I don't want to talk to his secretaries, but to him . . . He doesn't have time? He can't take my call? Oh, I understand, well, take down this name and show it to him . . . Rosina . . . Rosina Rivero Ayllón . . . Tell him that if he's interested, to call me at this number."

She hung up, but it was not two minutes before the phone rang at her house. It was Leonidas himself calling her without using any intermediary.

"No, of course not. This has been my name for many years, but that's because I bought it from a professional smuggler. He gave me the original documents, and I had to learn her whole life story. . . . You know how it is. Maybe you'd be interested in knowing that Rosina died a year after you left her, but I'm not calling to tell you that story. There's something else and it's very important. She had your son, Leonidas!"

There was silence. Evidently the man on the other end of the phone did not know what to say. Finally he said something, to which the woman responded by making a face and a negative gesture with her fingers as if he were present.

"No, it's not that. I'm not calling to ask you for money, much less on behalf of your son. No, your son doesn't need anything from you. Or maybe he does . . . Yes, of course he does. His name is Johnny Cabada."

Again, silence, but this time a much shorter one. Then the woman began to tell him the story of the young man running off with Emmita, and she gave him information that only the dead woman knew, thereby confirming the truth of everything she had told him.

"Do you have them with you? Tell me right now what you mean by Captain Colina has them. Who is he? . . . Of course, the girl's father is here with me, and he'll go with me to San Francisco immediately. Tell me where we should meet. At the captain's house? And where is that? . . . At the San Francisco marina, okay. And which way? Give me the address. I'm writing it down. . . . Of course, of course we can get there. We'll get there about the same time you do . . ."

Dante did not even have time to think. Rosina immediately started down the stairs when she hung up the phone.

"Is that your car? It's huge!"

"Get in, please. Next to Virgilio."

"And that donkey?" the woman asked.

"He's my friend. He goes everywhere with me."

"He's our friend. You must have seen him on the cover of our CD," added the Peregrino, who had not had a chance to say a single word.

After driving through Oakland, they took the fastest route on the highway, and a few minutes later they were about to start across the Bay Bridge when the traffic slowed down because it was rush hour.

"At this rate we'll never get there in time."

"In time for what?"

"It turns out Leonidas doesn't have them. They're with a crazy person who often gets out of hand and does worse things than what he's been ordered to do. Leonidas is calling him right now to tell him that the young man he has there is his son and not to dare touch him. . . . What worries me is that we don't know how the traffic will be on the road to the San Francisco marina."

There was no time for more explanations because they were almost over the bridge.

"Here, Dante. Take the highway to the right. I think it's the fastest way."

Rosina could not say anything more, because at that moment something began to happen that no one had ever seen and perhaps no one will ever see again in San Francisco. Tens of thousands of land and sea birds gathered at one point in the sky, forming a cloud and finally a shadow that covered almost the entire Bay Area. There were birds of all kinds and sizes: eagles, doves, hummingbirds, starlings, goldfinches, cardinals, pelicans, seagulls, terns, ducks, geese, and hawks. People heard them everywhere. They sounded like the whispering of migratory birds speaking in the sky, but it gave the impression that they were doing so in the next room. They concentrated in a point located west of the bay, and from that place they dove toward the exit from the bridge toward the marina. There they invaded the highway and obstructed the passage of all vehicles except for Dante's van.

The cloud interrupted radio and television signals and prevented the police from communicating and sending patrols to the marina. Besides, even if they had, they would have been blocked. Everyone's gaze was focused on the hypnotic point in the sky from where so many birds were emerging. The next day's papers would show in the photographs a single reddish spot in the sky that would be forever inexplicable. The Oakland and San Francisco airports would halt operations, and arriving planes would be diverted because there was nothing they could do in the face of the inexplicable.

The van moved along with all the speed that Dante could coax from it. A few moments later, they were in front of an old San Francisco house that had not been painted in at least half a century. Leonidas and his men had not arrived yet. The house did not have the usual steps leading up to the front door, and the door was on street level.

"Get out of the van, Rosina. Peregrino, get Virgilio out."

They obeyed without protesting, not even understanding what it was that Dante planned to do. In a very short time, they had seen and heard so many incomprehensible things that they were completely prepared for miracles and surprise.

Dante backed up, then sped forward and crashed his vehicle against a weak door that gave way upon being rammed. Then he got out of the car and proceeded to search for Emmita throughout Captain Colina's house. One of the bedrooms, the biggest one, had several stateroom-type beds where the thug's men often spent the night. There was another room in which his prisoners had probably spent the night, because its windows were boarded over with pieces of wood in the shape of a cross.

A typical house of this kind generally has many secret places and could even hide people in its cellar. Dante and his friends kept looking and stumbled upon Colina's bedroom. The sheets and pillowcases of the slept-in bed were decorated with Disney characters, as if it were a child's room. The nightstand and dresser were pink, and the latter had a mirror decorated with stickers of giraffes and elephants.

Taken aback, Dante looked to Rosina for an explanation, but she knew no more than he did. The papers, which would later write about Colina, would say that soldiers who fled their countries of origin suffered from depravity and that even the very torture they had performed had predisposed them to seek sexual satisfaction in the most perverse, complicated ways. An explosion interrupted their search. Suddenly they were surrounded by a group of armed men. The only thing Dante could feel was the icy barrel of a pistol against his right temple.

"No, don't do that. Leave him alone."

The man who was speaking approached him.

"You must be the girl's father. I'm Leonidas García, and you have nothing to fear. But we'd better get out of here and keep looking for them, because Colina has taken them elsewhere."

When he found out that Johnny was his boss' son, Captain Colina had been unable to resist the desire to make money off the situation. Much more than that, he felt that his time had come. Rage and revenge came together in him. He had told García: "I'm in control now, and you know it. Leave the money where I tell you, don't forget I want large bills. I'm taking the girl. I can leave you your son, but you know how much it'll cost you. We all have the right to a comfortable retirement, wouldn't you say?"

"They couldn't have gone far," García continued. "They must be here on one of the ships or pleasure boats; my men and I will go find them."

For Dante, this new search lasted much longer than all the previous ones, because every time they reached one of the possible hiding places, the group had already left it. It was obvious that they were dealing with a man who had experience in this business.

When all the predictable hiding places were exhausted, Leonidas's cell phone rang.

"You're an idiot, Leonidas. I liked you better when you made deals. Where do you want me to leave Johnny's body?"

All Dante would remember in the future was Leonidas' distorted face, his head hung for a moment and then gestured: "No. No. No! . . . I have the money."

The phone began to emit the sound meaning the caller had hung up. For Leonidas, that was proof that rage and revenge had been stronger than greed.

"Dead. They're dead. I think he already killed them."

The day had ended. Dante would remember, too, that the rain had begun to fall on the beaches before them and that an enormous moon painted the San Francisco houses yellow. Then came a shadow and then the shrieks of pelicans that alit on one side of the marina.

Dante shouted: "No, he couldn't have killed them. On that boat! Right there! They have to be there . . ." He was pointing to a craft moored to a dock to which the birds were flocking.

He would not remember why he associated the birds' presence with his daughter. Not knowing why, García and his men ran toward the boat.

Leonidas ran across the dock and leapt the few feet that separated it from the boat. He jumped onto it, shooting like he was possessed. His men did the same, and for quite awhile, only the roar of their submachine guns was heard.

"Don't shoot! We give up!"

Leonidas moved toward Colina, holding his gun in both hands. Then he left it in just his right hand and aimed toward the sky, as people do when they're going to carry out an order or a sentence. Then he slowly lowered his arm, a single shot was heard and the light of death was seen.

For an instant Leonidas stood there astonished, motionless. Then his knees buckled and he fell, but even on the ground, he kept trembling. His men retaliated by shooting their guns again.

Leonidas had underestimated the prowess of his enemy, skilled in betrayal, Colina had been quicker than he.

"García's dead," Colina shouted to Leonidas's men, but no one paid any attention to him and they kept shooting. Then he turned toward his prisoners, who had not been executed yet, and aimed his gun at them.

"Well, too bad, Johnny! This could have had a happy ending . . . Your father could have fixed everything with a little money, but he didn't want to . . ."

Colina's attention was distracted from Emmita, who took advantage of the opportunity to kick her feet and move her chair toward their attacker, striking him and preventing him from aiming at Johnny.

"How touching! . . . We'll see if . . ."

The captain never finished his sentence because the girl suddenly freed one of her legs and kicked him in the groin. The man's legs were spread and he didn't see the blow coming, but he reacted quickly and shot at her. Two men jumped between them, and one of them fell dead. The other covered Emmita with his body. They were Dante and the Peregrino, who had followed the entire search unarmed. Colina started to turn back toward the window and was hit by gunfire from Leonidas' men. It was a night of death. Leonidas, Colina, and the Peregrino de la Santa Muerte were dead. Up above, the stars burned like yellow and red butterflies for all eternity.

❧ ❧ ❧

The *Latino de Hoy* had asked me to do a story about Latino immigrants in Oregon, and it occurred to me to write the story of the Celestino family. The San Francisco press did plenty of stories on the facts that led to the death of mafioso Leonidas García, the former South American soldier Colina, and a famous *corrido* composer, but there are other inexplicable facts that intersect these stories and appear to be connected to them. Nothing more was said about the invasion of the birds because no one has found a satisfactory explanation, but there is plenty of material written about the Mexican who undertook an odyssey to rescue his daughter. What is not known is why he was always accompanied by a donkey.

I visited Johnny Cabada in the Oregon state penitentiary, where he is serving a six-month sentence. He was found guilty of some misdemeanors and will soon be released, transformed into a different person, he told me. He has organized a small Christmas tree purchasing and distributing business and says he will work hard to make it prosper.

"No, my friend, the best thing that can happen to anyone in life has already happened to me. Maybe all that led me to my previous life was the fear of believing that there was no one in my corner, that I had appeared out of thin air like those air eggs that hens sometimes lay. Maybe people take risks for fear of being nothing, because of a lack of love. It's different now. Now, I know who I am."

Emmita Celestino has devoted her time to teaching her father to read and write, and this year she will start school at Western Oregon University. Alex has proposed that father and daughter form a musical duo, and they're thinking about it. When I visited the Celestinos they served me a cup of coffee in the dining room of the house where an ornate picture in a silver frame shows Mary and Joseph fleeing to Egypt as a gentle donkey carries the newborn Baby Jesus.

I asked Dante if he's going to get a work visa, and then I realized that the universe does miracles but the Immigration Department doesn't. I asked if he considered any moment in his recent life miraculous, and it didn't seem so to him because miracles are a daily thing for him. I attempted to inquire about the four-legged animal that had accompanied him in his search, but Dante simply stated, looking at Virgilio, that it's a hardworking but stupid animal, like all those of its species.

At that moment, I seemed to notice a displeased look on the face of the donkey that had been present throughout our conversation and which, just at that moment, had deigned to cast me a quick, indifferent glance. Virgilio is small, furry, and soft, a donkey through and through, and no matter how much of a donkey he may be, transparent, silent, and light, there is no reason in this world for him to know how to read or for us to even think about him.

"If Virgilio could only speak!" Dante exclaimed laughing, as we were saying goodbye. He made me promise that I would attend the big party he is already preparing for Emmita's wedding.

A yellow, almost liquid sun was spilling over all of Mount Angel and permeating the yard of the house where we were talking. I asked Dante to go outside so I could take some pictures, and he agreed. But it was difficult for me because there was too much light here and there and everywhere, and that's why there are no photos in this text. Then I asked him to talk to me about Beatriz, and I no longer remember if he did. There was too much light, and it was spreading out over the city and the trees. I played with my fingers to see if they weren't soaked with light or gold, and while Dante talked, I don't know why, but I began to think about the love that moves the sun and all the stars.

Also by Eduardo González Viaña

American Dreams